The Malcolm Rose Collection

Three degrees of murder

Have you read this other chilling
Point Crime Collection?

1. The David Belbin Collection

Avenging Angel
Deadly Inheritance
Final Cut

POINT CRiME

The Malcolm Rose Collection

The Alibi • Concrete Evidence • The Smoking Gun

Three degrees of murder

■ SCHOLASTIC

Scholastic Children's Books,
Commonwealth House, 1-19 New Oxford Street,
London WC1A 1NU, UK
a division of Scholastic Ltd
London ~ New York ~ Toronto ~ Sydney ~ Auckland

First published in this edition by Scholastic Ltd, 1997

The Alibi
First published by Scholastic Ltd, 1996
Text copyright © Malcolm Rose, 1996

Concrete Evidence
First published by Scholastic Ltd, 1995
Text copyright © Malcolm Rose, 1995

The Smoking Gun
First published by Scholastic Ltd, 1993
Text copyright © Malcolm Rose, 1993

ISBN 0 590 54328 8

Typeset by TW Typesetting, Midsomer Norton, Somerset
Printed by Clays Ltd, St Ives Plc

10 9 8 7 6 5 4 3 2 1

Contents

THE ALIBI

Prologue

The car cruised to a halt by the hedge that separated the Burrages' back garden from the quiet street. Convinced that no one was watching, the driver leapt from the car and squeezed into the secluded garden through the laurels. It was a hot July afternoon but the figure, in trousers, baggy coat and hood, seemed to be dressed for winter. Stealthily, the stranger crept past the swimming pool. Without wind, the water was perfectly still, making a brilliant mirror for the house and the blue sky. The dark shadow of the uninvited guest floated across the pool's calm surface. By the back door, the figure hesitated, looked round and listened for a second. The garden was not overlooked. The intrusion had gone unnoticed.

A steady hand emerged from the coat and reached for the back door. The handle yielded to pressure. The door was unlocked. As it opened, strains of a Mahler symphony filtered through. Under the hood, only the lips of the intruder were visible. They curved into a smile. Music would deaden the sound of the approach. Like an angel of death, the cloaked figure slipped into the kitchen and shut the door noiselessly. On the table, there was a warm teapot, sugar bowl and biscuit tin. From the rack, the hand selected the knife that felt just right. Cautiously, the prowler slid out of the kitchen and into the hall. The study door was ajar. Inside the room, Stuart Burrage was absorbed in working at his computer, his back to the door, bombarded from all sides with classical music.

Knife in hand, the killer sidled into the study and tiptoed towards the victim.

It was only when the blade came over his head and appeared suddenly at his throat that Stuart turned his head. Startled and petrified, he was unable to react or save himself from the swift application of the knife. He issued a short gasp and a stifled cry as he collapsed on to the floor.

The posture of his assailant, kneeling by the body but avoiding the blood, exuded satisfaction. It was a clean and professional killing. One hand pulled back the shirt sleeve on Stuart's left arm to reveal his old-fashioned watch. The other hand still held the knife. The murderer prepared to break the watch by smashing down the handle of the knife on it but hesitated, then stood up and examined the computer instead. Again, the lips under the hood smiled broadly. Deciding against damaging Stuart's watch, the intruder discarded the knife, and retreated quickly – into the hall, through the kitchen and out into the beautiful, peaceful summer day. In seconds, the culprit had disappeared behind the hedge, climbed into the hired car and, undetected, driven away from the carnage.

1

Sea horses, queen angelfish and sergeant majors glided slowly and aimlessly across the screen. Crabs crawled across the sandy bottom and bubbles rose regularly to the surface. Artificial gurglings issued from the computer. In the centre of the screen, the water appeared to have turned crimson. Unconcerned, the fish swam through it.

The bloodstain should have been deep brown but the glow of the screen saver illuminated it from behind, turning it bright red, like a thin ruby curtain caught in sunlight. The blood had cascaded down the screen and dripped on to the keyboard below where its true rusty colour showed against the function keys. It had seeped between the buttons and congealed, gluing them together. Between the mouse mat and table lamp, there was a full cup of cold tea and two biscuits.

Unnaturally white, Stuart Burrage's body lay on the floor by the computer desk. His throat cut while he used the computer, he had toppled off the chair and hardly moved. He had not even tried to crawl towards the telephone to summon help. The blade had been applied clinically and accurately. Death had come quickly. Near his body, the carpet did not show an obvious stain but the thick brown pile was heavily matted with blood.

The study was large and luxurious. There was an easy chair and a huge filing cabinet. One entire wall was given over to cluttered bookshelves. Most of the volumes were sturdy hardbacks. Many were reference books on law. A few family photographs, none older than five years, were also displayed on the shelves. The other three walls were decorated liberally with valuable modern art, a family tree, framed qualifications and a newspaper clipping bearing the headline

"Surgeon Gets Life". Along with the leather-topped pedestal desk, there was an enormous antique clock, a cabinet containing expensive hi-fi equipment, two imposing speakers, and an ornate fireplace. The green lamps on the CD player and amplifier were still lit but the symphony had finished, the speakers dormant. The clock ticked rhythmically and its pendulum swung impressively but its weights were nearly touching the bottom of the case. For Stuart Burrage, time had already stopped.

His wife, Rhia, opened the front door and called into the house, "Stuart, darling? I'm back." She instructed the taxi driver to place her suitcase just inside the hall and paid him. Then she shut the door and, still wearing her elegant blue coat, headed for the study. From the doorway, she could see that the computer was on, but at first she did not see her husband. When she stepped further into the room, she spotted him slumped on the floor. She flung her handbag on to the armchair and dashed to his side. She did not need to check for a pulse. When she took his hand, it was leaden and cold. As she turned away, she noticed the kitchen knife under the chair. She buried her face in her hands and ran from the room.

Distraught and tense, Rhia sat in the lounge while the scene-of-the-crime team invaded the study. She had no wish to watch them going about their grisly job, like vultures picking over a carcass. The police officer in charge, Detective Inspector David Thompson, was a friend of the family. He tried to console Rhia and extract information at the same time. "I'm sorry, Rhia. It must be a terrible shock – and a terrible loss. He was a good man – and a great lawyer. I always respected Stuart. I enjoyed working with him." David Thompson had first encountered Stuart three years ago when they were both involved in the same case. Subsequently, they had met socially and the detective had struck up a particular friendship with Rhia. Now, he touched her arm gently. "I've taken personal charge of the investigation. I'll get whoever did it," he promised.

"But it won't bring him back," she sobbed.

"No," he murmured. "I can't do that."

Rhia sniffed and wiped her face with a handkerchief. "You have to ask me some questions, I think. Can we get it over with?"

Sympathetically, David replied, "Yes, of course." He cleared his throat, sighed, and began, "When did you come back and find him like that?"

"I don't know exactly. I didn't call straight away. I couldn't ... you know."

The police officer nodded considerately. "How long do you think it was?"

"About half an hour, I suppose, before I felt up to calling."

"That's OK," he replied. "I understand." He glanced at his watch to confirm the time.

Rhia's eyes were inflamed and her natural grace had been eroded by grief. She looked haggard and dismayed.

"Where had you been?" David queried.

"France. Paris. I just got back."

"Business or pleasure?" he asked.

"A little break, that's all. Stuart might have come as well but work got in the way – as always. Now I wish he had come," Rhia murmured.

"How long were you there?"

Rhia looked askance at him.

"I have to ask," he explained, "to establish the time of death. That's all. Presumably he was fine when you left. Between then and now…"

"Yes, I see," Rhia put in. "I went on Thursday. Four days. A long weekend really."

Seeing the family photograph on the mantelpiece, David was reminded of Rhia's stepson. He enquired, "Is Kieran around?"

"He's competing in Scotland. Swimming."

David asked, "When did *he* leave?"

"A few days before I went to Paris. He went with his girlfriend, Ali. She's a swimmer as well. They're due back on Wednesday."

"Ali? What's her other name?"

"Tankersley. Ali Tankersley." Rhia added, "She's a nice girl."

"Well," David concluded, "I'll need to talk to you some more, I'm afraid, but for now I need to attend to ... the study. And you need a rest. I'll get one of my chaps to make a drink for you. OK?"

Detective Inspector Thompson stood in the doorway for a moment and surveyed the scene. Immediately, one of his sergeants started to update him. He listened and, at the same time, prowled round the room. He stopped by the framed newspaper clipping and studied it for a moment. Tapping it, he muttered, "The infamous John Evans case. A surgeon turning the knife on his wife. He got life for it. A young Stuart Burrage was the barrister for the prosecution." He turned to his colleague and said, "Jim, check Evans is still tucked up at Her Majesty's pleasure." He hesitated, then added, "And trace all Burrage's cases for anyone who might bear him a particular grudge. Maybe he prosecuted someone who was later shown to be innocent. That sort of thing."

"I've already got someone on it," the efficient sergeant responded with a satisfied smile.

"Good. What about entry?"

Jim stayed beside David as he continued his slow tour of the room. "Not forced," he answered. "Probably just walked in through the back door. It wasn't locked."

"Pity," he mused. "Footprints in the garden?"

"Ground too hard. And no obvious tyre marks in the road."

"OK," David said, sighing. "Check door-to-door in case the neighbours have seen any suspicious vehicles – or people – out the back." Stopping by one of the forensic team, he asked, "Any decent fingerprints?"

"Lots. Mostly the same, though. Still checking."

Arriving at the computer, David watched for a while the fish swimming unconcerned through the polluted water. "Very calming," he remarked. "Didn't calm the attacker, though."

Jim inquired, "Do we turn it off and take it back for examination?"

"No," David replied urgently. "Certainly not. Best to examine it right here and now. Call in Kate. She's a computer buff. She'll relish this one. If it was left active in a document there'll be information about when he logged on and when he last edited it. That's probably when he died. Judging by the untouched tea, I'd say he'd just brewed it up, put on a CD, and sat down to work when he copped it. If we turn the computer off to take it away, we might not get back into it again. If he had a password to gain access, it would shut us out. Right now, it thinks he's still alive and working on it. Get Kate in quick. It'd just be our luck if we had a power cut."

"OK." Jim scuttled away.

Looking at the forensic pathologist kneeling by the body, David enquired, "Is it as obvious as it looks?"

"Yeah. Pretty professional slitting of the throat. Immediate loss of blood pressure, then massive drain into the carpet. Dead in seconds."

"When?"

The pathologist shrugged. "Still need more tests. Less than a week, more than thirty-six hours."

Frowning, David said, "Any ideas why his left sleeve's pulled up but not his right?"

"No. I've checked his left arm. There's nothing untoward. Perhaps he was looking at his watch when he was attacked."

"Mmm. Keep me informed." Then he called, "Someone bag this knife for me. I want to show it to his wife. See if it's home-grown."

David resumed his circuit of the room, aloof from the comings and goings of his team. He stopped by the family tree. It told him little more than he already knew about the Burrage family. Kieran was the sole offspring from Stuart Burrage's first marriage. He was seventeen years of age. After the death of his first wife, Stuart had married Rhia Swithenby five years ago. Rhia was an only child and she had not had any children herself. Her only surviving relative, her father, had died last summer. "Someone's done a lot of work on this. It goes back a good few generations of Swithenbys and Burrages," David mumbled to himself. "Saves a question or two." Nothing else in the room caught his eye.

Every time that David worked with Kate, he thought that she was more manic and more of a genius. With the flamboyant gesture of a maestro settling in front of a grand piano for a concert performance, the white-haired forensic scientist drew up the chair and flexed her fingers theatrically.

"Let's see what we've got," she began. "I doubt if he was actually typing when he was attacked. Some blood would have run down his hands on to the keys. He was twisting round, perhaps, to see who was creeping up behind him. Then the blood spurted from the side of his neck on to the top of the screen." Extravagantly, she demonstrated the effect by twisting her neck to the side and tracing with her hand the path of the gush from vein to monitor. "He fell off his chair before it got too messy. Most of it's in the carpet. Brown – good colour scheme for this sort of occasion."

Ignoring her gruesome sense of humour, David leaned over her and said, "What about the computer itself?"

"Let's take a look." Kate pulled on her nylon gloves and then moved the mouse a mere millimetre. Immediately the fish disappeared to reveal a document containing only a title and a few words. "It's Microsoft Word. The beginning of a report of some sort. But he'd hardly got started."

From behind her shoulder, David muttered, "Interesting. Look at the heading. *Re: Robert Tankersley*. Same surname as the son's girlfriend." He read aloud the start of the document. "It is with considerable regret that I have to report the..." He smiled ruefully. "Cut off in his prime."

"Not everyone leaves the culprit's name written in blood, you know."

"Shame," David retorted.

"Tankersley isn't your man," Kate deduced.

"Why not?"

"Because he wouldn't walk away from here leaving this clue. He would've deleted it," Kate answered.

"Maybe," David replied. "Or maybe he was in a panic – or at least in a hurry to get out. Or perhaps he doesn't know anything about computers."

Kate shrugged. "Bet you waste your time on him. Anyway," she continued, "let's see what other goodies Burrage left for us." She clicked on *Summary Info*, followed by *Statistics*. "He started this report at 3.21 in the afternoon of July the twenty-third. That was Saturday, wasn't it?"

"Yes," David replied.

"And this is the first version. He didn't save a longer document that someone else has partially deleted. What you've got is all there was. The computer's been churning away, it says, for 2,649 minutes. Let me think. That's ... forty-odd hours. It makes sense, doesn't it? It's 11.30 now, Monday. Almost two days later." Turning towards David, she concluded, "Your man died two days ago." She pointed to the cup of tea and uneaten biscuits and said, "He got himself settled with a cuppa, typed for a few seconds, didn't even live long enough to get a sip or nibble a Hobnob. Throat slit at twenty-five past three."

"More than likely," David responded cautiously, "but not necessarily. He could have opened the document and then got distracted. Did this and that, and then gone off to make the tea."

Kate frowned. "This is a professional man. A busy barrister. He'd work efficiently – no distractions. He'd make the drink and then start working. He wouldn't take a break as soon as he'd started a new document."

"Probably not," David admitted. "But I have to keep an open mind."

Kate laughed. "The proverbial open mind! Good excuse for not admitting the obvious. Bet you pathology confirms it, more or less." She took a good look at the cup of tea and commented, "See the brown ring at the top? That's scum – caused by a couple of days of evaporation."

"Can that be measured accurately so we can find out when he poured it out?"

Kate grinned. "No chance. The rate of evaporation depends on room temperature and atmospheric pressure. And there's so little loss that any measurement would be inaccurate *and* imprecise. Forget it. Believe me, the computer record's much more reliable."

"OK," David conceded. "But one thing seems sure. He was murdered in broad daylight. Interesting."

Kate turned her attention back to the keyboard and monitor. "What else did he do that day?" Under *File*, three other documents were listed. In turn, she opened them. Two were business letters and one was a financial report on a bridge club. Stuart Burrage was identified as the Bridge Club's secretary and treasurer. All three documents had been created on the 22nd July, the day before he was murdered.

"Running a bridge club's no big deal," Kate quipped.

David Thompson did not approve of her joke. He was too close to the victim to be amused. He agreed with her sentiment, though. "Probably not relevant," he said, "but can you get me copies of all these things?"

"I've brought a gadget. Wonderful things, gadgets. I plug it in to this system," Kate replied, patting Stuart Burrage's computer as if it were a faithful dog, "and it'll copy everything on to optical memory cartridges. And I do mean everything. It'll find even the hidden and protected files. Like extracting every last tooth. I'll take all his floppies as well. By the time I've squeezed all the juice out of his machine," she said with relish, "you'll need to demolish a rain forest to cope with the paperwork. But before you leave me in peace to get on with it, let's just check something else. I still believe in the human touch – well, mine anyway. You see, I wonder if he used e-mail." She left the file and examined the program manager. "Here we are. He's got a mailbox. Look. The last e-mail message was to someone called Daniel Allgrove. He didn't keep a copy of it but he asked for a receipt. Allgrove read the message at 2.55, it says. Half an hour before Burrage was killed." Kate looked at David and remarked, "I think you've got yourself another line of enquiry."

"Thanks, Kate," David Thompson replied. "I'll leave you to it and catch up with you when you've got all you can. Right now, I need to speak to his wife again."

"Good idea," Kate put in. "These affairs are usually domestic. Especially when kitchen knives are involved. Only the woman of the household would know where they are. Keep it in the family, eh?"

David grimaced. "I don't think so this time. I know her. And she'd need a long arm. She was in Paris at the time."

"I'm sorry to have to show you this," David murmured to Rhia, "but I really need to have it identified." He produced a polythene bag containing a black-handled kitchen knife. The blade was sharp, about ten centimetres long. "Is it yours?"

"I saw it before – in the study. Yes," Rhia answered, "it's one of mine."

"Sure?"

She nodded. "I use it all the time. It should be in the rack on the kitchen wall." She sighed wearily.

"OK." He continued, "I'll have to bring in an officer to take your fingerprints. We need to eliminate them. If we have yours, we'll be able to find out if there are any others on the weapon, door knobs and so on. He'll leave a kit so Kieran can give us his prints as well. Same reason."

Rhia muttered, "Fine."

Changing his line of questioning, David asked, "Daniel Allgrove. Doesn't he work with Stuart?"

"Yes. Stuart's junior partner. And a member of the Bridge Club."

"Did they get on OK?"

Rhia thought about it for a moment then replied, "Most of the time, yes. Stuart complained sometimes that Daniel had ideas above his station. It's just ambition, of course. Even so, Stuart had to put him in his place sometimes. You know, gave him the dreary divorce cases. Youngsters have to start at the bottom to learn the trade."

"So," David prompted, "Allgrove might resent Stuart, would you say?"

"Doesn't every junior partner feel he's being held back, peeved not to get the high-profile cases?" Rhia started to weep again. She had realized that her own husband would become the subject of a high-profile case.

"Do you want me to contact Kieran? If you know where he's staying, we can get him back straight away. He should be here. A bit of comfort for you."

Rhia nodded. Through her tears she stammered, "I suppose so." She wiped her cheeks again and remarked, "You know, Kieran and I have never really hit it off. I might as well be honest and admit it. He was close to his mother. He used to be close to Stuart as well but a little less, I guess, since I came along. Even so, he'll be upset. He admired his dad."

"I didn't know the first Mrs Burrage," David commented delicately. "What happened to her?"

"Breast cancer."

David nodded soberly. "I see."

He took a note of Kieran's address and organized for a counterpart in Edinburgh to go and break the bad news to him.

2

In the afternoon, the Intercity train from Edinburgh to Kings Cross lumbered round a bend at a rakish angle. Ali flopped to one side and her head lodged against Kieran's sizeable shoulder. Kieran hardly noticed. He was gazing out of the window, watching the ragged Northumberland coastline rush past. He felt queasy and strangely detached, as if the world around him had gone into overdrive, leaving him becalmed. A mere passenger. He was recalling a time when he was ten and confused. One night, instead of reading him a bedtime story, his mum sat on the edge of his bed, gently placed her hand on his chest, and talked about a lump that had appeared in her breast. Apparently, it had been there for a while but her own doctor told her that it was nothing to worry about. By the time that a specialist had corrected the diagnosis, it was too late. She tried to explain that there would be surgery and treatment but that one day soon she would die. Kieran was puzzled and angry. A little lump did not seem to be such a big deal. And surely modern medicine could deal with a stupid lump inside his mum. But it couldn't. For the next year, he watched his mum deteriorate and then die. It just wasn't fair.

The sea disappeared behind rocks. For no apparent reason, the train slowed and then stopped altogether.

The young Kieran knew that his dad was special because everyone told him so. He was becoming the barrister that everyone wanted on their side. Kieran was proud of his dad but the demands of a top-class lawyer and a top-class father were too much for one man. When his mum died, Kieran's life seemed to grind to a halt. His dad hired substitute mothers for a while so that he could continue his career without a guilty conscience and Kieran did not complain because his father was special. It would have been selfish to hamper his rise to the top.

His dad sued his mother's doctor for negligence. He won a sizeable settlement and Kieran discovered that a value could be placed on his mum's life. The compensation amounted to a third of a million pounds. That was the court's view of what she was worth. Kieran didn't want money. He wanted a mother.

With a slight jolt, the train began to move again. Within a few minutes, it was back to full speed and the countryside flew past once more.

At his precious Bridge Club, Kieran's dad met a woman called Rhia. Within weeks, she seemed to turn up at the house at all times – even first thing in the morning. Before long, his father was sitting on Kieran's bed, just where his mother had once sat, to explain that he was going to have a new mother. The barrister within his father presented a faultless case that night. All of the advantages were expressed logically and forcibly. The twelve-year-old Kieran had no defence to offer. After his dad left the bedroom, he cried till morning.

And so Rhia became one of the family. From the beginning, Kieran imagined her as a sultry stranger and gunslinger strolling importantly and mysteriously into town, shooting down everything that his real mother stood for. He could never bring himself to call her "Mum". At least Rhia was wise enough not to force the issue. "You're a big lad now," she said, trying to flatter him, "so why don't you just call me Rhia? It is my name after all."

Kieran had to admit that, at first, Rhia worked harder than he did himself to establish a relationship. Yet he resisted her approaches. She just wasn't *Mum*. She was nothing like Mum. She didn't smell right. She was an intruder. She was younger than Mum and very good-looking. Straight after the wedding she set about sprucing up everything. She spent a fortune on the house and herself. Kieran's mum didn't care about money. She cared only that the family was happy. Kieran watched disapprovingly as Rhia splashed out mostly on frills for herself. Worse, it was the compensation for his mum's life that she was using to make her own life cushy. If his dad had not held her in check, she would have frittered away the lot. Her meals were extravagant and perfect, as well. His mum's cooking was always a disaster. Meals prepared by his real mother were an ordeal and an endless source of banter. There were times when he could hardly eat the stuff for giggling. There was nothing funny about Rhia's food. Kieran was suspicious of her and he had remained suspicious of her to this day.

Sometimes, Kieran would be regarded as special as well. It was explained to him that a man of his father's stature and occupation would occasionally make enemies. When a particularly nasty case was going through the courts, Kieran was sometimes given a plain-clothes minder. As Kieran grew older, he began to question his dad's chosen profession. When he was defending the most obnoxious characters who were clearly as guilty as sin, his father regarded it as a matter of personal and professional pride to secure a not-guilty verdict or at worst a minor punishment. Over an immaculate meal, Kieran would thump the table and say, "But that man stole millions and you know it! He may have been a company director – and he used a computer rather than a sawn-off shotgun – but he was still a thief. And you got him off with almost nothing." His dad would smile in an almost patronizing way. "You don't understand, Kieran. There were mitigating circumstances. He was stressed at work – he was ill. And some legal technicalities came into it." Kieran shook his head. "In other words, you were cleverer than the other side – so he got away with it. Your arguments didn't reduce the crime, only the sentence. You get paid to win the case, not to find out the truth." It was then that his dad destroyed for ever his faith in the due processes of law. He replied, "Let's not get confused, Kieran. The court's there purely to enact the law. It's a court of law, not a court of justice."

Ali stirred, opened her eyes and clutched Kieran's arm. "All right?" she asked.

Kieran nodded. "I suppose so. I was just ... thinking."

"About your dad?"

"About lots. Mum, Dad, Rhia, crime."

Tentatively, Ali whispered, "What do you think happened? One of the crooks your dad put away got his own back?"

"I dare say that's what the police will check out, but..." He did not carry on.

"What?"

"It doesn't matter," Kieran replied. "Just that it's not the only possibility."

Ali looked at her boyfriend. He looked sad and wistful. She realized that he was grieving for more than his father. She squeezed his arm and murmured, "It'll turn out all right. Promise."

Kieran and Ali went to the same school but they only really took note of each other when their dads got together one night to discuss business at Kieran's house. After the meal, the two fathers retired to the study like men from a bygone age expecting cigars and brandy. Rhia and Ali's mother chatted together and so Kieran was forced to entertain Ali. They were both fifteen at the time. They talked about their common interest in swimming and played CDs. Suddenly more than distant members of the same school swimming team, they became friends. It was a couple of months later when they realized that they shared more than friendship. At school Ali watched as Kieran used his big frame, and his status among the boys, to rescue a bullied lad called Grant McFarlane. She was proud of him. Later, at a gala, Kieran watched as Ali's effortless, almost lazy, backstroke powered her to first place. He was proud of her. Recognizing the pleasure that they gained from one another, they became a couple. Even so, when they went out together, they were relaxed about it. In the playground, other kids embarked on wild relationships, declaring their undying love for each other, falling out weeks later, and stumbling into the next heated relationship. Kieran and Ali seemed to regard it as inevitable that they would grow apart sooner or later and so they never declared anything, did not expect anything, and kept clear of passion. Two years later, though, when all of their friends had dozens of broken partnerships in their wake, Kieran and Ali were still together. Still strong. They had fallen in love without noticing it. Neither of them would admit it, even though they both accepted that life apart was unthinkable.

"I bet the police come and see Dad," Ali groaned.

Kieran glanced at her and said, "I guess so. But you don't think..."

"No," Ali interjected. "At least, I don't think so. All I know is that two years ago they were as thick as thieves, your dad and mine." She hesitated and then added, "Perhaps thieves isn't the best term to apply to a lawyer. Anyway, in the last couple of weeks, your dad's name's been struck off polite conversation at home. Some falling out! I even felt like keeping quiet about it whenever we went out together – as if Burrage is a dirty word."

"I don't know what happened either," Kieran responded. "One moment, Dad was representing your father in some venture or other, then he wasn't."

Of course, they'd talked about the bust-up before. But then their only concern was whether the disagreement would endanger their relationship. Now, it had the potential to be much more sinister.

"Were you thinking of my dad when you said there were other possibilities?" asked Ali hesitantly.

"Not really," Kieran replied, still unwilling to expand.

Ali sighed. "It's Rhia, isn't it? You've never trusted her."

Kieran shrugged but did not deny it.

"She always seemed ever so nice to me. You only have a problem with her because she couldn't replace your real mum."

"Maybe," he replied. "But it's more than that." He hesitated before allowing his grievances to spill out. "She's into money in a big way. That's what I can't stand. I reckon she loves it more than she loves Dad. She got pretty rich when she married him, but Dad always stopped her going utterly wild with money. I think she'd do *anything* to get control over his cash. Now there's no one to apply the brakes, she's got everything she wanted. Suddenly, she's even richer, isn't she?"

"Possibly," Ali said. "But isn't it more likely that you are?"

Kieran frowned. "I ... er ... I don't know. I haven't thought about it. I wouldn't want to profit from all this."

"I know." Judging Kieran's need perfectly, Ali suggested, "Let's talk about something else – or just relax."

It seemed callous to engage in small talk under the circumstances so, as the train hurtled south, they were mostly silent.

Jim waved a piece of paper in his commanding officer's direction. "Something for you," he called in triumph.

"Already?" David responded. "What?"

"It's John Evans. He got parole two weeks ago!"

"You're kidding! How come?" He held out his hand for the report. Excitedly, he scanned it. "Oh, yes! This is good. I think you'd better get me a car, Jim."

"Already done, sir."

Cursing the traffic, Jim drove south into the London suburb of Balham. While Evans had been serving fifteen years of his sentence, his solicitors had looked after his assets. The Balham house was not as grand as the one in which the surgeon had killed his wife, but it was more than a home. After so much time in a cell, it was a palace.

David banged on the big door and waited. It was an old and large house, in need of much repair. When the door creaked open, both officers held up their identification. "Detective Inspector Thompson and this is DS Morrow," David announced.

John Evans looked briefly to the heavens and then groaned. "CID. It didn't take you long."

"What do you mean by that, Mr Evans?" David asked smartly.

"Out for two weeks and you're round already. I do know my rights, you know. I know what constitutes police harassment. Once on your records, always a soft target." There was a hint of hysteria in his tone. "You'll try to pin anything on me. My lawyer warned me about you."

"Look," David retorted. "We can come in and ask you a few questions or we can take you back to HQ. Either way, we need some answers. Please yourself. And call your lawyer if you like."

The surgeon was a tall thin man with little hair. His clothing was old-fashioned and looked baggy on him. His hands were large, white and steady. It was easy to imagine them wielding a scalpel. He stood to one side and mumbled, "Better come in."

The living room was spacious but shabby and sparsely decorated. When David dropped into an armchair, a small cloud of dust enveloped him. Jim stood behind his boss and kept his eyes on the suspect. "So," David began, "you join the real world again. Some would say fifteen years isn't long compared to a lifetime."

"I wouldn't," he snapped.

"No, I don't suppose so. Prison couldn't have been easy for a professional man like you."

John Evans eyed the detective with distrust. "If you'd come here for polite conversation you would've brought a bottle. You haven't – so what's it all about?"

"You left court all those years ago, screaming ... what was it?" David consulted Jim's notes. "'I'll get you, Burrage. You and your family.'"

"Did I?" murmured Evans, as if it were unimportant. "Perhaps, but I don't remember. If I did, it must have been the heat of the moment. The judge, bless him, had just told me I was going to spend the rest of my life behind bars. I'm only human – I might have let off a bit of steam." He scratched his bald head comically then stared directly into David's face and added, "Haven't you heard? Burrage is safe from me. The Assessment Board decided that I'm not a danger to the public. Prison cured me," he stated cynically. "I'm a good boy now! That's why I got parole."

"Yes. I know that." But Evans' dark eyes did not suggest sanity to David. The detective's intuition told him a very different story. He said, "I also heard that you saved the life of a warder in that prison riot last year. That didn't do your case any harm. In fact, I can picture you. Riot all around. Badly injured prison officer. What did you think? Here's a fellow human being who needs my help? Or here's my passport out of prison? Your medical knowledge allowed you to milk the opportunity for parole."

John Evans continued to peer at him defiantly and wildly. "It doesn't matter what you think. It's what the Board thought that counts."

Fifteen years ago, the surgeon's case was notorious. It was rare for a professional man like Evans to be found guilty of common murder. He was convicted because his fingerprints were on the knife, the stab wound was delivered by an expert, and he did not have an alibi – and because the prosecuting barrister was a persuasive performer. Under relentless questioning by Stuart Burrage, Evans broke down in court. He complained about pressure at work, where his mistakes had resulted in the deaths of two patients. He complained about pressure at home. He swore that he loved his wife, but admitted that she nagged him constantly. Because he loved her, he could not retaliate. He took it all, the hen-pecked husband, till he snapped. He wept helplessly in the dock and the prosecution got the result. For the rest of the proceedings, the defendant stared grimly at the floor. Only when he was led away did he look up. As a parting shot, he pointed at Stuart Burrage, threatening him and his family. If anyone in the courtroom was uncertain about the guilty verdict, that final act clinched it. The outburst seemed to prove that he was capable of suddenly flipping and destroying a family – his own or someone else's.

David sprang the important question on him. "Where were you Saturday afternoon between three and four?"

"Saturday afternoon?" John Evans gazed at the police officers with his head on one side. He was trying to deduce the background to the question. Slowly, a smirk began to appear on his face. "Do you mean someone's had a go at Burrage?" He raised his long arms, about to wave them in triumph and celebration, but decided to curb the impulse.

David merely repeated his question.

"Well, well, well. Sorry to disappoint you, Inspector, but I was ... otherwise engaged."

"Otherwise engaged?" David queried.

There was a short but telling pause before he answered, "I was here, watching the cricket." He nodded towards the television. "Not much else to do these days, thanks to you lot."

"Did you watch it on your own?"

"Yes." He barked his response as if he were issuing a challenge.

"Who was playing?"

Evans grimaced as if he found the question tiresome. "You'll have to do better than that," he mocked. "Middlesex versus Warwickshire. Warwickshire won again."

"As an alibi, it's hardly watertight," David Thompson remarked.

The surgeon shrugged. "It doesn't matter what I say. I know you. You'll pull it apart anyway if you want to – by hook or by crook. A man like Burrage must develop a lot of enemies, not just me, but if you want to blame me for something, I dare say you will. I'm not exactly heartbroken if he's copped it. In fact, nothing would give me greater pleasure."

David rose, declaring, "You'll be hearing from us." With Jim behind him, he made for the front door.

"Well," Evans prompted, "*has* Burrage gone to the great court-room in the sky?"

Tersely, Detective Inspector Thompson growled, "I think you already know that. I dare say it'll be on local news tonight and all over the papers by morning."

Back in the car, David quizzed his sergeant. "What did you make of our ex-surgeon, ex-con, then?"

Changing into top gear, Jim answered, "Mad as a hatter. Mad as the Parole Board."

"He did plug a hole in a prison warder."

"Only to buy his freedom," Jim rejoined.

"Mmm," David muttered, "I agree. It could be happening all over again. First, Evans' wife, now Stuart Burrage. Both stab wounds were precise. John Evans is an expert surgeon. He didn't have an alibi before and he hasn't got a decent one now. The only thing that's missing so far is his fingerprints on the knife."

"I'll check on that cricket match," Jim offered.

"Don't bother," David replied. "He was right. Middlesex trounced by Warwickshire. All it proves is that he's listened to the news or read this morning's sports pages. There was a *Daily Telegraph* on the table in the corner." He glanced at Jim and said, "You'd better check that Kieran Burrage and the Tankersley girl were really in Scotland on Saturday, though. It's a bit far-fetched but let's not miss anything. They were supposed to be on some sort of swimming club tour."

"OK," Jim responded. "What now?"

"Stuart's junior partner, Daniel Allgrove. I want to ask him about that e-mail message Stuart sent him half an hour before he died. And then I want to know if Allgrove could have got from his place to the Burrages' house within half an hour. After that, Robert Tankersley. See if we can find out what that last report was about. Let's see if we can collar both of them before the news breaks – while there's still an element of surprise."

It was late on Monday afternoon when the detectives were ushered into Daniel Allgrove's cluttered office. The lawyer, trying to look important behind his huge mahogany desk, was dressed to impress in an expensive suit and flamboyant tie. He was used to dealing with police officers. He regarded them with a degree of suspicion and contempt. He saw them as worker ants, crawling everywhere, doing the grubby and unpleasant jobs, to provide fodder for the queens of the legal profession, like himself. "Yes?" he said, waving them towards a couple of chairs. "What can I do for you gents?"

"You can tell me if you got an e-mail message from Stuart Burrage at the weekend."

The lawyer's face screwed up. "Now why would you be interested in that?"

"Did you?"

"Why not ask Stuart? He's working on a case at home today – and waiting for his wife to return from some trip, as I understand it. You could catch up with him at home." Glancing at the detectives' dour expressions, he hesitated and then asked, "Has something happened to him? It has, hasn't it?"

David saw no advantage in denying the crime or prolonging the mystery. He broke the news of Stuart Burrage's death.

Allgrove seemed surprised but not stunned. For a few seconds he was silent, gathering his thoughts, absorbing the implications. He shook his head woefully. Using a respectful whisper, he did his best to express regret at his senior partner's fate, but only succeeded in sounding relieved. "That's ... awful. Poor Stuart – and Rhia."

"Indeed," David replied. "He was murdered perhaps half an hour after he sent you a message, so naturally I'm curious about its contents. Did it arrive here, or at your house?"

"Here, but Stuart knows ... I mean, knew ... that I scan my messages from home with my computer there. So he knew I'd get it anyway. I was just putting the finishing touches to a piece of work when the computer bleeped me to tell me that a message had come in from Stuart. It was just before three."

"How come you know the time so accurately?" David enquired.

Daniel answered, "I was late, hurrying so I could go across to the school field and watch my boy play football. Local league. Three o'clock kick off. Parents have to take an interest, don't you think?"

"Did you go to the match or did the message stop you?"

"I read it quickly. Nothing urgent. He wanted my help with a copyright case. It's a messy and complex business these days, when two companies are at each other's throats over a copyright dispute. It needs careful research so Stuart turned to me. Nothing new in that. He often did when there were complications. I have a talent for it, you know. Anyway, there was something about the Bridge Club in his e-mail as well. A change in venue for the next meeting. That's it. Nothing to keep me from the game."

"Did anyone see you at this football match?"

"What are you suggesting, Inspector Thompson?" Daniel snarled.

"I'm following a line of inquiry – as thoroughly as a lawyer would wish me to."

"Yes, but I don't like your insinuation." He turned away with distaste but answered the question anyway. "Obviously my son saw me supporting on the touch-line. I exchanged words with his trainer late in the game – told him where he was going wrong – so he'd remember I was there as well."

"This message. Can you give a copy?" David asked.

"I don't see why not. But I don't see why I should either."

"It could be important."

"I doubt it," Daniel responded. "It's totally innocuous, I assure you. But, if you're adamant, I suppose I can print you a copy – if you think it'll assist your thorough inquiries." He turned to his computer, clicked the mouse a few times and then mumbled to himself, "Here it is." He clicked once more and then declared, "It'll be with you in a few seconds – for what it's worth." He nodded towards a printer in the corner of the room that had already begun to murmur to itself.

Jim strolled towards it and waited for the emerging piece of paper.

"I'm still ... a bit bewildered, to tell you the truth," Allgrove admitted. "I can't take it in. There'll be changes round here. Life without him is ... hard to imagine." He shook his head again.

Jim handed the print-out to his boss. David's eyes skimmed over it. "Thanks," he said to the lawyer.

"No problem," he replied. "Is there anything else I can do? I must go and see Rhia. Give her my commiserations."

"You can provide me with a list of people who might have reason to want Stuart out of the way. You know, disgruntled clients, violent crooks he put away. Jim here will help as well."

Allgrove shrugged. "OK. I'll put my mind to it – when I have time – and let you know." He exhaled loudly and added, "Now, if you gentlemen have got all you need, and I'm sure you have, I'd like to get on. As you'll appreciate, I have a busy time ahead of me. Important cases that will now be my responsibility. Clients to reassure."

David and Jim left. In the car, Jim declared, "Slimy, wasn't he? And arrogant."

"He's a young ambitious lawyer," David said with a wry smile. "It's part of the deal."

"He wasn't exactly devastated," Jim observed.

"No. Better contact his son's football team. Check out what he said. Right now, though," the inspector said, looking carefully at his watch, "I want you to drive to the Burrages' house. We don't need to go in. I just want to know how long it takes. Keep to the speed limit."

The journey took fourteen minutes. David muttered, "He could have left his house at three and made it here in plenty of time to commit murder. He'd be back by three forty-five. In time for the second half. He said he'd spoken to the coach *late* in the game. Interesting."

"The e-mail seems innocent enough, though," Jim put in. "Nothing to incite murder."

David read it again. "I agree. I doubt if we'd have got it quite so easily if there was something incriminating in it. Still, as junior partner, he already had enough motive." Tapping the paper, he added, "I'll take a look at this Bridge Club and the copyright case anyway. No stone unturned to get to the bottom of this one."

By the time that the detectives reached Robert Tankersley's house, all of the family had been reunited. Robert had come in from work and Ali had returned from Edinburgh with news of Kieran's father. DI Thompson had lost the element of surprise.

"I'm ... shocked," Robert stated as he paced the large lounge. "It's a disaster. We did business, me and Stuart. Not recently, but in the past. And, of course, Ali's going out with his son. I hope Kieran takes it OK."

"What sort of business, Mr Tankersley?"

"I sell electronic equipment. Stuart gave me legal advice."

"What sort of electronic equipment needs legal advice?"

Robert Tankersley stopped walking and peered at the detective. "Our equipment's used in all sorts of devices, but it includes missile guidance systems. There are strict – and complicated – controls on who you can sell arms to. Stuart kept my company on the right side of the law."

"But you hadn't sought his advice recently?"

"No. Once he'd put me on the straight and narrow, there wasn't any need. If the regulations on arms controls had changed, I would've been banging on his door again."

Behind David, Jim watched Mrs Tankersley and Ali. Mrs Tankersley sat stiffly, clearly nervous, but nodding almost continuously as if to support her husband. Ali frowned at her dad's last answer. She did not believe that he had told the truth.

"Can you explain", David pronounced, "why Stuart Burrage's last action was to begin a report that concerned you?"

"Me? Strange. No, I don't know anything about that, I'm afraid. What did it say?"

"Next to nothing. He didn't get the opportunity."

"I see," Ali's father replied, head bowed.

"Mr Tankersley. I'd like to speak to you in private for a moment," David said.

"I don't have anything to hide," he snapped.

"Maybe you don't. Maybe I do."

Robert shrugged, led the detective into a small study, and closed the door impatiently. "What is it?" he muttered, plainly annoyed.

David noted that, in the corner of the room, there was a desk and a state-of-the-art personal computer. Robert Tankersley also worked in electronics. Obviously he *was* familiar with computers. "What were you doing on Saturday afternoon?" asked the detective.

"What? Am I a suspect?"

"I am just trying to assemble a picture of what everyone was doing when he died. That's all," the police officer replied coolly.

"I assure you, Inspector Thompson, I had nothing to do with it."

"So where were you?"

"Shopping," he answered. "With my wife."

"Thank you," the detective replied. "Wait in here a moment, please."

David went back into the living room and asked Mrs Tankersley what she was doing on Saturday afternoon.

"What I always do," she answered timidly. "I go shopping in town."

"On your own?"

"No," she replied. "With Robert."

Fleetingly, Ali frowned again.

As the police officers left, David Thompson asked Ali, "Did you leave Kieran with Rhia?"

"Yes," she muttered. "They probably need time on their own – to sort themselves out. It won't be easy for either of them."

David nodded in sombre agreement. "True."

The taxi had pulled into Kieran's drive, dropped him off, and then whisked Ali away, back to her own house. Kieran had stood for a moment in the porch and breathed deeply before unlocking the door and going in.

The reunion with his stepmother was an awkward, unnatural event. She rushed to him and clasped him as if, suddenly and inexplicably, the death of his father had drawn them closer together. Kieran did not believe that it had. Reconciliation was not that easy. He did not reap any comfort from her embrace and he withdrew from her arms as soon as he could.

There were tears in Rhia's eyes and she sobbed, "Thanks for coming back. I ... I'm sorry. Sorry about your dad."

"Yes," Kieran mumbled. He could not cry. He had run out of tears when his mum died and later when she was replaced by Rhia. It didn't mean that he couldn't mourn his father but, for Kieran, it would be done with dry eyes and in private.

"I can see you're upset," Rhia whimpered.

"Yes," Kieran repeated. Utter turmoil would have been a more apt description. He felt that he ought to be even more anguished at the loss of his father. He thought that he might just have hugged the person who had murdered him. If so, she was putting on a convincing show of grief. He didn't want to be alone in the house with only Rhia – a stranger really – from now on. He didn't want to share his life with a stepmother that he resented. He wanted it to be like it was all those years ago – before his mum died and before his dad became famous and unapproachable.

"Where is he?" he asked quietly.

"Your dad? You mean, where have they taken ... his body?"

"Yes."

"The police took him away. There can't be a funeral until after the investigation." Fresh tears appeared again. "It's horrible." Her words came out almost as if she were underwater. Her eyes were red, set in a pallid complexion. She blew her nose and then muttered, "If you want to see him ... I'm sure David Thompson would arrange it."

Kieran didn't know what he wanted. And he didn't know what was expected of him. Seven years ago, he was with his mother in hospital when she died. Then, there were no choices to be made. He had not gained the experience needed to deal with his father's death. "I'm not sure," he said. "I'll think about it, I guess." He'd known enough about the manner of his mother's death to despise it. Now, he realized that he knew hardly anything about his dad's murder. "Where did it happen?" he muttered.

In reply, Rhia looked fearfully through the hall towards the door to the study. "While he was working at the computer."

The door was almost always open. Now, it was shut as if it could protect them from what had happened beyond. The study was sealed like a tomb.

"How did he...?"

Rhia sighed. "Didn't they tell you? They think someone came in through the back door, picked up a kitchen knife and..." Her hand shot to her throat as if she could feel the blade herself. She slumped into a seat. "Why didn't he come to France with me? Damn it!"

Kieran knew that he should go to her side and comfort her. But he didn't know how and he didn't feel inclined.

Rhia shook her head slowly. "I don't know what we'll do without him."

For a moment, Kieran was touched by her torment. "No," he said, almost tenderly, "but we'll sort something out, I guess." Then, still nonplussed by the situation, he added rather feebly, "I'll go and brew up some tea." He knew that tea was not a magical remedy for anything but at least, in making it, he would be doing something useful – and Rhia would interpret his action as kindness. Under the circumstances, it was the most sympathy that he could show her.

In the middle of the night, Kieran got out of bed and padded furtively to the study. He felt attracted towards it, like iron to a magnet. He didn't understand why but he wanted to be where his dad had drawn his last breath. It would be Kieran's personal commemoration for his father. He turned the handle of the study door slowly and quietly, as if he were the intruder. Silently, he opened the door and entered. The room felt colder than the rest of the house. It was nothing supernatural, Kieran knew. It was just that he felt chilled inside. He tiptoed, like his dad's assailant must have done, towards the desk. He touched the back of the chair but let go immediately. It felt like ice. He shivered. He could almost feel the presence of his father, working away, oblivious to everything around him. Once, it would have been Kieran, holding out a game or a school report, who would have remained unnoticed. On

Saturday, it was a murderer with a knife. Kieran's spine tingled. His dad did not deserve to die alone at the whim of some thug.

He turned and hurried away. The dismal study evoked the stale atmosphere of sudden and violent death. He could take it no longer.

3

The next day, a message arrived on David Thompson's desk. The Strathclyde Police had confirmed that Kieran Burrage and Ali Tankersley had taken part in a swimming gala in Glasgow on Friday evening. Kieran had come second in the individual medley and Ali had won the 200 metres backstroke. They were also seen at the team's party on Saturday night. It was not impossible for one or both of them to have returned to London between the two events but it was unlikely. They were probably both in the clear. Detective Inspector Thompson also received the pathologist's preliminary conclusions. After reading the findings, he felt that he had to return to Rhia Burrage and ask her another question. He was not looking forward to it.

In the Burrages' living room, feeling decidedly uncomfortable, the police officer coughed and then declared, "I'm sorry, Rhia, but I have to explore every avenue." To get it over with, he plunged straight in. "I have to ask you your whereabouts in Paris on Saturday afternoon."

Rhia was much more composed today but her innate poise, diminished by her husband's death, showed no sign of returning. As she listened to David's question, her neglected face expressed patience more than anger. She was disappointed that his duty outweighed their friendship but she realized that it would. The man trusted her, no doubt, but the detective in him could not afford to be swayed by familiarity. She expected David to become Detective Inspector Thompson and to investigate her movements. She was prepared for the questioning.

"I know you have to do your job." She sighed. "It means you've found out when he died, I suppose."

"Yes," the detective answered. "I've just had the report from pathology. It's consistent with the information from his computer. Both suggest three-thirty on Saturday afternoon."

Rhia nodded sadly. "Saturday. Let me think." She stared for a moment at the ceiling and then continued, "My art day. Pompidou Centre in the morning, the Louvre in the afternoon."

"And ... er ... I don't suppose Customs stamped your passport? In France, they don't really bother these days."

Before Rhia could answer, Kieran came into the room to see who had arrived. He looked pale and unkempt – as if he hadn't slept all night.

Distracted, the detective turned to him and murmured, "I'm sorry about your father, Kieran. And I'm sorry we had to drag you back early. We all thought it for the best, though."

"Yes, it's OK," he replied dully. "Am I interrupting something?"

"David's just asking me a few questions," Rhia admitted. "Mainly about where I was on Saturday afternoon. Three-thirty. That's when ... you know. Your dad's computer recorded the time, apparently."

"I see," Kieran mumbled. "Do you want me to make myself scarce?"

"No," his stepmother replied. "Not as far as I'm concerned anyway." She looked at David in case he objected to an audience. He signified his indifference with a shrug so Rhia continued, "Where were we? Passport. No. They looked at it, but that's all. If you need confirmation that I wasn't here, though, you can check with British Midland. I flew with them from Heathrow to Charles de Gaulle airport. They'll have records, I suppose."

"Yes, I'll have to do that."

Kieran did not interrupt. He leaned against the wall and listened. It was hardly a grilling. The detective appeared to be satisfied with Rhia's response. He did not seem to be considering that she could have sneaked back into the country on Saturday morning and slipped back to Paris in the evening. She could have made the extra journey easily, using a ferry or the tunnel. His closeness with her was blinding him to the possibility. Almost immediately Kieran lost confidence in David Thompson. Kieran did not know about French Customs policy, but he thought that a thorough police officer would have asked to see her passport just in case it had been stamped on Saturday.

"How's it going, in general?" Rhia asked.

David relaxed a little. "Well... Still checking. We've got a number of leads. We're looking at alibis and motives. There's one particularly strong suspect, just out of jail. Stuart prosecuted him for murder some fifteen years ago. Name of John Evans. And there's some other possibilities. Basically, no one's out of the reckoning yet – except you two, of course," he added quickly. "You were both miles away. Besides, I don't think for one minute..."

Rhia smiled limply. "You don't have to mother me, David. I won't be off your hit list till you've checked out my trip to Paris."

"That's just a formality, I'm sure." He was almost blushing. He pointed to a framed photograph of Stuart and Rhia and asked, "Do you have a copy of that – or something similar showing the two of you?"

"Yes. I'll get one for you." Getting to her feet like a doddery old woman and fiddling inside a cupboard, she enquired, "Do you need it for a picture of Stuart or me?"

"Well, for both really."

Giving him a photograph from an album, she commented, "That's your polite way of saying for me."

He did not deny it. Instead, he said, "There's a couple more things. Can you give me the names and addresses of the regulars at your Bridge Club?"

"The Bridge Club?" Rhia was amazed.

"Yes." The police officer explained, "One of his last communications was about the club so I need to check out the members."

Rhia shrugged. "OK. I can make you a list now, if you want." She went for a pen and paper.

"Thanks," David replied.

Once she had jotted down the details and given him the list, she added, "You said there were a couple of things."

"Oh, yes," he replied. "Did someone leave a fingerprint kit with you?"

"Yes," answered Rhia. "He put it in the fridge."

"Good." Addressing Kieran, the detective said, "Sorry about this but I need your prints – to eliminate them from any others we've found. OK? If you come into the kitchen, I'll help you through it right now. Then I can take them away with me. Get it over with."

Kieran shrugged and followed the officer.

Back at headquarters, David turned to Jim and said, "Well, we have to go through the motions. The Louvre must be riddled with video cameras. They'll have captured Rhia on tape. Get on to it, will you? I'll authorize a trip to Paris for you. Check the airports as well. Heathrow and Charles de Gaulle security cameras. You should look into her British Midland booking, I guess, but it won't mean much – not now Paris is just round the corner by train. Theoretically, she could have come back into the country on Saturday. It's more important to sort out the security pictures so we can eliminate her once and for all."

"There's something not quite right about all this," Ali commented.

Kieran put his hands on the side of the swimming pool, heaved and twisted. Dripping water that had been warmed by the sun, he sat next to Ali. His body was perfect. Training had given him broad shoulders, upper body strength and flexibility. His trunk tapered to a lean waist and his legs were slender but muscle-packed. Ali was shorter but built to the same design. Supple yet powerful. If they had been the same height and walking side by side, their ample shoulders would have kept them apart. Now, both of them were clad in swimming suits and dangled their legs in the pool. Kieran wiped the water from his face and enquired, "What do you mean?"

"I'm not sure," Ali responded. "But something strange is going on. Last night, after the policemen left my place, Dad disappeared straight away. He made a bolt for the study and occupied the phone for an age."

"So, he was telling all his business contacts about ... Dad," Kieran suggested.

"Possibly. But ... Oh, I don't know. Earlier, Mum and Dad lied to the police – twice maybe. I'm sure. Mum said she went shopping with Dad on Saturday. Well, Dad hates shopping. He always leaves it to Mum. And he didn't say that he'd fallen out with your dad, just that he didn't need his advice any more. And he implied there was no big bust-up by saying he would've consulted your dad in the future if need be. I don't believe that."

"Maybe not," Kieran replied. "But it strikes me he was just taking precautions. He didn't want to admit he's got a motive of some sort so he left out the argument. And he didn't want to admit to an opportunity so your parents agreed on an alibi. They must have worked it out after you told them about Dad but before the police arrived." Kieran swept his hand through his wet hair. "Perhaps they were lying but you can't really blame them – not unless ... but I can't believe that."

"I'm not so sure now," Ali said in a quaking voice. Her father's lies had persuaded her that he was a suspect. "Something funny's going on, I tell you, and it's about my dad, your dad, and business."

Kieran grunted. "Business," he murmured derisively.

Both Ali and Kieran were disillusioned with their fathers' trades. Kieran believed that lawyers were committed more to their clients than to the truth. Ali despaired that her dad's computer chips, so ingenious and so creative, were used to kill people. It was cruel and perverse. To Kieran and Ali it seemed that both of their fathers were prepared to sacrifice conscience for cash.

The same substitute of cash for conscience lay behind the pool. When Kieran began to develop a considerable talent for swimming, his dad had the pool built in the garden. It was a busy father's way of encouraging Kieran. Spending a few thousand pounds was much easier than giving up precious time to take a real interest in Kieran's progress.

"I've just had a terrible thought," Ali said, staring in horror at her boyfriend and shuddering as if the water had suddenly turned cold. "You don't think *you're* in danger, do you?"

Kieran shrugged. "I've been wondering that myself. It depends if Dad was the only target, I suppose." He put his hand on Ali's shoulder. "It depends what you believe about the motive. If someone's got something against the Burrages, yes, I might be. Especially if it's something against both Dad and me. But I can't be absolutely sure what we're dealing with. I suppose it *could* be someone with a grudge against Dad's firm. Maybe Daniel Allgrove is the one in danger. Maybe everyone is – it could have been a random choice by a serial killer."

"But if it *is* a family vendetta... Well, whoever did it, he could be watching us right now. It's scary."

Kieran tried to smile. He shuffled closer to Ali and put his arm round her shoulders. "I shouldn't think so," he replied in a reassuring voice. He kissed her forehead. As he did it, a movement in the window of Rhia's room caught his eye. He withdrew and whispered sullenly, "But I wouldn't be so sure it was a he."

"You're thinking of Rhia again," Ali deduced.

"Yes."

Glancing round to check that they were alone in the garden, Ali argued in a hushed voice, "But she seems desperately unhappy to me."

"I know," Kieran mumbled. Rhia had always been so immaculate, more like a perfectly programmed robot than flesh and blood, that it was hard to imagine her in distress. He had never seen her sick or scruffy or dishevelled. He had hardly ever seen her without the embellishments of make-up and jewellery. Now, she looked so drab that it came as a revelation to him that she could apparently suffer like a normal human being. "She's a social animal but she hasn't left the house. She just mopes around. She's either shocked and hurt – or good at pretending."

In Rhia's defence, Ali murmured, "I think you're too hard on her."

"Like you're too hard on your dad, thinking of him as a suspect?"

Ali managed a grin. "Yes. I suppose so. But, don't forget, Rhia was in Paris at the time."

"Yes, well, the police are checking that, so we'll know soon – if they do it properly."

Ali peered into his face and said softly, "You've been shaken by all this. You asked me out here because you thought you could swim it out of your system. You're more shaken than you'll admit to."

"Perhaps. It's just that…" He sighed. He had always been open and honest with Ali and, as far as he knew, she had always been the same with him. This was not the time to change. He needed her now more than ever before. "I know Dad didn't bother with me much over the last few years but, even so, I feel lonely without him, Ali. Like I'm a stranger round here. When Rhia moved in, she turned the house into *her* place. At least when Dad came home, he reminded me of how it was – the good times. Now he's gone, I'm a stranger in her home. It's as if there's no one to … to love me, I suppose."

Ali turned and hugged him. "Oh, Kieran! I'm sorry. But you've got me, you know."

"Yes. I don't want to lose you as well."

"Don't worry," she said into his ear. "You won't."

*　　*　　*

Kieran could not sleep on Tuesday night either. After hours of shifting position under a single sheet and peeping at the clock, he sat up and listened. The house was quiet. Rhia must be sleeping. Again, he was lured to the study. This time, it had more to do with Rhia than with his father. Even so, when he went in, trying not to make a sound, he felt apprehensive. It was illogical because the evil had long since gone, yet he could not help himself. In his mind, the room would always be blighted and spooky. He faltered for a few seconds but told himself that he was being silly. Regaining his resolve, he headed for the cabinet where his dad had kept all of the important documents. Slowly, he pulled the drawer open. It made a noise that was probably not loud but, in the silence of the night, sounded like thunder.

Kieran hesitated, waiting in case there were any tell-tale foot-steps from upstairs. After a minute, everything remained still. He sighed with relief. Before he resumed, he crept back to the door and closed it. He could not risk being discovered by Rhia. Besides, he would have to put on a lamp at some point. Closing the door would contain the light but it also reminded Kieran of being sealed in a crypt. Trying to ignore his discomfort, he returned to the cabinet and opened it further. He fiddled amongst the insurance policies, cheque books, birth certificates and other documents until he found what he wanted. He clutched three passports but, in the gloom, he could not distinguish one from another. Instead, he grabbed all three and took them to the computer desk.

Praying that the light would not give him away, he clicked on the desk lamp. Blinking in the sudden glare, Kieran selected Rhia's passport and flicked through its pages. Last year, she'd taken a holiday in Antigua. Kieran found the entry marked, "Antigua and Barbuda," but beyond it the rest of the pages were blank. Kieran was not sure whether to be disappointed or relieved. He was none the wiser. Rhia was right that the French Customs officers had not stamped the book at all. On Saturday, she might have returned home. Equally, she might never have been to Paris.

As he turned off the lamp and gathered up the passports, he contemplated the possibility that she had never left in the first place. He could not believe that Rhia would swear that she'd been to Paris if she hadn't. She'd know that it would be simple for the police to check on international travel. Surely, she would never get away with such a blatant lie. Shaking his head, he put the passports back into their place. As he did so, it struck him that a copy of his dad's will was likely to be somewhere in the drawer. Yet he decided not to search for it. It could take a while to find and even longer to understand. Besides, he considered it as private. While he remained suspicious of Rhia, he believed that it was legitimate to meddle with her things in the pursuit of the truth but he drew the line at prying into his father's will. It would be like grave-robbing. He closed the drawer, praying that it would not screech, and then slunk back up the stairs.

- He gasped aloud and nearly fell backwards when the landing light suddenly blazed.

Above him, Rhia appeared like a ghost hovering between one world and the next. Wearing an expensive silk dressing-gown, she was bleary-eyed and haggard. In a slurred voice, she asked, "Can't you sleep either?"

"Er ... no."

"The doctor gave me some pills to help, but they don't seem to do the trick all through the night." She yawned.

"Sorry if I disturbed you," Kieran stammered. "It's a muggy night. Just went down for a bit of fresh air."

"Did you go into the study?"

"No ... I mean ... yes." Kieran admitted it in case she had heard him coming out of the study.

More awake, Rhia murmured, "Nothing to be ashamed about. I go in sometimes. It's curious. Sort of haunted. Creepy, but at least I feel close to him there." She looked down at her stepson, still clinging to the banister. "I loved your father, you know, Kieran. And, while he didn't have the time to be much of a family man, I think you loved him too. We have that in common." She paused and added, "As well as an inability to sleep. So let's not fight each other. Agreed? We're on the same side."

Kieran could not bring himself to make peace but he was not sure enough of her guilt to make war. "Are we?" he muttered dubiously.

"Yes," she insisted. Not waiting for him to reply, she said, "Now, I'm just going to the bathroom, then back to bed. Are you going to try and settle?"

He began to trudge up the remaining steps. "I suppose so."

"Good night, then," she mumbled as she glided along the passage like a lost and tortured soul.

4

Detective Inspector Thompson drew a blank on the Bridge Club. If any member had harboured a dislike for Stuart Burrage, it was well concealed. The detective had failed to ascertain a single strong motive among the members. The only ill-feeling towards the Burrages resulted from the fact that they won all of the time. As David would have anticipated, Stuart was a class player. But no one kills an opponent for winning a game of cards.

In examining the contents of Stuart Burrage's computer, Kate had left no byte unturned. Even so, she had failed to cast any more light on his murder. The forensic report was disappointing as well. The scene of the crime was clean. All of the fibres identified so far belonged to Stuart, Rhia or Kieran. Only the Burrages' fingerprints were on the door handles. The keyboard, mouse, desk and chair were covered in Stuart's prints. As expected, the knife bore Rhia's fingerprints, but there were no others. The killer had been very careful. He could not have wiped away his own prints because the cleaning would have smeared Rhia's. He must have worn gloves.

Jim returned from France bearing a large box full of videotapes. "The good news is, I got all we need. Both airports and the Louvre co-operated. That's a lot of cameras. So the bad news is, there's several days of viewing here."

David grimaced. He had not joined the police force and risen to his current rank to watch a television screen all day. He delegated to his team. "OK," he replied. "Assemble as many people as you want – and the same number of TVs – so you can get through it pretty quickly. I'll get copies of a photograph of Rhia so you can tape one to each telly. Then get their heads down for the search."

Jim groaned and muttered, "It's excitement all the way in the police force."

"Remember the time difference, as well. They're an hour ahead of us over there." Leaving his sergeant to get on with the tedious sifting job, David went to consult Daniel Allgrove again.

Stuart's junior partner, suddenly in the hot seat of the business, seemed to be stressed. It couldn't have been easy for him to take on the responsibility of being in charge and, at the same time, to cope with two people's jobs. Consequently, he had not had much time to assemble a list of Stuart's enemies. "Before my time," Daniel said, "there was a surgeon who was supposed to have threatened him in court. Let me think. What was his name?"

David interjected, "John Evans. We're working on that lead already. Any more?"

Daniel Allgrove sucked in air audibly. "Several, but I doubt that many would be capable of murder."

"Which might?" the detective inquired.

"A couple of years ago, he helped a police officer out of a tricky situation when a suspect died mysteriously in his custody. The victim had a brother. Surname of Pascoe. Rumour had it that he was as bent as his brother. He'd bear Stuart a grudge, no doubt. But, personally, I would have thought the police officer himself was a more obvious target." Daniel stared momentarily at the ceiling and then continued, "He prosecuted a terrorist accused of murder. He was released after a few years because the forensic evidence was found to be flawed. I wouldn't dream of telling you your job but, even if terrorism isn't big business here any more, you might want to think about a revenge attack. I'm too busy to find the details but my secretary can supply them. There are a few other possibilities but, to be honest, I don't give them much credence. And I'm pretty astute in these matters. I think you're wasting your time."

"Perhaps," David conceded, "but I still want to check everything – even the remote possibilities – so I'd like your secretary's information."

"As you wish," the lawyer responded tersely.

"I also wanted to ask you about the copyright case mentioned in Stuart's message."

Daniel expressed surprise. "I hardly think there would be grounds for murder there," he replied. "We're talking respectable businessmen here."

"Tell me about it," David prompted.

"You're supposed to be an intelligent man so you'll appreciate the ... sensitivity. I have to preserve my client's confidentiality. But..."

Patiently, trying not to take offence, David reminded him, "It *is* for Stuart."

"Yes, I know," Daniel replied. "I can tell you this. We're ... I'm acting for Xenon Computing. The company's got good reason to believe that a copyright on one of its products has been breached by Megaware. When we show our proof, it's more than likely that Megaware will settle out of court. Xenon stands to pick up ten million. Now it's in my hands, I might secure an even better settlement. Big business."

"I haven't heard of either company. Are they well known?"

"No. They're both small outfits, employing a few computer whizz kids. But they supply some of the big players. Megaware's not independent, though. It's owned by CompuTech."

"And who's behind CompuTech?"

"No idea," Daniel admitted. "Stuart would have found out, I should think, but I didn't get a report from him and I've had no time to chase it up."

"Mmm." DI Thompson did not elucidate further. He rose and thanked Daniel for his time. "It's been interesting," he remarked. "I may need to speak to you again. I'll be in touch."

On Wednesday, determined to escape for a while from Rhia's homemade morgue, Kieran went with Ali to the coffee bar in the sports centre. There, half the swimming team and half of their school seemed to be a permanent fixture. Everyone knew each other. When Kieran walked in, the cordial buzz suddenly ceased. He could have been a conspicuous stranger strolling deliberately into the saloon in a corny western. The boy with no name. The boy with no father. He wanted to shout at them, "It's only me. Kieran. I haven't changed. No need for the hush." Of course, he didn't shout anything. He just smiled limply at all of the apprehensive faces that turned towards him. He didn't want sympathy or special treatment. He was trying to evade the regular reminders of his father's fate. He just wanted normal company. But his friends did not know how to react. They had all read about the murder in the papers. Commenting on it could upset Kieran. Ignoring it would be heartless. The uncomfortable pause continued until Ali broke the spell by nudging him and muttering, "Come on. Let's get a drink."

Seizing the opportunity to be the centre of attention, Mike Spruzen strode up to Kieran and asked, "How are you?"

Out of habit, Kieran merely grunted in reply.

Without listening, Mike responded, "That's good." He was an incomparable backstroker and an incorrigible pest. He never said hello to anyone. Instead, he always greeted people by asking, "How are you?" He wasn't interested in the reply, though. Responses of "Great, thanks," and, "Appalling," met with the same indifferent and distracted murmur, "Good, good." All of his acquaintances had long since learned that a proper response to his casual question was not worthy of the effort. Mike was concerned only for himself. He also seemed to believe that he looked cool and tough if he drank a few beers. He loved to recount his vast store of drunken adventures, over and over again, to impress anyone who would listen. With each telling a new, fantastic twist was added and the girl in his arms grew more and more stunning. Alcohol seemed to stimulate his imagination and his powers of exaggeration.

Rescuing Kieran again, Ali asked Mike, "How's your shoulder?"

Mike rubbed the injury that had kept him out of the Scottish trip. "Still sore," he said. "Did I tell you how I did it?"

"Yes," Kieran muttered.

Sitting down at their table, he began, "It was funny, looking back, but I wish I hadn't missed Scotland. I had to drink on my own." He giggled at a thought that would not stay private for too long. "It was drinking that got me injured in the first place. Wicked."

"We know," Ali and Kieran said in chorus.

"But did I tell you what happened after I fell down the bank?" Without waiting for a reply, he cracked on enthusiastically. "Well, I landed right by the track. I could've reached out and touched the rail if my shoulder hadn't hurt so much. Good job I didn't, though, because this Intercity flew past. Almost hit me, it did. That would have been curtains. You'd have had to scrape me off at Euston. And you should've heard this gorgeous girl I was with. Thought it had taken my arm off, she did. Scream? She was almost louder than the train! Anyway," he concluded, "I really came over to talk about you guys, not me. Sorry to hear about your old man, Kieran. Have the police got whoever did it?"

Kieran sighed. He did not expect a great deal of diplomacy from Mike but his flippant enquiry was hard to take. "No," he breathed. "They're investigating."

"Good job you two were in Scotland. Great alibi."

Kieran's mouth fell open but Mike's comment was so tactless that he could not reply.

Ali was less inhibited. "You oaf! Why don't you think before you speak? No one would accuse Kieran of ... hurting his own father. And if we'd been here maybe it wouldn't have... Anyway, just shut up, Mike!"

Normally, Ali let her life follow the line of least resistance. She wasn't lazy, just relaxed about life. That's what Kieran liked about her. When a whirlwind raged all around, she was the tranquil centre. But, when she felt someone had been wronged, she could let fly. Seconds later, she would be relaxed again as if she had rid herself of all her anger in one effective outburst.

"Just asking," Mike mumbled as he retreated.

Ali put her hand on Kieran's leg and whispered, "Still pleased you came, then?" She smiled mischievously at him.

"Well," Kieran replied, "I didn't know Mike would be here, did I?"

Some of the others made up for it. A few friends dared to approach their table and murmur in embarrassed voices, "Sorry about your father, Kieran. It's ... awful. If there's anything I can do…"

Kieran smiled and murmured, "Thanks. It's OK. I'm just trying to carry on. Moping around doesn't solve anything."

Each visitor would nod and reply, "Good for you."

After a while, he was pleased that he'd decided to return to normal life – if only for a few minutes.

Jim's team worked well into the night. It was easy to concentrate on the comings and goings on screen for the first fifteen minutes. It was even amusing. Some people's outlandish dress sense was fascinating. Suitcases that burst open in the airport lounge provided occasional distraction. Spotting the pickpockets became a spectator sport. But, after a while, the entertainment wore thin. It was like watching a tedious ice-skating competition in the hope of seeing a dramatic fall. The endless surveillance tapes numbed the eyes and brain.

It was worth the effort, though. The cameras had witnessed Rhia's departure from Heathrow, arrival at Charles de Gaulle airport, her return journey, and her visit to the Louvre at the exact time that her husband had been killed.

In the early hours, after he'd dismissed the rest of his team, Jim edited the various extracts on to one convenient tape, ready for DI Thompson in the morning.

5

"You look a bit rough."

"I know. I'm not sleeping much."

Ali looked at her troubled boyfriend with sympathy. "Is that because of your dad – or because of Rhia?"

"I don't know. A bit of both, I expect."

Ali shook her head. "You really believe that Rhia ... killed your dad, don't you? Despite the fact that she's obviously cut up about it – and she wasn't even in the country at the time."

"It sounds crazy but, yes, I do," Kieran admitted. He was convinced that Rhia's greed was sufficient to provide a motive for murder. "If she was out of the country, I just don't know how she did it, that's all."

"Neither do I," retorted Ali. She was surprised that Kieran clung to his hunch even when it was apparent that Rhia could not be the killer. "You're letting a grudge get in the way of your judgement," she suggested. "There's no evidence against her. Rhia's OK. And she couldn't have done it – even if you'd like to prove she did to get her back for taking your mum's place."

Kieran scowled. "It's not just that."

"What else is it, then?"

"Lots of little things, I guess," answered Kieran.

"Like what?"

"Well, like when she wanted to buy this really flashy Mercedes. Dad said we didn't need it, stopped her, and she went into an almighty grump. Same thing when she decided we should have a holiday villa in Antigua. Dad said we wouldn't use it enough to make it worthwhile. She hit the roof."

"That's supposed to convince me she'd kill for cash?" Ali responded. "Sure it's gross, but it sounds pretty flimsy to me."

"It's not the only thing. You know, the more I think about it, the more I realize I don't know anything about her. I don't even know what she did before she met Dad. She never talks about her past. Perhaps she's hiding something. And about this time last year, just after her father died, I think, she used to go off a lot. No idea what she was up to. She didn't talk about that either."

"Look," Ali said. "Why don't you ask to see that policeman when he gets proof that she was in Paris? David Thompson. I bet he'd talk to you about it. Maybe he'll be able to convince you that she didn't do it."

"No," Kieran replied. "I couldn't. Besides, he's Rhia's friend. I'm not convinced he'll do a proper job anyway. He *wants* to clear her name. Hardly unbiased."

"Maybe. But just because he's biased, it doesn't make her guilty."

In the event, Kieran didn't have a choice. His presence was requested at the police station. Detective Inspector Thompson apologized for inconveniencing him and explained that he'd received some videotapes from the airports and the Louvre in Paris. He was satisfied that the security tapes showed Rhia leaving the country on Thursday 21st July, returning on Monday 25th July, and strolling round the art gallery from two fifteen to four thirty on the Saturday in between. For the investigation, though, he wanted confirmation by someone close to her.

David positioned Kieran in front of a television and turned on the video. "We've got hours of tapes, but you're just getting the edited highlights," he quipped, clearly in a good mood. "The first few sequences are from Heathrow last Thursday. See?" He pointed to the screen where a woman in a white coat and carrying a single suitcase crossed the airport entrance. It could have been almost anyone but the woman did look like Rhia. Then the angle changed. The woman, definitely Rhia, approached the check-in desk. "Well?" David prompted. "This is the British Midland desk. Would you say that's your stepmother?"

Kieran nodded. "Yes, it is." Rhia walked out of camera shot but not yet out of Kieran's reckoning.

The next pictures showed Rhia arriving in Paris. The bottom right-hand corner of the screen showed the date and time. David Thompson reminded him that France was an hour ahead of British time. "Here we are," the police officer announced. "This is the important bit. The Louvre. Saturday. Three-thirty our time. Four-thirty over there."

There was no doubt whatsoever. Now draped in a pale green dress and a loose jacket, Rhia ambled into shot and then stood still in front of a huge canvas. She could have been posing but really she was just lost in admiration for the painting. Kieran nodded again and had to admit it. "Yes, that's Rhia all right."

Mechanically, he watched the clips of Rhia's return to England, again wearing the white coat, and declared a positive identification whenever David Thompson requested it.

When the final picture faded, the detective said, "Mmm. There we have it." He seemed relieved. "Don't get me wrong, Kieran," he added. "I never believed that Rhia ... was involved, but I had to prove it." Plainly, he had no wish to point the finger at a friend and, by eliminating her from his inquiries, he was one small step nearer the culprit.

In contrast, Kieran was almost disappointed, but he hid it from the police. Unlike David Thompson, he had always suspected Rhia.

"That's all I need," David said, putting his hand briefly on Kieran's shoulder. "Thanks for coming in. I know all this isn't easy for you."

Kieran stood up. "It's OK," he mumbled. It seemed that he wasn't the only one with a great alibi, to quote Mike. Rhia's was cast-iron. Before he left, he asked, "Did you get any fingerprints or anything like that?"

The detective shook his head. "I'm afraid not. The only finger-prints were yours, your dad's and Rhia's. Our man must have been gloved."

While a junior member of the team escorted Kieran out of the police station, David and Jim compared notes with two sergeants who had been given the brief of researching Megaware and CompuTech. They had delved into both companies and discovered something relevant. "Megaware's a subsidiary of CompuTech," they reported, "and CompuTech's owned – at arm's length – by Alpha Systems."

"And Alpha Systems?" David checked, expecting another twist. The officers grinned at him, plainly pleased with themselves.

"Alpha Systems has a managing director with the name of Robert Tankersley. Thought you might be interested, Guv."

"Tankersley?" he exclaimed. "You're not kidding I'm interested." He absorbed the information for a few moments and then thought aloud. "Stuart Burrage used to advise Tankersley. Now he doesn't. Stuart wouldn't have known Tankersley was hiding behind Megaware when he took on Xenon's case. Since then he must have found out that, at the end of the day, he was fighting Tankersley! Then it'd be a case of loyalty to a friend versus the case. Knowing Stuart, he'd stick with the case. He didn't like to drop anything. Like a dog with a bone. For him, letting go would smack of failure. He'd also confront the problem, you know. He was like that. Bet he went to Tankersley and admitted he was acting for a business that had got Megaware in its sights. They'd have fallen out, no doubt. Stuart would disassociate himself from Tankersley rather than lose the case to protect him."

Jim carried on the logic. "It makes sense. If Tankersley's daughter knew they'd had a bust-up, she wouldn't believe her dad when he said to us he would have done business with Burrage again. And she didn't, I'm sure. She didn't believe his alibi either, judging by her face. If there's millions involved in this case and it goes in Xenon's favour, Tankersley could be ruined. That's enough of a motive. And we've only got his wife's word on the alibi."

"Fascinating," David responded. "There's the beginning of that report on Stuart's computer as well. Perhaps, on reflection, Stuart thought it was best to give the case to his partner – to avoid any personal bias. That's why he e-mailed Daniel Allgrove and began a report that he could hand over to his partner!" He peered at Jim and added, "Time we paid Robert Tankersley another visit."

They both grabbed jackets and made for the door.

They found Robert Tankersley working at home and, in the lounge, they asked him if he wanted to add anything to his previous statements.

"How do you mean?" Robert Tankersley barked.

Sitting out of sight, half-way up the stairs, Ali knew that she should retire to her room so that she would not overhear the interview. Yet it was too good an opportunity. She could not turn her back on it. Feeling guilty and hardly daring to breathe, she snooped on her own father.

"We have information that suggests you and Stuart Burrage found yourselves in opposite corners."

"What are you talking about?"

"Xenon Computing versus Megaware. And Megaware's relationship to your Alpha Systems."

Ali heard the detective's speculation about why her dad and Stuart Burrage had argued. Then she heard her father sigh loudly and confirm it in a weary voice. He admitted that it was very likely that Xenon would have its pound of flesh from him.

"But," he stressed, "that's all there is to it. I bore him a grudge, I guess. It doesn't make me a killer, you know."

"So where were you on Saturday afternoon? Not shopping with your wife," David suggested.

"No. I was here. Simple as that. Pottering in the garden. As a precaution, I got Myra to say I was with her."

Sternly, DI Thompson growled, "It's called perverting the course of justice. A serious offence. It could land you both in jail."

"Look," Robert Tankersley declared, "we're not really like this. Especially not Myra. But we were scared when Ali told us the news. We may have lied, but that's all."

Shortly after, the police officers left and Ali padded upstairs. As far as the detectives were concerned, her dad had become a key suspect. As far as she was concerned, he was already a murderer. He was a murderer because his computer chips killed people. But killing Kieran's dad with his own hands – with a knife? It seemed too close and messy. His chips were weapons of death but the killing was well down the line, elsewhere. It was hard to imagine him wielding a knife as a weapon of death. Even so, she sat on her bed and trembled for a while. Trembled with fear and anxiety. She knew that he loved his business and she was no longer sure how far he would go to protect it.

Later on Thursday, Ali and Kieran had plenty to talk about. Kieran broke the news about the videos and Ali told him about her dad's revelations. "That's Rhia out of the picture," Ali concluded, "and Dad way up there." She grimaced.

Kieran frowned and mumbled, "Maybe."

Ali peered at him. "What's that supposed to mean?" she asked.

"Rhia's got an alibi and Dad hasn't."

Kieran shrugged. "They didn't find any fingerprints, you know. The police reckon whoever did it wore gloves, but there is an alternative explanation." Before Ali could interrupt, he added, "And when I got back on Monday, Rhia's coat was slung over the chair."

"So?"

Kieran remarked, "It was blue."

"Yes?"

"At Heathrow, she had a white one on."

Ali stared at him. Incredulous, she exclaimed, "Good grief, Kieran! You should know Rhia by now. She changes coats at the drop of a hat. Every time she stands in front of a different coloured wallpaper she has to change to look her best. She changed between the airport and here. That's all."

"She was wearing a green dress in Paris. I've never seen it before."

"So what? She wears a new outfit every day! You know that. She bought herself a new number in Paris, I should think."

"Yeah," Kieran replied. "I guess so."

"Besides, she was in Paris, Kieran. I know you don't like to let little things like facts get in the way of your imagination, but you can't deny she's got a terrific alibi."

"Cast-iron," Kieran muttered. As he admitted it, he was wondering if that green dress was in her wardrobe right now. If it were, and if it bore a French label, it would wrap up her perfect alibi. If it wasn't there, Kieran believed that something would not quite add up.

"I'd best get home," Ali proclaimed. "Not a pleasant prospect, but they'll get worried if I don't turn up soon." She groaned as if home had become unbearable. "You know, I really didn't think Dad was a serious suspect, but now..."

Kieran took her hand. "This is crazy," he remarked with a faint smile. "You're pointing the finger at your dad and discounting Rhia. Me, I'm the other way round. Do you think, when you live with someone, familiarity *does* breed contempt?"

Ali murmured, "Let's hope that's all it is."

They hugged each other and kissed briefly, too distracted by events and possibilities to put passion into it. Promising to get together again tomorrow, they parted.

*   *   *

Sleeping was not getting any easier. Kieran tossed and turned in his
sweat-soaked bed. The night was muggy and Kieran's brain was
overactive. He tried to relax, to concentrate on nothing at all, but
thoughts rushed immediately into the vacuum. Physically, he was
tired but, much to his annoyance, his mind would not leave him in
peace. To himself, he muttered, "This is boring. I might as well be
up, doing something."

He got out of bed and pulled on some shorts and a T-shirt.
Deciding to get some fresh air into his lungs, he left his stale bedroom and crept quietly downstairs. He unlocked the back door and
stood for a moment on the step, breathing deeply. It was a quiet,
empty and attractive night. He could see two full moons. One was
low in the sky in front of him. The other was a virtual image on the
surface of the pool. It was a harmless night so he ambled into the
garden.

The figure halted by the hedge that separated Kieran's back garden
from the quiet street. Convinced that no one was watching, the
intruder squeezed into the secluded garden through the laurels. It
was a hot night but the cloaked and hooded figure seemed to be
dressed for winter. Stealthily, the stranger headed for the
swimming pool where Kieran, in shorts and shirt, strolled. Without wind, the water was perfectly still, making a brilliant mirror for
the moon. Keeping out of Kieran's sight, the uninvited guest crept
up behind him.

Kieran sighed with relief. The air had banished his morbid
imagination and put him in a better frame of mind. He had no
doubt that, when he went indoors, luxurious sleep would come. For
a few minutes more, though, he wanted to take in the tranquillity.
There in the garden, he could be the last person on earth, un-
troubled by the hustle and bustle that surrounded both life and
death. By the side of the pool, he stretched and then began to
saunter towards the back door.

Suddenly, someone leapt at him. For an instant, Kieran saw a
cloaked figure like a vampire and a lunging knife. Instinctively, he
ducked and shrieked. The knife, aimed at his neck, flashed past his
eyes and the intruder slammed into him. Kieran grabbed hold of

his assailant and frantically held away the arm that wielded the knife. He couldn't see the face of the attacker but he had the strength of a man, he was taller than Kieran and he grunted with a deep male voice. Slowly, Kieran realized that he could not hold his arm for long. The man was stronger. The knife was getting closer to his face. Again, he cried out.

In the struggle, the man's hood fell back. The moonlight revealed an almost bald head and a face that Kieran did not recognize. "No!" Kieran bawled as the blade came within centimetres.

For a second, the intruder was distracted as Rhia appeared at an upstairs window and yelled, "What's going on?"

Kieran took the opportunity. He realized that the man would regain the upper hand at any moment, but he could tip the balance. There was one place in which he would have a natural advantage. He twisted and, still holding his attacker, threw himself into the pool. Both of them splashed into the water.

Underwater, Kieran was in his element. He could hold his breath for two whole minutes. He grasped his attacker and prevented him reaching the surface. Kieran kept a firm grip on the man till he stopped struggling. Then, freeing himself, Kieran kicked hard, still underwater. It served to propel him away from his assailant and winded the man at the same time. The knife glinted in the water as it sank to the bottom. In the rippling water, it looked like a weaving silver fish.

Kieran surfaced and realized that the stranger was in trouble. His coat, heavy with water, was dragging him down. He spluttered and gasped for air. Kieran swam to the edge of the pool and got out. He waited till the man had ceased thrashing about like a hooked fish, then he reached out and dragged his limp body, no longer a threat, to the side. Steeling himself, he heaved the man out of the pool. The intruder collapsed helplessly at the edge. Kieran knew exactly what he should do. He'd been trained in lifesaving. But he hesitated. He found it difficult to summon the desire to revive a man who had just tried to kill him.

Above him, Rhia stammered, "Are you all right?" She clutched his shoulder.

Recovering from the shock of her appearance, he uttered, "Yeah. I'm fine. But..." He pointed to the culprit-turned-victim and said, "He needs help."

Rhia groaned but got down on her hands and knees anyway. Efficiently, she adjusted the man's position and opened his mouth to check for obstructions. "A long time ago," she said, "I trained as a nurse." Then she started resuscitation. Between mouthfuls of air, she croaked, "I've called the police, by the way."

Kieran watched as Rhia inflated the man's watery lungs, again and again. By the time that he began to gurgle, gag and breathe again, sirens were spoiling the silence of the night.

Jim arrived in the second car. He glanced contemptuously at the sodden figure lying in the recovery position beside the swimming pool, and then turned towards Kieran. "Did you escape unscathed?"

Kieran nodded. "Who is he?"

"Don't you know?" he queried. Seeing Kieran's blank look, he pronounced, "This sad specimen is John Evans. A surgeon your dad put away for murder fifteen years ago. Our chief suspect. On a mission to eliminate the Burrage family, it seems." He turned briefly to the uniformed police officers and asked, "Searched him for weapons?"

"Yes. He's clean."

With a wry smile, he said, "He would be after taking a dip." Jim peered into the pool and enquired, "Is the knife in there?"

Kieran answered, "Yes. He dropped it when I dragged him in."

"OK," Jim said to the other officers, "who's going to get their kit off and salvage it?"

"I'll do it," Kieran volunteered. "I can't get any wetter. And I know where it went down."

Jim refused his help. "Only joking. Forensic will sort it out. We can't do their job for them. Let's get you inside, dried off, and then I'll need a statement." To his colleagues, he said, "Take Evans back to the station. Get the doctor to look at him and certify him fit to face some questions – and charges of murder and attempted murder."

As Evans was dragged to his feet, he stared at Kieran with wild eyes and uttered, "I'll be back. I'll get you Burrages yet! I'm going to wipe you all from the face of the earth." It was plain that resentment had been eating into him for years until nothing was left but insanity.

Jim grimaced with disdain and cried, "Take him away."

6

"It's all over," David informed Rhia on Friday morning. The detective was positively purring over the news. "Evans confessed. He … er … even bragged about it." He shook his head sadly. "Hate's been welling up in him for a long time. Not even satisfied with murdering Stuart, he'd set himself a bigger task, I'm afraid. If Kieran hadn't foiled him, he would've probably come for you next, Rhia. He destroyed his own family. Last night he wanted to finish off yours as well. He admitted it during questioning. His own family life was a disaster and now he says God whispers in his ear, telling him to devastate other families – starting with the Burrages. In other words, he's flipped. At least you can rest assured that he's locked up."

In her armchair, Rhia smiled weakly. "Yes," she said. "I feel a bit better now you've caught him. Somehow, I think I can begin to build my life again." She looked more relaxed than at any time since her husband's death.

David Thompson was preoccupied with Rhia but he did recognize Kieran's presence. The police officer glanced at him and checked, "Are you over last night's ordeal?"

"Yes," Kieran mumbled tersely.

"Good idea to dunk him in the pool. Saved your skin, I should think. Well done." He turned his attention back to Rhia.

Kieran's mind drifted. The case had been closed but his mind was still open. If Evans had killed his father, there were three things that Kieran did not understand.

Over a sandwich in the coffee bar, Kieran related last night's arrest to Ali and aired his reservations.

Once she had absorbed the shock of Evans' attack on her

boyfriend and recovered from the news, she remarked contentedly, "That's it, then." She was relieved because Kieran was out of danger and because it meant that her own father could not have committed the murder. "Suddenly, it's all over. Just like that."

Kieran hesitated and sipped his coffee before questioning, "Is it?"

"What do you mean?" Ali whispered as if Kieran were doubting the law of the land. "Evans has admitted it, hasn't he? That's what you said."

"Yes. That's what Thompson said. But when Evans was dragged away last night, he'd cracked. Totally. He was mad enough to claim that he assassinated Kennedy, as well as Dad."

"Hang on," Ali gasped. "Are you saying he didn't do it – despite the confession?"

"That's right. I think he was so besotted with the idea of murdering Dad that he imagines he has. He's probably proud of it as well." Noting that Ali was gazing at him incredulously, he added, "He really wanted to kill Dad but I reckon someone beat him to it. To get his own back, he had no choice – he had to go for me instead. He was deprived of Dad but he still wanted his pound of Burrage flesh. You see, if he … disposed of Dad, why did he yell, 'I'll get you Burrages yet,' last night? Sounded to me as if he'd still got a score to settle. It certainly doesn't sound like someone who's already killed a Burrage."

"Maybe not," Ali replied. "But, even so… Anyway, you reckon he was mad enough to say anything. If he's so crazy that he confessed to a murder he didn't commit, I'm sure he could suffer a slip of the tongue." She desperately wanted a neat and tidy end to the affair. She wanted Evans to be guilty. Otherwise, her dad would be back in the frame.

"All right," Kieran relented. "But what about the killer leaving evidence of the exact time of death? Careless or convenient, would you say?"

Ali looked puzzled. "How do you mean?"

"Well, Rhia…"

Exasperated, Ali interrupted. "You're not still trying to blame Rhia!"

"Just bear with me," Kieran muttered under his breath so that no one else in the café could hear. "She knew she could prove she was somewhere else at that exact time. She might as well have stood in front of the video camera and waved." He paused and then added, "Another thing. Why do it in the middle of the afternoon?"

"What are you getting at?"

"Surely, any self-respecting murderer like Evans would creep about in the middle of the night, like he did last night, not in the full glare of the sun."

"You think Rhia set it up somehow at three-thirty – and left evidence of the time – because she could arrange to be seen on video in France then?"

"Precisely. It would be much trickier to guarantee an appearance on video after dark," Kieran explained.

"What are you saying, Kieran? It was Rhia and, while she was in France, she used a hit-man or something?"

Kieran shrugged. "Possibly."

Ali sighed but decided to humour him for a while. "And how would you prove she hired some assassin?"

"I've been wondering about that," he answered, "and I think I know. Why does a hit-man carry out a murder?"

"For money. At least that's how it works on the telly."

"Exactly. That's the lead. I think I know where her cheque book is. You must admit, it would be ... interesting if she's made any big withdrawals recently."

"Well, it wouldn't prove anything but, yes, it'd be worrying. It *might* persuade me to take your theory seriously."

"There's the unknown dress thing as well," Kieran commented. He waved the remains of his last sandwich in the air. "Why don't you come round this afternoon and have a woman-to-woman chat with Rhia? You could ask after her now that the murderer's been caught."

For a second, Ali looked puzzled. Then her mouth opened and, feigning irritation at his cheek, she hissed, "So you can stick your nose in her wardrobe and cheque book while I keep her occupied! You want to use me as a decoy."

"I want you to come round anyway. It's no fun at home without you."

"Well…"

"Will you come?" Still she hesitated so Kieran continued, "Think of it like this. What if I'm right? Rhia killed him to get her hands on his money. If that's right – if she's a killer – will she want to share her new-found wealth with me?"

Startled by the thought that Kieran could be the next target, Ali submitted. "There's a lot of ifs in there but, OK, I'll come back with you. Just in case. I think you're barking up the wrong tree altogether, though." Her mind flitted impulsively to her father.

Kieran reached across the table and squeezed her hand. "Thanks. I know you don't agree with me – but that doesn't stop you helping out."

Ali added, "There's a condition. If you don't find anything while I'm doing your dirty work, distracting her, you give up this crazy notion about her."

Kieran nodded. "It's a deal," he declared.

Kieran found Rhia in the study. She was standing still, gazing wistfully at the family tree. Seeing him out of the corner of her eye, she turned towards him. She shook her head mournfully. "You know," she explained in a demure voice, "I was just wondering if I ought to have this ... updated now that we ... no longer have your father. It would acknowledge his passing. And it would be my way of finally admitting that he's gone." She wiped her eyes and asked, "What do you think?"

Kieran shrugged. "If you like." Unlike Rhia, he'd never taken an interest in family lines. It always struck him as a rather snobbish pursuit.

"Perhaps I will, then," she murmured, "but not just now. It's too much like rubbing him out."

Kieran nodded and then announced, "Ali's come. She's in the lounge. OK?"

Rhia pulled herself together. "Oh. I'd better come and say hello to her."

While Ali diverted Rhia with small talk, Kieran excused himself for a few minutes. First, he crept back into the study. This time, he had the luxury of daylight for his exploration. As quietly as he could, he opened the filing cabinet. It groaned as if loath to yield to him but, in the day, the sound seemed much more subdued than it did in the middle of the night. His fingers flicked through the files. He came across two different cheque books. One named Rhia alone and the other was for a joint account. The counterfoils of both cheque books revealed that small sums only had been paid out recently. Kieran mumbled a curse to himself and carefully closed the drawer.

Next, he tiptoed upstairs. Rhia's room was directly above the lounge so he knew that he'd have to avoid making any noise. Cautiously, he stepped into the bedroom that had once belonged to both his real parents. Then, it smelled faintly of his mum's cosmetics. Once Rhia had reformed his dad, it smelled of his after-shave and deodorant, Rhia's perfume and the herbs that Rhia placed in a bowl on her dressing table. Now, the sole fragrance was Rhia's. Kieran made straight for her wardrobe. The door, a full-length mirror, slid back silently to display a treasure-trove of clothes. One by one, he parted and inspected the garments, like searching through the papers in the filing cabinet. It was a dazzling spectrum of expensive skirts, blouses, suits, trousers, dresses and coats. Mainly blues, reds and whites. There were just a few green items but nothing like the dress that he had seen in the video. When he drew back the mirrored door, he saw a smile on his own face. Admittedly, he'd drawn a blank with the cheque books but the dress was still a tempting mystery.

Before he left the room, he glanced round it once more and felt an immense sadness. When he witnessed Rhia's expensive clothes and her jewellery, now lying idle on the dressing table, he saw only the profits of his mother's cancer. The compensation for her death paid for Rhia's extravagance. Kieran resented every trinket and every garment, bought with a bit of his mother's life.

When he returned to the lounge, Rhia said, "Are you feeling unwell, Kieran? You seem a bit peaky."

"Yes," he answered. "I ... er ... I guess I'm still feeling the after-effects of last night. Nothing to worry about, though."

Startling them all, the telephone rang insistently. Still standing by the door, Kieran was the nearest and so he answered it. A female voice asked, "Is Rhia there?"

"Yes," Kieran muttered. "Just a minute." He held out the phone to his stepmother.

"Who is it?" she enquired.

Kieran covered the mouthpiece. "No idea. I didn't recognize the voice. A woman."

Rhia frowned. "All right. I'll take it." She took the handset from him.

Kieran and Ali sat in silence while Rhia announced herself and then went quiet for a while, listening to the caller. When she spoke again, she said, "Thanks. Yes, it's been ... trying, unpleasant, but I'm getting over it now." There was a pause before she added, "Yes. Kieran's here. We keep one another company. It helps with the shock when there's someone else around." After another brief hush, she said, "Yes. Very soon. I'm sure I'll be able to arrange it soon." She breathed her goodbye and replaced the receiver. On her way back to her seat, she declared, "Another friend, wanting to offer condolences." She acted as if she were obliged to explain the telephone call. She hesitated before commenting, "And she was asking when the funeral's going to be. You're going to have to prepare yourself for it as well, Kieran. David Thompson told me they'll let us bury him soon. I'll have to put my mind to the arrangements."

Kieran grimaced. It wasn't a pleasing prospect.

Later, when they went out on their own, Ali asked, "Well? What did you find? Anything?"

Kieran grumbled, "I don't know what the going rate is for a hitman, or whether you have to pay before or after, but she's not taken out a cheque for more than five hundred in the last few weeks."

"Nothing there, then," Ali concluded. "What about the dress?"

"That's the good news. It's not there. No sign of it at all," he said brightly. "She hasn't got a green dress like the one I saw her in."

"So, she didn't like it after all and threw it out. You know what she's like. Easy come, easy go."

"Yes, but you might be wrong. The lack of that dress is evidence. I don't know what of, to be honest. It doesn't make sense. But it's good evidence," Kieran observed.

"Hardly," Ali retorted. "Perhaps the outfit's in the wash – or at a laundry."

"Maybe," Kieran responded in a dour tone. He didn't know how to interpret the absence of the green dress, yet he still tried to convince himself that it was significant. Deep down, though, he realized that he had nothing to go on and that Ali's explanations were much more likely.

"It's not enough, Kieran. Drop it. You promised."

It had been easy to promise before the experiment. Now, after failing to find evidence of a big pay-off, Kieran was reluctant to ditch his theory. Science lessons had taught him that facts and the results of experiments should shape theories. When the facts didn't fit the theory, it was the theory that had to go. He knew it was wrong to ignore the facts and cling to a discredited theory but he didn't have the detachment of a scientist. He had confidence in his intuition. He could not admit that his confidence might be misplaced. Frustrated, he grunted his unwilling agreement to appease Ali, but he hoped that he would stumble across some other facts that would resurrect his pet theory.

7

A week later, after training, several members of the club were stuffing themselves with carbohydrate in the café, replenishing lost energy. Ali nudged Kieran and whispered, "Grit your teeth. Grin and bear it. Here comes Mike."

The backstroker, slowly increasing his swimming sessions after his widely advertised shoulder injury, wandered up to them and uttered, "How are you guys?"

Neither Ali nor Kieran made a coherent reply but their shared indistinct murmur seemed to satisfy Mike. He plonked himself down and began to chatter. It did not take him long before he began to improvise on his favourite theme. "I was with this terrific girl a couple of weekends back," he enthused. "I meant to tell you. Hair like a shampoo advert. Face like a toothpaste ad. Figure like ... a slimming advert."

Ali interjected, "What was her brain like?" She tapped the side of her head.

"Brain? Er…" He hadn't even considered it.

"And what was her name?"

"Um…" Mike thought about it for a second and then dismissed her question. "Can't remember."

Grinning, Kieran said to Ali, "You're putting him off."

"Oh, that's right," Ali replied. "Sorry, Mike. You were telling us a story."

"Yeah. But if you don't want…"

"No," Ali interrupted. "We're champing at the bit, aren't we, Kieran?"

"Sure," Kieran muttered disinterestedly.

"Good. We went for a lunchtime drink or two or three, me and

... this girl. After, when we'd had a few, we went..." He paused before adding, "That reminds me. When we were hanging round outside the pub, as you do, I saw her."

"Who?"

"Your stepmother," Mike said to Kieran.

"Rhia?" Kieran queried, suddenly attentive.

"Yes, Rhia. Anyway," Mike continued impatiently, "she was a bit merry, this girl, and..."

Kieran interrupted. "When was this?"

"Saturday afternoon."

"Which Saturday?"

"Last but one."

"Saturday the twenty-third?" Kieran checked.

"I suppose so. Yes," Mike answered.

"Where was this?"

"In town, outside the Rose and Crown."

"Did you say anything to her?"

"No, I had better things to do – concentrating on that girl. Besides, she was in a car, waiting for the lights to change."

"What sort of car?"

"Er... A white Toyota, I think. Why the grilling?"

"Nothing. It doesn't matter," said Kieran, glancing significantly at Ali.

Mike continued his far-fetched saga about the nameless beauty but Kieran did not really listen. He was itching to escape Mike's clutches and talk over the new baffling piece of evidence that had suddenly emerged.

As soon as Mike finally left them, Kieran leaned over the table and whispered urgently, "What do you make of that then?"

"I think he's a complete prat. But I guess the world would be duller without him," Ali replied. "I do wonder what'll happen when he meets a girl he's serious about, though."

"No," Kieran gasped. "I meant what he said about Rhia."

"You're not taking that seriously, are you?" Ali uttered in amazement. "No chance. What do you believe? The videos and your own eyes or Mike's drunken fancy? Besides, I bet he hardly knows Rhia. He's probably only seen her a couple of times. He may have spotted someone who looks like her. There must be plenty of candidates with a passing resemblance to Rhia. And he said she was in a car. Tricky to see drivers clearly, I'd say." Ali hesitated and then commented, "She hasn't got a white Toyota anyway, has she?"

"No," admitted Kieran. "But it's possible to hire cars, you know."

"Yes, but would you call Mike a reliable witness, even when he's sober?"

"No," Kieran moaned. "I suppose not. But..."

"It doesn't add up, Kieran. She was in France and you know it," Ali snapped. "You promised to drop this idea."

Kieran exhaled noisily and then nodded. "Yes, I know. Guess I'm just clutching at straws."

Ali threw her arms round him and whispered in his ear, "Forget it. She's in the clear. Innocent. Even if you're right that it wasn't Evans, it's more likely to be my dad. He's got a motive and no alibi."

Kieran yielded to her common sense. Privately, though, he knew that his theory would continue to nag at him.

Kieran was surprised at the considerable hole that his father had left. It wasn't his absence that weighed so heavily. After all, Kieran was used to his dad's absence. Even when he'd been at home, he was usually working in the study – absent to Kieran. No. It was something else. It was the atmosphere. Home life had ceased to revolve around the needs of his father. There was a void. And his dad's influence no longer diluted the effect of Rhia. Once, Kieran could eat in silence, allowing his father and Rhia to chat between themselves. Now, if there was to be conversation, and politeness demanded it, he had to engage with Rhia.

For her part, Rhia talked to him much more than she did before her husband's murder. She also began to take up her social life again. She had been to the Bridge Club a couple of times but had burst into tears on the first occasion. Her second attempt was more successful. She didn't join in. She just watched awkwardly. She was not yet ready to think about a new partner. Her housekeeper did the mundane shopping but once or twice Rhia ventured into the best shops in the city to buy those special things that made her happy. Clothes and shoes mainly. She had her hair styled and began to apply make-up again. Once more, her eyes would glitter whenever she spotted a plush, expensive car.

The police released Stuart's body and Rhia had to cope with the funeral arrangements. She found herself in communication again with her circle of friends. She even began to talk about Stuart without flinching. Her friends started to come to the house without displays of acute embarrassment at her loss. Daniel Allgrove paid two visits. The first one was an official appointment to explain Stuart's will. It was too simple to take long. Basically, he had left everything to Rhia. When Kieran reached the age of eighteen years, a quarter of his father's estate would pass to him. He would take control of another quarter if and when he married. It was understood that, eventually, on Rhia's death, the other half would follow suit. Daniel's second visit had none of the starchiness of the first. It was purely social and he offered to help with the organization of the funeral.

The funeral itself was a dour affair. Kieran had to take a prominent place alongside Rhia and he hated every moment. He felt as if he were on show before all of his father's acquaintances. It seemed that he was presenting himself for inspection. He was expected to show dignity without coldness, remorse without melancholy. Even with Ali's support, he felt unable to deliver. He didn't feel brave or devastated. He felt empty, that was all. Maybe cheated as well, but he'd been cheated long before his father had died. Now, he wondered if his dad was also being cheated. He was not sure that the police had arrested the right person.

In the graveyard, he sneaked a glance at the massed ranks of refined mourners. David Thompson represented the police. He looked suitably sombre. Kieran wondered if it was true what TV detectives said. The murderer always turns up for the funeral. Furtively, as the vicar recited the words that he had spoken a hundred times before, Kieran scanned the faces but he was most suspicious about the one that was covered by a discreet black veil. Of course, without knowing it, he might have just seen Rhia's accomplice. If she was behind his dad's murder, she must have had an accomplice – or paid an assassin – to put her alibi into effect. It was the only solution to the riddle of her being in Paris at the time of the murder. She ordered the killing and then made sure of her foolproof French alibi while her accomplice carried out the murder at the agreed time.

For some reason, Kieran found himself peeking at David Thompson. The detective seemed to be infatuated with Rhia. And he had been very keen to blame someone else for her husband's murder. If he had participated in the killing, it was bound to be well planned. He had inside knowledge. He would have also known that John Evans had just been released from prison and was baying for the blood of the Burrages. It would be simple to pin the crime on him. And Thompson would not question Evans' confession too closely. Maybe Rhia and Detective Inspector Thompson had some sort of pact. After a decent period had elapsed, maybe they would get together. Kieran would then be living with two killers. He shuddered at the possibility.

Another option was Daniel Allgrove. An arrangement between Rhia and the lawyer was easy to imagine. Rhia had inherited the money and Daniel Allgrove had inherited the business. Mutual benefit.

Ali's father had not come to the funeral, but he was another contender. At first Kieran did not take the possibility seriously. Robert Tankersley's motive would have been to halt the prosecution of his company, but surely he would have known that the death of one barrister would not kill the case. There would always be another lawyer to take it on. But then Kieran remembered sheer spite. Robert Tankersley could have exacted revenge on Kieran's dad for abandoning friendship in favour of a lucrative prosecution.

Whichever way Kieran's thoughts turned, Rhia still occupied centre stage. She had not yet made a slip, there was no hard evidence that she was guilty, but perhaps carelessness would creep in as time went by. Kieran vowed to stay alert.

Shortly after the funeral, Rhia resumed her hectic social life. Step by step, her poise, self-indulgence and vulgarity returned. A newly acquired silver Mercedes C220 Elegance was parked in the drive like a showpiece. To Kieran, the car seemed to be an ominous statement of Rhia's class and financial independence. Within a month, the house always seemed to be teeming with her friends and increasingly Kieran felt like an outsider in his own home. Occasionally, the members of the Bridge Club would descend on the house and a smug David Thompson became Rhia's new partner. Resenting her occupation and lifestyle, Kieran spent more and more time with Ali. Once, when he and Ali walked into the lounge, Rhia was getting ready to go into the city. "Hello!" she chirped. "I'm just off." She slipped a small book into her handbag and joked, "Are you two going to be good while I'm away?"

In reply, they smiled weakly at her.

She looked sleek again, groomed to perfection. And she was festooned with jewellery. To Kieran, the ornaments were dead reminders of his mother's life. As soon as Rhia strutted out of the room, Kieran cried, "Of course!"

"What?" asked Ali.

"Well…" He didn't know how Ali would react to his thoughts but he wanted to share them with her anyway. "Did you see what she put in her handbag?"

"No. What?"

"A passbook for a building society."

"So?"

Kieran explained, "Remember I found out that she hadn't made any big payments from her cheque books? Well, they were just bank accounts. She'd keep bigger amounts in a building society, I bet. If she did pay someone, it would come out of a building society account. I didn't check that."

Ali's mouth remained open but she didn't respond straight away. After a few seconds, she stammered, "I thought you'd given up on…"

Interrupting, Kieran said, "Don't tell me you're not a bit suspicious now you've seen her remarkable recovery."

Ali shrugged. "I don't suppose I like the way she's carrying on but even so…" She did not finish because her resistance was low. She knew that Kieran had a good point.

"All I'm suggesting is that we check out her building society account."

"How?" Ali enquired. "She's got the passbook and you didn't find it last time. She must keep it somewhere else."

"True. But did you see the logo on it? It was the Westland Building Society. That's where Grant McFarlane works. Remember him?"

"Yes," Ali answered, frowning. "You saved his skin on more than one occasion at school. You're thinking he owes you one."

Grant had been bullied without mercy whenever Kieran wasn't around to afford some protection. Hating it, Grant had left school as soon as he could.

Kieran nodded with guilt written all over his face. He did not relish asking a favour of Grant because he would feel obliged to consent. To lean on poor Grant now, reminding him of the debt, would be almost as bad as the bullying in the first place. But Kieran was desperate for information. "Yes," he mumbled. "I guess Grant could get the details from a computer at work."

"It's probably illegal," Ali suggested. "Certainly unethical."

"So is murder," Kieran responded.

They planned to bump into Grant after work on the next day.

In the café, they plied Grant with coffee and asked how he liked his work at the building society. He was still amazingly thin and weak but he was dressed smartly. He looked more assured than he had ever managed at school. "It's good," he proclaimed. "Nice people."

Ali nodded sympathetically. She could imagine that he would feel safe behind a screen. He probably wished that he had conducted the whole of his life behind a screen.

Uncomfortably, Kieran said, "You know I've got a stepmother. Rhia Burrage."

"Yes," Grant answered. "And your dad died a little while ago. I saw it in the papers. Sorry."

Kieran shrugged. "It's OK. But we're supposed to be sorting out the accounts. You know. He left a lot of his money to me but ... er ... there's a possibility that my stepmother's draining the building society account for herself when half of it's mine really."

"Oh?" Grant muttered cautiously. "You should see someone about that."

"Yes," Kieran conceded. "But before I do, I need to know if it's true. I don't want to stir it up if I'm just imagining things."

Grant glanced at Ali and she nodded as if to confirm her boyfriend's words. She did her best not to blush.

"You want me to access the account?"

"Yes."

"It's not allowed." He peered at Kieran and remembered many past favours. He added in a whisper, "But she came in yesterday." He hesitated like a doctor about to break a patient's confidentiality. "I had to consult the manager about it. It's not often I get asked to make out a cheque for a hundred thousand pounds."

"What?" Kieran screeched. Then, more quietly, he asked, "Are you sure? Who was it made out to?"

Grant shook his head slowly. "That I can't remember. In a day I make out lots of cheques and see lots of names."

"Could you find out?"

"I … er … I suppose I could. It'll be in the computer record. I shouldn't, though."

"I know," Kieran said softly. "But I'd be ever so grateful."

Grant sighed. "OK. I'll check it tomorrow," he moaned.

Ali put in, "It'd be useful to know where the cheque gets cashed as well, wouldn't it, Kieran?"

"I guess so," he agreed. Turning to Grant, he quizzed, "Can you do that as well?"

Grant was as white as he used to be when some lads approached him menacingly. He nodded. "It'll take a good few days, though. And it could be up to six months."

Kieran smiled and, to lighten the mood as well as his own conscience, he quipped, "No one waits six months to cash a cheque for a hundred thousand!"

"I suppose not," Grant whimpered.

They arranged to meet again whenever Grant had news about the destination of Rhia's cheque.

"Ali, love! Do me a favour." Her mother's voice floated in from the kitchen. "Fetch me your dad's mug, will you? He's left it in the study, I think."

"All right," Ali called out. "I'm on my way."

She dragged herself away from the television and went into the study to collect the missing mug. It was lying between the mouse mat and a small pile of computer chips. She grabbed it and turned to leave when something caught her eye. Bending down, she confirmed that her eyes weren't deceiving her. In the bin, there was a pair of thin nylon gloves that had once been white. Now, they were stained brown with dried blood. Ali stared at them and swallowed. Suddenly, she felt quite sick. There could be any number of explanations for the bloody gloves, she realized, but there was one particular explanation that petrified her.

She jumped and issued a startled cry when her mum yelled, "Can't you find it?"

"Er… Yes. Just got it." She staggered to the kitchen and handed over the mug.

"Thanks," her mum said. Then she added, "Are you feeling all right, love?"

Ali knew that her cheeks were tellingly red. She could not hide her shock but she denied it anyway. "I'm ... fine. Thought I'd go and see Kieran."

"Fair enough. Looks like you need a bit of fresh air anyway."

Kieran was taken aback by her discovery. "You think your dad was in on the murder," he surmised. Kieran had never really believed that Robert Tankersley had murdered his dad. He had no real reason to count him out but he just didn't seem the type. Even so, Kieran knew that he did have a powerful motive. Vengeance. "You think he killed Dad, wearing those gloves, kept them till the fuss died down, and now he's getting rid of them."

"It's a horrible thought," Ali replied, "but, you must admit, it could be."

"Yeah, it could be. But it's a bit careless, isn't it, just leaving them in the bin for everyone to see?"

"Hardly everyone," Ali argued. "Only me or Mum."

"Did you take one?" asked Kieran.

"No. What for?"

"I'm sure someone could check if the blood's Dad's."

"The police could," Ali agreed. "But they've shut the case."

"True. I guess you'll just have to confront him."

Ali's mouth opened. "How do you mean?" she gasped.

"Ask him about the gloves. I bet there's an innocent explanation."

"It'd be like accusing him of murder," Ali objected.

"That's exactly what you're doing," Kieran observed.

"Yes, but ..." She sighed before continuing. "Not to his face. I couldn't say anything to his face."

"You'll think of something," Kieran commented confidently.

Later that day, Ali and Kieran got together again. "Well?" Kieran prompted. "Have you got an update on the gloves?"

Ali nodded. "I found a way of doing it," she said. "I told him I'd seen the gloves when I went into the study. I asked if he'd hurt himself."

"Good tactic," Kieran muttered. "And ...?"

"He said he had. Said he was trying out new chips. He wears gloves so he doesn't get grease on them. Can be catastrophic, apparently. Anyway, he turned one over – legs in the air, as he put it – and later put his hand down heavily on it. The legs went straight through the glove and into his hand. Drew quite a bit of blood. No great harm done, he said."

"Sounds reasonable," Kieran remarked. "But", he added, "you don't look much happier. Didn't you believe him?"

"I'm not sure. I thought I knew him well enough, but perhaps I don't. Perhaps he's been lying all along and I haven't twigged. He certainly didn't volunteer to show me the wound."

"He thought it was too trivial to show off," Kieran guessed.

"I sneaked back into the study," Ali told him. "I couldn't see a chip with blood on it. It wasn't on the desk or in the bin."

Kieran shrugged. "They cost the earth, don't they? He wouldn't just chuck it. He'd clean it up and use it again."

Ali still looked worried. "I don't know. Let's hope that's the answer."

"Bound to be," Kieran replied, trying to cheer her up. He touched her shoulder gently. "Besides, there's a much more likely culprit," he murmured.

Ali peered at him. Seizing the opportunity to talk for a while about a different suspect, she said, "I've been thinking about that as well. This hit-man idea. It doesn't really work, you know."

"Why not?"

"Well," Ali deduced, "if Rhia paid an assassin to … do the job, why did she feel the need to leave the country to give herself an alibi? A bit extreme, isn't it? She could have gone to a friend's house on the appointed day – just down the road. That'd be a lot easier and give her a perfectly good alibi. Better than relying on being caught on video."

"Yes," Kieran mumbled thoughtfully. "I hadn't thought of that." He stroked his chin and then added, "It doesn't mean I'm wrong about the hit-man, but I see your point. Going to Paris is a bit over the top. If it wasn't an assassin, perhaps she had another reason for paying someone a lot of money."

He was still intrigued by Mike's unlikely sighting of Rhia in a Toyota at the same time that a video camera recorded her in Paris. He knew that it made no sense. He knew that Mike was not reliable. He knew that a drunken Mike had not seen the woman clearly. But there was just a chance that Rhia *was* near home at the time of the murder. If she had fooled the cameras somehow, she could have committed the crime herself. Maybe someone had doctored the pictures to make it seem that they were recorded on the Saturday when in fact they were Friday's videos. Perhaps she posed in front of the cameras on Friday, bribed a security officer to interfere with the date, came back to England on the Saturday, killed her husband, and then returned to complete her trip. Then the enormous withdrawal from the building society would be the fee for tinkering with the videotape. The idea might seem absurdly complicated but Kieran decided to follow it up anyway.

When he explained his new theory to Ali, she frowned but did not try to knock it down. "So, how can you check it out?" she enquired.

"Not sure," he confessed. "But I think I'd better call a local car hire company."

Pretending that he was about to take a trip to France, he telephoned to enquire about booking a car for a day on his return to England. The assistant asked where he would enter the country. "Er ... I haven't finally decided," he answered. "It could be Heathrow or one of the ports maybe."

"Well," the woman responded, "we could have a car waiting at Heathrow for you. That's no problem. Some of the ferry terminals would be more difficult for us. You may need to contact one of the national companies. You'll find them at all major ports and the like."

"I see," Kieran said into the mouthpiece. "And if I definitely wanted a Toyota?"

"We don't deal with Toyotas at all, sir."

"Do any of those national ones?"

The woman was getting a little impatient. "Yes. Several," she answered abruptly.

"Thank you," Kieran said. "When I've sorted out exactly what I'm doing I'll call you back. Thanks again."

"You're welcome, sir," the woman replied in a tone that expertly disguised her irritation.

Kieran muttered a curse as he replaced the telephone. It was an impossible task to check every place that Rhia might have used to re-enter the country. And even if he made a lucky guess, he didn't know what name she would have used to hire the Toyota. Certainly not her own. Perhaps she'd had to pay for a forged driving licence as well.

"Oh, well," he said to Ali. "It wasn't wasted. At least we know she could've come back and hired a Toyota for the day." Even so, he was disappointed. He was forced to abandon the lead before he'd made any real progress. Instead, he had to rely on Grant tracing that cheque.

8

Kieran had to wait for ten days before he got any news from Grant. And when it came, it meant nothing to him.

Grant fidgeted with a pen and glanced round nervously before he announced, "The cheque was made out to someone called Sandra Jackson."

"Sandra Jackson?" Kieran looked blankly at Grant and then at Ali.

Ali murmured, "You don't know her?"

"No," Kieran answered. "Never heard of her."

"Where did she cash the cheque, then?" Ali asked.

"A bank in St Peter Port. High Street."

"St Peter Port?" Kieran repeated. "Where's that?"

"Guernsey. Channel Islands."

"Oh." Kieran scratched his head. Bewildered, he said, "I don't know anyone there, that's for sure."

"Rhia does," Ali interjected.

"So it seems."

"Well..." Grant muttered. It was his reticent way of asking for their permission to escape. Clearly he wanted to put the whole illegal episode behind him. Once Kieran had thanked him and apologized for applying pressure, Grant scuttled away like a small frightened animal.

"Sandra Jackson of Guernsey," Kieran groaned. "I'm none the wiser."

"So, what do we do?"

Kieran thought about it for a few moments. Then he pronounced, "We go to the reference library and check out a Guernsey phone book."

Ali said, "Have you got any idea how many Jacksons there might be in Guernsey?"

"No," he admitted. "None at all. Let's find out."

There were thirty-nine. "A manageable number," Kieran concluded in a hushed voice.

"Manageable for what?"

In the quiet of the library, he whispered, "We'll call them all and see if we can find her. We'll start with the S. Jacksons. There's only two of them."

"Yes, but if she's married," Ali pointed out, "the number will come under her husband's initials, I should think. So it's unlikely to be S. Jackson. It could be anything."

"I know," Kieran replied. "But we've got to start somewhere."

"And what will you say if you get through to her?" Ali breathed as Kieran took the directory to the photocopier. "Hello, Mrs Jackson. Are you a paid assassin or someone who fiddles video evidence? This is the son of your last victim. Have you spent your profits yet?"

Kieran shrugged. "Look, I'll copy the page so we can take the numbers home. I doubt if Rhia will be there. She'll be out with her mates. We can use the phone in peace. There's plenty of time to work out tactics before we get home."

"You keep saying we," Ali observed.

Kieran grinned at her. "It's OK. I'll do it. But you can hold my hand."

On the way home, Kieran remarked, "I think you're right. We can forget the hit-man. Have you ever heard of a female one – hit-woman? Unlikely. But she could have helped Rhia to sneak back to England, while still appearing to be in Paris. Some sort of security expert who can doctor video equipment – so it reads the wrong date."

"Don't you think someone in Paris would've noticed that?"

"I don't know." Struggling to keep his ailing theory alive, he commented, "All I know is you can do some clever things if you've got the right equipment."

Ali was sceptical, but she didn't try to cast further doubt on his hunch. Instead, her thoughts turned to the telephone calls. "All right, but what *do* you say if you get her on the phone?"

Kieran sniffed and considered it. "Perhaps just hang up. That way, we find out how many Sandra Jacksons there are and where they live. Then we can concentrate the investigation."

"Oh, it's an investigation now, is it?" Ali taunted him. "If you think like that, you ought to go to the police."

"We can't. We'd get Grant into trouble. Besides," he explained, "knowing Dad's business from the inside taught me that the whole thing's a game. The law's there to give the impression that justice is being done, but half the time I wonder if it is. It's about winning or losing an argument in court. It's not about finding out the truth. As long as there's a culprit who can be prosecuted successfully, the law's satisfied."

"I've heard this lecture before," Ali mentioned.

"Sorry. I'm just saying that Thompson's part of the game. He's happy because he's got someone behind bars and a confession. He won't waste any more time on it. On top of that, have you seen the way he sucks up to Rhia? He seems pleased to have Dad out of the way, milking the opportunity. If he really fancies her, there's a chance he was involved. If so, he's not going to open the case again, is he? But *I* think there's still a few question marks – a few things to investigate."

"OK, Chief Inspector Kieran Burrage. How exactly do you propose to investigate someone in Guernsey?"

"You haven't had your summer holiday yet, have you? Raid your piggy bank. I'm told the Channel Islands are nice at this time of year." Kieran grinned cheekily.

Exasperated, Ali cried, "Are you serious?"

"Yes. We can take your tent. It shouldn't be too expensive if we camp."

"And when you tell Rhia where you're going, what is she going to think?"

"Mmm." Kieran hesitated and then suggested, "There are plenty of Channel Islands, aren't there? We'll tell her we're going to one of the others."

Ali gave up objecting. She decided to take it a step at a time. There was no point worrying about a crazy scheme to go to Guernsey until Kieran had tried to trace the mysterious Sandra Jackson by phone.

His research did not get off to a flying start. Dialling the first

S. Jackson elicited the number unobtainable tone and the second one connected him with a sullen man called Steven. Having failed with the S. Jacksons, Kieran began to go through the other Jacksons in alphabetical order. His third call quickened his heart rate. "Is Sandra there, please?" he asked.

The female voice on the line sounded surprised and suspicious. "Sandra? You want Sandra?"

"Yes, please."

"On the phone?" the woman queried. "Are you sure?"

"Yes," Kieran uttered.

"Well, she's fast asleep and she wouldn't say much to you anyway."

"Oh. Why not?"

The woman's tone had changed. She almost seemed amused. "Because she's three months old."

"Ah. I see," Kieran stammered. "Sorry. I must have the wrong Sandra Jackson."

There was a chuckle on the line. "I think so. I'll tell her you called, if you like, but I doubt if she'll call back for a few years."

"Sorry," Kieran repeated.

"That's OK. It's cheered me up."

The telephone clicked and Kieran murmured, "Oops!" After he'd explained the call to Ali and endured more giggles at his expense, he tried more numbers and drew more blanks.

His enthusiasm for the task was beginning to wane when he had a lucky break. In response to Kieran's enquiry, the man on the other end of the line said, "No. She's out. She'll be back in about half an hour. Who is this?"

"It doesn't matter," Kieran replied. "I'll call back." With a hand that trembled, he put down the receiver as if it were red hot. "Phew! Got one!" he cried to Ali. He ran his finger down the list of Jacksons in the directory. "This one, it was. Listed as J.A. Jackson." He marked the entry with a cross. "She lives in St Peter Port as well. Handy for the bank," he remarked. "I'm going to have a quick rest. I don't suppose you want to…?"

Ali's firm shake of the head stopped him finishing his question. "It's your show," she said, refusing the telephone. "Your privilege." For a moment she considered him as he sat back in the easy chair, recovering from the shock of success. "You know," she said sadly, "I don't think I'd heard you lie till this investigation of yours. You lied to Grant. You're lying to these people on the phone, and you're proposing to lie to Rhia if you go to Guernsey. I know why you're doing it but don't make a habit of it, will you? I hate to see you getting good at it. I don't want you to lie to me – ever."

Kieran leaned forward and touched her leg. "Not to you, I won't. I'm not enjoying it, you know. It's just till I get to the bottom of Dad's death."

"As long as you can stop when it's over. I don't want you addicted to it like Mike. I'll want honest Kieran back again."

"You'll have him soon enough. But for now..." With a weary sigh of uneasiness, he picked up the receiver once more.

He discovered only two more Sandra Jacksons. Judging by the young voice, one was perhaps ten or eleven years old. Kieran noted from the list of names, addresses and telephone numbers that she lived in St Saviour. He marked the entry but discounted any notion that she was both a crook and the lucky recipient of one hundred thousand pounds.

For the final time, he asked, "Is Sandra Jackson there?"

"Speaking." This time it was a woman's voice.

Thinking quickly, Kieran feigned surprise. "Oh!" he uttered. "Sorry, but ... er ... you don't sound like the Sandra I was expecting. I'm calling to wish her a happy eleventh birthday. I must have the wrong Sandra Jackson."

The woman, sounding distrustful, muttered, "You sure have."

"Sorry," Kieran replied. He hung up. Turning to Ali, he declared, "That's the lot. Four Sandra Jacksons. Two underage and probably out of it. That last one lives in..." He scanned the directory and then added, "St Martin." While he highlighted the entry, he asked, "Is that near St Peter Port?"

"I think everywhere's close to St Peter Port on Guernsey. It's not a big place."

"And is everywhere called Saint something?"

Ali shrugged. "Sounds like it. But I guess you're going to drag me back to the library to find out – to look at a map," she surmised.

Kieran laughed. "You know me pretty well."

"Better than you think," she rejoined. "You're going to call in at a travel agent as well. Check out the cost of the ferry."

"No, I wasn't," Kieran said, wagging his finger at her, "but now you've suggested it..."

Ali grinned at him. "You can't fool me. You'd already thought of it."

"And you can't fool me," Kieran countered. "You're pretending you don't like the idea but really you're dying to get stuck into an investigation. You're not so laid back about it as you'd like me to think."

"All right, all right. We've proved we both know each other inside out," Ali replied, calling a truce to their banter. "If we've got to go, let's get on with it. Otherwise the travel agent's and library will be closed anyway."

Kieran put down his toast, gulped, took a deep breath and then peered at Rhia. "I ... er ... I need to get away for a bit," he proclaimed as if he were expecting an argument about it.

"Oh. What do you mean?" Rhia enquired.

Kieran's gaze reverted for a moment to the kitchen table, then he looked up resolutely. "After Dad and all. I need some time ... I don't know ... to get my head sorted out, I guess."

Even at breakfast time, Rhia was back to her most immaculate. She beamed at him and purred, "Sounds like a good idea to me. And something tells me you'll want Ali with you."

"Yes."

"Fair enough. She's a nice girl and I'm sure the two of you will behave." Rhia picked up her cup of coffee but before she took a sip, she asked, "Where were you thinking of going?"

Brashly, Kieran answered, "The Channel Islands. Ali suggested Jersey."

Of course, it could have been a coincidence but as soon as Kieran referred to the Channel Islands some coffee slopped over the rim of her cup and splashed on to the tablecloth. It was odd because Rhia was not normally clumsy. She didn't make slips without a reason. For a split-second she glared at Kieran but by the time that he named Jersey, she had recovered her composure. Dabbing at the stain with a napkin, she said, "Jersey? It sounds nice ... but why there?"

"*Because* it sounds nice. One of Ali's mates went there last year," Kieran fibbed. "She recommended it." Her fumble when he mentioned the Channel Islands justified the lie. The fact that she had spilled a little coffee would hardly stand up in court as evidence but, in Kieran's eyes, the jolt condemned her. She had been startled. More than ever, he was convinced that she had something to hide.

On reflection, he believed that he'd been right to announce his departure to the Channel Islands before he'd mentioned Jersey. It had allowed him to observe her reaction. Yet he was also aware of the peril. The woman sitting opposite him might have just realized that he suspected her. She might have guessed that he knew about the cheque. And she might have interpreted his holiday correctly as his means of investigating her. Kieran would have to watch his back from now on. He might also have to watch over Ali. Rhia would expect Kieran to share all of his thoughts and suspicions with Ali. Suddenly, both of them could have become targets.

Rhia smiled sweetly. "Excellent. It'll be good for you – both of you. I'm delighted. Whereabouts in Jersey?"

"Haven't decided yet. We'll camp so we can move around."

"Where did Ali's friend go?" Rhia persisted, as if she were testing her stepson.

"Ali knows. I'm not sure. We've still got to plan the details." It was like playing a tough game of chess, full of hidden hostility, after revealing his tactics to his opponent.

"I see." Rhia smirked. "When are you going? Where from? Have you planned that yet? And how are you getting there?"

"Next weekend. We were lucky. Some couple cancelled and we got their places on the boat at short notice. Because of that, it was cheap as well. It's just a week on Jersey. We take some sort of high-speed catamaran from Weymouth, early next Saturday morning. We'll get to Weymouth by coach the day before, I suppose." He hesitated and asked, "Have you ever been to the Channel Islands?" He tried to make it sound like a casual, innocent question.

"No. It's one of those places I've always meant to visit but never quite made it. Still," Rhia hissed, "I'm sure you'll enjoy it."

When Kieran left the table, he found that he was sweating. He had just hinted to her that he was on her trail, testing her alibi, trying to discover if and how she had committed murder. Unwisely, he had also told her his exact movements – but he had no option. He hoped that she would not check with the travel company which island was their real destination. The catamaran called at St Peter Port and then went on to Jersey, but it would do so without Kieran and Ali.

Until the weekend, he would have to live alongside a woman who might wish to dispose of him. Kieran felt nervous and uncomfortable – but safe. She would not try anything in her own house – at least not while she was around to face the accusations. Kieran believed that she had killed his father using some devious plan to avoid detection. He assumed that, if she was determined to rid herself of a threat – and an heir who would take away half of her husband's money – she would set up another intricate and ingenious scheme. Ironically, he estimated that he was not in danger while he stayed close to her. At the same time, he could hardly bear to be near her. He relished separation. Yet the distance could provide her with the space she needed to devise another murder and another alibi. To solve the crime, though, Kieran had to accept the risk. He longed to get away to Guernsey where he felt that the answer lay.

9

"Are you OK?"

Sandwiched between their bulging haversacks, Ali and Kieran sat in the lounge of the catamaran as it surfed the Channel, crossing the busy shipping lanes, dodging the other sea craft.

"How do you mean?" Kieran replied. "Of course I'm all right. I'm on my hols, aren't I? Everyone's OK on their hols."

"Not just a holiday," Ali remarked. "Anyway, I meant you keep looking round like a spy."

"Just ... er ... eyeing up the girls," he said with a grin.

She poked him in the ribs with her elbow. "I hope you get seasick, then."

From the open sea, the huddle of buildings growing out of the hillside looked like a toy town. Once Ali and Kieran had disembarked and walked into St Peter Port, it seemed like any other haphazard seaside town at nine-thirty in the morning. A curious mixture of locals going about their businesses and tourists beginning to clutter the narrow busy streets. The harbour road was awash with cars, taxis, delivery lorries and buses. Behind it, churches, shops, restaurants and pubs were clustered. On the pavements, blackboards announced fishing trips, guided tours, menus, special offers. In High Street, Kieran pointed to a round domed building that seemed to block the road. "That's the bank where she cashed the cheque," he remarked.

"Before we think about all that," Ali suggested, "let's establish base camp. We need to find out how to get to our site."

They bought a map from the tourist office and discovered which bus they needed to catch. It took them three miles inland and dropped them off between a wartime hospital built underground as a dismal concrete maze and a bizarre tiny chapel built from bits of broken pottery and shells. They strolled half a mile up a peaceful lane along the valley to reach the campsite. "London, it ain't," Ali observed. "Can't smell the exhaust fumes. Great!"

As soon as they had pitched the small tent, a dreary drizzle set in. They nestled inside where the rain on the taut nylon sounded like small pebbles. "I bet even the rain's clean here. It probably won't burn through the tent like the stuff at home."

After they had laid out their sleeping bags, they settled down to examine the map, made orange by the daylight piercing the fabric of the tent. Tapping the unfolded plan of the island, Kieran declared, "Doyle Road, St Peter Port. That's where one of the adult Sandra Jacksons lives." He marked it with a biro.

"Which one?"

"It's ... er ... J.A. Jackson. That's the husband, I suppose. The other one, W.A., is in St Martin. Jerbourg Road. Let's see." He peered at the names and numbers written among the tangle of lanes. "Here we are. Jerbourg Road. A number 2 bus will get us there, it says. It's not that far out of St Peter Port."

"And it's near Fermain Bay. My information says that's a really good beach," Ali hinted.

"Beach?" Kieran's mind was absorbed in other things.

"Yes," Ali cried, nudging him. "We are on our hols, remember. It's not all Jacksons and Bergerac, you know."

"Wrong island," Kieran taunted her. "Bergerac was the detective on Jersey."

"Don't try and wriggle out of it," she retorted. "Holiday equals beaches plus swimming. Look, there's a disco at Jerbourg. I'm not going to let you forget that we're here for fun as well."

Kieran smiled at her. "Sure. I know. But if we get the serious business done straight away, it leaves the rest of the week to play at tourists. Yes?"

"All right. But not now," Ali insisted. "I'm tired out after the travelling. We'll be budding Bergeracs tomorrow – especially if it's still raining. As soon as the sun comes out, though, I'm back on my hols."

As usual, Ali had the last word.

On Sunday, the two of them stood, feeling damp, foolish and unnerved, on one side of Doyle Road and gazed across at the

Jacksons' house. It was a terraced property, small and neat. A ramp led up from the garden to the front door.

"Well?" Ali prompted.

"Mmm. It isn't exactly what I expected for someone who's just banked a hundred thousand."

"No," Ali agreed. "The thing is, though, are we going to loiter here till the police take us away – on the off-chance that Sandra Jackson will come out like the prime minister to make a statement?"

"No, I guess not. But first we ought at least to get a look at her." Kieran pondered on it for a moment. He put his arm round Ali in the vain hope of buttering her up and said, "Back home, do you get visits from those religious nuts? You know, they always come in pairs like police officers and one asks if you've read the Bible lately and would you like to discuss your feelings about it. The other just stands there and smiles. Yes?"

Ali closed her eyes and moaned. "That's your plan, is it, to get her to the door?" She shook her head. "You want us to pay a door-step visit to talk about the Bible. What happens if she says yes?"

"No one says yes. We'll be safe. But I don't know what we do after. Let's take it a step at a time, though."

"And which is my role?"

Kieran squeezed her shoulders and grinned at her. "Just put on your best silly smile. Think of something nice while I talk."

"Tricky. I'll be shaking like a leaf," Ali answered. "We might be about to crash in on a hired assassin."

"You're exaggerating," Kieran complained. "We don't really believe the assassin story. Remember?" To lighten the burden, he added, "It's more likely to be someone who forges documents and manipulates video pictures."

"Still an accomplice, though. Anyway, if we're going to do it, let's get it done before I lose my nerve altogether."

Kieran pressed the door bell, breathed deeply, and waited. His pulse raced as if he'd just swum two hundred metres flat out. Ali's fixed expression was half-way between ecstasy and fright.

It was a man in his fifties that fumbled with the door catch and then appeared, a puzzled look on his face. "Yes?" he muttered.

"Good morning," Kieran responded in his best far-away tone. "We wondered if you had read the Bible recently and what you gained from it. What feelings did you have about it?"

Mr Jackson sighed. "My feelings would be unrepeatable, young man."

Behind him, there was a dingy hall and some sort of contraption at the bottom of the staircase.

Before Kieran could reply, there was a voice from inside. "Who is it?"

The old man turned and called back into the house, "It's them religious folk, telling us that the world's going to be perfect and free of suffering if only we follow the way of Jesus. Do you want to have a word, Sandra?"

"Yes," came the shouted reply.

Mr Jackson said, "Hang on a moment."

Kieran and Ali glanced at each other, barely able to sustain their smiles.

Mr Jackson withdrew into the hall and opened the door to the living room. Eventually, a woman in a wheelchair emerged, turned on the spot and headed for the front door. Kieran and Ali stopped smiling and simply looked ashamed.

Sandra Jackson examined the two callers and uttered, "Does your God, your Jesus, prevent suffering? Can He cure me? Can He take away arthritis?" She held out her hands, the wrists and knuckles deformed and useless.

Kieran felt sure that the real door-to-door evangelists would have a stock answer, but he had nothing to offer.

Sandra Jackson stared at them and then cackled, "No wonder you look guilty. If you don't mind, I'll pass on your perfect world." She closed the door on them before they could apologize, deeply embarrassed by the whole episode.

Despondently, they walked back towards the centre of the town. "Well," Kieran muttered, trying to break the black mood, "at least we can strike her off the list."

"Yes," Ali replied. "I hope we didn't upset her. Did you see her hands? They were ... mangled, really. It was awful."

"Horrible," Kieran agreed. "She's no assassin, that's for sure. And she's not up to anything that needs skilful hands, either."

"Poor woman," Ali murmured, still feeling sheepish about their blundering.

Recognizing that it was not a good time to propose that they should seek their second candidate, Kieran suggested instead that they should look around the castle next to the quay, followed by a thrash in the sea. Ali glanced at him with relief and gratitude.

"Thanks," she said, interlocking her arm with his. "Anything but more police work. I couldn't face another one like that just yet. Playing at tourists will put it out of my mind."

The following morning, Kieran attempted to sweeten Ali. Gently, he asked if she wanted the promised visit to Fermain Bay and the Jerbourg area, ending the day with the disco.

She saw straight through his suggestion, of course. "You mean, you want to chase up the next Sandra Jackson and make it up to me by having a bit of time on the beach like ordinary folk?" She paused and then murmured her assent. "Let's do the private detective bit first. I might need the beach and a dance to make me feel better afterwards."

Their first bus of the day took them into St Peter Port and the second meandered towards Jerbourg and St Martin's Point. Jerbourg Road was quite long and, from the bus, they could not locate the Jacksons' house. They alighted and walked until they arrived at the right number. It was a bungalow. The last in a row of cottages that had seen better days. The garden gate dragged on the path and Kieran had to lift it to open it properly.

"Same again?" he whispered to Ali. "Put on your best smile." He banged on the front door and waited. And waited. Then he banged again. "You know, I've got a bad feeling about this," he breathed. "I don't think there's anyone home." He used the knocker for the last time and then lifted the letterbox and peered into the bungalow. "Seems deserted," he concluded.

Ali sighed. "Now what?"

Kieran peered about. There was no one in sight. "We could walk round the back. Just in case she's in the back garden."

Ali did not like the sound of it but she did not want to have to return on another day. "Come on, then," she replied.

Feeling like crooks, they slipped down the side of the cottage and sneaked into the rear garden. It was well tended but also deserted. The second grown-up Sandra Jackson was proving elusive.

"Now we're here, I could take a look through the window." He stepped over a flower-bed and on to the patio. Pressing his face up to the glass and cutting out the reflections with his hand, he gazed into the living room. It was nothing special. Kieran expected it to be old-fashioned but the colours were modern and bright. A small neat room.

Suddenly, Kieran gasped and Ali whispered urgently, "What is it?"

Kieran beckoned to her. "Come and take a peek. Tell me if I'm dreaming or not. Over there," he said, pointing. "On the shelf."

Ali squinted and then uttered, "Good grief! You're not dreaming." When she stared at her boyfriend her face was white. "What does it mean?"

"I don't know. Why should she have a framed photo of Rhia in her living room?"

Still not quite believing it, they peered through the window again.

Both of them leapt and banged their heads on the glass when, behind them, a voice said pointedly, "Can I help you?"

Rubbing their foreheads, they turned. A burly man with a spade in his hands stood there. They were not sure if the spade was a weapon or whether he had just been doing some gardening. "You startled us," Kieran stuttered. "Are you Mr W. Jackson?"

The man frowned. "No," he snapped, examining them with curiosity and distrust. "I'm the next-door neighbour and you look like prowlers to me." Menacingly, he adjusted his grip on the spade.

"No," Kieran replied, trying to be nonchalant. "We're just looking for Sandra. We knew her quite well a while ago. She gave us her address and told us to drop in. We were in the area so we thought we'd pay her a surprise visit, but she doesn't seem to be in."

The neighbour hesitated. He seemed less hostile once Kieran had proved that he knew Sandra's name. Somehow, it made his explanation more believable. "You didn't know her husband, though, and you're not from round here."

"Er ... no. We're from England – and we only met Sandra."

"Mmm," the man mumbled. "How long is it since you've been in contact?"

"Months," Kieran lied. "Last year some time, I think."

"That explains it," he said, relaxing somewhat. He rested the spade on the patio. "She went on holiday on Friday. Asked me to keep an eye on the property."

"Is she taking a break on Guernsey?"

"No. Said she was off to London."

"And her husband?" asked Kieran.

The man shook his head sadly. "Died. If you'd been local, you'd know."

"Oh, I'm sorry to hear that. When?" Kieran queried.

"Just before Christmas last."

Ali nudged her boyfriend and said, "If she's not here, we might as well get going." She wanted to escape while their luck held.

"True." Kieran thanked the neighbour and apologized for the intrusion. "Pity we missed her," he concluded. As they walked away, the man with the spade watched them. His eyes escorted them from Sandra Jackson's premises. Kieran whispered to Ali, "Don't rush. Saunter."

"I feel like running," she replied, clearly shaken by the encounter.

"Too suspicious," Kieran muttered.

Once they were back on the main road, they scurried away as quickly as they could.

Safely on the footpath that led to Fermain Bay, they chatted about their uncanny discovery. Kieran was baffled. "What does that photo of Rhia mean?"

"No idea," Ali said. "But it tells us we found the right Sandra Jackson, even if she's not around at the moment. It tells us there *is* a Guernsey connection."

Thoughtfully, Kieran speculated, "It's quite a coincidence that she went on holiday just before we got here. I wonder if Rhia tipped her off. If Rhia realized we were on her trail and didn't want us to meet her… It's a possibility."

"And there's another coincidence," Ali put in. "Another woman with a husband who's died recently."

"Yeah. We can find out about that," Kieran replied.

Reading his mind, Ali interjected, "I know. He said anyone round here would've known about it. So I bet it got in the local papers. We need a trip to yet another library – to trace the story."

"You got it," Kieran chirped. "Let's…"

Ali interrupted him immediately. "Let's enjoy the sea and sand – and the disco. The library'll be open tomorrow."

Kieran would have preferred to follow the lead straight away but he gave in. "OK. I fancy a swim, I suppose. Looks like blue sky's making a comeback as well. We did agree to ease up when the sun does its stuff."

They found the library behind the bus station. One of the assistants led them to a microfiche reader and set it up for past copies of the local newspaper. They scanned down the endless columns of articles. "Here we go," Kieran mumbled. "December issues coming up. Keep your eyes open."

Kieran scanned down them until Ali cried softly, "Hold it!"

The headline on 22nd December read, "Local man dies in drugs mix-up."

Sitting side by side, Ali and Kieran read the report. Apparently, Mr William Jackson was 45 years old and not in the best of health. He was virtually house-bound and needed daily medication. He died while his wife was away, taking a short break from caring for him. She returned to find him dead on the floor of the living room. The post-mortem and analysis of the residue of the tablets showed that he had been given the wrong ones. The police did not understand how or why his treatment had been altered and his pharmacist had no record of a change in his prescription. It was evident that someone had tampered with his supply of drugs. Clearly the authorities suspected murder more than an accident, but motive remained a mystery.

The next day's paper relegated the story to page three. Sandra Jackson had been interviewed as part of the police investigation yet had been released without charge. She had definitely been in Britain when the culprit had interfered with her husband's medication. The police also seemed satisfied that she did not have the required medical knowledge. The article concluded that the case remained open and enquiries were on-going. Ali and Kieran searched three more weeks of newspapers but did not discover any further reports. It was an unsolved crime.

They removed the microfiche, turned off the reader, and looked at each other. Ali was the first to react. "It all sounds very familiar," she commented.

Kieran nodded. "Yet more coincidences. Wife away when hubby is murdered. She returns to find him dead. The police check out her alibi but seem satisfied that she's in the clear. Miles away. Cast-iron alibi. Like Rhia's."

"I'm ... worried, Kieran. This is telling us something, but I don't know what," Ali whispered.

"Yeah," Kieran murmured. "And there's that photo of Rhia. If I didn't know that she's lived in my house for the last five years, I'd say she had a double life. She lived here as Sandra Jackson and did in her husband at Christmas with a perfect alibi, then, as Rhia Burrage, she repeated the performance on Dad."

Ali smiled and shook her head. "Yes, but..."

"I know. It's a daft idea because it's impossible."

"True," Ali said. "But do you know where Rhia was just before last Christmas?"

Kieran inhaled and then slowly let out the breath as he thought. "Last Christmas. Well, on the day itself, she was at home. But ... er ... before it, she did go somewhere. We were deep in swimming training, Dad was working round the clock to clear the decks for Christmas, and so Rhia took herself off on one of her trips. I have a feeling she went to Edinburgh."

"What for?"

Kieran shrugged. "To do Rhia-like things, I guess. Shop a lot. Do the castle and art galleries."

"Mmm. The opposite direction from Guernsey," Ali remarked. "It's got me beat."

"Let's go down to the harbour," Kieran suggested. "We'll get a bag of unrecognizable seafood and slurp it down while we watch the boats come and go. Later, we'll find another club. Yes?"

"Agreed!"

They had a few drinks and danced until they'd missed the last bus. "Ah, well," Ali exclaimed, "Never mind. It was worth it. Good fun." A bit tipsy, she giggled.

"Taxi or walk?" Kieran enquired.

"It's a nice night," she answered. "Let's walk. Three miles won't take long – and it'll be all romantic and eerie along the dark lanes."

"Yeah," Kieran murmured as she snuggled up to him. "Let's hope we don't get lost."

The most arduous part of the walk was the haul up the hill from the sea-front. Once they'd found St Andrew's Road, it was a pleasant stroll in the fresh air. Very little stirred. Occasionally, a car would slice the darkness. Farm animals and rabbits foraged in the fields and by the side of the road. Ali thought she caught the flutter of a bat on its blindfolded hunt for food. Sometimes, a dog would bark briefly and birds hooted. Arm in arm, Kieran and Ali hardly noticed the distance. For once, they had both forgotten murders and mysteries. They concentrated on each other and on the tranquillity. Mostly, they ambled in silence, listening to the spooky sounds of the night.

They turned right by the folk club and followed the valley. There was no pavement so they walked in the narrow road. "Not too far now," Kieran whispered as if it was sacrilege to disturb the subdued pulse of nocturnal life.

"Listen," Ali murmured.

In the valley, an unseen band of crickets took on the role of a rhythm section for the frogs' irregular vocals. Kieran chortled softly. "I heard worse in the club tonight."

Ali stared up at the magical expanse of sky and declared, "There's a lot of stars."

"Don't," Kieran replied. "I always feel so small and insignificant when I think about such things. That's why I live in London. I can cope with mere lumps of concrete. Here, nature's so ... big. Overwhelming."

Ali laughed but, seriously, replied, "You'll always be significant to me."

Kieran stopped walking and hugged his girlfriend. "Thanks."

Suddenly, out of nowhere, a car roared down the lane towards them. Its harsh headlights caught them like a pair of petrified rabbits.

Transfixed, Ali yelled, "It's not stopping!"

Still holding Ali, Kieran dived with her into the hedge.

A few seconds later, it was all over. The car was swallowed by the night like a passing ghost. Ali and Kieran picked themselves out of the hedge and brushed themselves down. "That was close," Ali muttered in a quaking voice. "Are you all right? The driver mustn't have seen us – not expecting anyone to be here at this time of night."

"He must have seen us," Kieran grumbled.

"Forget it," Ali said. "No point dwelling on it. Let's just get back to the tent."

The spell had been broken. The rest of the walk seemed dreary and tiring, rather than idyllic and effortless. It was nearly two o'clock when they got to their tent. The site was quiet and unlit. Kieran and Ali stole up to their tent and unzipped the flap slowly so as not to wake the other campers. They clambered inside and closed the fastening again. Ali breathed, "Straight to bed for me."

Kieran agreed. "I'll light the lamp so we can see what we're doing."

He struck a match and turned the valve on the camping gas cylinder. At once, there was an exaggerated hiss of gas. Immediately, a bright yellow flame leapt from Kieran's hand to the canister. There was a loud whoosh and a fireball engulfed the gas cartridge, shot upwards, hit the roof of the tent and spread out in the shape of a mushroom. Kieran felt its heat sear his arm and face. He heard a human scream but did not know if it came from Ali or himself.

A second later, Ali bundled Kieran to the ground and smothered him with a sleeping bag. The tent was in complete darkness. The flash of flame had exhausted itself.

Ali was leaning over him, crying, "Kieran! Kieran! Are you all right?"

Confused, he opened his eyes and saw her silhouette. Tears were streaming down his cheeks but he felt unharmed. He wiped his face with his hand. His eyebrows had disappeared and some of his hair had been singed into short wiry curls. "Yes," he panted. "I'm ... OK. Just shocked, I guess." He sat up, resting on his elbows. He moaned with the effort and then observed, "Phew! There's an awful smell in here."

"It's the gas – and burnt hair," Ali told him. "I'll open the flap."

"The gas control must have been faulty," Kieran surmised.

Letting in some fresh air, Ali remarked, "It's been OK for the last couple of nights." She felt his brow and asked, "Sure you're all right?"

"Yes, I think so."

"We're very lucky, you know. We could've both been killed. The canister didn't have much gas left. And there's not enough air in here to keep a fire going. If the tent had caught, or the bedding ..." She sighed. Holding Kieran, she stammered, "Someone could have sabotaged it while we weren't here. Maybe whoever was driving that car." Chilled, she added, "I'm beginning to think there's something in your hunch, Kieran. Whenever Rhia or this Sandra Jackson go off on holiday, people have a habit of dying."

Kieran nodded. "I know. First the car. Now this. I get the feeling someone's trying to scare us off. I think we could be in danger."

In shared misery and exhaustion, they keeled over and fell asleep in each other's arms.

10

Ali blinked and shifted her position. It was light. She yawned and stretched. Undoing the first few centimetres of the zip, she peered out of the tent into the campsite. It was late in the morning because there was plenty of activity in the field. She closed the flap and watched Kieran. He stirred, let out a long moan, and opened his eyes. "Awake?" Ali asked.

"Mmm. Sort of."

By daylight, Ali assessed the damage. The back of Kieran's right hand was smooth, totally devoid of its down. The hair over his forehead had become frizzled and its nauseating smell still lingered. "You'd better wash it," Ali commented, "or no one will want to come near you." His face was bright red. She touched his cheek. "Does it hurt?"

"A bit," Kieran mumbled. "The only person who can get sunburn at two in the morning."

Ali tried a smile but it wasn't very convincing. She surveyed the tent. The gas light was blackened and its glass guard had shattered. Above it, there was a black mark in the ridge of the tent. The fireball had left dark streaks across the roof where it had scorched the fabric. The tops of the fibre glass poles at each end of the tent also had a thin layer of soot. Ali sighed. "You know when you wake up from a really horrible dream – a nightmare – and suddenly realize that it was just a dream, and there's nothing to worry about after all? Well," she said, "we've just done the same thing in reverse. My dreams were fine but real life … I've woken up to find it's a nightmare."

Kieran sat upright, bearing an expression of sympathy.

"I feel vulnerable in here," she continued. "It's not like bricks and mortar."

"I'll get breakfast," Kieran said, "then we'll talk about it."

"Careful, Kieran. Check the cooker first. I don't want to get paranoid about it but we don't know if anything else has been rigged up to kill us."

It was a pleasant day with a warm breeze. They sat outside on the grass, sipping black coffee and eating cereal. Ali began, "Someone's after us."

"Which means we're on to something," Kieran put in.

"Yes, but who is it?"

"I'll give you two guesses," said Kieran.

"Rhia or Sandra Jackson."

"Spot on, I reckon." He swigged back the dregs of his coffee and got up. "Time to find out which," he declared.

"How?" Ali queried.

Kieran extracted a telephone card from his wallet and waved it in the air. "I call home," he explained. "The camp office has got a phone. Won't be long." He jogged to the reception near the entrance gate.

Three minutes later, he jogged back again, unable to disguise the fact that his plan had worked. He plonked himself down on the grass and reported, "Well, it's not Rhia. She's at home because she answered the phone."

"You just hung up? You didn't say anything?"

"That's right," he answered. "My guess is, she contacted the ferry people and found we were coming to Guernsey. Then she told Sandra Jackson. Immediately, Sandra faked a holiday. She's not really in London – she's still here somewhere. Rhia must have told her which boat we were on. I bet she was waiting for us at the harbour, skulking around somewhere out of view. Followed us to here so she knew exactly where we were. That's how come she could sabotage the lantern last night – and try to run us down when she saw us in the lane."

Ali nodded. "Sandra Jackson," she groaned under her breath. Her distraught expression suggested that she believed her boyfriend's reasoning. "It means we've got to pack up and move on," she concluded. "Find another campsite to disappear into. Stop her finding us for three days. Then we go home."

"Mmm." Kieran thought about it for a moment and then countered, "You know what they say's the best form of defence?"

"Attack? What do you mean?"

"Tonight, I'd like to take a look inside Sandra Jackson's cottage. She's obviously not there, so why not?"

"Because it's breaking and entering!" Ali cried. "It's against the law."

"I think last night's events condone it."

Ali looked up at the sky as if seeking patience or courage. "I know how you feel," she said, "but..."

"How about a compromise?" Kieran suggested. "We pack up here and sneak into a new campsite in the hope that we'll lose her. Then, tonight, we'll try our luck at the bungalow."

Reluctantly, Ali murmured her agreement.

"We'd better buy a torch for the occasion," Kieran added.

Ali nodded and requested, "Make it batteries this time. No more gas, please."

The first campsite that they tried was full but they got a pitch in Torteval. It was three miles further out of St Peter Port, but they were next to the main road to the airport and the town so it had a good bus service. Anyway, they discovered that they could hire cycles from the campsite office. They gained freedom to ride any-where at any time.

They found it impossible to enjoy the day. They were too aware that Sandra could be stalking them. Even when they were erecting the tent, they stopped and looked round nervously at each unfam-iliar sound. They scrutinized the faces of everyone who came close. Ali was too anxious about Kieran's plans for the evening to relax in the afternoon. They trudged along part of the South Coast Walk, a cliff path, but they did not really appreciate it because it reminded them of their frailty. It would be easy for someone to push them over, down on to the rocks below where the waves crashed pitilessly.

Ali dreaded dusk and the start of their illicit investigation but, in another way, she welcomed it. Like a visit to the dentist with a relentless toothache, she hoped that she would feel better once it was all over.

It was a cool, airy evening. The wind came off the sea so, as they cycled along the south road, it blew across them. At midnight there were few cars and they could cycle side by side. Arriving at Jerbourg Road, they alighted, locked their cycles together behind a hedge, and walked the last hundred metres to Sandra Jackson's cottage. Their hearts pounded but it had nothing to do with the ride.

They did not linger at the front of her bungalow but crept directly to the back. "I hope no one saw us," Ali whispered.

Kieran glanced round. "Everyone's asleep," he assured her. The cottage was empty. There were no lights and the curtains were not drawn. Kieran tried the back door but it was locked. Next he checked out the old sash windows. The one into the spare bedroom was decidedly insecure. It was loose and the wood was rotten in places. He stumbled around the garden till he found an abandoned pitchfork. Jamming the prongs into the gap between the sill and the bottom of the window, he levered upwards. The wood of the sill splintered a little, then there was a small crack as the window catch gave way under the pressure. "We're in," he murmured.

As Kieran slid the window up and clambered into the deserted bedroom, Ali grew tense with nerves and guilt. If it had been light, her red face and frightened expression would have given her away. From inside, Kieran breathed, "Do you want to leave it to **me and** stay on guard here? You don't have to come in."

"No," she insisted. "I don't want to just stand here. I'd be scared stiff. I'm staying with you." She climbed on to the sill and let herself down carefully into the stuffy bedroom.

"The living room first," Kieran decided.

He took the small torch from his pocket. Making sure that he did not shine it towards a window, he led the way into the hall and then into the lounge. It had the musty smell of an unused room. First, he made for the photograph that he had seen before. He picked it up and shone the torch on it. The image did not look quite right. It had been taken a few years ago before Rhia had acquired her current elegance. Her hair was out of place and her clothes ordinary. "Before she married into money," Kieran muttered.

"Anything on the back?" Ali asked, her voice quaking.

He turned it over but there was nothing to see. He put it down again and looked round the room. There did not seem to be anything extraordinary. A small television, magazine rack, a mixture of classical and old sixties cassettes. Cheap and cheerful paintings of St Peter Port decorated the walls. Kieran opened each cupboard quietly and peered into each drawer in turn.

"You know," Ali whispered, "what isn't here is more remarkable than what is."

"How do you mean?"

A car sounded outside and Kieran snapped off the light, even though they were in a back room. Both of them held their breath but the engine's roar faded away. Ali sighed and answered, "Not even a video by the telly. Doesn't feel right for a video expert. And just one photo of Rhia. None of Sandra Jackson and her husband."

"If she killed him, she wouldn't want any mementoes, would she?"

"I suppose not," Ali murmured. "But... Never mind." As Kieran continued his search, she continued to brood.

"Wow," Kieran muttered as he opened another drawer.

"What?"

"A rifle," he answered.

Ali groaned and perspired even more. "Why's she got a rifle?"

"I dread to think. Perhaps it was her husband's. Perhaps he was once into clay pigeon shooting."

Ali was not convinced. The weapon made her feel even more uneasy.

"Here's something interesting," Kieran hissed as he rummaged in the next drawer down. "Bills, receipts and things." Barely able to contain his excitement, he said, "Here's one from a Weymouth car hire company. She hired a Toyota from the twenty-first to the twenty-fifth of July!"

Ali knelt down beside him. "That is interesting," she said into his ear.

Kieran stuffed the invoice into his jacket pocket and carried on his investigation. "Look, there's a phone bill – all itemized." He shone the torch on it. "Most of the long-distance calls are to my number. And the longest one was a chat with Rhia on the 5th July! She was certainly plotting something with Rhia."

"I think you've just converted me to your theory," Ali murmured. Thoughts of her father's involvement in Stuart's murder faded to almost nothing.

Kieran's heart stopped as he drew out the last item. It was an old photograph with a young man in the foreground. "That's a young William Jackson," he said. "I recognize him from the picture in the newspaper. But..."

Ali interrupted. "Yes. I see her."

In the background, a young Rhia had been captured, peering with admiration at William Jackson.

"I see her," Ali repeated, "but I don't know what it means."

"No," Kieran replied in a stunned hush. "Nor me."

They stood up. Ali said, "I've had enough. We don't want to be here much longer. Let's get going."

"OK," Kieran responded as he pushed the drawer back into position, "but let's take a quick look in her bedroom first. Just in case."

"All right. But turn off the torch because it'll be at the front and a light will be too much of a give-away."

They tiptoed down the hall and pushed open the bedroom door. The curtains were pulled back so that a little moonlight entered the room. As soon as they stepped inside, Ali and Kieran froze. They looked blankly at each other and then back at the bed in case their eyes were deceiving them. They could see that someone was sleeping under the bedclothes. The slightly fragrant smell suggested that the figure was a woman.

Ali put her hand over her mouth to stop herself crying out and waking the person in the bed.

Both of them backed out of the bedroom slowly and without a sound. In the hall, Ali's natural instinct was to run but Kieran grabbed her arm. "Quietly," he whispered.

Together, they padded down the hall and into the second bedroom. Quickly, and muffling the sound as much as they could, they climbed out of the window. Back out in the fresh air, Kieran pulled down the window again. He did not shut it completely in case it made a noise when it clicked into place.

Still moving stealthily, they walked round the cottage and back to the main road. There, they could contain themselves no longer. They burst into a run. Neither of them felt any relief until they were back on their bikes and cycling away at speed. Even then, Kieran was overwhelmed by embarrassment and Ali by disgrace. "Never again," she vowed. "My days as a policewoman are over."

"Yeah," Kieran muttered. "That was close. All that time we were in there and she could have caught us. Phew! But", he added between deep breaths, "you must admit, we found out some good stuff."

Ali did not answer. She did not want to admit to profiting from something that she knew was wrong.

When they settled down in the tent, neither of them could sleep. Ali had not shaken off her guilt and Kieran's brain was churning over incessantly. "I really didn't think she'd be hiding in her own place," he whispered. "Assuming it was Sandra Jackson, do you think that's how she did in her husband? She was lurking around – so she could do the dirty deed – but somehow persuaded the police she was somewhere else at the same time?"

Uncooperatively, Ali mumbled, "Could be." For the moment, she had lost her appetite for intrigue.

"With so many coincidences between them, maybe Rhia used the same method. Like Mike said all along, she wasn't in France that Saturday – whatever the videos seem to prove. She was in England, doing *her* dirty deed." Kieran paused and then muttered to himself, "But it was Sandra Jackson who hired the Toyota, not Rhia."

The door flapped and the nylon sides billowed uncannily as the sea breeze infiltrated the tent.

"You know," Kieran said in a hush, "I can't help feeling the answer's staring me in the face – but I can't see it."

Ali turned towards him. "I'll tell you one thing," she muttered. "We're in deeper trouble now. In the morning, she'll know we broke in. She'll see things disturbed. She'll be after us then. We'd better make ourselves scarce till we go home."

"I suppose so," Kieran replied. "But she may not know where we are right now."

"How many campsites are there on Guernsey? It won't take her long to find us."

"We could take a couple of boat trips. Like the one to Sark. She won't find us then. Even if she did, she couldn't do anything to us on a small launch with other passengers."

"Perhaps not," Ali moaned. "But you can bet she'll check which boat we're going home on. We can't do much about that. She'll book a place as well, if she can. Sooner or later," she said in distress, "she'll catch up with us. I wish we knew what she looked like. I'd feel a bit happier if I knew who to watch out for."

"It's all right," Kieran remarked, holding her arm comfortingly, "there's two of us and only one of her. She's outnumbered. She won't be able get us."

"She seems pretty cunning to me," Ali rejoined.

"We're not exactly stupid ourselves," Kieran contended. "We'll have to be careful and crafty as well."

Ali turned over to seek sleep. Kieran pondered on the photograph that showed that Rhia had met William Jackson many years ago. He could not deduce anything from it other than a connection between Rhia and another murder victim. It seemed that the men in her life were dropping like flies. Eventually he lapsed into sleep wondering if he was to be next.

On a map, Sark was a mere dot. In real life, it was a tall solid plateau jutting out of the sea. An hour-glass lump of rock. It consisted of a few houses, hotels and shacks, lots of horses and carriages, cycles, a couple of tractors and no cars at all. Ali and Kieran could almost taste the alien purity of its air.

The crowd of tourists coming from the harbour soon dispersed. Ali and Kieran decided to hire bikes and ride round the island. They headed south. At the neck of the hour-glass, La Coupée, the land fell away sharply on either side of the track. On one side, a steep path zigzagged down to a large sandy beach. On the other, the inaccessible precipice ended in rocks and the sea. They leaned on the rail on La Coupée and watched the few people who had undertaken the difficult trek down to the beach a long way below them.

"I've been thinking," Ali mentioned as she gulped the clean air. "Why do people keep photos of other people in their houses?"

Kieran looked puzzled but answered the question anyway. "Because they're fond of them in some way, I suppose."

"So who do you keep photos of?"

"Friends and family. What are you getting at?"

A yacht and a small motorboat came into view. The yacht was sailing straight past the island and would soon disappear behind the ragged cliffs that bordered the beach. The launch swung into the calmer waters of the bay. A few tourists walked past Kieran and Ali on the precarious narrow track. Ali and Kieran both turned and examined them, expecting the worst. It was a perfectly normal family and not a psychopathic killer.

Once the family was out of earshot, Ali continued, "Just bear with me. Think of your own house. How many of the framed photos out on show are of friends?"

Kieran thought about it. "Now you mention it, none. They're all family photos, I think."

"Same in my house," Ali remarked. "The ones on display are mainly me, Mum and Dad. There's one of Grandma and Grandad on my mum's side. That's about it."

Out in the bay, the boat dropped anchor. The scream of a hungry baby on the beach drifted up the headland.

Kieran nodded slowly. "I think I see what you're saying. You think, because of that photo in Sandra Jackson's place, she's related to Rhia?"

"Exactly," Ali uttered.

Kieran exhaled. "Sandra Jackson's part of the family?" He hesitated and then argued, "I doubt it. Remember the newspaper article on William Jackson's murder? It said he was forty-five. If Sandra Jackson's much the same age – which is likely – that's more or less the same as Rhia. But in Rhia's family tree, there's no one who'd be the same age as her. It can't be right."

Ali glanced at her boyfriend and shrugged. "Oh well, it was an idea. You'd better start thinking why else Sandra Jackson might keep a photo of Rhia, then."

Somewhere, there was a bang followed by a thud in the rock below them.

"What was that?" Ali asked.

"Sounded like a car backfiring," Kieran replied.

Ali stared at him and exclaimed, "There aren't any cars on Sark!"

It happened again and a few centimetres from Kieran's hand, something twanged against the rail, making a dent in it.

Kieran grabbed Ali's hand and yelled, "Run!"

They dashed back along the track till they were hidden behind the rocks that rose up on either side. They propped themselves against the rock until they got their breath back.

"Someone was taking pot-shots at us!" Kieran cried. "Probably from that boat."

"And I can guess which rifle was doing the shooting," Ali gasped.

From behind the wall of rock there was the sound of a motor starting up. Kieran walked back up the track until he could see over the bank. "Careful!" Ali shouted.

"It's all right," Kieran called back. "Come and look. The boat's heading back to Guernsey. She's given up."

An old man, wandering along the path, scowled first at Kieran and then at Ali. Still grimacing, he lengthened his stride to get past them faster.

Kieran put his arm round Ali's shoulder and together they watched the launch until it disappeared from view. "Sandra Jackson won't find us on Sark, you said. We'll be safe," Ali mumbled. She wasn't angry with Kieran. She was afraid.

"She must have guessed our tactics," Kieran reasoned. "She must have been keeping watch on the harbour and spotted us this morning. Still, we're safe for now, though. We've just seen her retreat. We can enjoy the rest of the trip."

"Yes, but what about when we get back? She'll be waiting."

Kieran answered, "Maybe. But remember, according to that neighbour, she's supposed to be in England. We know she's only pretending – she's still here – so she won't risk being seen *too* much or she'd blow her cover, as they say. It's one thing to keep a discreet eye on the harbour but it's another to actually do something to us in St Peter Port. Too many people about. All we have to do is make sure we're not followed when we cycle back to the tent. That's easy." He tried to sound certain to give Ali strength and confidence.

"Oh yes?"

"The roads are busy, right? We wait till the traffic comes to a complete standstill and then we ride through it as fast as we can and away. In a car, she'll be stuck."

Ali sighed but seemed reassured by his words. "All right. But don't you think it's time we went to the police?"

"With what?" Kieran asked, clearly doubting the wisdom of her proposal.

Ali shrugged. "Well, you've got that car rental thing."

"Yes," Kieran admitted, "but hiring a car in Weymouth isn't against the law. We've only got theories. Outlandish ones, the police will think. And we still don't know how they did it. There's nothing to back up the video fixing idea."

Ali accepted his argument. They would seem like a couple of hysterical, imaginative kids.

They trudged back to where their bikes lay by the side of the track. "Follow me," Kieran chirped, still trying to cheer her up.

"We'll aim for something called the Venus Pool. The guide says it's a natural swimming pool in the rocks at the end of the island. We can relax a bit there."

They spent their last full day in the vicinity of the campsite, biding time, keeping out of Sandra Jackson's way. On the following morning they returned their cycles, packed up the tent and caught the number 14 bus into St Peter Port. The nearer they approached the town, the more edgy they became. Kieran was still trying to convince himself and Ali that, even if Sandra Jackson saw them at the harbour, she would not be able to harm them. With plenty of on-lookers, it would be too chancy for her.

They made sure that they waited for the catamaran where there were lots of other people. A café full of witnesses. When the boarding began, Kieran and Ali first surveyed the territory and then sprinted across the road to join the queue in the ferry terminal. They felt protected by the long line of passengers.

On the boat they took two seats at the back of the lounge so that they could see everything happening in front of them and so that no one could creep up unseen behind them. When Ali grasped his arm, Kieran enquired, "Glad to be going home?"

"You bet," she responded. "But I'm worried in case she's on the boat with us." She glanced round and mumbled, "She could be anyone."

"She can't do anything here – as long as we don't ask for it by leaning over the rails once it gets going."

Ali smiled weakly. "Wild horses won't drag me on to the deck."

Once the catamaran was skimming across the sea, Ali left her seat only to visit the toilet. She was making her way back to Kieran when she caught sight of a mother struggling with her two young toddlers who had both decided to have tantrums at the same time. For some reason, quite involuntarily, Ali halted to observe the rumpus for a while. As the woman muttered and cursed more heatedly, the kids seemed to enjoy making her life yet more awkward and embarrassing. At first, Ali did not see the significance of the family feud. She didn't understand the impulse that made her linger and watch. A plastic frog hurtled across the gangway and landed at Ali's feet. She bent down and picked it up. Taking it to the harassed mother, she knelt down beside her and shook it in front of the toddler who had thrown it. It rattled pleasingly. The child snatched it back and the mother said, "Thanks."

"They're a handful," Ali remarked.

"You could say that." As Ali stood up, the woman advised her, "Never have two at once!"

While Ali smiled sympathetically at her, the flying frog thwacked into the side of her head.

The mother screeched, "Gemma! That was naughty!"

Ali said, "Never mind," and rushed away.

Kieran rose when she approached. "Are you all right?" he asked anxiously. "You've been a while – and you look like you've seen a ghost."

"Sit down," she ordered, plonking herself back into the chair. "Sit down and listen." She grabbed his arm and shook it in agitation. "It's obvious. You said the answer's been staring us in the face. You were right."

"What are you talking about?"

"A couple of days back, you said it was almost as if Rhia had a double life. Rhia and Sandra could be the same person, you thought, but really you knew they couldn't be. You weren't far out, though. The real answer explains everything – the photos in Sandra Jackson's cottage. The French videos. The car hire in Weymouth. Mike's sighting. It all makes sense!"

Frustrated, Kieran uttered, "What does? You haven't told me yet!"

"You were right all the time, Kieran. Rhia did kill your dad. But she hasn't got a double life – she's got a double!"

"A what?"

"A twin," Ali explained. "Rhia and Sandra are identical twins! It's obvious. Those photos in Sandra Jackson's house weren't of friends *or* family. They were Sandra Jackson herself – on her own and with her husband."

Kieran's eyes were bright as he nodded. Infected by her excitement, he said, "Yes, of course. The two of them fooled us all. The police videos showed Sandra masquerading as Rhia."

"That's right," Ali replied. "I'm sorry I doubted you about the dress. Rhia didn't have that green dress because she wasn't the woman in the green dress."

"And Rhia gave Sandra a pay-off of one hundred thousand

pounds for posing in front of the cameras at the time they'd arranged – when Rhia left her hiding place, went home and murdered Dad. That's why she left evidence of the exact time of the murder and why the only fingerprints on the knife were Rhia's," Kieran concluded. "Sandra came over to England, hired the car, met up with Rhia and took her passport and tickets, I guess. Rhia took Sandra's driving licence and the hire car. It was Sandra Jackson flying from Heathrow, pretending to be Rhia. When she got back, they'd have exchanged documents again and Sandra would have travelled back to Guernsey. Neat. Really, they just swapped places for a few days!"

"Bet it was the second time they'd pulled that trick," Ali added. "Remember Mr Jackson's murder? Sandra had an alibi. The newspaper said she was in Britain. My guess is that she seemed to be on video in Edinburgh at the time. That would have been Rhia's pre-Christmas trip. Actually, Sandra never left Guernsey. She was holed up somewhere on the island, on hand to poison her husband." Abruptly, Ali's flow came to a halt. Disappointed, she spotted the flaw in her own logic. "But she didn't have any medical knowledge. She wouldn't have known enough about drugs to kill him like that."

"No," Kieran put in. "But Rhia would. Ages ago, she was a nurse. She told me. She could have got her sister the pills and given her instructions – as well as an alibi."

"Yes!" Ali was breathless with her discovery and conclusions. She slumped in the chair, almost exhausted.

"Trouble is," Kieran said, "I don't know how we prove it. You must admit, it's clever. They've got a good double act, providing one another with perfect alibis."

"Yes, but at least it means we'll be safe from them here on the boat," Ali estimated. "You were right. Before we left home, Rhia must have phoned Sandra Jackson and told her we were on our way. From that moment, Rhia stayed around London, seeing friends to provide her own alibi and, no doubt, getting herself on video at some London tourist spots for Sandra's alibi. That would have left Sandra in the clear if she had got us on Guernsey. She wouldn't follow us on to the catamaran, though, because it would take her too close to Rhia. Their little scam is only convincing if they're in different countries."

Kieran nodded but did not reply. He did not wish to scare Ali with his thoughts. He was wondering if Rhia would pretend to be away when they returned. He wondered if Rhia and Sandra Jackson were planning it right now. Rhia could buy a ticket to Guernsey and tell everyone that she was visiting the Channel Islands. Then she would hide out somewhere, ready to pounce on Kieran and Ali. On Guernsey, Sandra Jackson would apparently return from her own phoney trip to London and make herself visible at the exact time that Rhia swooped. The thrill of solving the puzzle gave way to gloom.

"I know why Rhia never mentioned her twin," Ali added. "If anyone else knew she existed, the alibi wouldn't work. But how come she kept it secret for so many years? She couldn't have plotted all this from birth."

"No," Kieran replied. "She's fascinated by genealogy or whatever it's called – her family tree and all that – but Sandra Jackson doesn't appear on it. Strange."

11

The catamaran glided sedately up to Weymouth's harbour wall and the workers on the quay secured the craft with ropes. Customers with cars hurried to the vehicle deck, hoping not to be the last passenger to spill out on to the crowded and narrow streets of Weymouth. Ali and Kieran joined the line of travellers waiting to disembark via the walkway. Ali whispered, "You know as soon as we set foot on dry land we're back in danger, don't you? Rhia this time, not Sandra."

"Yes," Kieran answered. "I know. I've been thinking. There's something I want to do before we get out into the big wide world and face her, though."

"Oh?"

"A telephone call might be interesting."

Before Ali could query further, the queue shuffled forward.

Once on solid ground in the terminal, Kieran made for one in a row of telephones. First, using Directory Enquiries, he found the number of the Guernsey police headquarters in St Peter Port. Then he called the station and asked for the officer in charge of the William Jackson case. When, after a couple of minutes, a female voice came on the line, he stressed, "I need to speak to whoever's heading the investigation into William Jackson's murder."

"And so you are," she replied sharply.

"Oh. Right. Well ... I don't know what you've found out but I imagine Sandra Jackson's alibi was being in Edinburgh. And I guess you've got videos from security cameras to prove it."

There was a barely noticeable pause before the detective said, "Who is this?"

"I can't tell you that yet, but am I right?"

"Yes," she replied cautiously. "But that information was never released. How did you know?"

"Because I'm ... acquainted with her identical twin sister who was in Edinburgh just before last Christmas."

This time, there was a stunned silence. Before the police officer had worked out all of the implications and could ask another question, Kieran hung up. "Yes!" he said, fisting the air. "You were right. Rhia *did* provide a Scottish alibi – just like Sandra Jackson came up with a French one for Rhia."

Kieran soon sobered up. He was going home to a killer who wanted him dead. As he ambled with Ali towards the exit, he said, "I just hope that the Guernsey police take Sandra Jackson in for questioning now. She can hardly carry out any plan for Rhia if she's in the nick."

Ali stopped and stated, "It won't make any difference to us – or to Rhia. She's just as dangerous because she won't know about it. It's only *after* she's ... you know ... got rid of us that she'll find her alibi's collapsed."

"We'll be OK," Kieran responded. "Just that we've got to plan for ... every eventuality. Come on," he urged. "Let's crack on – and get on with our lives."

In their week away, they had become accustomed to the clean air of the Channel Islands. As they emerged from the terminal, they could sense England's atmosphere of dilute exhaust fumes. Kieran took a deep breath and said, "Smell that? We're home!"

"We're from London," Ali rejoined. "I'll give us two minutes and we won't even notice the pollution any more. You don't when you're in it all the time."

Simultaneously, they froze. "Talking of pollution..." Kieran mumbled. In front of them, standing by a Toyota, Rhia was waving at them to attract their attention.

"Oh, no," Ali groaned.

Thinking quickly, Kieran turned to a lad standing next to him. He was athletic, about thirteen years of age. "You've got broad shoulders on you," Kieran commented. "Bet you'd make a good swimmer."

The boy was wary but smiled at Kieran's flattery. "Already am," he boasted. "Junior champ, me."

"Yeah?" Kieran replied. "That's impressive. What stroke and distance?"

"Hundred metres breast-stroke."

"I bet you're good with numbers, names and faces as well."

"Not bad," the boy mumbled.

"Do me a favour, then," Kieran said to him. "Remember me, Kieran Burrage, and Ali Tankersley here. And remember that lady over there by the car. Her name's Sandra Jackson and she's from Guernsey. Most of all, remember her car's registration. Can you see it?"

The boy was bemused but nodded anyway. He recited the registration for Kieran's benefit.

"Good. If anything happens to us, if you see it on the news or in the papers, go and tell the police that she picked us up and tell them her car's number plate. Will you do that for me?"

The lad shrugged and said, "All right."

Kieran slapped him on the shoulder. "Thanks. And keep up the swimming."

As they continued to walk slowly towards Rhia, Ali whispered fearfully, "Planning for the worst again, I note. I hope it doesn't come to that. But you could have told him who she really is."

"Perhaps," he answered. "But if I did, Thompson would check who's hired the car, probably find it was someone called Sandra Jackson, and assume that the kid's messing about. End of the line. My way," Kieran explained, "that lad's story and the car rental would match. If the boy remembers the bit about Guernsey, Thompson would have it on a plate."

"Even if you're right that Rhia's used Sandra Jackson's name and licence to hire the car, the trail would only lead to Sandra Jackson. Rhia's off the hook."

Kieran glanced at her and replied, "I don't think so. How strong do you reckon sisterly loyalty is? Do you think Sandra Jackson will take the blame for murders she didn't commit? There'll be no honour between these two, I bet. One will take the other one down with her." There was another reason why he'd refused to name Rhia for the second time in a few minutes. Some instinct told him that he should confront her himself, before he informed the police. It was his right and his duty.

Rhia looked impeccable, like porcelain, and innocent. It was impossible to believe that she could be involved in anything sordid. Yet Kieran and Ali had to believe the impossible, because they knew.

Beaming at them like a delighted mother, Rhia chirped, "Hi! Welcome back."

Neither Kieran nor Ali could reply. They just stood there foolishly with their mouths open.

"I checked with the ferry company when you were returning," she explained. "I thought I'd meet you off the boat and give you a lift home. I knew you'd appreciate it. For such a big occasion, I wanted a more ... comfortable car, but this will have to do. Still, it's much more friendly than a coach or train."

"Not the Mercedes, then?" Kieran said pointedly, his tone ringing with sarcasm.

"No," she answered sweetly. "It's being serviced."

Really, Kieran thought, right now she doesn't want to be seen in a car registered in her own name. He shivered.

"Get in," she invited them politely. "I'm dying to hear if you've had a nice time."

Any passers-by would have taken her to be a bubbly parent who had been separated for too long from her loved ones. Presumably, that's why she put on the performance – to convince witnesses that all was well.

Still dumbstruck, Ali and Kieran stood inert on the pavement as she opened the passenger doors for them. "Ali can keep me company in the front," she chimed. "Kieran, you can sit in the back."

Ali clung to Kieran's arm, refusing to budge.

"We'd like to sit together in the back," Kieran declared.

Rhia's mood changed. "No," she barked. "I told you the seating arrangements. Don't make a fuss." Deliberately, she put her hand into her jacket pocket, gripped something inside, thrust it towards Ali, and motioned towards the car's front door.

Kieran groaned. "I think we'd better do what she's suggested," he said to Ali.

The bulge in her pocket could have been a packet of sweets, a pen, almost anything, but Kieran thought that it really was a gun.

Kieran took Ali's rucksack, ushered her, visibly shaking, into the front seat and closed the door. He shoved both bags to the far side of the rear seat and then slipped into the remaining space himself. Leaning forward, he whispered to Ali, "No real choice. It'll be all right. Don't worry."

He looked back towards the ferry terminal and noted with relief that the young swimmer had taken him seriously. The boy was watching every move.

Rhia got into the driver's seat and started the car. It purred into life. Before she pulled away, she said, "Now, let's not have an unpleasant journey. And remember, Kieran, it would be ... unwise to try anything silly when your precious girlfriend is next to me." With one hand on the driving wheel, she tapped the pocket containing the gun to show that, even when she was driving, she could threaten Ali quickly and easily.

"Charming!" Ali cried. "And to think I was the one who tried to persuade Kieran that you were as pure as snow."

"I think you two might have the wrong end of the stick," Rhia responded. "You appear to be assuming my guilt – without a sliver of evidence, I suspect."

From the back seat, Kieran put in, "Are you speaking as Rhia Burrage or Sandra Jackson now?"

"Sandra Jackson?"

"Come on," Kieran blurted out. "Your twin sister must have been on the phone about us. That's why you arranged this little reception, no doubt."

Rhia braked as some traffic lights turned to red. "Twin sister?" she said, twisting round in her seat. "Can you prove that?"

"No, but we know she is. And I've just called the Guernsey police to tell them that she's got an identical twin. I think they'll find that ... interesting. They might begin to question the value of her alibi of being on video in Edinburgh. They might think it's worthy of further investigation."

"You're bluffing," Rhia murmured.

"He's not," Ali emphasized.

"The lights have changed," Kieran prompted her.

Rhia accelerated away from the town towards the A31 and the M3 motorway to London, muttering, "It doesn't make any difference."

Kieran leaned forward. Watching him in the rear-view mirror, Rhia tensed immediately and her right hand dived into her pocket. "I just wanted to ask something," he murmured.

"What?" she snapped, her hand still lingering near the gun.

"It's the only thing we don't understand. How come you kept your twin a secret all these years?"

Rhia sneered. "It wasn't me that kept it secret. It was Father." Abandoning any thoughts of denying that Sandra Jackson was her sister, Rhia decided that she might as well satisfy their curiosity. "Mother died when I was born," she declared, as if she had a divine right to sympathy. "I was brought up by Father. He died last summer, as you know. Just before he passed away, he told me something. He told me that I had a twin sister. He'd kept it from me until the very last moment, too ashamed to admit that he hadn't been able to cope with both babies and so he'd abandoned one. Sandra was adopted." She sighed heavily and with irony. "Funny. I'd always felt there was something missing from my life. Not just a mother. Something else. I tried to make up for it, I suppose, by working out my family tree. For me, it was like a religious calling. But I still didn't feel ... fulfilled. It gave me some experience at tracking people down, though. When Father told me I had a sister, I knew I had to find her straight away. First, I traced the family that had adopted her and then I found Sandra herself. It wasn't easy. Her adoptive family hadn't told her about me, either. She thought they were her real parents. I think Father and the people who adopted her must have made a pact to keep silent."

"That makes sense," Kieran muttered. "When you found her, you worked out a plot to get rid of each other's husbands," he surmised. "And that required you to keep her a secret."

"You make it sound ... cold and calculated," Rhia objected. "But you don't understand. You don't know what it was like. Sandra's life was dreadful, stagnant, held back by poverty and an awful, oppressive husband. He was disabled. Everything she did, she did it for him. Together we decided it was time she had her own life. I helped her to get rid of the shackles. That's all."

"That is cold and calculating," Ali retorted.

Before Rhia could turn on Ali, Kieran said, "No doubt you painted a certain picture of Dad for her, as well. To get her co-operation, you probably presented him as some sort of monster."

"If I painted a picture of him, it was accurate. Sandra was more concerned that, if I were free of your dad, I'd be able to help her financially so that her new life would be ... comfortable."

"So", Kieran concluded, "this was the deal. You posed as Sandra in Edinburgh while she murdered an overbearing husband – after you'd sorted out the drugs. In return, plus a hundred thousand pounds, she agreed to stand in for you in Paris, allowing you to kill Dad and inherit a lot of money."

"You *have* been doing some research," Rhia replied.

"It stinks!" Kieran growled.

"All I know is that I've saved my sister," Rhia maintained. "Now, she can look forward to a real life. As long as you two don't spoil it for her. And there's only one way I know that will ensure you don't make nuisances of yourselves…"

"What do you mean?" Ali cried.

Kieran muttered, "She's thinking of removing a threat and getting even more money for herself – by getting rid of me."

"You are cynical, Kieran," his stepmother responded coolly. "I'm not thinking of myself, only Sandra."

"Sure," Kieran uttered. "And I'm second in line for the throne."

Ali murmured, "You won't get away with it."

Rhia glanced at her watch and then announced, "Look, this is the New Forest. It's a lovely place. We'll take a detour somewhere – to see more of it."

Ali glanced back at Kieran. Her expression suggested alarm. Both of them knew that Rhia was plotting more than simple sightseeing.

She turned left on to a track that led deep into the woodland. "There's a gorgeous place up here," she informed them.

"And what have you got in mind?" Kieran barked.

"A break in the journey. A bit of relaxation," she lied.

Kieran did not persist in his questioning. He had a good idea what was on her mind. He had to wait until he had an opportunity to strike back.

She drove carefully along the pot-holed trail until she pulled into a secluded parking place. The car was hidden by a screen of ancient trees.

"Let's get out," she said. Her tone fell somewhere between a command and a suggestion. "There's a beautiful spot just through these trees. Bring your backpacks."

Kieran and Ali looked at each other anxiously but obeyed.

Well away from the main road and with the car engine off, there was a deadly calm. Only the birds among the upper branches went about their business, uncaring of the feud between three insignificant human beings.

"You'll love it," Rhia announced, as she took a heavy bag from the boot.

Standing side by side for protection in the dense forest, Kieran and Ali shuddered. Neither of them moved.

There was no pretence any more. Rhia yanked the gun from her pocket and waved it in the direction that she wanted them to go. "Some people have to be encouraged to enjoy themselves," she observed.

Kieran took Ali's hand and set off among the trees. There was no path but the comings and goings of squirrels and ponies had kept the way clear. Immediately, he had to let go of Ali because there was not enough room for two abreast. After just a few seconds of walking, trees surrounded them, isolating them utterly from the rest of the world. They were trapped in a murky microcosm of their own with a murderer. Without Rhia it would have been a pleasing screen from prying people. With her, it was claustrophobic and menacing.

As they trekked into the forest, they became aware of the sound of running water. Shortly after, the trees thinned a little and a river appeared in front of them. Really it was only a stream but, at this point, there was a bend in its course and erosion had widened it. Nearer to the inner bank, the water was slack and inviting. Kieran and Ali halted. Rhia had been right. It was lavish and lonely, like a natural temple encircled with trees. To either side of the curve, both upstream and downstream, the trees grew impenetrably right down to the banks so a riverside walk was impossible. Rhia leaned against a trunk, put down the bag and said, "You can make camp here."

"What?" Kieran exclaimed.

"Packs off," she ordered. "Pitch your tent by the river. It's a super place for it."

Kieran sighed. He remembered that, several years ago, he envisaged Rhia as a sharpshooting stranger imposing herself on the Burrages. He did not realize how accurate the image would turn out to be. Rhia was propped against the tree, gun in hand, as if she were in a wild west saloon, expecting trouble.

Dragging the folded tent out of Ali's rucksack, Kieran tried to work out the cruel plan that was in his stepmother's brain. "What are you trying to set up here?" he murmured, not expecting a reply.

"We got back from Guernsey, perhaps out of money. No coach or train fare. Maybe we hitched a lift this far – found this remote spot and decided to camp overnight." As they assembled the poles, Kieran deduced, "You're setting up some sort of accident! Just in case. I bet in Weymouth you bought a ticket for the ferry but didn't use it. That way, the travel company's registered that you're in Guernsey. You've probably got Sandra working on an alibi right now."

Rhia was smirking. She checked the time as if to confirm that she was working to an agreed schedule.

Kieran continued. "Really, you could kill us anyhow – you could just shoot us – but you're making it look like some accident in case the alibi doesn't hold up, in case the police are on to Sandra. Besides, you don't want to overuse the twin sister trick. This way – manufacturing an accident – you may not need her to double for you."

Ali had stopped helping to erect the tent and was staring at Kieran, hoping that his horrifying logic was the product of a warped and hyperactive imagination. The sight of Rhia toying with a pistol dismissed any hope that he was mistaken. She shook her head and fought to keep back tears. She was determined not to show her weakness in front of Rhia. Ali was praying that Kieran had a plan to get them out of trouble – or that something would occur to her. Really, she wanted to collapse inside the still sagging tent, hide, cry, and only emerge when it was safe – when her world had righted itself and, unharmed, she could carry on her normal, uneventful, carefree life.

Slowly, Kieran lapped the site, tightening the guy ropes, pulling the tent into shape. When he'd finished, Rhia called, "Well done. Now spread out your things inside as if you were staying overnight. Keep the flap open so I can see." She moved into a position where she could keep an eye on them.

Inside, manhandling the sleeping bags, Ali whispered to Kieran, "She's going to kill us! What are we going to do?"

"Wait to see what she's got in mind," he breathed. "Wait for an opportunity."

From outside, Rhia's sarcastic voice muttered, "Very cosy."

Kieran and Ali scrambled out and stood, like sentries, either side of the door. They stared at Rhia, awaiting orders.

Rhia glanced once more at her watch. Her smile suggested self-satisfaction. "Now, Ali, you get back in and strip off."

Ali cried, "What? Why?"

"Get into your swimming costume," she commanded, pointing the gun at her to show that she meant it. "As you surmised, Kieran, you've just arrived here, pitched the tent, and, to relax before an evening meal, Ali's decided to take a dip in the river. It could hardly be more attractive for it. But don't think you're being left out," she said to her stepson. "You're going to have a swim as well. You'll keep your clothes on, though."

Kieran responded, "If you've got it in mind to have us drown, it won't look very convincing. You know we're both strong swimmers. Even if one of us had a problem, the other would sort it out."

"I know," Rhia groaned. "Do you think I'm a complete fool?" Once more, she waved the gun at Ali and snapped, "Go on, then, get in and change." To Kieran, she said, "You've decided to have a nice cool drink before joining her." Walking backwards so that she could keep the gun trained on him, she went for the bag.

She returned and put the bag down close to Kieran. Then she backed away from it and told him to extract the contents.

Kieran peered inside and then took out the six cans of beer. He glanced at Rhia suspiciously.

"Take a couple down to the stream and put them in the water to cool them down," she directed him.

While Rhia watched him carefully, he negotiated the bank with two of the cans in his hands. The slope down to the river was gentle and bore the signs of animals. Birds had hopped around and ponies had come to the water for a drink. He placed the cans securely in the stream where the flow was lazy.

"Right," Rhia called. "Back up here. Erecting the tent was thirsty work. You need some refreshment. Drink one of the beers. All of it."

At last, Kieran understood her plan. Ali was to go for a dip while he had a few innocuous drinks. Ali would get into trouble and Kieran would spring into action. But he would be in no fit state to help her. His drunken attempt to save his girlfriend would result only in his own drowning. Two victims rather than one.

He opened the can and gulped some of it down.

"Faster," Rhia demanded.

As Ali clambered out of the tent with one arm behind her back, Kieran finished off the beer.

"Good," Rhia uttered. "Put the empty can by the door to the tent and then open another."

Kieran scowled at her. Holding his stomach, he muttered, "I can't. I'm all bloated already."

Rhia aimed the gun at his head and cried, "Don't try your luck! Of course you can. Get on with it."

Kieran shrugged, dropped the first can near Ali's feet and then fetched another one. As he bent down and all of Rhia's attention was on him, Ali lifted her arm and threw their peg hammer directly at Rhia.

She was too far away, though. Rhia had the time to side-step. She took the blow on her thigh. "Ow!" she squealed. But the hand that held the weapon did not waver. She cursed Ali but almost immediately she laughed aloud. "What a silly impetuous girl you are," she mocked. "Right. Finish that drink, leave the tin near the last one and bring the other two down to the bank."

She instructed Ali to get into the water and Kieran to sit on the edge of the bank and begin the third beer. Then she called to Ali, "Swim up and down. Enjoy it – like training. I want to see you go fast. You're supposed to be good so show off to me."

Kieran mumbled to himself, "She wants Ali to be tired out before she organizes the drowning! Lower her resistance."

After a while, Kieran could feel the effects of the alcohol. He began to feel detached from the horrible situation that Rhia had set up so efficiently. When he glanced from Ali in the river to Rhia standing further along the bank, his eyes took longer than usual to focus. His stomach was full and queasy.

"Drink!" Rhia yelled at him.

Blinking and lolling, Kieran lifted the can to his lips and gulped yet more of the sickening liquid. His legs dangled from the overhanging edge and swung erratically. He regarded Ali with sympathy and love. In the water, no one could distinguish her tears from river water. She was being punished simply for being with him. This whole affair had nothing to do with her. He had dragged her into it and now she was about to be killed just for being his girlfriend.

Ali reached one end of the pool yet again and stopped momentarily to catch her breath. At once, Rhia barked, "Swim! Faster."

Behind them, beyond the tent, there was a rustling in the under-growth. Kieran's head twisted round and he fought to bring his eyes to a focus. He was hoping to see the cavalry, charging to the rescue. But it wasn't. It was just a couple of wild ponies approaching the stream.

While Rhia was distracted, Kieran decided to make his move. He scrambled to his feet and began to hurtle towards Rhia. Almost immediately, he slipped and tumbled over. It was a laughable, pathetic attempt. When he looked up towards his stepmother, he saw the barrel of her gun pointed directly at his head. Even if he hadn't been befuddled, he would not have been able to take her by surprise. The decoy was feeble and the distance too great. Rhia sniggered and the ponies retreated into the forest.

"Excellent," Rhia declared. "The alcohol is getting to you. To show such recklessness – and bad judgement – you must be nearly ready. Finish off the last pint."

Kieran's grip on reality was becoming ever more slender. He could no longer arouse any worthwhile opposition. He lurched back to his place on the crest of the bank and swallowed the remaining beer in a single draught. In a slurred voice, he pronounced, "Done." It was an admission that he had consumed the drink and that he was helpless.

"Good," Rhia replied. "It's time you joined your girlfriend. Into the river with you."

Kieran obeyed blindly. He stumbled down the bank and waded into the cool water.

Gasping for breath, Ali joined him.

"Now," Rhia said with an ugly grin, "I want you to pick up anything heavy from the bottom."

Kieran stared at her for a few seconds, unable to comprehend. "What for?"

They stood there like fools in the sluggish part of the river, one intoxicated and one exhausted. They clung to each other and tottered together.

"Because you're going to crack her over the head with it – the sort of injury she could have sustained if she'd dived in carelessly."

Even his confused brain registered revulsion at her demand. "No!" he protested.

Rhia grimaced with frustration. "I thought this was where you might draw the line." Keeping the finger of her left hand on the trigger and maintaining her aim, Rhia bent down and picked up a massive bough in her right hand. "I'll do it instead!" Without warning she flung the bough violently at Ali's head.

Intuitively, but still in a daze, Kieran put out his arm to protect Ali. The branch thwacked him painfully and knocked his arm backwards on to Ali. Both of them toppled over.

In the instant that Kieran plunged into the river, the cold water revived him. At once, he could make dreadful sense of their predicament. With his mind cleared, he decided what they had to do. He dragged Ali back up to the surface and whispered to her. "Deep breaths! And get ready to hold one."

Ali had been stunned. In a broken voice, she murmured, "No chance."

"Do it," Kieran dictated. "It's the only way."

Rhia was heading for them with a rock in one hand and her gun in the other.

Kieran positioned himself in front of Ali. "No, Rhia. I won't let you hurt her."

Rhia raised her arm to hurl the rock.

"Now!" Kieran cried. He grabbed Ali's arm, turned and dived out into the rapidly flowing part of the stream as if he were in a vital race. Ali lunged after him. Staying underwater, they swam as best they could and let the river carry them away from her.

Kieran felt the rock thud on to his back but the water stripped it of much of its force. Even submerged, Kieran heard the crack of the gun. There was a ping in the water as the bullet zipped past his head. It wasn't difficult to keep underwater. Kieran's heavy clothes dragged him down. The second bullet sliced through the river and into his leg just above the ankle. He opened his mouth to cry out in agony but instead he choked. He kept going for as long as he could but then he had to fight to reach the surface. Coughing and spluttering, he was amazed and relieved to see Ali still by his side. Her face was red with the effort of holding her breath, but she had surfaced at the same time and was swimming breast-stroke. His plan had worked. He turned on to his back, letting the current complete his escape. Rhia and the curvature of the river were out of sight. "We made it," he called to Ali. "Let's get out here. She got my leg."

They swam across the flow and scrambled out on to the opposite bank. Ali was weak but she helped Kieran hobble on to dry land and behind some trees where they were out of view.

"She won't find us here," Kieran groaned. "There's no path by the river so she can't follow us – and she can't swim." He turned his head to one side, coughed and then vomited until his stomach had rejected all of the beer. He was shivering with cold and shock.

Crashed out in the undergrowth, Ali asked, "Are you OK?"

"Better for being sick," he answered. Gingerly, he pulled up his trouser leg to inspect the damage. Watery blood had seeped down his left leg and into his sock.

"Oh, no," Ali moaned.

"It's not too bad," Kieran assured her. "I think it's gone right through – just under the surface. Too messy to be sure, but I think it looks worse than it is."

"I hope you're right. It looks awful to me."

Kieran rubbed his arm gently. "This isn't too good either. It's where the branch got me."

"I hope it's not broken or anything."

"No," Kieran replied. "Quite a bruise, I should think, but I'll live."

"I'm glad about that." Ali surveyed the wreck of her boyfriend sympathetically. He was trembling, pale and saturated. Slowly recuperating herself, she said, "I hate to say this, but what now? Rhia won't give up, you know. Maybe it'll take her a while, but she'll find us."

"Yes," Kieran agreed. "I think the main road's that way," he said, pointing behind her. "We should head for it and get help."

"Really?" Ali muttered questioningly. "Can you walk that far? And it's exactly what she'll expect, surely. She could be making her way there now – to cut us off."

"True," Kieran admitted. "So what do you suggest?"

Ali shrugged. "I guess we do what she'd least expect us to do."

"What's that?"

"Go back. Go back and look for help in the other direction. That way, we can nip into the tent. You need warm dry clothes."

"But..." Kieran sighed. "You're probably right."

"How's the leg?"

"I think you were right about walking. It's not going to hold up for long."

"There's no way through this wood anyway," Ali said. "How about swimming?"

"Less painful than walking," Kieran estimated. "But how about you? It'd be against the current. Not easy."

Ali tried to raise their spirits. "Remember the four by one hundred relay in Glasgow? I swam the last leg. My best ever. I hit the water in seventh place. By the end of the first length, I was in third. Everyone thought I'd burnt myself out, but I kept going."

"Yes," Kieran murmured. "But ... you didn't win."

"No, but pulling the team from seventh to second was pretty miraculous." She grinned. "I'll make it back upstream. I'm more worried about you. Still, as long as you can swim to the tent, you could rest there while I go for help. That track we drove along must go somewhere in the other direction. I'll give it a try."

Kieran limped back to the stream and gently lowered himself into the cold water. Ali followed him. The current hadn't carried them a great distance but, even so, the return journey was laborious. Without a sound, they swam into the slack water of the bend and stood, breathing hard. The site was deserted. Their orange tent looked lonely and out of place.

Kieran stepped forward and winced with pain. His leg was getting worse. "Let's get you inside and wrapped in something warm," she said, offering her shoulders to lean on.

Together they staggered to the door of the tent, squatted down and unzipped it. Inside, her knees drawn up to her chest, Rhia was sitting and waiting. She was grinning insanely and holding the gun in both hands on top of her knees.

12

"Chasing you was hopeless," Rhia proclaimed. "Besides, I didn't think you'd get far with that wound. I had an inkling you'd double back." She squeezed the trigger.

Ali pushed Kieran one way and leapt the other way herself. The flap of the door closed and then twitched as the bullet pierced it, flew past Ali's ear and slammed into a tree.

Instinctively, as she fell sideways, Ali kicked as hard as she could at the base of the fibreglass pole. The support fell in and the front end of the tent collapsed. Inside, Rhia swore and fired again. The shot ripped through the fabric and screamed harmlessly into the far, eroded bank of the stream.

Ali and Kieran lay low either side of the deflated tent while Rhia tried to disentangle herself from the nylon. From outside, it looked funny. If it had not been a murderous adult, it could have been some silly kid pretending to be a ghost draped in an orange sheet.

"Quick!" Kieran called to Ali. "Unhook the guy rope on your side. Throw it to me."

Guided by the direction of his voice, Rhia took aim and fired through the material again. Kieran shrieked as the bullet grazed his arm. Ignoring the pain, he caught the rope with his other arm. As quickly as he could, he bound it securely to the peg on his side, trapping Rhia in the bottom half of the tent. She was as good as tied up. But she was still able to fire the weapon. Even if she could not see to aim, she was a threat, like a caged animal. Kieran knew very little about guns but, if films were anything to go by, he calculated that she had one shot left. He crawled away to a different position. In silence, Ali joined him and together they watched Rhia labour like a wasp trying to emerge from its pupa. Ali was cowering and uncertain. Next to her, Kieran shook with cold. He was bleeding from three wounds and light-headed. Neither of them was in a fit state to run away. They were entranced by the strange spectacle of the frenzied creature writhing inside the tent.

Suddenly, their worst fears were realized.

Rhia had got hold of their kitchen knife and used it angrily to slash through the nylon. From the bottom to the top, the fabric was slit by the sharp blade. And Rhia burst from her cocoon like an enraged demon. She had dropped the gun to cut her way out so she stood there, surrounded by the remnants of the tent like a discarded dress, with the knife in her hand.

With one final effort, Kieran struggled to his feet drunkenly and squared up to his stepmother. "Just like the knife you used on Dad," he commented.

Rhia glanced at it and her lips twisted into a smile. "Yes," she admitted. "And I'm not finished yet."

Kieran stood in front of Ali who was too startled to move from the ground. "Come on, then," Kieran challenged her. "Let's get it over with."

She did not need the invitation. She charged at Kieran like a savage soldier with a thirsty bayonet.

Kieran stood his ground until the very last moment. As she lunged at him, he dodged out of the way. She flashed past him and then screeched as she tumbled over Ali. Her shrill cry turned into a hideous scream when she crashed to the earth. She did not attempt to rise.

Ali, nursing her shin where Rhia had kicked it, peered anxiously at her boyfriend. He returned her look and then they both stared at Rhia, still stricken on the ground. "I think she's ..." Kieran approached her cautiously.

"Careful," Ali muttered fearfully.

He knelt down, a metre away from her. She was sprawled on her side and there was a moist red stain near her stomach but her chest still rose and fell weakly. Her eyes were closed and strange little gasps issued from her mouth. The bloodied knife lay in front of her. Kieran leaned forward and moved it out of her reach. "She's alive," he called to Ali, "but in a bad way."

Ali forced herself upright and staggered towards him. "Get the car key," she suggested. "She put it in her jacket pocket."

Kieran felt like an impatient vulture. Revolted, he picked carefully at her pocket. As he drew out the key, Rhia's eyes flickered open. In a croaky voice, she whispered, "I guess it's all over."

Kieran lowered his gaze as if he were the guilty one. He nodded. She swallowed and grimaced, clearly suffering from her injury. All trace of her veneer of elegance had been stripped away. She was a wreck – a sad victim of her own making. "I really wanted to help Sandra, you know." She closed her eyes again, coughed and clutched her stomach. "*Did* you tell the police about her?"

Kieran murmured, "Yes."

Rhia sniffed and sighed wearily. "It's over for her as well, then. But, I tell you, the police won't have her. Not Sandra."

Puzzled, Ali and Kieran glanced at each other. "Come on," Ali said, taking his arm and dragging him up. "We've got to get moving. You need help. She needs help, I guess, even if she doesn't deserve it. I've had a couple of lessons so I can probably drive the car."

"It doesn't seem right to leave her like this," Kieran mumbled.

"Go," Rhia interjected. "I want to be on my own."

Kieran shook his head despondently, groaned and then nodded. "OK," he consented.

When the way through the trees was too narrow for Ali to support Kieran, she found him a stout stick to lean on. Slowly, like the wounded returning from war, they shuffled back towards the car. It wasn't far but it seemed like a marathon.

At last they reached it. Kieran rested against the passenger's side of the Toyota while Ali went to the driver's door. Just before she used the key, there was a loud bang from the direction of the river. Birds scattered nervously from the trees. In horror, Ali and Kieran stared at each other over the top of the car. "Oh no!" they uttered together.

Rhia Burrage had used the last bullet on herself.

Ali and Kieran fell into the car and wept with exhaustion and pity. Eventually, Kieran wiped his face and murmured, "Now it *is* all over."

Separated for most of their lives, unaware of each other, the twins still shared more than their appearance. Both were prepared to kill to liberate themselves from their husbands and neither was able to cope with the thought of a trial for murder. On Guernsey, Sandra Jackson took her husband's rifle, hired a motor launch and set out to sea. First she shot a hole in the boat and then in herself. Both twins found the same way out.

Wanting to kill Stuart Burrage was not an offence but John Evans still faced a charge of attempted murder. Because he had also confessed to a murder that he didn't commit, it was likely that he would be declared unfit to stand trial. He would be treated rather than punished. Ali's father, Robert Tankersley, was made bankrupt by the out-of-court settlement over his infringement of copyright. Ali believed that it made him a better person. No longer did he trade in people's lives.

A few days of rest cured Ali of the physical effects of Rhia's attack. Kieran needed longer but his injuries were not serious. The bone in his arm had been chipped but both bullets caused only flesh wounds that were soon treated in hospital. There was another type of damage. The nightmare of being hunted like animals by Rhia would stay with Ali and Kieran for ever. That scar would never heal.

Not yet fit, Kieran sat in the auditorium and yelled his support for the team. Ali had already won the 100 metres backstroke and she was about to complete the double by taking the 200 metres race as well. The water rushed past her as she surged down the final length. How could he ever have believed that the current of a river would get the better of her? She touched home a full second before her nearest rival. Standing in the water, she waved triumphantly towards Kieran in the crowd. There was no comparison with the person who had stood in that stream, exhausted and numbed with fright. He cheered her victory.

Afterwards, when they met in the café, he kissed her and murmured, "Great stuff!" When among friends, they had never before shown their affection. They had not tried to hide it. It had simply not been uppermost in their minds. Now, their relationship had been set in stone by sharing and enduring adversity. They became even closer.

Sitting over a glucose drink, Kieran murmured, "You know, I do wonder if it would've been different if I'd tried harder to get on with her."

"Oh, Kieran. I'm not having you think like that," Ali declared. "It had nothing to do with you. Rhia was after your dad's money. Full stop. Even if you'd been her best buddy, she'd still have been after the loot."

"I suppose so," Kieran responded. "I went down to the cemetery today," he whispered, reddening. "It sounds silly, but I suppose I told Mum all about it."

Ali reached across the table and took his hand. "That's not silly," she replied softly. "Did it help?"

"Yes, I guess so."

"Then it was perfectly sensible." She smiled at him.

With an excited bound, Mike Spruzen arrived at their side. "Just heard!" he bellowed. Addressing Kieran, he babbled, "You were shot twice! Amazing." He grabbed a chair and plonked himself down. "Reminds me of something that happened to me once. You'll understand this now. I was with this girl. Absolute stunner. Film star and supermodel league. Well, as you do, we tried to creep back to her house in the middle of the night, you know." He winked at them. "Trouble was, her old man spotted us. He belted downstairs. 'What do you think you're doing with my daughter?' he yells at me. Then, he pulled this gun out of his dressing gown pocket. Don't know what sort it was. Probably a semi-automatic..."

Unable to maintain straight faces any longer, Ali and Kieran burst out laughing. "Nothing changes!" Ali exclaimed.

With a puzzled expression, Mike uttered, "What's got into you two? It was serious. I could have been topped for that girl."

Ali smiled at him. "Sorry," she said. "We didn't mean to spoil your story. Carry on. We know it's no fun. We had to face just an ordinary gun. It must have been awful if he had something special."

"You're not kidding!" Mike pronounced. "Anyway, I'll tell you how I got out of it. Real cool, I was..."

Ali and Kieran allowed him to outpoint them. His comic-strip adventure was too divorced from reality to offend them. He lived in a parallel fantasy world where it was possible to be cool under fire, where no one got hurt, where endings were always happy.

CONCRETE EVIDENCE

1

Thump! Thump! Thump! Thump! Kelly looked up from the kitchen sink and smiled. "He'll wear out our view, will Evan, if he keeps that up," she remarked.

Tea towel in hand, Sarah glanced out of the window. "The wall's in a bad way even without our beloved brother's help," she said. "There's a good few cracks already and they're getting wider – subsidence or poor workmanship." She hesitated, then added, "You know who built it, don't you?"

"Yeah," Kelly replied glumly. "Henderson's."

The sisters resumed the washing-up in thoughtful silence. *Thump! Thump! Thump!*

Six months ago, they could see the industrial estate from their kitchen window, and hear the traffic and the machines. Not a great view, but at least they'd felt part of the real world. Then their mother lost her long, hard battle over planning permission and, almost overnight it seemed, the extension to the video factory appeared at the bottom of their garden. Now the estate, traffic and machines were hidden behind a bland concrete wall, but it wasn't an improvement, as their mum had anticipated all along. The factory owner's solution to the Keatings' worries had been to paint a giant mural on the concrete monstrosity. Now they had a view of two-dimensional rolling hills and, of course, the goal mouth that Evan had added with an aerosol so that he could practise shooting and ball control.

Evan was the only one who approved of the wall. Every day he spent an hour kicking a ball rhythmically against it. Sometimes he would stop and stare at the mural as if he were sizing it up. No one knew what was going through his mind when he wore that faraway expression, but then the moment would pass and he would resume the clockwork kicking. Volley with the left foot against the wall. Control the rebound on the right thigh. Volley with the right foot. Control the rebound on the left thigh. Volley. *Thump! Thump! Thump!*

Without warning, Kelly shrieked and dropped a clean plate back into the soapy dish-water.

A car, out of control, had ploughed straight through the hedge on the right-hand side of the garden, bounced up on to the lawn and was careering towards Evan and the wall. "Evan!" the sisters screamed in unison.

A black cat padding across the lawn let out a yowl and sprang out of the way. Less agile, Evan spun round and the football hit him on the back as he dived to one side. The car shot past him and slammed into the concrete hills with a sickening crash.

Glass shattered, metal crumpled, shrapnel flew. The front end of the car was crushed. The engine stalled. A second or two later, part of the wall leaned, tottered as if it were trying to keep its balance, and then collapsed. Great chunks of concrete fell on to the grass and the car's bonnet in an unearthly clatter.

When the dust settled, the lawn was littered with fragments of painted poplars, people and hillside. The car was smothered with rubble and the gap in the wall revealed machines that churned out videos by the hundreds.

Evan was staring impassively into the mess at his feet when Kelly and Sarah dashed towards him, calling, "Are you all right?"

He didn't respond. His face was grey, speckled with dust. His gaze was fixed. He had retreated into his own private world.

"Evan?"

Kelly's eyes followed Evan's stare. Suddenly, her hand darted to her mouth. Beside her, Sarah screamed at the top of her voice. "No, no!" she cried. The three Keatings were gaping at a body lying among the rubble of the collapsed wall. It was the remains of their mother.

Her legs were still encased in concrete but the rest of her body had broken free of its cruel cage, like a life-size statue emerging from its mould. Much of her clothing had stuck to the concrete and ripped away from the body. Her skin was as grey as parchment, and lay like a taut shroud over prominent bones; her hair was like straw and her eyes were sunken and black. The remains had begun to decay and the putrid smell was revolting. Even so, they recognized their mother – their mother who, just over five months ago, was supposed to have run off with another man. Now misshapen, she lay on the ground and hundreds of woodlice, made homeless by the collapse of the wall, crawled all over her.

The doors of the car creaked open and the two young joyriders staggered out. Smiling, obviously on a high, one chirped, "Fantastic! They build these cars well. Stronger than concrete."

"Great things, crumple zones," the other replied.

When they saw that they weren't alone in the garden, they were surprised – even disappointed not to be the centre of attention. Then they saw the body and they turned and fled, unnoticed by the Keatings.

Sarah clutched her sister, using Kelly's shoulder to muffle her uncontrollable sobs. Neither sister had seen a dead body before, and now they had to confront not just the hideous sight of death but their own mother's corpse.

Evan wiped his face with the sleeve of his green jumper, picked up the football, turned his back on the relic of his mother and walked away in silence.

Eventually, Kelly separated herself from Sarah. "Come on," she said. "Let's go in. We can't do anything for her out here, that's for sure. We'd better call Dad – and the police."

2

"It's what's known in the trade as a cock-up," Detective Chief Inspector Neil Tatton said to his new sergeant as they sped towards the Keatings' house. He used flippancy to cover up his annoyance. His last case remained unsolved and now a mistake in an old inquiry had come back to plague him. He wasn't looking forward to the inevitable dressing down from the Superintendent. He sighed and opened Mrs Keating's file on his knee.

"October, last year. Mrs Barbara Keating. Husband reported her missing on the morning of Saturday the fourteenth. She never came home after work on the Friday. In door-to-door checks, some local bobby with a photo found a restaurant owner, at The Seafood Spree, who identified her. She'd taken an early evening meal in his place – with a mystery man. We christened him Mr Fish. Keating and Mr Fish were the first customers in the restaurant that night, so the owner remembered them quite well. A lovers' tryst, he thought. Scheming going on between them. Nervous and excited, he said they were. All lovey-dovey too, like a couple of teenagers planning to elope. That was the last sighting."

He turned over a page then continued, "The husband, Clive Keating, didn't admit to knowing his wife was being unfaithful, but the kids knew all right. Kelly, Sarah and Evan. Ages of ... let's see ... eighteen, sixteen and fifteen. The lad was big for his age – and a bit of a screwball, if I remember rightly. As slippery as a fish himself, but he virtually admitted that he knew his mum had got herself a bit on the side. He was smarting over it, I reckoned at the time. He said he'd had an argument with her on the Friday morning. 'You're breaking up the family so you don't love me any more' – that sort of thing. Then she vamoosed. It looked straightforward," the detective said as he closed the file, "especially backed by the best piece of evidence available at the time."

"What was that?" Detective Sergeant Vicky McCormick asked.

"Think about it," DCI Tatton replied unhelpfully.

The sergeant took a right turn then glanced triumphantly at her passenger. "No body," she concluded.

"Bingo! If Keating knew about the lover and did his wife in or if the kid, Evan, got carried away, there'd be a body. Crimes of passion always provide a body."

"But now we have one," Vicky murmured.

"Right. An open and shut case is open again, and I think we can assume it's a murder inquiry."

"Want me to jump the lights, Neil?" she asked as she neared a crossroads.

"No. The body's not going anywhere. It'll wait for us."

As she brought the car to a standstill at the red light, Vicky inquired, "Ever identify Mr Fish?"

"No," Neil answered. "They didn't book the table in his name. It was early enough in the evening to just drop in."

"How about payment? A cheque or Visa sales voucher with Mr Fish's real name and signature?"

"Unfortunately not," he grumbled. "Paid in cash. They didn't eat much. Not a big bill."

"I thought everyone paid by plastic these days," Vicky commented, taking a left turn past the canal. "Still, my husband hasn't taken me to a decent restaurant for so long, I wouldn't know." Her voice was deep, almost like a man's.

"The best we got out of the restaurant owner – Daniel Perriman – was a description. And that was a bit vague, a bit average. You know: white, average height, average mousy hair, no distinguishing features. Could have been me or thousands of others. I think the owner paid more attention to Barbara Keating. They left together, Keating and Mr Fish."

"Last person to see her alive, possibly."

"Yes. I'd quite like to speak to our Mr Fish," Neil said, in a tone overflowing with understatement.

When they arrived, the scene-of-the-crime team was crawling all over the place. Two officers with a very long tape measure were noting the distances between the road, the smashed hedge and the wall. From their measurements, a detailed plan of the area would be constructed later. Some other workers were shoring up the stricken part of the wall, making the building safe. Picking his way through the debris towards the body, DCI Tatton stopped by the car and watched a young forensic scientist dusting the surfaces for fingerprints.

"What are you doing that for?" he barked.

"The boss said make a thorough job of it."

"Well, I'm the governor now. And I imagine the victim was already dead when the car hit the wall. The rest of us are after a murderer, you know, not a joyrider. Your time would be better spent tracing the car's owner so he can give his insurers the bad news."

"Yes, sir."

DCI Tatton barely glanced at the victim. He had always found examining bodies distasteful. Besides, his job was to police the living, not to take care of the dead. Instead, he asked the pathologist, "What have you got for me?"

"Not a lot. Female. About forty years old. Partly mummified, partly decomposed. From the inside. Consistent with being buried in the wall for some months."

"The daughter called us," Tatton said. "We know who the victim is. And building records will tell me when she was dunked in concrete. Friday 13th October last year would be my guess. In the dark, probably. So are you going to give me anything that I don't already know?"

Vicky had not known Neil Tatton for long, so she wasn't familiar with his character and moods, but this morning the signs of irritation were hardly subtle. Clearly, she thought, this case was giving him the creeps. Trying to put the pathologist in a better frame of mind, she interjected, "Any obvious cause of death?"

He shrugged. "No sign of physical damage as far as I can see. No blood stains, no broken bones."

"She wasn't shot, knifed or battered, then," Neil declared. "Strangulation?"

"This isn't a fresh body, Tatton. I can't look for bruising, you know. The skin's like leather and covered in concrete in places," he replied. "The neck's intact, though – I can tell you that. Maybe a closer examination in the lab will reveal something."

With a grimace on her face, Vicky asked, "Was she alive, do you think, when she went into the concrete?" It wasn't a pleasant thought.

"I don't think so," the pathologist answered. "The inside of the mouth and nose are free of concrete so she didn't gasp for air. She was probably dead or unconscious."

Sergeant McCormick paused then added, "Found her bag yet?"

"Don't ask me. I'm a bodies man, not a handbag man." He called to one of his colleagues who shouted back, "No. Not yet."

In turn, Vicky yelled, "Keep looking. With women there's always a bag – somewhere."

"OK. That's all for now," Tatton muttered. Turning to Vicky, he said, "Come on. We'll get on with our job and let these guys get on with theirs. We'll get their report soon enough." Heading towards the house, he asked, "Tell me, Sergeant McCormick, what do you make of this method of disposing of the body?"

"Typical gangland stuff," Vicky answered. "Perhaps she was mixed up in some organized crime. Drug dealing, possibly. It also tells us that someone didn't want the body to be found."

"Mmm." The Chief Inspector pondered for a moment. "Could be that our man is simply off his rocker."

"I didn't deduce that the culprit was male," Vicky retorted.

"They're usually male," Tatton replied. "And dumping bodies in concrete is a particularly macho thing to do." Changing the subject, he asked, "Have you decided who we need to interview?"

"I think so."

"Well?"

"The family, obviously. Especially the husband. And the lad, Evan. The building site workers – they'll need to be traced. And the manager of that restaurant."

"Why him?" he asked, obviously testing her.

"We need Mr Fish. Badly. Perhaps we can jog the owner's memory for something else. More information."

"After five and a bit months?"

"I know it's a long shot, but even so…"

"OK. Is that it?"

"No," she responded. "I think we'd better have words with Mr Eric Henderson."

"Henderson?"

She smiled cockily. "Henderson of Henderson's Builders. He got the building contract on this factory, I think."

Hesitating before he knocked on the door to the house, Neil queried, "How do you know that?"

"My so-called better half works there. In one of those rare moments when we actually speak to each other, he told me about this site, I'm sure."

"Henderson, then. And don't look so pleased with yourself, Sergeant. It was hardly great detective work. Just the right connection, that's all."

"Isn't having the right connections one of the hallmarks of a good detective?" she replied.

The Keatings remembered Detective Chief Inspector Tatton. Those few months ago, he was the one who'd broken the news that Mrs Keating had been seen with another man in a restaurant in town. To a different extent, each of the Keatings had resented him for bringing into the open what, in private, they all knew – Mrs Keating was seeing another man. Somehow, once their secret had been announced as a fact by an outsider, they felt more cheapened, sullied and cheated.

While her unfaithfulness had remained unspoken, there was always the chance that it might suddenly stop and there would be nothing to be ashamed of any more. Neil Tatton had shattered that hope. None of the kids could deny that it looked as if their mother had deserted them, but their dad, too proud to admit the truth, had mounted a feeble protest. DCI Tatton was certain. He had told them calmly and clinically why he believed Mrs Keating had run off with another man, and why he was closing the case. He'd seemed eager to finish the business quickly and get on to another, more exciting, case.

Now he sat in front of them again. He still bore the expression of someone who would rather be somewhere else, doing something else. He did not appear to be embarrassed, but he was clearly disgruntled at having to admit to an error.

"I won't ask you lots of questions now," he was saying, "because I know you've had a shock. But I do have to make fresh inquiries, of course. I'll come back tomorrow."

"What for?" Mr Keating mumbled.

"I realize it's difficult for you," Tatton answered, with just a trace of impatience in his tone. "I'll have to ask you all to cast your minds back to October, just before Mrs Keating disappeared."

"Fresh inquiries?" Mr Keating snapped. "What does that mean? Are you now saying she was murdered?"

"I haven't ruled it out," DCI Tatton responded dryly. "The manner in which the body was disposed of suggests murder, I'm afraid."

"Last time," Clive Keating complained, "the lack of body suggested she'd run off. I told you she hadn't. I was right. You made a right old cock-up."

With considerable difficulty, Vicky kept her face straight as her partner objected, "I don't think that's entirely fair, Mr Keating. It was the best interpretation of the evidence at the time. It looked watertight. But now we have a new piece of evidence, so we have to think again. It's a process of refinement and reconsideration till we get to the truth."

"Perhaps you'd better reconsider if there ever *was* another man."

To Kelly, her father seemed rather sad, perhaps even a little desperate. To Sergeant McCormick, it seemed possible that Clive Keating was trying to suggest that he lacked the motive of jealousy. If his wife had never had a lover after all, he would never have had cause to take his revenge. The sorrow and anger in his eyes could be the result of seeing the remains of a loved one but, equally, he could be regretting a crime that had come back to haunt him.

The boy was different. He was handsome but his eyes told her nothing. Behind them there could be a little angel or a little devil, or maybe both. Maybe he was an angel who endured dark moods, periods when the devil would rule.

The two girls appeared to be much less complex. They were genuinely shocked by the find but, as they looked sadly at their father, it was plain to see that their sympathies lay with him, not with their mum. Vicky estimated that they knew they'd lost their mother some time before she even went missing. They looked worldly enough to recognize a mother who was sharing her affections with an outsider. Kelly, the older sister, probably mothered the family now. Vicky knew that the male of the species did not have a monopoly on murder, but she could not regard either sister as a serious suspect.

"I think we'll call a halt to this conversation for now," Tatton said, rising from his chair. "We'll talk again tomorrow when you've all had a bit of time to get over the initial shock. My officers will soon finish in the garden and leave you in peace."

"What about ... er...?" Sarah uttered. She still couldn't bring herself to mention her mum's corpse.

"They'll remove the body for examination. And they've got in some contractors to take care of the wall. It won't be left unsafe."

"We'll make sure they tidy up," Vicky added, "so you don't have that to worry about as well."

3

Mr Keating ran a small newsagent's shop in the suburbs. It ticked over on sales of magazines, newspapers, cigarettes and confectionery, but would never make the family wealthy. Before her death, Mrs Keating had topped up the family income by working part-time as a secretary at Henderson's Builders. When they weren't at school, the girls would often help in the shop and their brother earned extra pocket money by taking on the newspaper round. It always took the promise of payment to drag Evan out of his permanent state of detachment – the whiff of money acted like smelling salts to him.

The next day, Evan sat alone in his bedroom and the girls whispered nervously to each other while police officers interviewed their dad in the dining room. After a restless night both sisters were on edge.

"How are you?" asked Kelly.

"Rough."

"No sleep? Nor me," Kelly said. "Thinking about Mum."

Shivering, Sarah replied, "Yeah. Horrible." Banishing the unwanted image from her mind, she added, "Now we've got to face the police. What do you think? Will it be all right?"

Both Sarah and Kelly had been questioned by police officers before, almost six months ago, but then it all seemed straightforward – an inquiry, not an inquisition. Now the police were trying to trap a murderer and anyone they interviewed was under suspicion to some extent. That made them feel like crooks under threat of discovery.

"Just tell them what you know," Kelly advised her sister.

"Not much," Sarah replied. "But what if they ask about Dad, or Evan?"

"There's nothing you can do but tell the truth. They'll notice if you try to lie."

"But do you think Dad...?"

"He loved her, Sarah. I'm sure he did."

"So if he found out she was seeing someone else...?"

Kelly shrugged. "I still don't think he'd ... you know."

Listlessly, Sarah wound a lock of hair round and round a finger. "What about Evan?"

Her sister sighed. "He's a law unto himself. I'm not sure he's got it in him to have a go at anyone, though. At least, I hope not."

"He was upset that day, you know. And he did argue with Mum. Remember? What was that all about?"

"I don't know. He wouldn't say. I'll tell you one thing, though," Kelly said, "I bet the police try to squeeze it out of him."

"They'll be lucky!"

Vicky McCormick sat opposite Mr Keating at the dining table while Neil Tatton skulked round and round them like some subtle parasite. "How would you have described your marriage?" he probed.

"How do you mean?" Mr Keating squirmed.

"Happy, harmonious, troubled, stormy?"

Mr Keating shrugged. "It was like many a twenty-year-old-marriage, I suppose."

"And what's that like?"

"It means rather more respect than passion. We weren't spring chickens."

"I see what you mean," DCI Tatton replied. "A middle-aged marriage."

"Yes."

"So," he asked, looking for once into his suspect's face, "did either of you try to find passion elsewhere?"

"We've been through all this before!" Mr Keating exploded.

"True. But I wondered if you'd changed your view in the light of this new development."

"No," Clive retorted. "I wasn't aware of my wife seeing anyone else. Despite your evidence, I'm not inclined to believe that she ... strayed," he said proudly. Even so, a little sweat appeared on his brow, as he sat bolt upright in perfect military posture.

"Mmm." Annoyingly, the detective completed a lap of the dining room before he asked another question. He stopped pacing and inquired, "What about you, Mr Keating?"

"What about me?"

"Did you try to rekindle the flames with someone else?"

Clive Keating was taken aback by the unexpected question. After a split-second pause, he declared, "Certainly not."

"Many men of your age do."

"I've got my hands full with the shop. Even if I'd wanted to, I'd never have time for an affair. Too busy. I was quite happy with my circumstances, I assure you."

Changing tack without warning, Tatton asked, "Run again through your movements on the evening of Friday 13th October."

"I ... er ... I was in the shop till closing time."

"When's that?" Sergeant McCormick put in.

"Seven," he answered. "Then I had quite a lot of sorting out to do. I didn't leave the shop till after seven thirty. I got home about eight. Barbara wasn't here so I warmed up a pie or something, and ate."

"Did any regular punters come into the shop? Ones who could confirm that you were there?"

In a weary voice, Clive Keating muttered, "How am I supposed to remember that after five or six months?"

"OK," Neil Tatton conceded. "Who else was at home when you got back?"

"No one. They were all out. Kelly was off to one of those all-night dance things."

"A rave," Vicky commented.

"Yes," Mr Keating added. "That's it. But I don't know about Sarah and Evan. If you want to know what they were doing, you'll have to ask them."

"We will," the detective replied tersely. "Carry on from the dinner."

"I watched the nine o'clock news, then a film."

"Which film?" asked the sergeant.

Mr Keating grinned. "That's easy. They showed *Friday the Thirteenth*."

Vicky nodded. "Ah, yes. Nearly Hallowe'en as well. Out come the horror films. I wanted to watch that one but ... I missed it, I'm afraid. It was the one where Donald Pleasance chases a psychopath and Jamie Lee Curtis nearly cops it, wasn't it?"

"No," Clive answered. "It's the cheap rip-off of the film you've got in mind. No big stars, as far as I remember, just blood and gore. Teenagers getting hacked to pieces in a summer camp."

The DCI took control of the questioning again. "BBC or ITV?"

Clive Keating sighed. "I *have* got an IQ above ten, you know. If I was making this up as an alibi, I'd have checked my facts first. So do these tests prove anything?"

"BBC or ITV?" Tatton repeated.

"The film followed the BBC news and there were no adverts."

"Did you notice any activity on the building site that evening?"

"The men were working late by floodlights when I first came in and made the meal. I ate in front of the telly. By the time I washed up, the lights were off. I wouldn't say I saw anything odd."

"When did you wash up?"

"Er ... after the film. About eleven, I suppose. Eleven thirty at the latest."

"And had the kids returned by then?" asked Vicky.

"Kelly was still out. Sarah and Evan came back just before the end of the film, I think."

"Together?" Neil Tatton queried.

"No, separately."

"OK," Detective Chief Inspector Tatton announced. "That's enough for now. You can go. But we'd like a word with Evan next. Can you tell him to wait outside till we call him in?"

"Well, Vicky," Neil muttered when they were alone, "what do you think? Did he know his wife was carrying on, or didn't he? And if he knew, would he have killed her for it?"

"Yes, he knew," Vicky replied. "I'm sure he did. But he won't admit it – even to himself. And if he wouldn't admit it to himself, he wouldn't have a reason to take it out on her. If he denied himself the truth about his wife, he had no motive."

"Mmm." Neil pondered on the matter. "Maybe," he added. Then, without warning, he asked her, "What about *your* husband? If he was cheating on you, would you know?"

The Detective Sergeant hesitated. She didn't like the intrusion into her private life but knew that Neil wasn't really interested in it

– he was just using it to assist the inquiry. "With this job, I hardly ever see him," she quipped. "Sometimes, I reckon I'd have trouble picking him out in an identity parade. Anyway," she continued, returning to the matter in hand, "what are you getting at? That Keating may have been so preoccupied with his business that the marriage fell apart without him noticing?"

Neil shrugged. "You didn't answer my question."

Abruptly, Vicky replied, "We're investigating the Keatings' marriage, not mine, but I think a husband or wife always knows when their partner's having an affair, even if they're busy or trying to pretend it's not happening. Deep down, they always know."

"Mmm." Neil sat down. After a pause, he asked, "By the way, did he get that stuff about the film right?"

"Yes. And he knew the difference between *Friday the Thirteenth* and *Halloween*," she answered. "That part of his story holds up."

"You must have a good memory for these things."

Vicky smiled. "Bit of a movie buff. Besides, I *did* want to see it, but duty called that night."

"It often does. Too often," Neil remarked. He cleared his throat, then asked, "Have you got kids?"

"No." The sergeant looked a little disappointed.

"So you don't know how an affair would affect the kids?"

"Not first-hand, no."

"Well, the textbook sentiments are jealousy and resentment. That's our Evan, I think. You can expect the children in a broken family to be confused and angry ... or, like Evan, simmering. They can even blame themselves for the break-up. But one thing's for sure: they don't want to take second place behind an outsider. They feel betrayed, especially when it's the mother who's doing the betraying. And lads tend not to share their feelings. The girls would talk about their troubled home life, but Evan would bottle it up. The question is, just how angry was he? Angry enough?" Neil stood up again sprightly. "Let's try to break down his defences and find out."

Evan bit his nails and fidgeted in his seat as he answered the police officers' questions in monosyllables. He rarely looked into his interrogators' faces.

"Where were you", DCI Tatton queried, "on the night of your

mother's disappearance between, say, eight and midnight?"

"How should I know?" Evan muttered. "It was ages ago."

"We know it's difficult," Vicky interjected, using a softly softly approach, "but try to cast your mind back."

"Everyone knows where they were and what they were doing when really big events took place," Neil Tatton added. "For you, there can't have been a much bigger event than your mother's disappearance."

"I was out."

"Out where?"

Evan shrugged. "Walking."

Incredulous, the detective responded, "For four hours on a cold, wet night?" He hadn't believed the story five months ago and he didn't believe it now.

"That's right. Or nearly. Till about eleven, I think."

"Well, what did you do? *Where* did you walk?"

"I can't remember," Evan said. "I went into town for some of the time."

"Did you join up with anyone?"

"I saw a few friends outside the youth club."

"Did you stay with them for any length of time?" Vicky inquired.

"A few minutes, that's all."

Tatton had been trained to remain detached. He neither liked nor loathed suspects in case his feelings clouded his judgement. He regarded the people that he interviewed simply as tools of his trade, not as fellow creatures. He was a trespasser on the privacy of reserved characters like Evan. He didn't enjoy it, but gate-crashing other people's hearts and minds was all part of the job and he didn't easily tolerate those who made his job harder. Clearly, Evan had no alibi for that night. Even if his friends confirmed that they had seen him for a few minutes on Friday night, he could not be eliminated as a suspect. He could have killed his mother, dumped the body, and gone into town specifically to be seen. Tatton did not even bother to ask for the names of the friends Evan claimed to have met that night.

"Let's go back to this argument with your mum," Tatton said, rather irritably. "What did you say it was about?"

"I told you."

Standing behind Evan, Tatton put his hands on the back of the seat in which the boy sat slouched, leaned over him and whispered menacingly, "Tell me again."

Evan chewed at his fingernails as he tried to steel himself. Or maybe he was trying to contain his frustration: an angel trying not to turn into a devil. Still he said nothing.

"Who started it?" Tatton prompted.

"She did," Evan mumbled.

"What did she say?" asked Sergeant McCormick.

"She told me it wasn't my fault."

"What wasn't?"

"That she had a boyfriend."

"She thought you might be blaming yourself, then," Neil Tatton said.

Evan nodded. "I suppose so."

"How did you know she was having an affair?" asked Vicky.

"Because I saw them once. Out on the paper round."

"How do you know they were having a love affair?"

"They were kissing."

"I've kissed lots of women without being ... romantically attached," DCI Tatton commented.

"Not like they were kissing."

"OK," the policeman said. "Tell me what he looked like."

"I didn't see his face properly. Quite a bit taller than Mum. Black hair." He shrugged.

"Black hair? Not mousy?"

"Well, it was dark, at any rate."

"Was it long, curly, or what? Was he white, thin, big nose, young, old?"

"It was a long time ago and I only saw him for a second," Evan replied. "He was white, about the same age as Mum, I suppose. He wasn't fat or thin. Average, really. Looked quite smart."

"Did you know him?" Vicky asked. "Had you seen him before?"

"No," Evan answered.

"Let's go back to the argument," Neil said, standing in front of Evan. "*Did* you blame yourself for your mum's behaviour?"

"Why should I?"

"Did you?" Tatton insisted.

"Not really."

"So, how did the conversation go from there?"

Evan shrugged again. "*I* blamed *her*, I suppose. Said she couldn't think much of us."

"And?"

"And nothing. That was it."

"That was it?"

"We both got a bit annoyed, but that was it."

"OK," DCI Tatton responded wearily. "What happened then?"

"She went to work. I went to school."

"You didn't see her again?"

Evan shook his head.

"When you came back to the house that night – after this walk – who was in?"

"Just Dad."

"What was he doing?"

"Snoozing in front of the telly," Evan answered.

"No sign of Sarah or Kelly?"

"No."

"All right, Evan, you can go," Tatton said. "But think about something before we see you again: you have a duty to cooperate with us. There's a law about obstructing police officers in the execution of their duties, you know. Think about it."

Evan did not reply. Relieved, he got to his feet and left the dining room as quickly as he could.

DCI Tatton slumped into a chair.

"Doesn't waste his breath, does he?" he grumbled. "Tight as a clam. There's still something he's not letting on about that argument and his walkabout."

"Yes," Vicky agreed. "But it could be purely innocent, or just irrelevant. I'm sure that fifteen- year-olds get up to plenty that they wouldn't want to tell the police. It doesn't have to be murder."

"Mmm." Detective Chief Inspector Tatton sighed, then said, "Go and drag in the daughters. Not that it'll do us much good. Another dose of *déjà vu* for me. Kelly first."

He was right. They learned nothing new from Kelly and Sarah. Any one of a number of friends could confirm that Kelly had been dancing herself silly that night. She only chilled out in the early hours. Sarah's boyfriend, Matt Smith, could confirm that they'd watched a film in town that night. She'd returned at eleven thirty. Neither daughter had seen anything but both had guessed that their mother had a boyfriend. In their separate ways, each revealed her feelings about her mother's death. Kelly remained stiffly solemn as if scared to betray her emotions in front of strangers, while Sarah fidgeted and trembled on the verge of weeping. After the interviews Neil Tatton left the Keatings' house with nothing extra to show.

The manager of The Seafood Spree, Daniel Perriman, was a different kettle of fish. Years of making clients feel welcome and comfortable had fashioned his face. Like an airline steward, he wore a permanent professional smile and exuded friendliness. Behind closed doors, though, he probably ranted and raved at his staff if he found a speck of dirt on the cutlery. Vicky imagined a taskmaster who was nervous and demanding in private, and an unflappable host in public.

He escorted the police to a discreet table and, out of habit, took hold of the back of the chair as if he were about to invite Vicky to sit. "As I recall, this was the lady's place," he said. "The gentleman sat opposite. So, you see, my staff and I could see her clearly but the gentleman had his back to us. He leaned across the table and took her hand now and again."

"Did they come together or did they meet in here?" Tatton inquired.

"They came in together, I think. Most do."

"And they left ... when?" asked Vicky.

The restaurant manager shrugged and answered politely, "It was over five months ago, you know."

"You said they came in at about six and left at seven thirty originally. Your first customers," Neil reminded him.

"Then I'm sure I was right," Mr Perriman replied. "I remember it was definitely early."

"And you said the man had mousy hair."

"Did I? You have to understand that I've had thousands of customers since then. I really don't know for sure."

Neil persisted. "Your statement referred to mousy coloured hair. Not, say, black."

"Well, I hope I got it right. I could describe the lady much more accurately."

DCI Tatton smiled wryly. "I don't need a description of her, only him."

Mr Perriman's expression conveyed helplessness. "I'm sorry."

The manager was ten times more talkative and cooperative than Evan but he knew ten times less, the detective thought. As a result both of them were equally unhelpful as witnesses. Neil Tatton hadn't expected anything else. He was relying on Henderson's Builders and the forensic report to supply him with new leads.

4

Evan shuffled impatiently from foot to foot as he waited for someone at the other end of the line to pick up the phone. In agitation, he drummed on the window of the call box with the ragged fingers of his right hand. "Come on!" he muttered into the receiver.

Eventually, the ringing stopped and a male voice said bluntly, "Yes?"

Evan recognized the brief response. "Mr Warr," he breathed. "Evan Keating here."

"Oh." The man seemed to anticipate trouble.

"Have you heard?"

"Of course I heard," Trevor Warr replied. "No one drives across your garden and knocks a whacking great hole in my factory wall without me knowing about it. I've been to see the damage."

"But that wasn't all."

"Yes. I heard," he said. "I'm sorry. Sorry about your mother."

"But what are you going to do now?"

Warr didn't answer immediately. The question took him by surprise. "Get the factory fixed and back in action as quickly as possible. What else?"

"What about Mum? Have the police been to see you?"

"What do you mean, Evan? I can do nothing about your mother. That little problem has nothing to do with me. And yes, a constable came to see me, as you'd expect, but only to tell me about the wall."

"What about the planning permission row and ... you know?"

"I imagine your mum made herself unpopular with a whole number of people, not just me." Warr's tone suggested annoyance as he added, "I repeat, I had nothing to do with her death."

This time, Evan hesitated. He simply did not believe Warr. But he hoped that the owner of the video factory could convince the police of his innocence if they ever got close to him. He dreaded the possible arrest and conviction of Warr. He needed him. "OK," he said into the mouthpiece. "Good. But I ... er ... need some weekend work. Any going at the moment?"

Warr laughed. "You've got to be joking! Not unless you're a budding builder. I've had to close down the operation till the wall's replaced. Even then, with your mother and all ... it's a bit of a risk for me."

Evan crammed both the receiver and his fingernails up to his mouth. "Look, I'd come in, wouldn't ask any questions, and do whatever you want me to do. I won't be any trouble and I need the cash. Please!" he pleaded.

"Calm down, Evan. When the building's fixed and the fuss has died down a bit, we'll be back up and running. I'll think about it then. But get this straight: I'm not promising. There are plenty of people out there who'd take on a bit of extra work for something straight into their pockets. We all need it these days."

"Yes, but..." Evan ran out of reasoning and resorted to threats. "The cops are coming back to talk to me again. You wouldn't want them to learn about your ... arguments with Mum, would you?"

Warr snorted. "They'll unearth our disagreements over planning permission sooner or later."

"But it wasn't just that, was it? She found out about my work for you. She didn't ... approve."

Warr became defensive. "She didn't see me about that, so don't try and make out that she did."

"But the police—" Evan began.

"You won't get my sympathy with threats," Warr interrupted him. "You won't tell the police any more than you have to, not if you value the money you get from me. You need it too much to let on to the law."

Evan knew that it was true. He could not reveal his suspicions about Trevor Warr to the police without telling them everything. Then where would he be? In trouble himself.

"I'll be in touch", Warr whispered into his ear, "when I have some news – when we're back in operation."

Evan thumped the tattered telephone directory. "All right," he muttered, admitting the weakness of his position. He put down the phone and went home, where the scaffolding in the garden prevented him from taking out his frustration on the wall with a football.

5

The police officers pulled into Henderson's yard and parked between a concrete mixer and a dump truck. Amid the chaos of his office, Eric Henderson was both wary of the police and yet still slick.

"How's the construction industry?" Tatton asked him. "As bad as they say?"

"Probably worse. I've laid off quite a few workers, I'm afraid. Every contract is priceless these days – and fought for. You have to run a lean operation to stay in business."

"You didn't make Mrs Keating redundant, did you?" Vicky asked, well aware that she was addressing her own husband's employer.

"No. But look at this office. I needed someone like her full-time to keep it in order. She only worked part-time here. And her replacement does just two days a week."

"Any good jobs on at the moment – or in the offing?"

"A few bridges. One over the canal and three for the new ring road. Not huge contracts, but they'll keep us afloat for a bit."

DCI Tatton showed as much sympathy as he could muster. "Tough times," he remarked.

"True," Eric Henderson replied. "But you haven't come to chat about the troubles of the building trade. I suppose it's about Barbara Keating and, from what I read in the papers, a rather gruesome find."

Neil Tatton nodded. "And in your wall too."

"Yes. That was one of our contracts. Clinched it in September, and started shortly after. It was for a Mr Warr, a video manufacturer, extending his business premises, in a hurry." The builder shook his head and added, "Ironic really, getting that contract."

"Why do you say that?"

"Well, Barbara Keating fought for ages over the planning permission. She didn't want it erected. Then, by working here, she found herself helping to build it – in an indirect way, of course."

"Did she ever talk to you about the extension?" asked Vicky.

Henderson thought for a moment then replied, "Not as I recall."

"If I were her," Neil Tatton suggested, "I might have tried to persuade you not to build it. I might have thought about sabotage."

"Sabotage?" Henderson queried. "You mean, she was up to something that night? Fell into the cavity and knocked herself out? Next day my lads tipped concrete mix…" He did not continue.

"It crossed my mind," the policeman said.

"Possibly," Henderson replied. "It's a horrible thought but I can't comment one way or the other. All I know is, she didn't approach me about the building site. She knew I needed the work and if I'd broken the contract we'd all have been out of a job and someone else would have built it anyway. If she wanted to halt the building, she'd have had to nobble Warr, not me. There was a queue of builders wanting the work. There always is these days. Only Warr could have stopped it. Perhaps you'd better talk to him."

"We will." DCI Tatton tried a different line of questioning. "How well did you know Barbara Keating?"

"She was a work colleague. I wouldn't say I was close to her."

"Did you ever meet socially?"

"No."

"How do you think she got on with her family?"

Eric Henderson frowned at the police officers. "She didn't bring her problems with her to work – if she had any," he added smartly, "so I've no idea."

"For a moment there, it seemed you were suggesting that she *did* have problems at home."

"Well," Eric said, realizing that it was futile to deny the policeman's allegation, "there were rumours about an affair."

Eagerly, Tatton asked, "An affair with who?"

"I've no idea. I don't even know if it was true. And I wasn't bothered to find out. She could have been married to ten separate men for all I cared. Her personal life was her own business, not mine."

"Did you ever see her with another man?" Sergeant McCormick queried in her low-pitched tone.

"Sure," he replied, barely disguising his contempt for the question. "I saw her with your husband." He paused for effect, looking directly at Vicky, then added, "And with Ted, the warehouse manager, and Graham from Personnel. She'd even been seen with me. Need I go on?"

"I meant", she said, "obviously romantically involved."

"When she was here, she was involved with letters, phone calls, orders, dealing with visitors. That sort of thing. Any romance she enjoyed was out of hours. So I wouldn't know about it."

"Thank you," Vicky responded.

Before they left Henderson's, the two police officers talked to three of the men who had worked on the video factory the previous October. They remembered the night of Friday the thirteenth. They'd joked about it. They were behind schedule, and working late under floodlights. They'd just started pouring in the concrete when the generator failed – typical for Friday the thirteenth. They couldn't remember exactly when they gave up and left the site – probably about eight thirty. They finished the concreting at first light on the next morning. And, no, they hadn't looked into the cavity before they filled in the remainder with concrete.

On the way back to the police station, Neil Tatton thought aloud for his colleague's benefit. "What have we got, then? A rotten Friday for Barbara Keating, I suppose. But a picture is emerging. First, a breakfast row with her son. A day at work. Then, at about six o'clock, she met her lover, Mr Fish, and together they went for a meal. And a scheming discussion. They left the restaurant together at seven thirty. An hour later, the labourers had left Warr's new factory. That gives ample time for a murder and travel to the building site. Her body could have been dumped there in the dark any time after eight thirty and before dawn on Saturday."

"But only by someone who knew about the site," Vicky put in.

"So which of our suspects does that rule out?"

"None of them," Vicky admitted. "But it implies that Mr Fish *did* know about it, if he's our man."

"True," Neil replied. "But he might not be. She could have left him and gone home. There was still plenty of time for her husband to do her in and dump the body before the kids came back. His alibi's hardly worthy of the name."

"The daughters seem to be in the clear, though. Their alibis held up."

"Mmm. Unlike Evan's. And", Tatton continued, "he's big. Powerful enough to drag a body up a few ramps on the building site."

"But the boy seems the most cut up about her death," Vicky noted. "It's got the girls down all right and Keating himself is angry, but Evan could be in real shock."

"I doubt it," Tatton argued. "He's just uncooperative. And remember, they've all had months to get used to the idea of being motherless. I wouldn't expect them to be devastated."

"What about Warr?" Vicky tried. "There's a new suspect. He'd probably keep an eye on progress at the building site, so he'd know there was scope for dumping a corpse there."

"Motive?" Neil inquired.

"If planning permission was such a nightmare, perhaps he came to blows with Barbara Keating over it. It would've been very convenient for Warr to get rid of her."

"But she copped it *after* she'd lost the battle over planning permission."

"Ah, yes. Perhaps she was taking her revenge on him, then, but he turned the tables on her."

"You mean, she attacked him in some way, and he killed her in the struggle? Then he hid the body because he was scared."

"Who knows?" Vicky replied.

"Mmm," Tatton murmured thoughtfully. "Remember there wasn't an obvious weapon. No knife wounds or bullet holes. So she didn't have her own weapon turned against her. That suggests she attacked him with bare hands. Let's go and take a look at him. If he's some muscle-bound hunk, I think we can forget it. She wouldn't risk it."

Trevor Warr was fifty, balding, and a bit of a wimp. His house made up for it, though. It was enormous, full of strong colours and beautiful objects. Neil looked round the lounge. "Nice house," he whispered to his colleague. "Business must be booming."

After the detective had explained to Warr why they wanted to question him, Tatton said, "The British public must be snapping up videos if you think a bigger factory is viable."

Warr was dressed casually but expensively, with an outlandish medallion around his neck. "Yes," he answered with self-satisfaction. "There are worse businesses to be in."

"What exactly do you make in your factory?"

"We manufacture videos, thousands of copies from a master tape. Under licence, you understand. Then we distribute them. When you browse around in your video shop, there's a good chance you'll pick up one that my company's produced."

"You don't do the actual filming, then? Just distributing other people's films."

"That's right. It's like publishing. Taking a story someone else has written and churning out the books. In my case, the story's on tape."

"Interesting," DCI Tatton commented in a tone that suggested the opposite. "Your new place, it's been in operation for a few months now. Did you go on to the site when it was being built?"

"Not much."

"But you did?"

"Yes. I must admit to being a workaholic," the small man replied. "I went in now and again to see how the building was getting on. Couldn't wait to get going, you see. The builders were behind schedule and I went to chivvy them along."

Vicky imagined that a man like Mr Warr was more likely to antagonize the workers than speed them up, but she kept the thought to herself and asked, "So were you there in the early part of October?"

"Probably. I can't be sure, though."

"Did you get planning permission easily?" Tatton queried.

"No," Warr sneered. "A local woman kept trying to block it, but I got there eventually."

"And do you know what happened to that local woman?"

"Yes," he answered. "I read about it in the newspapers. I'm sorry, but I can't say I'm heart-broken. She seemed to me to be a most obstructive and unpleasant individual."

"Did you ever meet her? Face to face?"

"Only across various council rooms during our little tussle. That was close enough."

"Where were you on the night of Friday the thirteenth of October?"

"You don't think I..." Warr paused, then added, "Of course,

you're just doing your job and I can see why I might be regarded as a suspect. Just a moment." He took a diary from a bureau and immediately put it down again, mumbling, "Last year's, not this." He searched for a while then, from the bottom of a pile, drew out another desk planner. "October thirteen," he muttered as he flicked through the pages. "During the day", he announced, "I had a meeting in London at the BBC. Plans afoot to release a certain series on video. I can't say which. Hush hush."

"But you can tell us who you met."

"Yes. A Mr Harding in Publicity."

"What time did you get back?"

"Late. I stopped in London to do some research round the cinemas."

"Research?"

"Watched a couple of new films. But neither was suitable for video, by my estimation." For the police officers' benefit, he recited details of the films and the cinemas that he had visited.

"And you got home when?" Vicky queried.

Warr breathed in deeply then exhaled while he considered. "I don't really know. Not far short of midnight, I shouldn't wonder."

"You made this trip alone?" Neil inquired.

"Yes."

"Can I see your diary?"

"Of course."

The scribbling in the box for 13th October appeared to confirm Warr's trip to the BBC but there was no record of watching films. DCI Tatton queried this.

"No. I was in London and unexpectedly I had the time after my meeting. The films that I wanted to view were on, so I went. Spur of the moment decision. No plans, so it didn't get into my planner."

"I see," Tatton said, rising from his chair and calling a halt to the interview.

"Have you got all you need from me?" Warr checked.

"For the moment," Tatton replied, with a hint of malice in his voice.

As Vicky accelerated out of Warr's drive and rain began to splash on to the windscreen, Neil turned to her. "Another one without a good alibi for Friday night," he commented. "But I'm still not convinced about his motive. I'm going to pay the forensic team a visit. We need a lead – or a lucky break. Perhaps they can provide one. You check out the London films."

The Chief Forensic Scientist was dragged out of the laboratories to speak to Neil Tatton. She had a manic mass of pure white hair reaching down to her white lab coat, and an obvious passion for her work. "Keating?" she chirped. "Yes. Messy, eh?"

"But what have you found, Kate?"

"Come this way," she said brightly, indicating the way to her disorderly office. "I'll show you my new toy – a LIMS."

"A what?"

Kate beamed. She was enjoying her ability to bamboozle Neil, and was just waiting for an opportunity to show off her new gadget. She waved her arms vigorously in the air as she spelled it out, "It's a laboratory information management system."

"You mean, it's a computer."

"Yes. Here it is."

As they sat in front of the screen, Neil said, "What happened to the good old days when someone just told me the findings? You know, when we used to *talk* to each other."

"Much more sophisticated now. The tests are specialized. Lots of different expertise needed, so you'd have to speak to the Toxicology Lab, the analytical chemists, microscopists. It's endless. But this", she said, patting her electronic box of tricks as if it were an obedient dog, "knows it all. Every result from every lab is recorded in a file in here. Immediate access. No messing," she enthused.

She tapped out a password and the screen came to life with a plan of the Keatings' garden and details of Barbara Keating's death. "Microscopy's reporting fibres found on the body and clothing. Some from the seats in The Seafood Spree restaurant, and some grey-blue fibres possibly from a Peugeot car seat. But", she warned, "there may be other sources. There were also some green woollen fibres, probably from a jumper. Pathology seems to be bemused. No detectable physical injury and no sign of a struggle. The cause of death isn't obvious."

"What about poisoning?" Tatton asked.

Kate clicked the mouse on the toxicology icon. "Here we are. Everything at your fingertips. Good stuff, eh? Anyway," she noted from the screen, "nothing of significance found but any poison is likely to have degraded over a few months, so the lab wouldn't be able to detect it."

"Great," Neil uttered sarcastically.

"I doubt if you're interested in the contents of the gut, barely recognizable after this time, but analysis suggested muesli for breakfast – wheat grain and oats still in the stomach. There was some evidence of a shrimp salad as well."

"That figures," Neil muttered. "Anything else?"

"Bound to be," Kate replied. "Let's try chemical analysis." She clicked on two more icons and another report appeared. "No. Nothing unusual in the body or in the handbag. But that reminds me – there was something in her bag that'll interest you," she commented tantalizingly.

Neil's ears pricked up. "Really? What?"

"Just a second." She accessed yet another computerized report – a list of the contents of Mrs Keating's handbag. Among the traditional items – make-up, purse, tissues – there was one that had been highlighted. A piece of paper, 6 cm by 3 cm, printed with "Dinner Date. 10. 6."

Kate looked into Neil's face and muttered, "I was right, wasn't I? You're intrigued."

"Mmm." He was fascinated but, if he had deduced anything of importance, he kept it to himself. "Anything else of interest?"

"Not really," Kate replied. Then she added, "Well, there was a used envelope, addressed to Henderson's Builders. Nothing in it."

"I'll take it – and that bit of paper."

It took the forensic scientist a couple of minutes to find the items and hand them over – an ordinary envelope and the scrap of paper, both sealed inside plastic bags. Neil thanked her and hurried away to find Sergeant McCormick. They needed to pay the Keating family another visit.

Kelly looked at Sarah and Sarah looked at Kelly. Then they both looked at the blank faces of their father and brother. On the small piece of paper that DCI Tatton showed them, "Dinner Date" had been typed at the top. Underneath, it was inscribed with the figure ten and, under that, six. "No," Mr Keating muttered. "No idea what that's about."

Tatton turned to the youngsters. "What about you three?" he said. "Any ideas?" Kelly shrugged and the other two mumbled, "No."

"OK," DCI Tatton replied. "Have any of you got green woollen jumpers? Or did you have one five or six months ago?"

"Yes," Kelly answered. "Why?"

"Because it might explain some fibres we found on your mum's body. With your permission, we'll take a few fibres from your jumper before we leave, so we can test for a match with the ones we found."

"All right," Kelly murmured.

"What make of car have you got?"

"A Cavalier," Mr Keating answered.

"What type of seats, or seat covers, does it have? What colour?"

"Some sort of plastic – dark colour."

"And did you have it in October?" asked Vicky.

"Yes," Mr Keating replied testily.

"How about this?" The detective showed Clive Keating a tatty envelope, with Henderson's business address typed on it.

Clive smiled wryly. "Over there", he said, pointing to the sideboard behind Sarah, "there's still a drawer stuffed full of them." Sarah leaned back in her chair, yanked a bulging polythene bag of used stamps torn from envelopes from the drawer, and dangled it in the air. "Barbara collected them for charity," her father explained. "When I remember, I keep them as well."

"Mmm." Chief Inspector Tatton stood up. "For breakfast, was your wife in the habit of eating muesli?" he asked.

Clive's face betrayed amazement and anger at the same time. "What's that got to do with it?"

"Probably nothing," he replied. "But I'm curious. Just making sure that it checks out with what we've found."

"The answer's yes," Clive snapped. "She did."

"Thanks," Tatton said. Turning to Kelly he added, "Can you fetch us that jumper? And a bit of sticky tape."

"Tape?"

"We'll just press it against the material for a moment to take a sample of the fibres."

"Oh, I see," Kelly said. "OK." She went upstairs to get the jumper while Sarah fetched a roll of Sellotape and scissors.

*   *   *

Two days later, shortly after Kate reported that Kelly's jumper did not match the fibres found on her mother's body, the meagre pieces of evidence became irrelevant to the investigation. With a heart-felt sigh of relief, Tatton wrapped it all up. He was able to go to the Keatings early on Friday morning with the good news that the murderer had confessed. The case was closed.

Sergeant McCormick was on compassionate leave, so he turned up at the Keatings' house with a different side-kick.

"Oh," Kelly said as she answered the door. "It's you."

"May I come in? I have some news that you'll find ... interesting."

The sparkle in the detective's eye told her that he'd solved the crime. She stood to one side. "OK," she replied. "We're having breakfast, but you'd better come in."

Looking like the cat that got the cream, DCI Tatton stood in front of the family in the dining room and announced, "Late last night, we found Mrs Keating's killer, a man we called Mr Fish and whose real name I'll come to in a minute." He looked at his stunned audience as if he expected applause.

Kelly was the first to find her voice. "You arrested him?" she asked.

"Not exactly," Tatton replied. "There was no need." Too impatient even to sit, he looked down on them like an actor in full flow. "Let me tell you the events of Friday the thirteenth last year." Looking directly at Clive Keating for a moment, he added, "It might even give you some comfort." He cleared his throat and declared, "I believe things came to a head for Barbara Keating that day. She was under pressure from her boyfriend, Mr Fish, to leave all of you and go away with him." The detective returned Clive's stare, saying, "Yes, there *was* a lover, as you will hear in a moment. But first, there was Evan." Evan stopped chewing his fingernails and cocked his head. "You and your mum had your ... discussion. Being accused of unfaithfulness and not caring about the family only added to her feeling that she had to make a decision. In fact, Evan's comments probably tipped the balance. At work she got a note from Mr Fish, saying they should meet for a dinner date. Remember, I showed you the slip of paper."

Kelly interrupted, asking, "What about the ten and six? What did they have to do with it?"

"I don't think it's a coincidence that The Seafood Spree is 10 Tanglefoot Road and that they met there after work at six o'clock. Anyway," he continued, "Mr Fish gave her an ultimatum – it's either them or me." Neil paused for effect. "She decided then and there. Her argument with you, Evan, made her realize how much she'd hurt you. Hurt you all, I imagine. She called off the affair."

Clive blurted out, "How do you know all this? You're just guessing. It could be nonsense."

"I don't think so. We have Mr Fish's word for most of it," DCI Tatton replied. "That night, Mr Fish was so upset by her decision that he killed her. He couldn't bear to lose her, so he decided you wouldn't have her either. It was after the meal, dark. They left at seven thirty. He drove over here in his Peugeot and dumped the body, some time after eight thirty, in the cavity where the concrete was about to be poured. He knew all about the building site, you see." He warded off their questions by raising both hands. "I'm coming to who he is in a minute. He resumed his normal life – and his work at Henderson's Builders where he'd met Mrs Keating – but couldn't forget what he'd done. We know from his own wife that he'd been miserable since October, and acting oddly, so it all fits." He coughed, then continued. "The discovery of her body brought it all back to him. Guilt." He shook his head. "He couldn't live with what he'd done. For five months or so he'd tried, but failed. Last night, at nine o'clock, he committed suicide." The detective took a photograph out of his pocket and showed it to Evan. "Is this the man you saw with your mum?" he asked.

Evan took a look and hardly hesitated. He nodded. "That's him."

"You're sure? There's no doubt at all in your mind that it's the man you saw kissing your mum?"

"No. It's him."

"I have to tell you", the detective said, putting the photograph back into his pocket, "that Mr Fish was Detective Sergeant Vicky McCormick's husband. He didn't match the restaurant owner's first description particularly well, but when I showed him McCormick's face, it jogged his memory. Like Evan, he identified McCormick as Mr Fish."

The detective's performance was nearly at an end. For an encore, he read from McCormick's suicide note. " 'She promised she would leave her husband. But she changed her mind. She did not want to see me again. I did not mean to kill her.' We found this – and more besides – on his computer screen. It seems that the word processor's taken over from writing in all walks of life, even suicide notes. Anyway, it's a clear confession. Everything fits. I'm closing the case." He looked pleased, pleased to wash his hands of the whole business and get on to another case. It was a swift and tidy ending.

Again, Kelly looked at Sarah and Sarah looked at Kelly. This time, it was not surprise but disbelief that they exchanged through their expressions. Their dad and Evan simply looked relieved.

"So", Kelly piped up, "Mr McCormick had a green jumper?"

"The fibres weren't from your jumper, but the forensic service is overworked," the policeman replied. "Now there's a clear-cut outcome, I won't be wasting their time on unnecessary work. All in all, it's best to let sleeping dogs lie. A sad and sorry affair, but at least it's over."

As soon as they closed the door on the policeman, the sisters shot upstairs to Kelly's room. Carefully closing the bedroom door, Sarah ventured, "What do you think?"

Kelly shook her head wearily. "We lost Mum ages ago. She wasn't coming back. She loved someone else. I don't believe it."

"Nor me," Sarah said. "I can't see her wanting to try again with Dad."

Kelly plonked herself down in a chair. "There is a problem, though. If not, lots of problems."

"Oh?"

"If we don't believe she was going to start again with Dad, we don't believe the suicide note. If we don't believe the note, we don't believe it was suicide."

"You mean, Mr McCormick was murdered as well?"

Stuffing her papers into her school bag, Kelly nodded. "The suicide note was typed, he said, not hand-written. So there was no writing to check against Mr McCormick's. Anyone could have typed it into his computer."

"I suppose so," Sarah murmured.

"But there's something else."

"What?"

Kelly looked puzzled. "If McCormick was her boyfriend, why didn't he report her missing? All the time, the story in the papers was that Mum had run off with someone. Obviously he knew that was wrong, so why didn't he say so? Perhaps we're wrong about all this."

Sarah thought about it then replied excitedly, "No, we're right. He wouldn't go to the police because of his wife. She's a policewoman. He didn't want his wife to know about the affair."

"Yes. Could well be," Kelly agreed. "But if McCormick didn't kill Mum, who did?"

"And", Sarah added, "who killed Mr McCormick and faked the suicide note?"

The girls looked at each other helplessly.

"I think we'd better try and find out," Kelly said, as they made for the front door.

6

Physically the two sisters were quite unalike. Kelly was tall and thin, with fair hair cut short, scraggy and boyish to offset the natural delicacy of her pale face. She had never felt delicate but she had been cursed with those features. Sarah was shorter but, like their mother, more robust. Her hair was longer and darker. Despite appearances, she was more sensitive than her older sister.

In Kelly's room after school, Sarah was sprawled on the bed. "It's all very well playing cops and robbers – cops and murderer, actually – but it just doesn't seem right, this ... picking over Mum's bones." She sighed heavily. "Poor old Mum."

Kelly touched her arm lightly. "I know, but it beats moping about. It's something we *can* do for her: find out what really happened. We can't do much else."

"I suppose not," Sarah mumbled her agreement. She sniffed and said, "All right. But what do we do? Where do we start?"

Kelly shrugged. "I'm not exactly an expert at this sort of thing either. My only qualification is watching cops on the box. And who knows how realistic they are?" She hesitated then suggested, "We could make a list, though. You know – suspects and clues. Stuff like that."

Sarah disentangled the fingers of her right hand from her hair and smiled sadly. "OK. Sounds sensible, I suppose." She scrambled off the bed and over to Kelly's desk.

Clearing a space among the bottles and jars, Kelly put a piece of paper in front of them. Her Biro hovered over it.

"Well?" Sarah murmured.

"Suspects," Kelly said. "I was just thinking."

"I suppose", Sarah muttered gloomily, "you're going to tell me that if we're going to do this properly we've got to start with Dad and Evan."

Kelly nodded. "I suppose so."

"What about you and me?" Sarah asked.

Kelly grimaced. "I think we can leave ourselves off. Besides, we've both got alibis for the night Mum died."

"True," Sarah responded rapidly.

"That reminds me," Kelly added. "What about last night? If McCormick was killed last night at nine o'clock," she said in a whisper, "have Dad and Evan got alibis? That would mean we don't have to put them down."

"Dad was working. Late night Thursday opening, then he'd be off doing the rounds collecting newspaper money from his old dears. That takes till about nine. The trouble is," she added, "we can't be sure that he went on the rounds last night. Sometimes he does it every other Thursday. And Evan – he was doing whatever Evan does, no doubt. Hanging about."

Kelly had no reason to hesitate further. She headed the list with her father and Evan. Against each person on their hit list, the sisters added a possible motive. Against their father there were just two words: unfaithfulness, jealousy. Evan's motive was put down as an unknown argument. Looking for other suspects, Sarah asked, "Who was the man Mum clashed with over the video factory?"

"Warr," answered Kelly. "I'll put him down under planning permission argument."

They also included Eric Henderson. They didn't know of any reason why he would want to murder their mum but noted that he would be no stranger to the building site and so had the knowledge to dispose of her body.

"Then there's Vicky McCormick," Kelly added. "That's if she knew about the building work as well."

"But she's a policewoman," Sarah objected.

"So what? I don't suppose the police are immune to crimes of passion."

"She killed Mum because she was … stealing her husband. OK," Sarah agreed, "but why would she kill her own husband?"

Kelly pondered for a moment. "I know. McCormick – Mr McCormick, that is – didn't go to the police even when it was reported that Mum had run off with someone. Right? He couldn't.

But he'd be curious, surely. Maybe he did some investigating himself instead. The detective said he'd been behaving strangely for a good part of the last six months."

"Yes," Sarah interrupted in her eagerness. "If he got close to the real murderer, then he might have got himself killed."

"Exactly," Kelly joined in. "His wife might have killed him and faked his suicide if he was about to turn her in."

"True. But it could have been anyone. If he found out who killed Mum, then the killer would have to get rid of him as well. It could have been his wife – or anyone on the list."

"Or someone who's not on the list," Kelly interjected. "We might not have thought of him yet."

"Or her," Sarah added.

They left a few blank lines on the page in case they needed to add more names later, then wrote down some clues that they would need to follow up: a green jumper; Evan's argument; the Dinner Date note; the seafood restaurant owner's description that didn't quite fit; knowledge of the building site; McCormick's murder at 9 pm on Thursday; the 5½ month gap between murders; a Peugeot car.

"A Peugeot?" Sarah queried.

"Don't you remember? A couple of days ago, Tatton was into car seats in a big way when he questioned us. This morning he said McCormick drove a Peugeot. Not just a car but a Peugeot. They must have found something from Peugeot seats on Mum."

"Yes, you're right," Sarah said. "But there are plenty of Peugeots in this world. And even if Mr McCormick didn't do it, she might still have been in his car before ... you know. Perfectly innocent."

"I know. But there are even more green jumpers in this world and that's on our list. By the way, Evan's got a green pullover, though he didn't admit it to the police. Still, let's not worry about that just now. On its own, each of these things I'm writing down isn't very helpful, but we're chasing someone with the right combination. Yes? We're building up a picture."

"You mean, someone in an environmentally friendly jumper who can change his appearance and drives around in a Peugeot?"

Kelly grinned. "OK, I take your point, but you know what I mean."

"So do we now borrow Dad's car and cruise the back streets for this chameleon?"

"I don't think so, somehow. Let's keep it in the family."

Feeling glum about the prospect, Sarah asked, "You want to start with our very own black sheep?"

"Can't think of anything better," Kelly admitted.

Deprived of the concrete wall, Evan was juggling the football and counting at each kick, "Ten. Eleven. Twelve."

"Tricky," Kelly said, buttering him up. "I don't know how you do that."

Evan didn't lose his concentration easily but, unaccustomed to praise, he faltered. The ball hit the ground at fourteen. Even so, he didn't appear to be upset that they had spoiled his record attempt. In fact, he was always so docile that they had never seen him annoyed. That was one reason why neither sister really believed he was guilty of murder. If he ever did get angry, then he did it in private or at least out of sight of Kelly and Sarah. Now he squinted suspiciously at his sisters and prompted, "Yes?"

"You're really skilful with a ball, Evan," Sarah said. "Why don't you join a team? I bet Matt would get you a place in the Scorpions."

"I prefer it on my own," Evan returned.

"You know this investigation?" asked Kelly.

"The one that's over?"

"Sort of."

"What do you mean?"

"We", Sarah said, nodding towards Kelly, "don't think the police got it right."

Evan sighed. "It's over. Let it go."

"Do *you* think Tatton got it right?" Kelly insisted.

Evan bounced the football twice, then replied, "That's got nothing to do with it. I'm just glad the law won't be snooping around any more."

"So", Sarah deduced, "you think there's more to it as well. McCormick isn't the whole answer."

"So?" Evan mumbled, increasingly disgruntled with his sisters' attitude.

"So we ought to try to find out what really happened," Kelly replied.

"Why?"

"Because ... because we want to know the truth. There's a

murderer out there somewhere. Who knows who else is on his hit list?"

Reinforcing the point, Sarah added, "Maybe we are."

"Don't be daft," Evan said disdainfully. "What are you anyway? A couple of Miss Marples?"

Kelly shrugged. "Something like that." And before Evan could pour more scorn on them, she said, "You know this row you had with Mum?"

For an instant, Evan looked amazed and disgusted. "You don't think I..." His voice faded away and immediately he began to juggle the ball again. "One. Two. Three." It was his way of avoiding the issue.

Now Sarah decided to have a go. "You're not the sort to have a real row," she said.

"Well," Evan replied, still keeping the ball off the ground, "perhaps it wasn't a real row, more an exchange of views."

"But what was it about – really? Not what you told the police."

In frustration, Evan kicked the ball out of reach. "It was exactly like I told them."

"Was there something else, then? Something you didn't tell?"

"That's my business. And Mum's."

Kelly and Sarah stole a glance at each other.

"Come on," Kelly persisted. "You can tell us. It might be the key to this whole thing."

Evan strolled across the lawn to pick up the football. When he returned with it, he walked straight past his sisters, mumbling, "No. I don't think so."

"Do you know who killed Mum?" Sarah called after him.

When Evan looked back without stopping and muttered, "No idea," neither Kelly nor Sarah believed him.

In desperation, Kelly shouted, "Mum would want you to tell us. She'd want us to get to the bottom of it. See it from her point of view."

Evan hesitated, turned, and said, "She doesn't have one any more." He slouched back into the house.

The two sisters shrugged at each other. "Oh, well," Kelly murmured, "could be worse."

"I suppose so," Sarah replied. She exhaled loudly as if she were tired. "What about Dad? Should we check him out somehow?"

Kelly thought about it. "No green jumpers, no Peugeot. And ... well ... it's Dad. I'd have trouble believing that he could..."

"Yeah," Sarah agreed. "I know."

"And I don't know what to ask him. 'Did you kill Mum?' seems pretty heartless! As well as pointless. I couldn't do it."

"Let's ignore that angle for the moment, then. He's not a prime suspect."

Kelly smiled. "You've been watching too much telly," she said.

Together they went indoors to discuss their next move.

7

The next move, they decided, was to put pressure on Evan. Neither Kelly nor Sarah were keen on this tactic, but they recognized that he was their best lead. They had little choice. Yet it seemed doubly underhand to investigate Evan: he was their brother and he was vulnerable.

They decided not to follow him on Saturday morning when he got on his bike, delivered the newspapers and then collected his earnings from the shop. Late in the afternoon, though, when he headed for the town centre, they went in hot pursuit. They ended up at Revolvers – a popular Saturday-night spot for kids. The place was throbbing with music and Kelly and Sarah had to shout to make themselves heard. Roller skaters charged up and down, round and round the rink, occasionally skating into the family area, zipping expertly hither and thither among tables and chairs. A cluster of youngsters was gathered round the large TV screen showing a soccer match. If the music hadn't been so deafening, they would have heard the thump and clatter of ten-pin bowlers and the crack of snooker balls upstairs in the club.

Evan did not join the queue for roller skates or bowling shoes. He bought a packet of crisps from the bar, then sat at a table near the television and watched the football, slowly eating crisps and occasionally nibbling at his fingernails. Kelly and Sarah took up a position at the other side of the family area and kept an eye on him from a distance, while skaters criss-crossed their view.

"What's he up to?" Sarah yelled into her sister's ear.

"Well, right now he's scratching his head as if he's got nits."

"Don't muck about! What's he really doing?"

Kelly shrugged. "Strikes me he's watching the soccer on the

box," she said with dry humour.

"Yes, but…"

"I know," Kelly replied. "He could've watched it at home. Perhaps he likes the atmosphere. Perhaps he's meeting someone. A girl, maybe."

Sarah smiled weakly. Kelly's comment reminded her that she was snooping on her own brother, and she blushed. If he had come to meet a girl, Sarah would feel mean and guilty for prying into his private affairs.

On the big screen, the soccer match ended and the scene switched to a race course. Long-legged horses, only just under control, were being paraded before the race.

Still Evan watched avidly. No one joined him, but at one point a beefy male acquaintance walked past him, nodded a greeting, and paused briefly to take a crisp from the bag that Evan offered him. The man smiled his thanks and walked away. Evan finished the crisps and threw away the empty packet.

A few minutes later, the same man ambled past Evan and thrust his own bag of crisps towards him. From where they stood, Kelly and Sarah could see the words "fair exchange" on the man's lips. Evan's hand dipped eagerly into the packet, but he did not eat the titbit that he took. Instead, he slipped it into his pocket.

As the man with the crisps walked briskly away, Sarah said, "What was all that about?"

"I don't know," Kelly answered, "but not just an exchange of crisps. I've got an idea. Not a nice one. Keep an eye on Evan – I'll be back in a minute." She shot after Evan's friend.

"Careful!" Sarah called after her.

On the television, the horses shuffled into line under starter's orders.

Three or four minutes later Kelly returned and, sitting close to Sarah, shouted into her ear, "He took a crisp from a girl over there, then got into a Peugeot and sorted something out on his lap. I couldn't see what. Now he's come back in."

The sound of the music was mixed with the thunderous pounding of hooves.

When the race was over, Evan seemed to lose interest. He nodded glumly towards his acquaintance and sauntered towards the exit.

Kelly nudged her sister. "Come on," she said. "We might as well tackle him. Now's as good a time as any."

Outside, she suggested, "You go to the left. I'll catch him up on this side."

Evan's eyes were wide and alert, like a threatened animal's, as he spotted his sisters closing in. "What are you two doing here?" he stammered.

Kelly saw no reason to delay. They might as well move in for the kill, while he was still suffering from the shock of being ensnared.

"I don't suppose", Kelly teased, "I imagined an MI5-style exchange of cheese and onion crisps, did I?"

Evan blinked at her, then said, "I don't know what you mean."

Lowering her voice, Kelly asked, "Could it be that you put some money in your crisp packet so the fella with the blue Peugeot could take it without anyone knowing? Then, after he'd checked it, he handed something to you in return, using the same trick." She paused, then added, "You're not into drugs, are you?"

"Drugs?" he exclaimed. "You've got to be…" His eyes flitted around. Outside the club several youngsters were drifting like lost souls. He didn't want them to overhear, so he replied, "I'm not saying anything. Not here."

"Let's go for a walk then," Kelly suggested.

They crossed the road and took the path that skirted round the artificial lake. On a windy day, the lake would be packed with sail-boards, like colourful sharks' fins. Now, in the gloom of early evening, it was calm and still. The ducks reclaimed the water and paddled in safety, looking for food. The wind surfers were probably confined to the pub on the other side of the lake.

"Come on," Sarah said. "Let's have the truth."

"The truth?"

"Yes," Kelly added. "If you don't, we'll use our own imagination – and we'll probably imagine something much worse than it really is."

"You already have." Evan stopped walking and leaned on a fence overlooking the lake. Keeping his gaze on the lighted windows of the pub, he mumbled, "You've got it all wrong. It's nothing serious."

"What is it then?" Kelly persisted.

Unwillingly, Evan murmured, "Sometimes it's soccer scores. Sometimes horses. It's even been ice-skating."

"What has?" Sarah asked, bemused.

"I put a bit of money on the results," he admitted.

"Gambling!" Kelly surmised.

Evan nodded.

"I get it!" said Kelly. "You checked out the horses on the screen, then you told that bloke what you're backing while he took your money, disguised in a crisp packet, and gave you ... what? Some sort of receipt?"

"A betting slip. Prints out a proper record on a computer – probably in his car."

"He *is* well organized, isn't he?" Kelly exclaimed in exasperation. "But one thing's for sure – it's against the law. He won't have a licence or whatever."

"No," Evan confessed. "It's not exactly above board."

"When you say, 'a bit of money', what do you mean?" Sarah added.

Evan blushed. "Not much. And I win sometimes."

"How much did you just lose?"

Evan mumbled, "He takes a fiver as a minimum bet."

Sarah cursed.

"You lost a fiver – or more – just like that? Evan!"

"You sound just like Mum sometimes," he countered.

Kelly didn't have time to be stung by his comment. Her thoughts had raced ahead. "I'm beginning to understand," she said. "That morning, Friday the thirteenth, Mum found out about this gambling business didn't she? You had a row about it."

Evan nodded again. "Found a betting slip in my trousers."

Suddenly it became clear to Kelly. "Dinner Date! They give horses daft names. Did you bet on a horse called Dinner Date?"

"It came in second," he admitted.

"The ten and the six?" queried Sarah.

"A tenner at six to one," Evan answered.

"Ah." The Keating sisters nodded knowingly at each other. "I see now," Kelly declared. "You couldn't tell the police you were really arguing about gambling because it's not legal at your age. Thought they'd do you for it. They'd do that bloke inside as well – preying on youngsters. Anyway," she continued, "when you'd finished arguing with Mum, she took the slip off you. That's how come it was in her bag."

"Yes," Evan whispered.

"It's obvious, then," Sarah commented.

"What is?"

"Mum and this boyfriend. They met to talk over what she should do to stop this little earner. Somehow, that bloke inside found out and ... put an end to it. First Mum, then McCormick."

"He did get into a Peugeot 405," Kelly added, "so it might fit. But right now, what are we going to do about you, Evan?"

"Me? What do you mean?"

"I'm worried about you. It may not be as bad as drugs, but you've got to stop."

"Why? It's my money."

"Because it's almost as addictive as drugs. And you never know what it can lead to. Debts. Thieving to support the habit. That sort of thing."

"I know," Evan muttered unconvincingly.

"So, do you reckon you can stop?"

"Sure," he responded in a tone midway between confidence and indifference. "I could quit any time."

"Why do you do it, Evan?" Kelly queried.

He shrugged. "The adrenalin, I suppose. You get really high during a race. You wouldn't understand if you haven't done it."

"Perhaps not. It just seems like a waste of money to me. Still, I've done enough preaching. I don't suppose any more will help."

Evan looked away.

After a pause, Sarah asked, "What's that man's name?"

"No idea," Evan replied. "Everyone calls him Pete, that's all."

"Pete," Sarah repeated. "That's the one."

Kelly nodded slowly, thoughtfully. "Could be," she murmured.

In front of them, a duck upended itself. As it probed unseen in the mud at the bottom, its backside wobbled comically in the air.

"We're going to have to dig up some dirt on him," she concluded. "Does he always hang about in Revolvers?"

"Weekends and most nights, yes. They pipe in a sports channel all the time so it's convenient enough for him. Sometimes he does other places. He arranges afternoon betting parties now and again."

"Have you been bunking off school?" Sarah asked.

"Not much," Evan muttered.

Kelly sighed. "And you wanted to know why you should stop! You're hooked."

"What about Thursday nights?" Sarah questioned. "The night McCormick copped it."

"He used to meet clients down beside the canal, under the old bridge, before taking them to a gambling den. Now they're building a new bridge, he puts in another night at Revolvers instead."

"Did you see him on Thursday?" Kelly continued. "That would give him an alibi."

"No," Evan replied. "I was somewhere else."

"So", Kelly concluded, "he's got to go on our hit list. I think we'll have to do something about him."

"You can't mess with him, Kelly," Sarah warned. "Seriously. He's probably raking it in. He'd go a long way to protect his interests. Maybe he has already."

"So", her sister asked, "what do you think we should do?"

Sarah breathed in deeply, then shrugged. "I don't know. Turn him in to the police for running an illegal gambling business?"

"That won't help with the murder," Kelly commented.

A car roared into life in the car park beside the pub, and cast two parallel beams across the water. As it pulled away, the beams swept over the lake as if searching out waterfowl.

"How are you going to prove it was him?" asked Sarah. "Put him under a spotlight and interrogate him?"

Kelly grinned at her sister. "No, I wasn't thinking of that."

"What then?"

It was Kelly's turn to look helpless, but only for a moment. Her face brightened and she turned to Evan. "Has your Pete got a proper job, do you know?"

"Not sure," he answered. "Someone told me he had something to do with the building trade."

"Ah! He doesn't work for Henderson's, does he?"

"I don't know."

Even Sarah had to admit that they had a lead now. "We could ask Mr Henderson if he employed this Pete for the video factory."

"How?" Kelly asked. "Half his builders are probably called Pete, and we can hardly say Pete the bookie."

"I suppose not."

Kelly tilted her head to one side as she thought about it for a moment. "What we need", she proclaimed, "is a photo of him. Then we could take it to Mr Henderson."

Sarah took up the logic eagerly. "And if he identifies Pete as one of his crew, that'll just about sew it up. This Pete would have the motive *and* it'd come naturally to him to..." Her voice lost its fire as she finished the sentence, "To get rid of a body ... like that."

"Why wait six months before going after McCormick?" Kelly wondered aloud. Then, answering her own question, she said, "Perhaps Pete was checking out our family. He'd have to have done that to concoct that suicide note." Turning to Evan, she inquired, "Has he ever asked you about Mum and Dad?"

"Hardly said anything to me. Or me to him."

"He could have been snooping without us knowing about it," Sarah put in.

"Yes," Kelly agreed. "Or maybe McCormick was snooping on *him*. Doing a bit of research, getting evidence, before telling his wife all about him. If McCormick got a bit too close – curtains."

"So", Sarah insisted, "it *is* risky to mess with him."

"It's Sunday tomorrow. He'll be back here at the centre. I reckon I can snap him without him even knowing. It shouldn't be too difficult, with Evan's help."

Both sisters turned towards Evan. He looked at them, then turned away, pretending to be interested in a passing moorhen. After a few seconds of silence, he shook his head dejectedly. "All right," he murmured. "What do you want me to do?"

8

The three Keatings each chipped in some money. They changed it into a ten-pound note and Evan folded it to the size of a postage stamp and slipped it into a small sheath. "That", he said to his sisters, "goes into the crisp packet. He'll take it with a few crisps."

"Hope he doesn't swallow it," Kelly quipped, despite her tingling nerves. "He'd have a bit of a wait before he got his money back."

"Have you got your camera?" Sarah asked.

"It's in the bag," Kelly replied, tapping her handbag. "So let's get cracking."

The girls went into Revolvers first. Fifteen minutes later, Evan strolled in, bought a packet of crisps and sat down two tables away. As instructed, he did not even glance at them. He sat and scratched the top of his head, which was the signal that he wanted to place a bet with Pete. Then he chewed his fingernails mercilessly as he studied the list of runners for the heats of a 5,000-metre race at some athletics event.

Kelly used Pete's first approach to Evan to gauge the angles, then manoeuvred herself into what she thought was the right position, ready for his return. She hoped her hand wouldn't shake too much to get a decent photo when he passed the betting slip to her brother.

The three of them waited tensely. Kelly checked the camera setting for the third time.

Sarah's eyes darted to the entrance and nervously her lips formed the words, "He's coming."

Just as Pete hesitated by Evan, bent down and offered him a smoky bacon crisp, Kelly clicked the button. There was a flash.

Pete straightened up. Anger and panic were clear on his face even in the semi-darkness. All he saw was a young woman beckoning to her sister and yelling, "Stand up! I'll take another like that. Hold your drink up!"

Sarah yanked her fingers out of her hair and got to her feet. Lifting her glass towards the camera, she mouthed, "Cheers!"

There was a second flash.

Pete relaxed a little but moved away as quickly as he could.

Kelly had taken a photograph of Pete, then turned rapidly and directed the camera at Sarah. Pete had not looked up in time to see the change of angle. He was unaware that his image had been captured on film.

The girls plonked themselves down into their seats and sighed. It took a few seconds before they were capable of smiling at each other, and almost a minute before they stopped trembling. Then Kelly put her thumb up and Sarah lip-read her message, "Got it."

They waited for twenty minutes before they left the club, shortly after Evan's departure. The race had finished and he had lost again. Kelly was driving her dad's car and she pulled up at the end of the street to let Evan get in.

"Well done," she congratulated him. "It worked. It's in the can, as they say."

In the scruffy reception of Henderson's Builders, Kelly's eyebrows rose. "Faye!" she cried.

"Kelly!" the secretary replied.

They had been at school together. Kelly had stayed on, Faye had left at sixteen. She'd married, had one kid, and got divorced, all within two years. Now she just about supported herself and her boy by working part-time as Mrs Keating's replacement at Henderson's while a friend took care of the baby.

"What are you doing here?" Faye asked.

"Just ... er ... some unfinished business with your boss. Do you think we can see him?"

Sarah stood beside her sister and Evan cowered behind. They'd managed to drag him along because he knew Pete better than they did.

"I suppose so," Faye replied. "He hasn't got anyone with him at the moment." She rose and headed towards Mr Henderson's door.

Kelly caught her arm. "Thanks. But first, why don't we get together again? Say tonight?"

"That'd be nice," Faye answered. "But it's difficult. You know, with the baby." She looked disappointed.

"You could come to our place," Kelly offered. "Bring the baby."

"Well…" Faye had always been a bit scatty and indecisive. "I don't know."

"Tell you what," Kelly said to encourage her, "I'll pick you up and drive you across. No problem."

The smile was a long time coming to Faye's attractive but worn face. Eventually she nodded. "OK. I'll jot my address down and give you it before you go."

Kelly and Sarah returned her smile.

There weren't enough chairs for them all to sit in Eric Henderson's office so Kelly took the seat in front of his desk and the other two stood behind her like bodyguards. Mr Henderson wore an expression of curiosity and surprise. He had a big bushy beard that gave his face a comical appearance. None of the Keatings was fooled by this impression. His manner and the hardness of his eyes suggested a ruthless businessman.

He cocked his head on one side and said, "I agreed to see you out of respect for your mother. What do you want?"

Kelly had rehearsed her piece in the car on the way to Henderson's. "We're concerned about a loose end in the investigation into Mum's death. We have reason to believe that this man", she held out the recently developed photograph, "might hold the key."

Eric Henderson still looked puzzled. Barely glancing at the photo, he asked, "What do you mean? What sort of key?"

Kelly had hoped he wouldn't quiz her along those lines. "We think he might have been with Mum just before she died."

"Look," Mr Henderson replied, "it's over. George McCormick couldn't take rejection, it seems. Simple as that. I lost two good employees and you lost a mother. Let's leave it at that."

"But this man", Kelly persisted, "might have been in on it. We want to get to the truth. His name's Pete. Do you know him?"

"Why should I?"

"Because he's a builder," Sarah put in.

On the other side of the desk, Henderson sighed heavily and

examined the photograph. Pete was bending over Evan so it had not caught his full face, but there was enough: a stocky man in his twenties with cropped mousy hair, a broken nose and thick eyebrows.

Henderson laid the photo on his desk and looked into Kelly's eyes. "If you think he's one of my men, you probably think he worked on the video factory. That means you think he was involved in killing your mother – or at least in getting rid of the body."

Kelly nodded. "Well?"

He returned the photograph. "Sorry, he's not one of mine."

Kelly wanted to look away but forced herself to keep her eyes on Eric Henderson's face. There was a silence as she gazed at him, assessing his character. He was obviously annoyed to have his time disrupted by kids who were trying to dredge up an old relic that should be allowed to rest, but his reply was direct and sincere. She thought he was probably telling the truth. "OK," she said, reclaiming the photograph and standing up. "We won't bother you any more."

Before they shuffled out of the door and returned to the reception area, Mr Henderson called after them, "There's been enough tragedy. Let your mum rest in peace."

Back inside the borrowed car, Evan finally spoke. "What about showing the photo at that seafood place? In case the owner saw Pete hanging around that Friday while Mum was inside."

His interest took his sisters by surprise. They both turned in their seats and peered at him. "That's a good idea," Kelly declared. "If they'll speak to us."

Evan did not reply. He had lapsed into disinterested silence again.

The visit to The Seafood Spree turned out to be a waste of time. They did get to see Daniel Perriman but his shallow smile soon faded when it became clear that the party of three was not Tuesday evening's first group of customers. In fact, when he realized their true mission, he turned out to be rather grumpy.

"Look," he snapped. "This death has brought me enough bad publicity what with police visits and everything. I've done my bit. I answered their questions and identified a body. Now I've put it all behind me. I'm a caterer, not a crook."

"Just a quick look," Kelly said softly. "It won't hurt, surely."

Grudgingly, the man put on his spectacles and glanced at the photo. He did not even take it out of Kelly's hand.

"No," he said impatiently. "I've never seen him. And now," he added, pushing his way to the door and opening it, "I bid you goodbye."

"Thanks, anyway," Kelly muttered on the way out.

"I don't know why you thanked him," Sarah commented. "He almost said no before he looked."

"I know," Kelly replied. "Just my upbringing, I suppose."

The third person to examine Kelly's photograph that day was Faye. She held baby James on her knee with one hand and the photo in the other.

"Mr Henderson said he'd never seen him, but have you?" Kelly prompted.

"Don't know," Faye replied. A few more moments of consideration brought a more definite response. "No," she said. "There's someone at work quite like him but no, it's definitely not him. This bloke's not been around while I've been there." She handed back the photo.

"All right," Kelly conceded. Changing the subject, she asked, "Do you like it at Henderson's?"

Faye shrugged. "It's a job." She seemed reluctant to show any enthusiasm and her cheeks reddened.

"It's all right," Kelly said. "You don't have to be embarrassed about replacing Mum. It wasn't your fault."

"Yeah. But…" She fiddled with the baby's clothes rather than finish the sentence.

"It's not going so well, I understand. Not much building work."

"True. That's the reason I got the job, I reckon. I'm not a fast typist and I'm not the most organized, but he doesn't have to pay me as much as someone experienced like…"

"Like Mum."

Faye nodded. "He has to cut corners to survive. I only do two days a week. It just about keeps us going, me and the baby." She jogged him on her knee.

Kelly wondered whether Henderson's predicament had anything to do with her mum's fate. The two murders had become so prominent in her mind that she scrutinized everything people said for relevance but she could not make any connections here.

"Did you know Mr McCormick?" she asked. "The one who ... killed himself?"

Faye squirmed uncomfortably in her seat. "George? Yes," she said glumly. "I wasn't surprised, mind. He wasn't the life and soul of any party. Miserable, he was, but angry as well. I can't honestly say I liked him, but I'm sorry he ... you know."

"He didn't happen to ask you about this man, did he?" Kelly waved the photograph in the air.

"No. Didn't ask me anything other than normal work stuff – you know, wanted this or that file, or a bit of typing."

They chatted for a while longer but the evening petered out. Faye wasn't a good talker and, with the baby to occupy her, she wasn't a good listener either. When Kelly gave her a lift home, they vowed to keep in touch. In Kelly's case, politeness demanded it. For Faye, the evening had been a real break from her daily routine. She had enjoyed the evening and was grateful to her friend for suggesting it. She was looking forward to a repeat performance.

On Wednesday, Kelly and Sarah stood in the doorway of Evan's bedroom like a nervous double act on a ludicrously small stage.

"You're in tonight," Sarah stated.

"No. I've just come on in the last five minutes to score the winning goal at Wembley," Evan replied with a blank expression. He could have been indulging in ridicule or humour; it was impossible to say.

"What she means", Kelly put in, "is that we're pleased you're staying in."

"Oh." He didn't need to ask why. His sisters knew that if he stayed at home, avoiding Pete, he couldn't gamble. And that would please them because they had begun a crusade to get him to kick the habit.

Evan's craving for excitement had started when he first realized that his mum had found a lover. The exact reason for turning to gambling was never clear in his own mind. In spite of what he'd told the police, he thought he might have been responsible for his mother's need for someone else. The thrill of the race and the high stakes helped him to forget the guilt. At times he knew it wasn't his fault and he just felt angry with her, but he kept a lid on his resentment. Instead of proclaiming his fury from the roof-tops, he discovered that he could punish her by turning to something outside the family.

Because his mum forced him to play second fiddle to some boyfriend, Evan made her the poor relation to his gambling. Now, there was little point in punishing the dead, so he saw the sense of his sisters' crusade. He would try to live without the element of risk, without abandoning himself to luck, without the elation of winning. Besides, he didn't relish another meeting with Pete, in case he realized that there had been a conspiracy against him. On top of that, Evan no longer had the cash.

"It struck me", Kelly continued, "that betting's an expensive business, even if you did win now and again. How did you afford it?"

Evan noted her use of the past tense but didn't object. "Paper round. And pocket money. That sort of thing."

"But ... er ... surely that wasn't enough."

Evan's head drooped as he hesitated. He'd never told anyone about his other way of making money.

"You see," Kelly explained, "we've put Pete the bookie on our list of suspects but we've come to the end of the road with him – for the moment. We were wondering if there was anything else we should know about." She took up a position on her brother's bed as he nodded.

"I suppose I might as well tell you now," he mumbled. "I didn't tell anyone before because I needed the cash. I couldn't risk letting on about the videos, or the source of money would've dried up."

"What do you mean?" Sarah inquired.

"I didn't want Mr Warr taken away for murder, did I?"

"Why should he be?"

"Because someone at Mum's work told her they'd seen me in ... one of his videos."

"*What?*" Kelly exploded.

"Sometimes I did a bit of work for Mr Warr. His proper business – distributing videos – is legit, of course, but he runs a scam on the side. That's how he funded the extension. A racket in making videos."

"Don't tell me you starred in some of them!"

"No, not really," Evan stammered. Then he conceded, "Well, yes. A bit."

"A bit?" Sarah cried. "Either you did or you didn't."

"He's got a studio where he makes the films. I help out, lugging props around the place – that sort of thing. But sometimes, if he needs a crowd or a passer-by, he gets me to join in. It's not really acting, it's just being there."

Kelly sighed. "Let me get this straight. You earned a bit on the side by helping Mr Warr make these videos. What sort of videos are we talking about, Evan? Why aren't they legitimate?"

"It's not what you think. They're OK videos – more or less. Just cheap. A bit of horror, science fiction, supernatural – anything that can be done in a studio and put together on a shoestring. It's the type of operation that the tax office doesn't get to hear about. Struggling actors, moonlighting unemployed – he uses those sorts of people. Ones that need some cash in their pockets without all the complications of national insurance, tax and stuff."

"He uses underage kids as well," Sarah remarked irritably. "It's called slave labour." She seemed to have developed an instant dislike for Mr Warr and his dealings. It didn't help that she couldn't forget the unhappiness he had caused her mother when the planning permission row was in full swing.

"Yeah. I put in more hours than I'm supposed to. I did quite a few nights and weekends. Took a bit of time off school as well. But I had to – for the pay."

"That's bad enough, but isn't there a law about schoolkids performing in films? Doesn't Warr need some sort of licence?" Kelly checked.

"I think so," Evan answered. "But … er…"

"He didn't bother with that either," Kelly deduced. "Some racket! You only mix with the best, don't you? Pete the bookie and now Warr. Anyway," she said, "someone at Mum's work saw one of the videos and spotted you – passing by or whatever. Told Mum what you were up to. Then she had that row with you. Have we finally heard what it was really about, that argument? You doing this video stuff to fund the gambling?"

Her brother nodded.

"And you didn't tell us or the police because you'd lose the job," Sarah deduced. "And the income that went with it."

"Yes."

"This is important," Kelly put in. "After that row, Mum could have threatened to expose Warr – to stop your little game. To stop *her*, he might have killed her."

"Yes," Evan agreed in a subdued voice. "I know. I think he did it. I phoned him about it, you know."

"You accused him of murder?" Sarah exclaimed.

"Nearly. He denied it, of course."

The three of them fell silent for a moment, then Kelly murmured, "Is that the lot? You haven't got any more nasty surprises for us, have you?"

"No," he replied. "You know it all now."

"Well, what do we do? Warr looks like a real suspect, suddenly. He could've easily put the body in the wall. And he might have had a go at Mr McCormick as well if he'd been poking his nose in, trying to get evidence on Warr's racket."

"And now you want us to snoop on him too," Sarah moaned.

Kelly shrugged. "Let's hear some better ideas," she said.

She didn't get any.

Admitting defeat, Sarah asked, "What have you got in mind? A raid on his wardrobe for a green jumper?"

"No. But we could check out his car, at least. Do you know what he's got, Evan?"

"Something big and showy, like a Daimler, I think."

"Not a Peugeot?"

"Not that I know of. But he's rich. He's probably got more than one."

"And *have* you ever seen him in a green jumper?"

Evan looked blank.

"Evan's a boy," Sarah put in. "Boys never notice clothes."

"I don't suppose you were working for him on the night Mum died, were you?" Kelly asked.

Evan shook his head. "I was at Revolvers, I'm afraid. Waited around all night but Pete didn't show. I can't rule either of them out."

Changing the subject so that none of them had to dwell on that evening, Kelly murmured, "What about last Thursday? I'd like to know what Warr was doing that night as well." Looking at Evan, she inquired, "You didn't call him then, did you?"

"No. It was before that. But", Evan added, "I think I know someone who could help. Someone called John."

"What are we waiting for?" Kelly commented.

"Because John's... Well, you'll see what he's like. Just don't be put off. He's OK really."

They found John in a dingy sports club. He was clinging to the ropes of the boxing ring and shouting childlike encouragement to whichever combatant seemed to be getting the worst of it. Unlike Kelly and Sarah, he did not wince each time a punch thudded home. He was built like Humpty Dumpty with muscles – or a Mr Universe pumped up like a balloon. His layer of fat made him look much older than he probably was, but his chubby face was soft and young. It was a face that could never be clouded by unhappiness.

"Evan!" he called when he caught sight of his friend. Letting go of the ropes, he waddled across the room, dodging the medicine balls and table tennis tables, with a baby's exaggerated expression of joy on his face. "How're you doing, old son?"

"All right, John. You?"

"You know me," he chimed. Turning to Kelly and Sarah as if he'd known them from birth, he said, "Last time I seen Evan, he was covered in blood! Heh, heh, heh!" His laugh could have brought all the activities in the hall to a stop, but the punters were used to him. "Remember?" he chortled.

Evan could hardly forget. He had been in charge of a knife attached to a tube that delivered red liquid to the plastic blade when it apparently bit into flesh – a standard prop for a horror film. That day, though, he had applied too great a pressure to the liquid and when it was pumped through, the knife leapt out of the actress's hand and snaked, like an out-of-control hose-pipe, spurting fake blood everywhere – over the actress, who howled with laughter; over Evan, who was too shocked to see the funny side of it; over Warr; over John and the rest.

"Yes," Evan muttered. "I remember."

"Explosion in a red paint factory," John giggled. "The bread knife massacre! Great stuff. Anyway, I ain't seen you much these days."

"Keeping a low profile," Evan replied. "Are you still doing work for Mr Warr?"

"Sure am. Went quiet, it did, while he got the factory sorted. Now he's started up again. Still likes me, he do."

It wasn't true, of course. Evan knew that the film-maker did not so much like John as take advantage of him. Whenever some heavy scenery needed shifting, John provided the muscle. He'd even performed a few feats of strength on film, but he wasn't an aggressive type. He once got a job as a bouncer at a night club because he looked like a man who could move mountains, but two weeks later he got the sack because he couldn't bring himself to harm a fly.

It also occurred to Evan that, if the studio was back in action but he hadn't been asked to take part, Warr must be avoiding him. In Warr's eyes, Evan had probably been tainted by his contact with the police. It would be too dangerous to give him any more work, despite what he'd said to Evan on the telephone.

John beamed at Sarah and invited her to feel his biceps. She patted the enormous mound of flesh and muscle in his upper arm and, with as much admiration as she could muster, murmured, "Mmm!"

"Good, eh? Good for lifting tree trunks!" Seeing an expression of disbelief beginning to form on Sarah's face, he added quickly, "In films, like. Not really." His chuckle almost made the earth move.

"Making a new video, is he?" Evan asked.

"Yep," John replied. "Haunted house or something."

"What is it? Filming just at weekends, or on week days?"

"Behind schedule, he says, after the wall collapsed." He laughed again, not thinking of what it might mean to the Keatings, then continued, "So we're at it most afternoons and nights."

"Like last Thursday?"

"Last Thursday?" John repeated. "That were years ago," he cried happily. "Let me think."

Evan caught an errant table tennis ball and threw it back to one of the players while they waited for John's brain to tick over like an unwilling engine on a winter's morning.

"Yes," he pronounced eventually. "Thursday. One of the girls, she were going on about seeing some group on *Top of the Pops*. Great, she said they were. That's Thursdays, ain't it?"

"Yes," Evan answered. "And was Mr Warr at the shoot?"

"Sure."

Sarah looked disappointed. She would have dearly loved to nail Warr for murder.

"All the time?" Evan asked.

"I don't know," John replied. "He … er… No. The producer were cursing him at some point. Heh, heh! Couldn't get on. Wanted Mr Warr to decide on something but he'd scarpered early, like."

The Keatings glanced at each other triumphantly.

"What time would that be, John?"

"It's no use asking me about time," he sniggered. "Never notice it. Eight? Nine? I don't know."

"OK. Never mind. Just one more thing," Evan said. "You've done stuff with him for ages, haven't you?"

"Yep! He knows good prime beef when he sees it. Always wanted me on the set. A film star, me."

"You've probably seen him driving around a bit. You know that big car he's got?"

"Mercedes. Cracking set of wheels."

Evan nodded. "Ever seen him in another car? Ages ago, maybe."

"Er…" John scratched his head with stodgy fingers. "He's had a VW, I think. And a Peugeot."

"A Peugeot?"

"Yes. Sure. Red, it were."

Evan grinned at him. "Thanks," he said.

"Are you off now?"

The Keatings nodded.

"Pity," John said. "Still, maybe you'll come in and help out soon, eh?"

Evan returned his smile. "Maybe," he said. "Look after yourself, John."

"Sure will!"

Outside the club, Sarah was furious. "It makes me so angry!" she bawled. "He's just a … big buffoon. And Warr's taking advantage of him."

"He didn't even ask why we wanted to know all those things," Kelly said, agreeing with her sister. "He's in another world, the poor chap."

"I know," Evan said. "But it's only the filming that allows him to make a living. You've got to give it that."

"I know what I'd like to give it," Sarah cried.

"It's time to do something about this Warr," Kelly added. "He could be our man. He might have control over life and death in his films, but not in real life."

Sarah agreed. "He deserves everything he's got coming to him."

"Like what?" Evan pondered.

"We'll flush him out into the open," Kelly replied.

"What do you mean?" asked Sarah.

"Well," Kelly explained as she opened the car doors and they all piled in, "what was his motive for murder?"

Sarah shrugged. "Mum threatened to expose his illegal filming. McCormick probably found some evidence to take to the police, so he copped it as well." She hesitated, glancing at her sister. "Oh, no! You're not thinking of threatening him ourselves!"

"Why not?"

"Because we'd be dead meat."

"How else are we going to flush him out?" Kelly argued. "Besides, I know how we can confront him *and* be safe while we're doing it."

"Oh yes?"

"It's a nice irony. We meet him at the centre of the indoor market," she proposed. "You know, where there's seats."

"Where's the irony in that?" Sarah asked her.

"It's monitored by video, remember? To catch shoplifters or whatever. He can't do anything to us – he'll be under surveillance at the time. It'll all be on video."

"And when we leave the market?" Sarah queried. "The cameras don't follow you home, you know."

"We'll just have to be careful."

9

The circular market was a colossal concrete cake in the centre of the town, constructed in the boom years when buildings were big, bold blots on the landscape. In those days, there was enough money around for Henderson's to build it solidly, like an impregnable fortress. By the time its bad architectural style had been recognized, it would have cost another fortune to knock it down and start again. With money in short supply, the blemish was likely to stand till doomsday.

Inside, the stalls were arranged in rings. Customers could walk round and round for ever. Newcomers were easy to spot. They negotiated the market like a maze: they knew roughly where they had entered, but weren't sure where they wanted to go or how to get there, and they ended up shuffling round in a state of bewilderment.

After school on Friday, Kelly, Sarah and Evan strode past the lost souls and converged rapidly on the hub of the market. There, seats and tables were laid out and drinks and hot dogs were being served from a kiosk. They each bought themselves a coffee and then sat at one of the tables, glancing nervously towards the shoppers who circled them. Waiting for Warr to emerge from the crowds, they felt exposed, expecting a solitary and dangerous predator to come at them from any angle like a shark.

"He'll make for you," Kelly said to Evan, "because he doesn't know me or Sarah."

"Yes." Evan looked at his watch. "Nearly four," he muttered.

By telephone, Evan had persuaded Warr to agree to meet them in the market at four o'clock. Warr's resistance towards the meeting had been broken down once Evan had convinced him that he had no further desire to take part in his illegal videos. With that decision, Evan had become a threat in Warr's eyes and had to be taken seriously. The boy could blab to the police if he no longer lived in fear of losing the considerable amount he earned through backstreet filming. If Evan really could do without the money, Warr had lost his hold over him. The whole operation was in jeopardy because of an out-of-control and underage ex-member of his underground crew.

Above their table in the market, among the dangling strip lights, there hung a small dome with four camera lenses aiming in different directions. In the centre of the dome, a red light flashed on and off to bring shoppers' attention to the video surveillance.

When Warr finally stepped into the arena at four-fifteen, he was turned out immaculately. Even though Kelly and Sarah had never seen him before, they recognized him immediately. In such a down-beat place, he was like a fish out of water. Sarah nudged her sister and whispered, "Bet that's him. Very posh."

"Yeah," Kelly replied. "Remember, not all villains look like scarecrows and wear stockings over their heads."

Behind the carefully preened exterior, Warr's face suggested a worried man. Taking a seat opposite Evan, he nodded towards Kelly and Sarah and declared, "I didn't expect an audience."

"My sisters," Evan retorted.

"Yes," Warr snapped. "I can see the resemblance. But what I want to know is, what do they know?"

Kelly interjected, "We're not dumb. We can speak for ourselves. And Evan's told us everything."

Warr unbuttoned his jacket slowly. "I see." Still not addressing Kelly or Sarah, he looked at Evan and remarked, "I suppose they made you change your mind about working for me."

Sarah was about to comment that Evan could stand on his own two feet, but she stopped herself. If it was true, she'd better let him at least speak for himself.

"Maybe," Evan grumbled. Then, looking straight at Warr, he added, "But I think I'm entitled to change. What with Mum's body falling in front of me and all."

Warr regarded Evan intently for a moment before replying, "I suppose so." He levered himself into a more comfortable position in the plastic seat. "So why not just disappear from the scene? You didn't have to call me."

"Because we know all about you," Evan responded.

"What's that supposed to mean?" asked Warr. "Is it money you're after? A golden handshake?"

"No," Kelly blurted out.

"What then?" he said, peering at the girls this time.

"Our mum was driven around in a Peugeot before she was killed. You had a Peugeot. Her body was dumped at your building site. You'd know all about that—"

Warr interrupted. "Not again!" He gave a loud but hollow laugh. "You want me to break down and confess to a murder. I don't believe it. Three kids! You have to be joking! It was absurd enough when Evan tried to blame me over the phone. Listen. Let me spell it out for you. I had nothing to do with..." He leaned forward and lowered his voice, but it still retained its harshness. "...with your mother's death. Why should I?"

"Because she heard about Evan working on your videos. We think she had a go at you for it. Probably threatened you. Plenty of motive."

"But—"

Before he could defend himself, Sarah exclaimed, "And there's last Thursday night."

"What about it?" Warr queried, agitatedly.

Evan explained that, despite the police's suicide verdict, they believed his mum's boyfriend had been murdered on that night, presumably after he'd investigated her death.

"But ... how many times do I have to say it? Your mum didn't approach me about the videos. I hadn't got a clue that she was seeing another man, and why would I want to kill him?"

"You would if he threatened you as well. You know all about murder," Sarah said, scratching her arm nervously. "You've staged it in films."

"Yes. True. But let's not confuse fact and fiction. If this boyfriend was murdered and you say it was made to look like suicide, that requires skill. It's not easy to fool police pathologists, you know. You should be looking for a real expert."

Kelly plucked up enough courage to reply, "We don't believe you. Unless you've got an alibi for Thursday night."

The factory owner hesitated and then sneered at them. "As a

matter of fact, I have." Keeping his voice to a whisper, he explained, "I was on a set last Thursday, filming."

"The whole evening?"

"Yes."

"Well, we have information that you left early."

Warr's eyes opened wide with surprise. "You what?"

"You heard."

Recovering as if from a blow, he shrugged like a boxer pretending he hadn't been hurt. "I don't have to answer to you."

"No," Kelly replied, "but you'll have to answer to the police."

"You're going to tell them?"

The three Keatings nodded.

"You'll make fools of yourselves," Warr said to his accusers. "On Thursday, I went out for a meal – with a young lady acquaintance." He seemed proud of his liaison with her.

"Not The Seafood Spree," Sarah blurted out.

Mr Warr looked surprised at her comment. "No. A Chinese meal, actually."

"Well, you *would* say you were somewhere else with someone else, wouldn't you?" Sarah said, still hostile towards him.

"I wouldn't want to give the police her name, but I will if I have to – to clear my name."

"So you get a friend to swear blind that she was with you. Not very convincing."

"Look," Warr said, banging his fist on the table so that Evan's empty polystyrene cup fell over, "I'm not an unreasonable man. I can see why you think I might have … had it in for your mother. We weren't the best of friends. And you three are desperate to find someone to blame. But there's no need to get paranoid about it."

"We're not," Sarah declared. "It all fits and you deserve—"

"Just a minute," Warr interrupted. "It all fits, you say. But does it?" He suddenly looked pleased with himself. He adjusted his bright flowery tie to make his audience wait and wonder. "Your mum heard about the videos. That's what you claim. As a result, she came after my blood. But you're forgetting something. Did you tell her *I* made the videos?" Looking directly into Evan's face, he added, "Did you say to her, 'Trevor Warr did the filming'? I doubt it. Not if you valued your earnings from me. I'd hazard a guess that my name was never mentioned."

"I ... er..." Evan blushed.

"Well? Did you tell her?"

"I can't remember. It was nearly six months ago," Evan muttered.

"You'd better think about it, my lad," Warr said, rising to his feet and wiping his hands together as if to remove the grime of the market-place. "Because if you didn't tell her, she'd hardly come pounding on my door. She wouldn't know it was me. And", he added, wagging a finger unpleasantly, "before I leave you with that thought, rest assured that if any of you talk to the police about this, or about my video work, you'll regret it." He swanked away from the table and vanished among the mass of bargain hunters.

Kelly and Sarah sat stunned, staring at Evan, with the same word on their lips. "Well?"

Evan looked at them and shook his head. "I don't think I did ... but she heard about the video at work. Whoever told her might have known Warr was behind it."

His sisters looked doubtful but were keen to clutch at straws. Sarah nodded and murmured, "Possibly."

"Yes," Kelly agreed. "Or we might have got carried away a bit because – let's face it – we don't like him because he exploits people like Evan and John."

"But there's evidence as well," Sarah objected.

"True, but he doesn't look the green jumper type."

"I wouldn't put it past him to have a green suit," Sarah retorted.

Kelly sighed. "I reckon we've got to think again. He might have done it but – like Pete the bookie – we'll have to park the idea for a bit. Unless we get any more info." They got up and trudged dismally out of the maze.

On the way home, Kelly kept thinking about something that Warr had said to them: "You should be looking for a real expert." His words haunted her. Perhaps he had a point, she thought. And on her list of suspects, she had only one expert in police work.

10

It was Faye who provided Kelly with some unexpected clues. At her request, they met at the Keatings' house again on Saturday afternoon. Evan was absorbed in the sport on television and baby James tottered round the room, investigating everything, falling over and screaming at regular intervals. Clive Keating was minding the shop and Sarah, conscious that she'd been neglecting her boyfriend lately, was out with Matt.

"That photo you showed us," Faye said.

"Yes?" Kelly replied, trying to goad a more useful statement from her guest.

"Well, it's been on my mind," she began. "You know I said there was someone at work who looked a bit like the fella in your picture? Roger. I took more notice of him after I seen you last and ... er ... outside the yard, I think Roger met the chap in the photo."

Kelly sat erect and attentive and Evan turned his head away from the television. Then James tripped over a chair leg and cried as if his entire world had been shattered. Kelly had to wait till his mother had picked him up and calmed him down before the conversation could be resumed.

"I seen him in a car. Well, he was standing by it. Waiting, at going home time, to pick up Roger. When I seen them together, they looked like brothers. Perhaps they are."

Trying not to get too excited, Kelly asked, "Was it a Peugeot? Blue?"

"I didn't notice it much. It could've been. But, yeah, it was blue."

"What about this Roger? What does he do?" Kelly queried, with the fingers of both hands crossed.

"He's one of the builders."

"And did he work on the extension to the video factory?"

Faye turned her attention momentarily to James. "Better? Want to go walkies again?" She lifted him down to the floor. Looking at Kelly, she answered, "Yes. Roger would've done that job."

Kelly's sigh was almost audible. She uncrossed her fingers. Suddenly, Pete was back in the frame in a big way. He certainly would have had a motive if her mum had tried to intervene in his gambling scam. Now, it transpired that, through his brother, he would have had the knowledge to dispose of her body at the building site. He looked like a strong suspect.

There was something else that Kelly had been considering and it was possible that Faye might be able to throw some light on it. "At Henderson's," she questioned, "do you ever hear of videos doing the rounds?"

"Videos?"

"Yes," Kelly responded. "Nothing too nasty. Just cheap stuff. Hauntings and horror."

"Well," Faye said, "you do hear of all sorts going round the men."

"Do you know where they come from? The videos, that is."

"Come away, darling," Faye said to James. "Evan's trying to watch that. Yes, good boy." Addressing Kelly again, she answered, "It's ... er ... rumoured they're made not a million miles away from here."

Kelly tried to extract more from her. "Where exactly?"

Faye kept her gaze on her son as she spoke. "The bloke at the video factory. He's supposed to be behind them, according to the rumours."

"Interesting," Kelly responded. "I just wanted to know what Mum might have heard on the grapevine. Do you think she would've known that as well?"

Faye shrugged. "Well, I heard, so I guess she might have."

Kelly nodded slowly and exchanged a knowing glance with Evan. Warr could have been lying when he said that their mother hadn't pestered him. And if she knew that he'd made the videos, she could have told George McCormick in the restaurant. Then, after her disappearance, he might have gone looking for evidence against Warr. That could be how he got himself killed.

*   *   *

Later, when Faye and James had left, Kelly managed to prise her brother's attention away from the football results. "I've been thinking," she told him. "Mum was in The Seafood Spree with McCormick. We have the manager's word on that. As we don't think he killed her, she was safe then. Yes? At some point that evening, though, she got into the hands of the killer. Right? But how?"

"What are you getting at?"

"When and where did she leave McCormick? From that moment she was vulnerable to attack. So, when did she stop being with McCormick and become a victim of ... whoever?"

"How should I know?" Evan wasn't in the best of moods. He really wanted to watch the football results and not act as the great detective's sounding board. Yet the television coverage only reminded him that he was missing out on the real excitement at Revolvers. Often, when a result was announced, he thought to himself, I could have predicted that. I'd have been twenty quid up by now. His fingernails were taking extra punishment as his system reacted to emptiness.

Kelly continued her reasoning. "Mum was a woman. I doubt if McCormick would just let her make her own way home – or wherever she was going. He'd give her a lift. But if she was coming home..."

Evan showed some interest by mumbling, "Yes?"

"Well, he wouldn't give her a lift to the front door, would he? They might have been seen by Dad. So, he'd have dropped her round the corner or something."

"Yeah. Possibly. That's if she *was* coming home."

"I know. Let's assume that she was for now. The police asked everyone around here if they'd seen anything. No one reported a struggle on the street or someone yelling for help, so, if she was picked up by the killer near here, she didn't create a stir in the process."

Evan looked away from the TV screen for longer this time. "You're saying she was whisked away by someone she knew. Or she came home and Dad..."

"Let's not think about what Dad might have done. I can't imagine..." She shook her head. "No. But if your Pete had tried to drag her away, surely she'd have created a fuss. Someone would have noticed something. She'd seen Warr before, though. He might have enticed her into his car without her raising the alarm. And..."

"And?"

"Recently, I've been thinking about Vicky McCormick."

"I doubt if Mum knew her."

"No," Kelly agreed. "But two women are less likely to fight on the street. Mum wouldn't have been so wary of another woman."

"And Mrs McCormick could have played the police officer, anyway," Evan suggested. "Got out of an unmarked car, flashed her identity card, and asked Mum to get into the car with her. 'I'm afraid your husband's been in an accident, Mrs Keating. Please come with me. I'll take you to him.' That sort of thing."

"Yes! You're a genius, Evan, when you put your mind to it. She might even have been driving the family Peugeot. That would tie in with what we know. You might have got it."

"And", he added scornfully, "we might be barking up the wrong tree altogether. Perhaps she wasn't on her way home at all." He turned back to the television to watch some more sports news.

Wandering out of the room, Kelly murmured to herself, "Maybe. I have a hunch, though. I'm certain Vicky McCormick could make murder look like suicide. But", she wondered, "how do you investigate a police officer?"

Yet it wasn't just Vicky McCormick. Kelly's chief suspects still included Trevor Warr and Pete the bookie. All three of them had a connection with the building site and she could easily envisage a different motive for each of them. It surprised her how many people might have wanted to be rid of her mother. Was she such an ogre? To Kelly, she was just a normal mother who'd got bored with her life and her marriage. Taking on a job and a local businessman over planning permission had apparently not been enough to spice up her life – she'd needed a lover to do that.

The Keatings' situation had hardly been novel. Several of Kelly's friends at school were trying to cope with broken families. She'd been one of the few, though, with a mother who'd strayed; mothers were usually the devoted victims of wayward fathers. Now Kelly was unique amongst her friends; she was the only daughter of a murder victim. Even worse, she had inherited enough of her mum's obstinacy to want to solve the crime.

When Sarah returned, her boyfriend Matt was with her. He was a big lad with cropped hair, polite but uncomfortable in Mr Keating's presence. Despite being brash and outgoing, he had not yet disgraced himself in front of Sarah's father so Mr Keating tolerated him.

As soon as he sat down Matt struck up a conversation with Evan as if he were under instructions to do so. "Are you still practising ball skills?" he asked.

Evan shrugged in reply.

"The Scorpions could do with more of that."

"Oh?" Evan responded. "Is the team in trouble?"

"No. Fifth in the league. Not bad. We can keep goals out but we can't score. That's the problem. We were wondering if—"

"No," Evan put in quickly. "I'd rather not."

"OK." Matt's tone suggested that he'd kept his side of a deal but wasn't too upset by failure. He glanced at Sarah and shrugged.

Keen to follow up her new evidence, Kelly asked her sister how much she'd told Matt about the deaths.

"I don't keep any secrets from him," Sarah told her, patting Matt on the leg. "He might as well know what he's mixed up in."

Now that she felt free to talk in Matt's presence, Kelly outlined her conversation with Faye. Then she tried to get her brother and sister to agree on a way forward. "First," she proposed, "we've got to chase up our number one suspect."

"Who's that?" Sarah queried.

"Who do *you* think?" Kelly replied.

"Warr," she answered without hesitating.

"Mmm. Maybe. But I'm beginning to wonder about Vicky McCormick. What do you think, Evan?"

Evan pondered on it for a moment, then said, "I'll go with McCormick."

"Why?" Sarah retorted. Clearly she'd expected Evan to support her own choice. "You said you thought Warr had done it."

"Well, if you must know the truth," Evan muttered, staring at his own feet, "I'd just rather it wasn't Pete or Mr Warr. If either of them killed Mum, it'd be my fault. It was because of me that Mum might have tangled with them."

Both sisters looked sympathetically at him but he didn't see their concern.

"OK," Kelly said. "I can understand that."

"But we can *do* something about Warr. We could take a look at the factory for clues or try and find this woman he said he was seeing that Thursday night. See if she backs up his story. Vicky McCormick's a real problem," Sarah objected. "We don't know anything about her. Where does she live? I bet police officers don't put themselves in the phone book. How do we get to her without going to the police?"

"You're right," Kelly answered. "We don't know anything about her, but it's not such a problem because we can find out about *Mr* McCormick instead. I imagine Faye can put her finger on his telephone number and address. They'll be on file at Henderson's. Then we can go and talk to her; exchange sympathies now we have a bereavement in common; see how she reacts."

"Maybe," Sarah mused. "But I still think Warr's more ... you know."

"If I can make a suggestion," Matt put in, "you don't have to just go after your number one. There are four of us and three suspects. We could split up. Sarah and me, we could check out Warr's alibi. You could hunt down this policewoman, and Evan could follow up the bookie."

"Well, I'm not sure about Evan going after Pete," Sarah remarked, alarmed by the suggestion.

"Hang on," Kelly pronounced. "He might have a point. It doesn't have to be dangerous. Look," she said, "you don't have to go after Pete himself, Evan. You've just got to mix with your mates and find out if any of them saw Pete a week last Thursday. If so, when and where. We can rule him out if he was doing business that night. Can you do that? Can you do it without getting tangled up in more gambling? I don't want you to do it if you're going to get hooked again."

"No, I'll do it," Evan agreed. "And I won't get involved again."

Kelly smiled at her brother. She believed him. "And you two," she said to Matt and Sarah, "you don't have to do anything risky either. In fact, I suggest you go out for a meal tonight instead of following Warr around. Maybe even three meals."

"What are you on about, Kelly?" her sister probed.

"Remember, Warr said he went for a Chinese that Thursday. I think there are three Chinese restaurants in town. He's bound to have reserved a table for two. He's that type. Wouldn't turn up on spec. So all you've got to do is to see their booking lists for that night. Go into all the restaurants, try to make a booking, and sneak a look at the list."

"All right," Sarah agreed, glancing at Matt. "We'll give it a go."

"That only leaves you," Evan said to Kelly in a rare display of concern for one of his sisters. "Seeing Vicky McCormick could be dangerous if…"

"Yes, but I'll make sure I tell her straight away that you three know all about my visit. Then she can't do anything to me, because you'd go to the police immediately."

The four of them accepted their tasks and, with a renewed sense of excitement and trepidation, went their separate ways.

Kelly persuaded Faye to sneak into work that same evening to look up the McCormicks' address. Once she knew where the policewoman lived, Kelly decided to pay her a visit straight away. She was eager to get it over with.

She expected the house to be elaborate. It wasn't. It was one of a terrace of big, old and untidy houses – ideal homes for those with time to dedicate to their upkeep. Evidently the McCormicks did not have much spare time.

At the front door, Vicky was taken aback. She hesitated, then said, "You're the Keating girl. Kelly."

"Yes. Can I have a talk with you?"

Vicky glanced up and down the street before she replied. "Er … I suppose so. Come on in." She stood to one side to allow her guest to enter the dingy hall that ran the length of the house. She guided Kelly into the front room – a lounge containing bookshelves, a midi hi-fi system, a huge pile of cassette tapes, a couple of desks and a computer. Presumably, this was the machine on which McCormick's killer had left the note. There was also a photograph of the McCormicks standing together by a lake in happier times.

The police officer wasn't dressed in black but there was an air of sadness about her. Now that she was on her own, the big old house must seem eerie and forsaken. She cut a forlorn figure but, Kelly wondered, was her sorrow faked?

Vicky inquired how Kelly had found out her address, then she asked, "Why have you come?"

"I spoke to Evan and Sarah about it. We thought I should. Because of ... your husband and my mum. We have something in common now, don't we?"

"Apparently so," Vicky replied guardedly.

They sat opposite each other and looked blankly at one another for a few seconds.

"I need to know who I'm speaking to," Kelly began hesitantly. "Sergeant McCormick the police officer or Vicky McCormick the wife and ordinary person."

"Which would you rather talk to?"

"The wife of George McCormick."

"Well," Vicky said with a weak and wry smile, "I *am* on leave for a few days yet. Besides, if you want to talk about your mum and George, you can. It's a closed matter as far as we're concerned. My superior has tidied it up."

"OK," Kelly replied. "I'm sorry about your husband. It's awful. But ... do you believe Mr Tatton's version of events?"

Vicky stood up and turned away, lost in thought. When she looked again at Kelly, her eyes were red. In a fragile voice, she said, "I'll put the kettle on. Fancy a coffee?"

"OK. Please."

While Vicky was out of the room, curiosity drove Kelly to examine the stack of cassettes. Each box was labelled with its contents – classical music – and the spine of each case bore the date of recording. They were organized in chronological order. She noted that the most recent tape bore the index, "St Petersburg Philharmonic: Sibelius Violin Concerto in D minor; Rachmaninov Symphonic Dances. BBC Radio 3." It bore the date of Thursday before last. An idea formed in her mind and she scanned back through the pile of tapes recorded last year. Eventually, she spotted what she wanted. It was there! One cassette had been logged on the thirteenth of October. "Ulster Orchestra: Schubert Symphony No. 5; Mozart Piano Concerto No. 12 in A; Schubert Symphony No. 6."

"George's collection," Vicky explained as she came back into the room with a couple of steaming mugs. "Not my thing, but he was mad on classical music. If he'd been here now the room would be throbbing with Beethoven or something." She looked haggard as she spoke. She probably loathed his obsession when he was alive and now lamented its absence.

Before taking the mug, Kelly stole a glance at the cassette recorder. It was a simple model and did not seem to have a facility for automatic recording at a pre-set time. Joining Vicky in the centre of the room, she clasped the mug. "Smells good," she said. "Thanks." She sat down again.

Vicky sipped her coffee and murmured, "Do I agree with the DCI's conclusion?" Gazing straight at her guest, she answered, "I don't have a reason not to. Like you, I'm sorry as well. Sorry about your mum. And as far as George was concerned, we still loved each other, you know, but we tended to lead separate lives. I regret that now. I didn't know he'd taken up with your mum, but it didn't come as much of a shock. It's no great surprise to me that he got mad when she rejected him, either. He was like that, I'm afraid. Now it's all over, I'm just trying to forget it. I've got to get on with my life; there's not much else I can do. Wipe the slate clean and start again. I don't want to see it raked over."

Kelly thought she detected a hint of threat in Vicky's voice, but she wasn't sure. "I just thought it might help us both to come to terms with it if we had a chat," she said.

Vicky looked piercingly at her guest. "Is that all?" Steeling herself, she added, "You don't believe that George killed your mother and then himself."

It wasn't obvious to Kelly whether Vicky had made a statement or asked a question. In reply, she said, "You can't help wondering."

"Wondering what?" Vicky leaned forward. "It's all right; the case won't be reopened. You can say what you like."

Kelly took a gulp of coffee. Sooner or later she had to come to the point. She couldn't spend the afternoon skirting uselessly around it. "What if Mum *didn't* reject him?"

Without noticing it, Vicky slipped into her role of police officer. "You think someone else killed your mum?"

"And then maybe your husband."

Vicky shook her head. "What's your evidence?"

"We haven't got any. It's just…"

"Speculation?" Vicky suggested.

"Yes," Kelly agreed. Plucking up courage, she asked, "How did he die?"

"Drug overdose. He'd been on sleeping pills for some months. He took the lot."

"So, someone could have forced him to swallow them. The suicide could have been faked. Yes?"

"I can't disprove that," Vicky admitted. She shuffled in her seat and then continued, "It'd take some proving, though."

"When did he … er … you know?"

"He died at nine thirty. Pathology could be reasonably precise," she reported. "Besides, the time of his suicide note was recorded automatically by the computer. It was entered at five past nine." She let out a long weary sigh. "It's the police officer in me talking again. I want to forget the whole episode but … it rubs off on you, police work. It's not a job, it's a way of thinking. And it doesn't leave a lot of time for family life. Criminals don't keep a nine-to-five schedule, I'm afraid. Call-outs round the clock. Not ideal for family life and certainly not for having children. He'd have loved kids, but… Don't get a job in the police force, Kelly. It's not worth it."

If Vicky McCormick was an actress, she was a good one. But Kelly already knew that. If she'd committed two murders, her performance during the investigation was brilliant. It would have to be. Any murderer who wasn't a good actor simply got caught.

Kelly wound up the visit as soon as she could. She thought she wasn't going to learn any more from Vicky, and besides, she was keen to follow up the two solid facts that she had learned.

Matt was in his element. He strode into The Jade Garden with Sarah in his wake, with all the assurance of a man with an American Express Gold Card.

"Table for two," he told the receptionist. "Booked earlier. The name's Jones. Vincent Jones."

The little man on the desk ran his finger twice down the booking list, mumbling to himself, "Mr Jones." Eventually, he looked up apologetically. "I'm sorry, sir. Did you make the reservation today?"

Matt gave a groan. "Yesterday. I called yesterday to reserve a table for tonight. In the name of Jones."

The receptionist flicked the pages, clearly at a loss. "I'm sorry, sir," he repeated. "There seems to be some sort of mistake."

"Look," Sarah put in nervously. "I'm sorry about this, but can you show me to the ladies' room while you sort it out?"

"Certainly," the man said, eager to prove that there was some-thing he could do correctly.

As soon as the receptionist turned his back, Matt delved into the pages of the book of reservations. A week ago on Thursday – there it was. A reservation for two, listed as Mr and Mrs Warr, nine thirty. There was a tick beside the name. Matt took it to mean that the couple had turned up for their meal.

Returning to Matt, the receptionist said to him, "Sir, I've checked with the manager and I think we can accommodate you – to make up for our error. If you could just wait here a moment."

Scanning the menu, Matt took fright. The prices were out of his league. When Sarah returned he nodded to indicate that he had the information they needed. He also indicated the price of the meals. Sarah gulped. "Leave it to me," Matt said with a wicked glint in his eye.

When their host returned, Matt said to him, "It's a pity about this booking problem. I'd heard that The Mandarin was an excellent establishment."

The man gawped for a second, then replied indignantly, "Sir, this is The Jade Garden!"

"Oh! Sorry," Matt returned. "Wrong place."

The receptionist was still agape as Matt took Sarah's arm and led her swiftly out of the restaurant.

11

The Keatings got together with Matt after his match on Sunday afternoon, to compare notes. They knew that McCormick had died on the Thursday before last some time after nine o'clock. By car, the Chinese restaurant was probably fifteen minutes away from George McCormick's place. Trevor Warr could have left his studio at about eight thirty, driven to McCormick's house, committed a devious murder, then shot off to collect his young woman and arrive at The Jade Garden for nine thirty. It was possible, but not very likely.

Still keen not to dismiss her number one suspect, Sarah commented, "We don't know that he got to the restaurant on time. He could have been late. It may not have been such a rush."

"No," Kelly agreed. "But, as alibis go, it's not bad. That'd be a busy night by anyone's standards."

Evan had kept a low profile at Revolvers but had still managed to talk to a few of Pete's customers. One of the lads and a girl remembered doing business with him on the Thursday night of the murder. Both were uncertain about the time. "They're more worried about who's crossing the finishing line than checking the time," Evan explained. "One said he thought it was at least ten because he'd already had a few drinks at a club. But Laura – she's well addicted to it. She said she sold Pete her watch. It was a present from her dad, worth fifty quid at least. Pete gave her a fiver for it. The gambling bug gets you like that. And as soon as she's sold everything she's got, she'll start nicking things. She probably already has. Anyway," he declared, "she thinks the watch said twenty past nine when she handed it over. If that's right, Pete would never have got from McCormick's place to Revolvers that fast. So I reckon he's off the hit list."

"Yes," Kelly agreed. "If we can rely on this Laura."

"What about you, Kelly?" Sarah put in. "What's the verdict on Vicky McCormick?"

Kelly beamed like a messenger with good news. "Well, I found out some really useful stuff. The trouble is, I still don't know about the woman herself. She's either innocent or she's guilty and a cracking liar. Anyway," she continued, "McCormick died after an overdose of sleeping pills. If you believe police things on telly, it's hard to shoot or stab someone and make it look like suicide, but anyone could have stuffed him full of his own pills. The murderer could have looked in the bathroom cabinet or wherever and seen the bottles with his name on them. Ideal."

"The one who'd be bound to know where they were is his wife," Matt remarked.

"True," Kelly responded. "She didn't act like I imagine a murderer would, but I suppose murderers don't."

"As you said, she could be a cracking actress."

Kelly shrugged. "Anyway, I think I've got proof that he didn't commit suicide. Most nights, from seven thirty to nine, Radio 3 has a programme on classical music. Famous orchestras going through their paces. I looked it up in old newspapers. Thursday last week, George McCormick recorded it."

"So?"

"No one records a programme then kills themselves. Why bother with a tape if you're never going to hear anything again?" Kelly glanced at her audience and noted, with pleasure, their unspoken accord. "And that's not all. He had another cassette recorded on the thirteenth of October last year. That programme went out in the same slot as well. I checked by phoning the BBC in London. Seven thirty to nine." Kelly stressed the time, then stopped talking to let the information sink in.

"But he was—"

"It doesn't mean anything," Evan objected. "He could have been miles away at the time. He could have used a timer switch."

Kelly grinned at her own foresight. "No," she retorted. "He didn't have one. I checked. It doesn't mean he was at home every minute from seven thirty till nine, but he must have been there at seven thirty."

"He was supposed to have left The Seafood Spree at seven

thirty, according to Tatton," Sarah reminded them.

"Maybe he missed the first part of the concert," Evan suggested.

"Possibly," Kelly replied, "but I don't think so. The cassette started with Schubert's Symphony No. 5 and the BBC told me that was the first piece on the programme."

"This is ridiculous," Sarah put in. "We know he was in the seafood place."

"Maybe the owner – Perriman – didn't get the time right," Kelly suggested. "That's one explanation. But even if he was half an hour out, McCormick would still be pushed to bring Mum back – if he did – then drive home in time for the programme. There *is* another explanation, though."

"What's that?" Sarah queried.

"He wasn't in the restaurant."

"Hang on!" Sarah uttered. "The owner identified him."

"But his first description was a bit wide of the mark, if you remember what Tatton said. Perriman may have made a mistake. Maybe Mum was with someone who looks like George McCormick."

Trying to lighten the mood a bit, Matt said, "That probably rules out Vicky McCormick."

Kelly ignored the humour. "I saw a photo of him with his wife in his house. He looked tall. Judging by her height, I'd say he was six foot or thereabouts. With very dark hair. Almost black."

"That's what I told the police," Evan mentioned. "It certainly rules out Pete. And Mr Warr. He's too short and hasn't got enough hair. I haven't seen anyone who looks like McCormick."

"Henderson's got that beard, so he's not our man," Sarah commented.

"I don't know," Evan returned. "A beard isn't a permanent fixture. He may not have had it last October."

"He did," Kelly confirmed. "I remember Mum used to joke about the boss's big beard."

"What about your dad? He's nearly six foot, I should think, and he's got black hair," Matt observed.

None of the Keatings replied immediately. It seemed too preposterous. Eventually, Kelly said, "No. There's a resemblance, I grant you, but it couldn't be. He'd be in the shop at that time on a Friday. He said so. And he wouldn't lie about taking his own wife out for a meal. Why should he?"

"Only trying to help," Matt rejoined.

"The whole thing's a puzzle," Kelly concluded. "And we don't even know if the man she had a meal with is the one who killed her. It's just a guess."

The others sighed. There was almost too much to contemplate.

"No one said this detective stuff was easy!" Kelly remarked. She seemed to be enjoying the challenge.

That night, Kelly examined her list of suspects again. Dad and Evan still occupied the top slots. Even after her findings so far, she had no good reason to discount either of them, but she was convinced that Evan was innocent. He wouldn't be throwing himself into the investigation so whole- heartedly if he had something to hide. Next came Trevor Warr. He'd have to be fleet-footed to be a serious suspect now. Eric Henderson? He was the only one on the list not known to have clashed with her mum. She worked for him and she had one of his envelopes in her handbag when she was killed, but so what? Kelly couldn't imagine a motive. Vicky McCormick, police officer and Oscar winner? "Perhaps," Kelly mumbled to herself. "She was certainly keen to keep the case closed." Pete the bookie? According to Evan, he knew all about computers. He could have organized the fake suicide note on McCormick's computer. But lots of people worked with computers and Pete seemed to have an alibi for the night Mr McCormick died.

It struck Kelly for the first time that she had assumed that McCormick's and her mum's murders had been committed by the same person. Why? Because they were too closely linked to be separate issues. Too much of a coincidence. "It's a good assumption," she deduced. "At least, I think it is."

Glancing at the list of clues, she realized that she'd made some progress. She could explain the note on Dinner Date in the handbag. The topic of Evan's argument had finally come out into the open. But the Peugeot ... "Forget it," she mumbled. "Mum had been in a Peugeot shortly before she died. Doubt if it was Pete's or Mr Warr's. So, she'd been in McCormick's car. No great surprise. But if it was on the evening of the seafood meal, it would implicate Vicky McCormick. The trouble is, there's no way of telling. Then there's the green jumper. Same problem. Could be anyone's. She'd probably come into contact with Evan's that same morning." One way or another, all of her suspects were familiar with the building site. "Vicky McCormick would have known about it through her husband." It left the poor description of her mum's dinner companion. "Why on earth did Perriman make a mistake?" She shook her head in frustration.

Matt was right, of course. It was uncomfortable to have to admit it, and she had only her memory of a photograph to rely on, but her father *could* be mistaken for George McCormick in poor lighting by someone who knew neither of them well. "Which", Kelly reminded herself, "was exactly how Perriman had seen one of them." She couldn't imagine, though, why her dad should shut up shop early, take Mum out for a meal, and then deny that it had happened. It made no sense to her. Unless … unless he had some reason to distance himself from her that evening. The thought made her shudder so she tried to shut it out of her mind by changing direction.

If George McCormick hadn't been with Kelly's mother on Friday the thirteenth, the long gap between murders made more sense. Kelly fancied that McCormick would have undertaken quiet investigations into his lover's disappearance. They would have taken time if he'd got no information from her that day. He might not have known where to start. Rather like us, Kelly thought. She didn't even consider how they were going to avoid the same fate as McCormick if they ever did catch up with the villain.

She added what she now knew about the timing of both crimes to her list. It didn't cast any new light on the circumstances.

The facts were still swimming round her brain like tireless goldfish in a bowl when she went to bed.

12

After a hard day's work in his shop, Clive Keating liked to relax in front of the television. Not that he saw a great number of programmes. Some time after the news, his eyelids would droop and he would become increasingly drowsy until his mouth opened and his head lolled. When Barbara Keating had been in the house, she'd often gone unnoticed in the evenings as well. This Monday's batch of repeats was enough to send a hyperactive child off to sleep, but even so, he wasn't snoozing. The television was on but he was simply lost in thought, his gaze fixed on the coffee table to the side.

The police had returned his wife's property. Her dishevelled handbag now sat on the table like a sad, unwanted relic, and he stared at it from a distance, tears blurring his eyes.

Evan had been given the task of quizzing his dad about his movements on the night McCormick had been murdered. He wasn't looking forward to it. Now, surveying the scene in the living room, he was put off altogether. Something told him it wasn't the time to tease information from his dad.

"Oh," he muttered. "Mum's handbag."

His dad sniffed and replied, "I didn't want it, but they didn't give me a choice. They shoved it straight into my hands. Your mum's stuff." He exhaled loudly.

"Shall I take care of it?" Evan volunteered.

Mr Keating looked up at his son and nodded. "Yes," he answered. "You put it with the rest of her things."

For the last six months, Clive Keating had acted as if his wife were simply on an extended holiday. He'd not thrown out any of her belongings. He'd occupied only half of his own bedroom. It seemed that he had expected her back any day. Or perhaps he'd wanted to give that impression. None of his children had believed that one day she'd walk through the door and carry on as if nothing had happened. But maybe it had been too painful or too incriminating for their father to excise her from his life.

He shook his head then added, "There's something else. They said they can release the body now they've finished all the paperwork."

"The body? What are we supposed to do...?" Evan stopped himself as he realized that he was about to ask a stupid question.

His father answered him anyway. "Give her a proper funeral."

"Yes," Evan responded. "Of course."

When Evan prised open the handbag in his bedroom, a small cloud of white dust blew into the air. It was like exposing an ancient tomb. Inside, the artefacts were all individually wrapped in plastic wallets. Presumably the police had sealed them like that and hadn't bothered to take them out again before returning the handbag.

Evan set about removing the articles one by one and extracting them from their packaging: a purse containing a modest amount of money, a couple of credit cards and her driving licence; various items of make-up; the infamous betting slip; a ring with a key to the house, a car key and another small key; a wad of tissues; a comb and a Biro; the envelope that Tatton had already queried, its postmark so smudged that Evan couldn't even tell where it had come from; a small mirror and an emery nail file. Nothing remarkable.

His bed littered with his mum's meagre possessions, he suddenly felt depressed. He never wanted to see her corrupt body again, so sitting among her things was the closest he'd ever get to her now. He felt hollow. He didn't blame himself entirely for the fact that she was dissatisfied with her humdrum life but, just by being her son, he had contributed to the millstone around her neck. Ironically, when he'd added excitement to her life by getting involved with crooks, that life had been cut short. If the dead still had desires, she'd probably now prefer the role of bored wife and mother.

He raked through the contents of her handbag again, hoping she had left a clue, but the only hopeful item was the keyring. What did the small key unlock? Evan didn't know.

After proving his expertise at the Chinese restaurant, Matt had taken Sarah to The Seafood Spree to try his luck with a photograph of her father. It was the most recent picture they could find, and showed him and his wife together.

Sarah hadn't dared to go into the seafood restaurant after Mr Perriman's display of impatience last time. Thinking that Matt would stand a better chance of success on his own, she'd lingered outside and waited for him to do the business. He wasn't exactly booted out into the street, but he didn't get a very warm reception. Mr Perriman had glanced suspiciously at the photograph of the Keatings, recognized Sarah's mum, denied ever seeing her dad, then ordered Matt to leave. As they'd walked away, Sarah had peeped over her shoulder to see him standing in the window of his restaurant scowling at them.

Kelly had visited Faye in an attempt to squeeze yet more facts out of her. Despite her prompting, Faye couldn't remember hearing any rumours that Eric Henderson and Barbara Keating had had disagreements. Kelly had also asked if George McCormick had behaved differently during the period between the discovery of her mother's body and his "suicide". Faye hadn't noticed anything particularly strange. "He came into the office a few times – maybe more than normal – and took away papers and computer disks," she'd reported, "but there's not much new in that."

Back at home, as soon as Evan showed Kelly the small key, she identified it. "It's either her jewellery box or vanity case. Or maybe her briefcase." Excitedly, she added, "You don't think she hid something in it, do you? Something that'll tell us what happened?"

Sarah shrugged but Matt answered, "No. That'd be too easy."

"Only one way to find out," Kelly murmured. "I suggest you go downstairs, Sarah, and keep Dad occupied. Evan and I can slip into their bedroom and try it out."

"All right," Sarah replied, both pleased and disappointed to be left out of the real action.

Kelly and Evan tiptoed into their parents' bedroom. It reminded Kelly of jaunts on Christmas Eves of years ago when, as an over-excited and naughty girl, she would sneak downstairs to take a premature peek at her presents under the tree. In their mother's half of the bedroom, it also seemed appropriate to whisper and make hardly a sound. Respect demanded it.

"Here's the briefcase," Kelly breathed. She was about to extract it from the gap between her mum's wardrobe and her unused bedside cabinet when she groaned and left it to gather yet more dust. "No key'll fit that," she said. "It's got a combination lock. Let's try her vanity case. Over here. See, it *has* got a lock."

Evan tried the key but it didn't fit. "That's not it," he said in a hushed voice.

"Oh," Kelly murmured in disappointment. Treading softly towards the dressing table that had remained undisturbed for six months, she murmured, "Try this." The jewellery box had a layer of dust on it. "I think it's a safe bet that no one else has checked it out," Kelly muttered as she blew across the lid, producing a small puff of dirt. She handed the box over to Evan and pointed to the brass clasp.

"If there's a clue in here," Evan whispered, "it must be small." The key slotted into the lock and, after a couple of attempts, it turned and the clasp sprang upwards. Evan smiled and gave the box back to Kelly. It didn't seem right for him to forage in his mother's jewellery.

In silence, Kelly emptied the box, item by item, on to the dressing table. Familiar earrings and brooches tumbled out. There were two lockets. One contained a tiny photo of their dad, the other bore a picture of George McCormick. "No wonder she kept this under lock and key," Kelly commented softly.

"Yes. Let's hope Dad didn't see it. If he did, he'd have good reason to ... Well, let's hope he didn't."

Kelly took the locket in her palm and examined it closely. On the back, it was engraved. Her eyes widened as she read, "Happy birthday. Love, G.M."

"Her birthday was the tenth of October so he must have given it to her just before she died," Evan mumbled. "You don't think Dad spotted it, do you?"

"No idea," Kelly answered. "But perhaps she *has* left us a clue." She looked dejected as she said it. Unwillingly, she was trying to come to terms with the fact that her own father had become a serious suspect.

They cleared up noiselessly, replacing everything in the jewellery box, locked it again and left the room as quickly as they could.

"Hey, Dad," Kelly said, bringing her father back from the edge of sleep on Tuesday evening. "Made a mug of tea for you."

"Oh," her dad murmured. He wiped his eyes, sighed and, a little more awake, took the mug. "Thanks. Thanks very much. Do you want to borrow the car again?"

Kelly laughed. "No. I was in the kitchen feeling thirsty and made one for you as well." Actually, she had also been sieving through the television pages of the stack of old newspapers tucked away in a corner of the pantry. "There's something you can do for me, though," she added. "Cast your mind back to Thursday, a couple of weeks ago. You know, the night before we had that last visit from Inspector Tatton."

"Yes?" he queried, glancing at her suspiciously.

"Well, one of the girls at school videoed the new Bond film that night. She's invited me round to see it. Says it's great. But I'm not that bothered, unless it's really good. It started at nine, ITV, so you'd have got back in time for it – or at least only missed a few minutes. Knowing you, a sucker for that sort of thing, I bet you watched it. Was it any good?"

Her dad thought for a moment. "Thursday, you say?" He took a sip of tea, then said, "Yes, you're right, it was on. But ... er ... you should know what I'm like in front of the telly. It can't have been that good. I must have drifted off because I don't remember it."

"Not even a bit?"

He shrugged. "Bond jetting all around the globe, trying to stop a power-mad baddie. I think he was a drug dealer in that film. Lots of stunts. A chase with petrol tankers near the end."

Kelly smiled. "Sounds like a familiar plot. Perhaps I won't bother." She concentrated on her own drink of tea but she was thinking about her dad's reply. His description was vague enough to fit almost any Bond film. Perhaps he hadn't seen much of it at all. The only part he remembered distinctly was towards the end. That would be well after the time of McCormick's death.

Kelly was beginning to worry about her father. Had Mum's antics hurt him so much that he'd turned into a murderer? She hoped not. If she found proof of his guilt, she'd have to face a terrible dilemma. Should she keep quiet and let him get away with his crime of passion because he'd suffered enough? Or should she turn in her own father? She didn't want to have to make that decision. Yet she had worked out a method for checking her dad's movements that Thursday night. It would have to wait till this

Thursday evening, though. She thought that she could persuade Sarah and Matt to take on the task, and she hoped they'd be able to clear his name.

The telephone rang on Wednesday, before Clive Keating got home. Kelly answered it – she was alone in the house.

"Is that one of the Keating girls?"

"Yes, Kelly," she replied, her face crinkling into a frown.

"Kelly," the caller repeated. "Good."

Her ear froze to the phone as she listened. She had never had a threatening call before and its impact was like a sudden right hook to the head.

"Stop messing in things you don't understand," the muffled male voice whispered.

It was like receiving a call from a dim and distant world. Yet the whisper into her ear somehow made the caller seem alarmingly close. "Who is this?" she stammered.

"Never you mind. Just listen. It's over. You can't bring back your mum or McCormick, so let it be."

The more she heard and the more the horror of the situation was displaced by curiosity and reason, the more she realized that she could be listening to a woman. If so, the female caller was using a voice as low-pitched as possible to make herself sound like a man.

"No more prying. You don't want to end up—"

The voice broke off from its threat. Kelly could just make out footsteps in the background. She could tell that the person on the phone was still on the line but he or she was waiting. There was the characteristic sound of a door opening then closing with a crash. It could have been a shop door, Kelly thought with a sinking feeling. A newsagent's door. Desperately, she tried to find alternatives. It could have been a restaurant door, the door at a builder's yard or even at a police station.

The unearthly voice started again. "You don't want to end up like your mum."

Her face pale, Kelly swallowed.

"They'll be pouring concrete into the bridge over the canal soon. If you carry on sticking your nose in where it's not wanted, you'll end up propping up the road. Understand?"

"Yes," she mumbled.

"Good. Just do what I say. Back off."

The phone went dead.

Quaking, Kelly flopped into a chair. She closed her eyes and breathed deeply for a minute. The telephone call had shocked her but, once she'd recovered, it made her more determined. It could even be considered a good sign. She must be getting close to the killer. Obviously she'd have to be careful from now on, but she hadn't been put off the investigation. In fact, she had learned something. The caller knew all about another building site and, in following one of their recent leads, they were barking up the right tree. Although Eric Henderson would know the building site best, they hadn't hassled him at all. He could be in the clear. Much more likely was Vicky McCormick or ... But would her own father threaten her like that?

Kelly was pleased to have spared Sarah the phone call. It would have scared her sister silly. If Sarah had taken it, the investigation would have been abandoned by now. Kelly decided not to tell anyone about it. It was a risk, she realized, to keep it to herself, but it was difficult enough to track down a murderer without having to do it on her own because the others had been frightened off.

Evan had put his mother's handbag away in one of her drawers but he'd thrown away the betting slip and left out the envelope. It was lying around in his bedroom, waiting to be taken downstairs and stored with the rest of the charity collection. He grabbed it and went down to the living room, then hesitated before he slipped it into the bag of stamps. Every stamp in the polythene bag had been torn from an envelope. The one in his hand was the exception, the only complete envelope. Why bother to bring home a whole envelope when only the top right-hand corner was wanted? It was a waste of space in her handbag. Evan glanced inside the envelope to make sure his mum hadn't concealed a clue there. It was definitely empty. Turning it over, he examined the back. Nothing had been written on it. No murderer's name scrawled in blood. The address of Henderson's Builders on the front looked correct and unexceptional. Along the edge on the left-hand side someone, probably his mum, had written in small figures, "0101". Evan stared at it for a while then shrugged. "What's that?" he mumbled to himself. "The start of a phone number?" He didn't know and he had no way of finding out. It's probably nothing, he thought. Even so, he didn't put the envelope in the bag; he took it back upstairs to his bedroom.

Most of the people on Clive Keating's newspaper round came into the shop to pay their bills but a few, mainly the old folk, found it difficult to leave their houses. For these customers, Clive collected their newspaper money each Thursday evening. It would take an hour, from eight to nine o'clock normally. He was always thankful for volunteers to do the collection but would not let Evan or the girls do it on their own on dark nights. This Thursday, though, Sarah offered to take on the chore with Matt as bodyguard and her father accepted gratefully.

At one house, an old lady answered Sarah's knock and came to the door with the correct money already in her bony hand.

"Thanks, Mrs Hegarty," Sarah said as she took the cash and filled in the small receipt. "Dad was going to come," she said, "but he's busy. He can't always do it himself like he did last week. Kelly came round the week before, if I remember." She looked at the woman to see how she reacted.

Mrs Hegarty shook her head. "I don't think so, dear. It was Mr Keating who called two weeks ago, I'm sure. He's a good man, your pa. Always has time for a few words."

"I must have got it wrong," Sarah replied. "When did he call?"

"Oh, I never take notice of time. It doesn't do to watch clocks at my age. It's always about this time, though."

In the next street, Mr and Mrs Sweeney were more helpful. After Mr Sweeney had answered the door, his wife called from the sitting room, "Who is it?"

Mr Sweeney bellowed into the house, "Mr Newsagent's daughter, after the money." His wife must have been deaf. He went to get some cash.

Once he'd paid, Sarah asked him, "When's the best time for us to collect the money?"

"Now, love, and not when your father does, that's for sure. I sits down to watch the news and ... ding dong on the doorbell every Thursday. A right nuisance. When you does it you gets here just before nine. I reckon he natters too much on his way."

"More than likely. Did he come just after nine last week?"

"Yes. And the week before. And the week before that."

From inside, Mrs Sweeney bleated, "What's Mr Newsagent saying?"

"It's his daughter, Edie. She's ... er ... she's asking after your health." He grinned wickedly at Sarah. "It perks her up when people ask after her."

She returned his smile. "Well, thank you, Mr Sweeney. Thank you very much. We'll have to see what we can do about the timing in future."

Sarah hurried home with the news that her dad could be struck off the hit list. At the time of McCormick's murder, he was probably standing on Mr Sweeney's doorstep, keeping him from watching the start of the news.

"So," Kelly said, "Dad's out of it. That's a relief. And what's more, I think I can figure it out now." With her father off the hook, she could eliminate all of her chief suspects, apart from one.

"Oh?" Sarah responded. "Do tell us ordinary mortals."

"Well, like Dad, Pete the bookie and Mr Warr have both got alibis. Not perfect ones, but reasonable. Henderson's not a hot prospect—"

Evan interrupted. "Why not?" he demanded.

"No motive," Kelly answered. "And ... That's it, really – no motive." She still didn't want to tell them about the phone call from the harassed killer.

"Leaving?" Sarah quizzed.

"Detective Sergeant Vicky McCormick," Kelly announced. The policewoman with the deep voice, easily made to sound like a man's. "She's got the motive – and the Peugeot. She could've picked up Mum that night. On top of that, being in the police business, she wouldn't have much trouble faking her husband's suicide."

"What happened to the theory that it wasn't her husband in the restaurant with Mum?" Evan queried.

Kelly shrugged. "Perhaps Mr Perriman just made a mistake after all. He does see a lot of folk. It'd be easy to get confused."

Sarah and Evan gazed at their sister in silence. Eventually, Sarah said, "All right, but what do we do next?"

Kelly knew perfectly well what she was going to do next but, after the phone call, she didn't want to put anyone else at risk. "Not sure," she fibbed. "Let's think about it. It's Thursday now. We could tackle it at the weekend. Pool any ideas then. OK?"

The others nodded their agreement.

But Kelly's mind was made up. She would confront Vicky McCormick. It would have to be somewhere public, to make sure she'd be safe. The policewoman could hardly do a repeat performance in front of a crowd. With a wry smile, Kelly thought of the ideal place. Tomorrow, Friday 13th April, she'd meet Vicky at The Seafood Spree. It might bring back Vicky's memory of that night six months ago.

Kelly reminded herself of Vicky McCormick's telephone number from Faye's notes, then checked that no one was within hearing range and picked up the phone. It rang six times before Vicky's throaty voice came on the line. "Yes?"

Taking a deep breath, Kelly inquired, "Is that Mrs McCormick?"

"Yes. Who is it?"

Kelly identified herself and continued, "I think we should meet again, don't you?"

"I've already told you what I think," Vicky replied, clearly irritated. "The last thing I want is to resurrect it all. Back off, Kelly."

Kelly listened carefully. The voice was different from yesterday's, but that was being muffled deliberately. It could easily have been the same person. The accent was much the same. And, if Kelly remembered correctly, yesterday's caller had also told her to back off. "I know," Kelly responded uneasily. "But I think I need to see you once more. That should do it."

"And are you after me myself, or me the police officer?"

"You."

Sergeant McCormick sighed. "I really think you should stop messing..." She paused, then added, "But I expect your mind's made up."

"Yes."

Vicky relented. "OK. It's your decision. When and where?"

Kelly arranged to meet her the next evening at six o'clock in The Seafood Spree.

Just one last thing to do. She dialled the restaurant and announced herself to Mr Perriman. At first he sounded peeved. "Don't worry," she reassured him, "I just want to come for a meal this time."

"Really?"

"Yes. Tomorrow at about six."

Mr Perriman sounded less harsh. "Well, I can certainly accommodate you at that time. You don't need to book a table. Just come along."

Kelly put down the phone, feeling relieved. Yet she told herself that the serious business was only just beginning.

13

Kelly hesitated as she made for The Seafood Spree after school in the early evening of Friday the thirteenth. She had a few misgivings, she was nervous, but she was also determined. She was fifteen minutes ahead of schedule yet she did not linger for long. She strode along the streets towards the restaurant.

It was six thirty when the doorbell rang insistently. Only Sarah and Evan were at home and Evan got to the door first. Sarah flew down the stairs in case Matt had arrived. She stood behind Evan and her jaw dropped as the door opened to reveal Kelly's number one suspect, Vicky McCormick. Neither Evan nor Sarah said anything. They just waited for the policewoman to explain herself.

"It's Kelly," Vicky started. "She arranged to meet me at six in The Seafood Spree but she didn't turn up. Is she here?"

"She was meeting you?" Sarah queried over her brother's shoulder.

"Yes. She arranged it last night, by phone. Can I come in?"

"Just a minute," Evan objected, still blocking her way in. "Why was she seeing you?"

"I'm not sure. Something about your mum and my husband, I imagine."

"And you say she didn't turn up?" Sarah checked. Like her brother, she was thinking that it would be very easy for Vicky McCormick to claim that she hadn't seen Kelly. The truth could be much more serious. She began to fiddle with the pendant round her neck.

"That's right. I went to the restaurant. I was a bit late and Kelly wasn't there."

"Perhaps she'd left," Evan suggested. "Didn't want to wait."

"That's what I thought but Mr Perriman – the manager – hadn't seen her either. If she set out for the restaurant, she didn't get there. I got worried about her. Thought she might be here."

"No," Evan answered. "She could've forgotten. Maybe she's at some party. She likes parties."

"Kelly doesn't forget things," Sarah commented.

"Then I *am* worried," Vicky said. "I think you'd better come with me while I sort this out."

Evan glanced back at his sister. She was frowning. If this woman at the door had captured Kelly, she might be after both of them now. He turned to their visitor again and muttered, "This isn't official, is it?"

"You mean, is it police business?"

"The police always go around in twos. This isn't official."

"No," Vicky admitted. "But I think I'd better follow it up."

"Without us," Evan announced. He felt that the detective sergeant might be conning them. "If it's not proper business, you can't force us. We won't come."

Vicky McCormick looked surprised and disgruntled. She exhaled, then shrugged. "You're right, I can't force you. Not yet. But – never mind, I'll do it myself." As a parting shot, she said, "I think Kelly's been dabbling in things best left to the police. Let this be a warning to you. Don't you two start as well."

The off-duty police officer walked away and Evan closed the door. He was left looking at a pale, trembling sister.

"What do we do?" she uttered.

"First, we have a think," Evan replied. With Sarah in his wake, he slipped into the living room.

As soon as he sat down, he got up again. "*Yellow Pages*," he mumbled.

"What?" Sarah inquired.

"I'll call the fish place and check out Vicky McCormick's story."

"Good idea."

Mr Perriman came to the phone eventually and confirmed what the policewoman had stated. "Your sister," he complained. "She phoned to say she was coming and then she doesn't appear. It's not good enough."

Evan didn't answer the criticism. He simply said, "Thank you."

He nodded at Sarah and told her, "She wasn't lying. Not about that anyway. Kelly didn't show up. But", he added, "maybe she didn't show because Vicky McCormick waylaid her."

Sarah was on the verge of panic. "Don't tell me Friday the thirteenth's repeating itself, this time *before* a meal at the seafood restaurant. We've got to do something. Kelly could be ... I don't know. She could have been kidnapped on the way there."

"Yes," Evan agreed thoughtfully. "By Vicky McCormick, or..."

"Or who?"

"Or anybody."

"Like?"

"Any of our suspects. We've no idea where they are now and what they're up to. Not even Dad."

Sarah's mouth hung open. She was lost for words.

"But it's probably Vicky McCormick," Evan continued, partly to put Sarah out of her misery, and partly because his father wasn't his prime suspect.

"That's right," Sarah retorted at last. "We've ruled out most of the others, including Dad."

"One thing's for sure, though," Evan said. "It strikes me that we need to solve this right now. Kelly could be in trouble."

Sarah agreed. In the midst of her anxiety, one thing pleased her: Evan was speaking like one of the family. For the last few months he wouldn't have shown such brotherly concern. Now the Keatings were beginning to operate like a unit again. Yet she was scared. She feared that they were about to lose Kelly just as they had all started to pull together as a family should, especially one that had lost its mother.

"So", Evan continued, "it's time I was on my bike."

"What do you mean?"

"It won't take me long to pay a few visits on my bike. I'll call in at the shop and check out Dad. I reckon I know where Pete and Mr Warr will be, so I can take a sneaky look at them as well."

"Pity you can't pedal fast enough to chase Vicky McCormick in her car," Sarah commented. "That would be more useful."

"I'll leave that to you. You need the Matt Mobile. Why don't you give him a call? The two of you can drive to McCormick's place. Kelly wrote down the address – it'll be in her room somewhere. See if you can spot anything suspicious at the house."

"Like signs of Kelly?"

Her brother nodded. "OK?" he asked.

"I suppose so. You be careful."

"And you," he replied as he headed for the garage.

His bike was doubly locked. It was shut inside the garage and its front wheel was anchored to the frame with a combination lock. Too many bikes disappeared from the district to take risks. Evan knelt down by the front wheel and dialled in the code to release the lock: 2511. It was easy to remember the number because it was his birthday: 25th November. Before he lined up the third digit, he dropped the lock and stood bolt upright. He remembered that it was his mother who had suggested the birthday code. And, Evan reasoned, if she'd suggested it for him, maybe she'd used the same system herself. That would be 1010 in her case. And upside down, it would look like 0101! Evan gave up on the idea of taking to his bike. Instead he flew back into the house.

In his bedroom, he grabbed Henderson's envelope and turned it the other way up. It was there. Written down the side. 1010. His mother had left a clue after all.

"Sarah!" he yelled.

His sister bounded up the stairs as if his bedroom were on fire. "I thought you'd gone," she said when she saw that there wasn't an emergency.

"Nearly. But take a look at this first." He handed over the envelope and pointed to the hand-written number. "I think that's a message from Mum. And I bet it's the combination that opens her briefcase."

"Really?"

"Yes. Do you want to find out?"

Sarah looked unsure. She didn't like the idea of delving into her mum's things.

"If it is a clue, she wrote it because she wanted us to find it," Evan insisted. "She wouldn't have left the combination – if that's what it is – if she didn't want us to use it."

"No, I suppose not," Sarah replied. "All right, let's go and get it over with. For Kelly's sake.'

In their father's bedroom, Evan dragged the dusty briefcase out of its niche. "It's not heavy," he said with some disappointment. "I hope there's something in it after all."

"She didn't use it much," Sarah commented. "Occasionally for work. Put a newspaper and sandwiches in it. That's about all."

Evan balanced the case on a bedside chair and thumbed the ratchet till he had dialled 1010 on the left-hand clasp. He pulled back the fastener and the lock sprang open. He glanced at Sarah and said, "Told you!" He lined up the same number on the right-hand catch and opened it. Hesitating before lifting up the lid, he muttered to his sister, "Keep your fingers crossed."

The briefcase wasn't quite empty. At the bottom there lay a single piece of A4 paper. It was a letter from a supplier of building materials and it was addressed to Mr E. Henderson of Henderson's Builders. Evan picked up the letter and held it up so that both he and Sarah could read it.

The first paragraph confirmed an order for hundreds of tonnes of aggregate at a discount cost.

"What's aggregate?" Sarah queried.

"I think it's added to cement to make concrete," Evan answered.

The second paragraph was much more interesting.

We are obliged to point out that this aggregate can be supplied at this low price because its quality restricts its use. It is excellent for concrete that does not bear stress. Concrete made with this material has medium compressive strength, as shown in the accompanying technical data, but, if it were to be used for load-bearing walls, its limited tensile strength would provide little resistance to impact. Such concrete failed controlled impact tests.

Evan and Sarah looked at each other. They realized that they had read something significant but the message was slow to sink in.

"What does it mean?" Sarah muttered.

"I'm not sure," Evan replied. "But…"

"Has it got anything to do with Mum? And Kelly?"

"I wonder if we've been ignoring the one real piece of evidence we've got," Evan said. "It's been staring us in the face and we've ignored it."

Sarah interrupted his thoughts. "What are you talking about?"

"Concrete evidence!" Evan declared. "Literally."

"You mean, why did the wall fall down?"

"Exactly," Evan cried, becoming more animated as he worked it out. "It's not normal for cars to knock down a concrete wall when they crash into it at no great speed, is it? The car should have come off worse. The wall was weak. It had lots of cracks. I don't know exactly what this letter means but it's definitely a warning not to use this aggregate stuff in important walls."

"You're saying Henderson used it anyway," Sarah deduced. "He was warned it wouldn't stand up to impact but he used it anyway."

"That's right. It was cheap so he used it. He was cutting corners. It's almost like…" He paused, then continued, "… like Mum was trying to tell us something when she fell out of the concrete."

Sarah groaned and turned away, but soon looked back at her brother. "It was built badly. So what?"

"Not just badly, it's probably criminal. And Mum knew."

Sarah nodded slowly. She peered closely at the letter and commented, "This is a photocopy. She must have seen the letter at work one day. She knew the place was being built badly, so she copied the letter as proof and brought it home to keep it safe."

"Yes. She brought it home in her handbag, in the original envelope. That's why the envelope was still complete. She took the letter out, dumped it here and the envelope stayed in her handbag. Then she'd have gone to put pressure on her boss. Blackmail him. Threaten to tell someone about dodgy workmanship if he didn't drop the building." Evan paused only to get his breath. He continued, "She could have blackmailed Henderson to stop the work going ahead. And if Warr tried to get someone else to carry it on, she could have planned to threaten him with leaking information about the videos. She must have believed she could halt the building."

"Henderson…" Sarah mumbled. "Do you think he killed Mum to stop her talking?"

"It fits," Evan concluded.

"I must admit, it might explain something that's been bothering me. We've been guessing that George McCormick spent five months or so investigating her disappearance and getting nowhere. Then, a few days after the wall collapsed and Mum … you know, he got close enough to the killer to get himself killed. It was too much of a coincidence for him to sort it out just then. But he was in the building trade. He'd know that the wall shouldn't have collapsed. That was his big clue. He saw it, we didn't."

"Could be," Evan agreed. "He can't have found this evidence," he said, waving the letter, "but he might have challenged Henderson anyway, just because he knew that something was wrong with the wall."

Sarah was thinking back to the information that Kelly had gleaned from Faye on Monday. "Didn't Kelly say that Mr McCormick went to Faye after Mum's body was found and asked for lots of files and floppy disks? Perhaps he was looking for proof."

"Yes, I think she did. I doubt if he found anything. Perhaps he tackled Henderson anyway – out of frustration."

"Hang on," Sarah put in. "It still doesn't quite fit. Henderson wasn't with Mum in the sea-food restaurant that night. She was with George McCormick or someone who looks like him. I never saw George McCormick but, if he looked like Dad, Eric Henderson's nowhere near."

"That's true," Evan conceded. "Henderson's much shorter and tubbier, and he's got that great beard."

"There's something else. Why should Kelly disappear? She was after Vicky McCormick, not Henderson. If she wasn't threatening him, he wouldn't be out cruising the streets trying to grab her. It doesn't make sense."

"I see what you mean," Evan replied. "But ... er ... I wonder if it makes sense if Vicky McCormick's in on it as well."

Sarah's brain went into overdrive. "Now that's a real possibility. They both stood to gain. Henderson removes the threat to his livelihood by killing Mum and Vicky McCormick gets rid of an un-faithful husband – and his lover. Vicky could have called Henderson to tell him that Kelly was hounding her. Together, they'd want to get her off their backs. I think you've cracked it, Evan!"

"Yeah," Evan murmured, without enthusiasm. "It means Kelly's in deep trouble."

They both jumped and then ducked down below the level of the bedroom window as the doorbell suddenly chimed.

"Is that Vicky McCormick back again?" Sarah whispered urgently.

"How do I know?" Evan responded. Keeping low, he sneaked up to the window and carefully peered down on to the street. Then he let out a groan. He stood up, turned to Sarah and said, "The Matt Mobile's out there."

"Phew!" Sarah sighed. "Matt's arrived. Good. We need him."

"Well," Evan retorted, "we need his car at any rate."

At the front door, Matt chirped, "Sarah Keating? Your taxi's here." Then he saw her face. "What's up?" he said.

"It's Kelly," she began as she let him into the hall. "And we think we know who did it."

Once they'd updated Matt, he asked, "So where do you want to go?"

"McCormick's place, I should think," Sarah replied.

"There are alternatives," Evan declared. "Like Henderson's yard. Or…"

"Or what?"

"Let's assume that McCormick and Henderson have got Kelly," Evan reasoned. "If they've got a choice, they wouldn't take her to either of their houses or to the builders. It'd be too risky, in case they were seen with her. They'd take her somewhere else."

"Like?" Sarah encouraged him.

"It *is* Friday the thirteenth again."

Sarah and Matt glanced at each other and then they both stared at Evan. "You don't mean…"

"I mean, they could have taken her to a building site. Just like they did with Mum."

The full horror of Evan's words was still hitting Sarah as Matt said, "So where's Henderson building stuff these days?"

"Down by the canal," Evan suggested. "They're putting up a new bridge."

"What are we waiting for?" Matt responded. "Let's go."

14

From the back seat of the car, Evan pointed over Matt's shoulder. "Park there," he called. "We can walk down the towpath to the site. If anyone's about, they won't see us coming if we're careful."

It was seven thirty and the April evening was overcast. The gloom made it seem later. It wasn't cold but rain threatened. As they approached the ancient brick bridge that had come to the end of its useful life, they wished it was darker.

"The new bridge is going up on the other side of this one," Evan said as they lingered out of sight behind the old one. "Once we're out of its shadow, we'll be in the open. There's a fence round where they're building, but some of the kids at school come down here and mess around. They say you can get under it in one place on this side. We'll have to find the hole, and hope we're not spotted."

"OK. Do you want to lead?" Matt asked Evan.

"All right. Follow me. Quietly."

"Do you want the torch?" Matt said, holding it out to him.

"No, you keep it. The last thing we want right now is to announce that we're here."

They stole out from the dinginess of the bridge, Evan first, and crept towards the wire fence. Beyond it, there was a steep slope up to a wide muddy track, that one day would be a proper road, leading to the edge of the canal. A big truck was parked on the embankment. Where the track stopped there was a wooden tower surrounded by steel scaffolding – a mould into which concrete would be poured to form a support for the new bridge. On the opposite side of the canal, the other support had already been erected. Once the second concrete pillar had been completed, the beam of the bridge would be lowered into place by the crane, which stood waiting like a giant guardian of the silent building site.

"No one's about," Sarah whispered.

"Good," Matt replied.

"But Kelly could still be here. She might be in this tower."

"She'd be yelling for help."

"Not if she's gagged," Evan speculated. "Or knocked out."

"Charming!" Sarah muttered.

"He's right, though," Matt said.

"Let's check out this fence," Evan suggested.

The three of them crouched down and inched their way along the perimeter, stopping sometimes to tug at the wire webbing to test its sturdiness. About fifty metres away from the towpath, Evan grabbed hold of the fence, yanked, and found himself flat on his back in the mud. He sat up quickly. "Here it is." The wire netting had come away in his hand. It wasn't a big hole, but it was enough to crawl through. Evan went first, then Sarah, and finally Matt slipped into the compound. They stood on the wrong side of the fence and their hearts beat faster. They had become trespassers.

"Up here," Evan breathed.

They scrambled up the bank and on to the mud track that ended suddenly with the tower at the edge of the canal. Feeling very exposed, they crept along the track, pausing by the lorry, where they were shielded from the housing estate on the other side of the mound.

"I'm sure we're being watched," Sarah muttered, imagining prying eyes everywhere.

"Think of Kelly," Matt said. "We haven't got a choice. It's not far to the end. Even if someone's watching, we can get her out – if she's there – and leave here in a few minutes."

There was a small gap between the end of the track and the wooden frame. It was bridged by a plank.

"You go on and check," Evan murmured to Matt. "You've got the torch. We'll keep watch in case anyone comes."

Before he put his whole weight on the plank, Matt tested its stability by pressing on it with his foot. It seemed perfectly safe so he walked its short length and peered over the wooden frame and down into the murky depths of the tower. He couldn't see to the bottom so he called into it, "Kelly?" He concentrated, trying to hear the faintest reply, but there was nothing, only the echo of his own voice coming out of the hollow. He switched on the torch and directed its beam into the cavity. It picked out the rough wooden sides, some steel rods that would reinforce the concrete and, at the bottom, gravel. There was no sign of a victim of abduction.

Over his shoulder, Matt cried softly, "She's not here."

Sarah and Evan looked at each other and shrugged.

"Just as well, really," Matt reported as he crossed the plank, "because I can't see how we'd have got her out of there."

Sarah was crestfallen. "What now?" she mumbled.

"We get out of here for a kick-off," Matt answered.

Evan led the way down the embankment, through the hole in the fence, and back on to the towpath. Standing underneath the old bridge, he said, "Of course, there are other places where bridges are being built. I don't know if it's Henderson's that's putting them up, though. She could've been taken to any one of them."

"You mean the new ring road?" Matt checked. "You're right. There's at least a couple of bridges going up for it."

"Back to the car, then," Evan concluded. "We'll have to take a look."

Sarah disliked the idea. She'd had enough. Yet she also knew that they had little option. She confined herself to a low moan and plodded after Evan.

For a short distance on the outskirts of town, the old road ran parallel to the new. The ring road itself was not far from completion but some bridges were still under construction. Matt stopped the car at a bus stop that was separated from the first building site by a small field. The sun had gone down but, by the spotlights of the works area, they could see that the great concrete columns and arch were almost finished.

"Not that one," Evan said without even getting out of the car. "Let's try the next."

Matt pulled away from the kerb. "The next one's about half a mile down the road, I think," he said. "There's a track for the lorries, cranes and the like to get to it."

"Fine," Evan replied. "We'll take it as well."

When he came to the track, Matt turned left, past the sign that read "Construction vehicles only". It was a bumpy driveway and he crawled along it in second gear despite wanting to put his foot down to get out of sight of the main road as quickly as possible.

The landscape was unreal. Motionless machinery lay everywhere, like petrified dinosaurs in a barren terrain. Heaps of sand and gravel stood on a half-made road that ended abruptly a few metres short of an artificial cliff – a chasm soon to be spanned by concrete. A fluorescent ribbon fluttered as a warning of the sheer drop. Here and there steel skeletons like playground climbing-frames poked out of the foundations, waiting to be enveloped in concrete to form unimaginable structures.

Matt brought the car to a halt and Evan got out and glanced around. It was like stepping out of a spacecraft to help in the construction of a lunar colony. But the crew that should have been there had vanished mysteriously, leaving tools scattered all around.

"Weird!" Sarah exclaimed.

Only the distant strings of street lamps and rows of house lights reminded them that they were not far from familiar territory.

"Well," Matt said. "Here we go again."

Side by side they walked towards the heart of the compound. Suddenly, they froze. Harsh spotlights had come on and blazed down unforgivingly on them as if they were footballers in a stadium at night. Instinctively, they all ducked down.

"Over here," Evan whispered. He led the way and they crawled behind a dump truck, where they were shielded from the worst of the glare.

Leaning against one of the enormous tyres, Sarah muttered, "Someone's seen us."

"I'm not so sure," Matt responded. "I don't think anyone's here. It's more likely to be a security system: infrared detectors. They sense movement and turn on the main lights automatically. I think we've just got to carry on, ignore the lights, and hope for the best. Otherwise we might as well give up and go home right now. We'll have to hope no one can be bothered to report that the lights are on."

Evan shrugged. Making the best of it, he said, "At least we won't need a torch."

They got to their feet and, still uncomfortable in the dazzle, headed towards the first of two huge wooden structures. In a day or two, they would be filled with concrete and then stripped of their framework to reveal supports for the bridge, designed to be strong enough to take the weight of four lanes of traffic over the river below. Where the tarmac of the new dual carriageway stopped, compressed earth sloped gently up to the top of the temporary towers. Tomorrow, lorries would trundle up the ramp and pour concrete sludge into the cavities.

Taking a last look about them, Evan, Sarah and Matt put their hands on the top of the wooden wall and peered over. The security lights pierced most of the cavern below them, revealing a network of thick steel wires that would strengthen the concrete pillar. They cast ominous shadows on the inside surface of the frame, making it look like a cage.

"Can you see to the bottom?" Sarah asked.

"Just about," Matt replied.

"I don't think there's anything in here except these cables, but it's a long way down," Evan added

"The torch won't help a great deal," Matt commented. "It's not powerful enough to make much of an impression down there."

Sarah called into the hole, "Kelly? Are you there?"

Nothing. It was as if she had shouted down a deserted mine shaft. The void swallowed her words.

"Let's try the next one.'

They ran down the ramp, crossed on to what would become the second carriageway and hurried up the next slope.

Inside, the cavity was the same: hollow, eerie, and riddled with steel bars. It reminded Evan of a dreadful prison. Otherwise, it seemed empty. "Kelly!" he cried into it.

His lonely voice bounced back.

Sarah sighed, fighting to keep back tears of weariness and dismay. She couldn't bring herself to admit it aloud but she was wondering if Kelly was lying unconscious or even dead at the bottom of one of these grim holes. Her own sister, so full of life, condemned in one of these awful pits! Sarah wanted to run away but she wanted to stay too. She hated the building site but leaving it meant giving up.

"I'm not sure if there's another place like this further down the road," Matt said. "There might be. We could try—"

"Shush!" Evan snapped. "Listen. I heard something!"

They peered as far as they dared over the belly of the earth and concentrated in silence. It seemed like a minute but it was only a few seconds before Matt murmured, "Wishful thinking."

Frantic, Sarah called, "Kelly?"

At first, there was no answer. Then they heard it: a weak but definite clang.

"Yes!" Matt confirmed when they looked at each other. "There's something."

The metallic noise sounded again.

"It's Kelly!" Evan cried. "She's down there! I can't see anything; she must be in shadow. But she's banging on the cables."

Sarah wanted to roar with relief and scream with horror at the same time. Instead, she muttered, "What are we going to do? She must be in trouble. We've got to get her out."

"Give me the torch," Evan said to Matt.

"Why?" Matt asked.

"Why do you think?"

"You can't—"

"What are you two talking about?" Sarah put in.

Evan took off his coat, handed it to Matt and snatched the torch. "I'm going down," he said.

"But..." Sarah looked over the edge again. "How? It's not possible."

"These steel bars – they're like a ladder. I can use them to climb down."

"You can't be serious!" Matt spluttered. "You can't even reach one from here."

"I can," Evan replied. "I'm going to stand on the edge and you're going to steady me. From there I can jump and catch that nearest cable. The rest is easy." He slipped the torch into his trousers' pocket, ready for action.

"No!" Sarah yelled. "You'll get yourself killed. It's a long way down."

"Yes," Evan answered. "That's why I don't intend to miss that steel bar. Well, are you just going to stand there or are you going to steady me before I jump?"

"I can't help you kill yourself."

"Look, I'm a good climber. And if you've got a better idea to get Kelly out, I'll listen to it."

Neither Matt nor Sarah could reply.

"Right," Evan said. "While I'm down there, you try and find planks that'll stretch from here to the steel frame. I'll need them to get out when I come back up with Kelly. We haven't got the time to look for them now. I'd rather jump and get it over with. Help me up."

"I'll say one thing," Matt murmured as he gripped Evan's arm, "you've got guts enough for two."

"Just don't let me fall before I jump," Evan replied as he clambered up on to the edge of the frame. "And when you feel me take off, let go straight away. Whatever you do, don't hold me back."

Matt held Evan steady by his right arm and Sarah clasped one of his legs as he stood on high like a man on the gallows. She could feel his leg trembling – or maybe it was her own arm shaking.

Evan breathed deeply. "Get ready to let go," he whispered without looking at them. Perched on the edge, his gaze was fixed on the steel skeleton. All his concentration was focused on one of the rods. He did not look down to see the great chasm between him and the steel bar.

He flexed at the knees and then threw himself forward with all his strength, like an Olympic swimmer diving into a pool. He leapt out over the void.

Sarah screamed.

Evan let out a cry as he hit the network of cables with a tremendous thud. His fingers closed round the first horizontal rod but, with the force of his collision and the sweat on his hands, they could not keep a grip and he slipped. With nothing below his legs he began to fall. Desperately, he clutched at the second bar. This time his fingers made contact and he got a hold. He shuddered to a halt, wrenching his arms, but maintained his grip so that he dangled alarmingly in mid-air. Flailing his legs till he found a firm foothold, he clung on to his make-shift ladder while his frenzied heartbeat slowed to merely wild. He fought for his breath as if he'd just completed a marathon.

"Are you OK?" Sarah called across the divide.

"Yeah," he answered without turning his head. "A good few bruises, but I'm OK. It's just like a climbing frame, only bigger. I'm going down. It shouldn't take long. You go and find a plank or two. I don't fancy being stranded here when I come back up."

"All right," Matt responded. "Good luck."

Evan began to descend into the pit. It was like going down an endless ladder but the rungs were further apart and not so regular. Sometimes he had to stretch with one of his legs to reach the next bar. When he stopped to relax his aching muscles, he yelled into the blackness below, "Hold on, Kelly, I'm coming." Out of the brightness of the floodlights, it got darker and darker as he slowly made his way down. The air smelled stale and damp.

Eventually his foot, probing for the next rung, made contact with solid ground. It was the concrete foundation for the pillar, and the vertical rods that he'd used as a ladder were embedded in it. He took out the torch and flashed it around. "Kelly?" he called.

She was behind him and all she could do was moan. There was a handkerchief gagging her mouth and her wrists were tied by a short length of rope. Her trousers and jumper were stained and torn. She looked like a white-faced scarecrow.

Evan put down the torch so it illuminated her, knelt down and untied the gag first.

"Ugh!" She spat out the taste of the handkerchief.

"Are you OK?" Evan asked as he began to work on the rope.

Kelly was in no fit state to answer. She simply stammered, "I can't tell you what I felt when I saw the lights come on and heard your voice." She threw her freed left arm around her brother, hugged him tightly and cried without restraint.

Eventually she regained her composure, wiped her face and sniffed. She muttered into his ear, "Thanks."

"I guess it was Henderson," Evan said.

Kelly nodded. "He pushed me down."

"You fell all the way down here?" Evan was amazed.

"Yes."

"So how come you survived? It's some drop."

"I've got some bad news for you," she muttered. "I hit these wires on the way down. I couldn't keep hold with my hands tied, but I did enough to break the fall by grabbing a few cables."

"Wow. Sounds painful."

"Yeah. The trouble is, I can't move my right arm," she admitted. "I think it's broken. It hurt enough, but now it's just numb."

Evan groaned. "Can you stand?"

She held out her good arm as an invitation to be pulled to her feet.

Evan drew her up gently till she was standing shakily. "Well," he said, "that's a start. But you can't climb a difficult thing like this with one hand. It's not possible."

Kelly looked apologetic. "Sorry," she mumbled.

"It's not your fault," he replied. "But ... er ... we've got a problem. We can't wait for help to arrive. Henderson could turn up any moment with those security lights blazing away. We need to crack on. So, how are we going to get you back up?" He paused before continuing, "I know. You can't climb with one arm but you can have a piggy- back. You can hold on to me with your good arm."

"What?"

"Look. I'll need to keep my arms free for climbing. They'll be up here." He demonstrated by holding both arms up in the air. "You can thread your left arm round my shoulders and cling on to my waist or something with your knees."

"You can't clamber all the way up there with my weight on your back!"

Evan looked up towards the light, turned to Kelly and shrugged. "Piece of cake," he lied. "But if you think your arm hurt before, by the time we get to the top, it'll be torture."

"I know." She tried to smile at him. "It won't be easy for you either. But I guess we haven't got much choice."

Evan turned his back and held his arms up. "Come on, let's get cracking. Just keep your bad arm sandwiched between your chest and my back. Keep it as still as you can. I'll try not to jolt about too much."

"Never mind me," Kelly replied, climbing awkwardly on board. "Just concentrate on getting up. I'll try not to groan too much in your ear."

Evan reached up for the first rod and stepped on to the lowest rung. It was then that the enormity of the task struck him. Kelly wasn't heavy but she wasn't light either. After a few metres she'd seem unbearable. She also restricted his movement so much that climbing wasn't going to be easy. "OK?" he asked her.

"Yes," she said in a voice that ached to cry, No! I feel like I'm dying.

"Hang on. I'll go as fast as I can."

With her knees she gripped his hips. Her left arm looped round his shoulders and sometimes slipped against his neck.

"Sorry," Kelly mumbled.

"It's all right," Evan replied, coughing. "I know you've often wanted to throttle me, but I'm not sure this is the right moment."

"If you get us out of this, I promise I won't say another cross word – ever."

Evan stopped to get his breath back. "Can I have that in writing?"

"Yes, if you've got a piece of paper, a pen and a right arm you can lend me."

At first, it was a struggle to haul up himself and Kelly when there was a big gap between steel rods. It soon became a struggle even with the small gaps. Much of her weight lay on his shoulders. His quivering arms and the backs of his legs ached. He seemed to be carrying the world on his back.

When he next stopped to gather strength, he yelled upwards, "Can you hear me?"

Sarah's voice drifted down, "Have you got her?"

"Yes. Sort of. She's in bad shape. Have you got a plank ready?"

"Nearly," Matt answered. "I've found a metal sheet that'll reach across."

"Good," Evan called. "Don't rest it on the top cable. Try and put it a few rungs down so I can climb above it."

"Why?"

"You'll be able to see us soon. Then you'll see why. I need to lower Kelly on to it. And I think you'll have to help her across it. OK?"

"Yes," Matt boomed. "We'll get it into position now."

Evan lapsed into silence as he put all his effort into dragging himself and his sister up towards the light. At one point he heard a gasp from above. Sarah must have seen them. She was obviously startled but Evan was reassured. They must be near the top. It was certainly getting lighter and he thought it might also be colder and less damp, but he was too hot and sweaty to be sure. On his back, Kelly was weeping to herself. Between sobs, she muttered, "You know, Evan, I never told you before. You're some brother. Full of surprises. Hidden depths."

Panting, he replied, "I'm not doing this every day, you know."

She looked up and whispered, "I can see Sarah's face. She looks petrified. Not far to go."

"Just as well," he gasped. "I can't do much more."

Kelly sniffed and, through tears, said, "You can make it. I trust you."

His body was throbbing with exhaustion. Cramp threatened to grip his left leg but he hoped to reach fresh air first.

Kelly shifted her position a little and a stabbing pain in her right shoulder made her scream.

"Are you OK?" Evan said.

At the same time a voice – much closer now – called down, "What's happened?"

"It's all right," Kelly muttered. "I've just nobbled my shoulder as well, I think."

Matt's practical tones floated down to them. "Not far, just a few metres. Keep coming straight up, Evan, and the plate will be on your left."

"Good. As long as I don't come up and bang my head on it."

"No. I'll warn you if you drift underneath it. I'm on it now, ready to grab her."

"OK," Evan replied, trying to keep moving slowly and steadily. Between wheezes he shouted, "Keep clear of her right side. Broken arm – maybe shoulder as well."

He heaved on the next rod and planted his foot securely on another rung. He was so drained of energy that he wanted to be sick, yet his stomach felt tormentingly empty. He swallowed several times to try and get rid of the foul taste in his mouth and throat.

On his back, Kelly was barely conscious. "Kelly!" Evan yelled. "Don't drift off. You might let go." He coughed, then added, "If you fall back down again, I'm not coming to get you."

Kelly managed a brief, strained giggle. "Don't you love me any more? Or is it back-seat drivers that you can't stand?"

Evan moaned theatrically. Refreshed by Kelly's quip, he reached up and tugged.

A few minutes later, his head emerged from the hole and he saw Matt astride a steel plate on his left.

"Twist round a bit," Matt said, "and I'll take her. I can get her by her good side."

When the weight lifted from his shoulders and hips, Evan felt so light – so giddy and insecure – that he thought he would float away. He clung to the giant frame, unable to move.

Matt steered Kelly into her sister's arms and came back to pluck Evan off the skeleton of steel. As he guided Evan along the plate and back to solid ground, he said in total admiration, "That's the bravest thing I've ever seen."

From the ramp, another voice responded, "I agree. None of my chaps would be brave – or stupid – enough to try it."

It was Eric Henderson and he was wearing a green jumper and wielding a length of heavy iron pipe. He looked like a policeman with a truncheon.

15

Sarah reacted first. "You!" she cried, taking a step towards Henderson as if to protect the others. "We know all about you. We know why you killed Mum."

The builder looked askance at Sarah, took a step towards her and proclaimed, "You know why I'd have liked to get rid of your mum, that's all. I didn't kill her."

Sarah hesitated. She wasn't sure what to believe. He seemed to be irritated in the same way that she would be irritated by a false accusation, yet there was a lot of hard evidence against him. On top of everything, he'd thrown Kelly down a pit and left her for dead. She squared up to him. "You're lying," she said.

"Listen." He walked right up to her and spoke slowly and firmly. "I had nothing to do with your mother's death."

Sarah stared into his face and knew that he was telling the truth. The realization unnerved her. She opened her mouth to reply, but her lips couldn't form any words.

Matt stood by her side protectively. "But you disposed of the body," he said. "This business with Kelly proves it."

"Yes," he admitted. "I can hardly deny that."

"You know who killed her, don't you?" Matt retorted.

Eric Henderson nodded.

"We think we know too," Sarah told him.

Curious, he cocked his head on one side. "Oh?"

"Her."

"What? Who?"

Sarah pointed behind him. "Her. Your accomplice. Vicky McCormick."

The police officer had crept up quietly while they talked.

Henderson hesitated, not sure if Sarah was playing a trick on him. Then he spun round, holding the pipe high above his head, and brought it down sharply.

Vicky McCormick dived to one side but she wasn't fast enough. There was a sickening crack as the metal hit the side of her head and bounced on to her shoulder. A small moan issued from her mouth. She was unconscious by the time her body thudded into the mud.

"No!" Sarah screeched, staring in horror at Henderson. "How could you—"

Impatiently, he interrupted, "She must have followed you. Waiting in the wings, no doubt. She was letting you do the hard work, so don't feel sorry for her. Thought she'd just have to turn up at the end to grab the glory."

Matt knelt down beside the policewoman and felt her chest, neck and wrist. "I ... er ... I think she's dead."

Henderson simply shrugged.

Standing up and returning to Sarah's side, Matt remarked, "It wasn't her you were working with, then."

Mr Henderson grinned unpleasantly. "Her? You've got some strange notions in your heads. She's a cop." Still holding the bloodied metal tube, he declared, "Anyway, this is very convenient. I've got all the people who suspect me together in one place."

"You can't get rid of all of us," Sarah exclaimed. "You won't get away with it."

"We could run," Matt said. "At least one of us will get away."

Henderson laughed. "I can't see Kelly or Evan doing much running, and you two won't leave them."

From behind Sarah and Matt, Evan pushed himself upright and barked, "I can still run. Besides, it's all over for you. We've got a copy of a certain letter. It shows that you've been cutting corners with building materials. We've left it with a friend, as insurance. It goes to the police if we don't show up soon. And it makes you look as guilty as hell."

"You're bluffing."

"Does this sound familiar?" Evan asked. "Something along the lines of, 'We must point out that this aggregate is cheap because of its poor quality. Concrete made from it will fail impact tests.' Does it ring a bell? I think you know the letter. I'm not bluffing."

Mr Henderson glared at Evan for a few seconds, then relented. Reaching into a pocket, he pulled out a mobile phone. Still keeping an eye on his captives, he punched in a number and waited. Someone must have answered because he spoke. "It's me. We've got trouble." He listened to a reply, then said, "No, there's no choice. You'll have to come. Ring-road site. Take the track opposite Salt Lane. You can't miss us." He put the phone away and said, "The person you want will be here in ten minutes. For now, we stay here and talk. I have a little proposition for you."

"What do you mean?" asked Evan.

"I'll give you the killer on a plate – and the evidence you need. In return, you give me the letter. That's the deal. Of course, you forget that Sergeant McCormick was ever here as well."

"Who is it and what's the evidence?" Matt demanded.

"Do we have a deal?"

Indignantly, Sarah snapped, "After what you've just done to Kelly!"

"I did try to warn her."

"You did?"

"I heard from … a certain person that you lot had been nosing around. I volunteered to warn you off. Didn't you tell them about the phone call?" Henderson directed his question over Sarah's shoulder to Kelly, who was still propped against the wooden structure.

Kelly shook her head. "No," she responded weakly. "I didn't tell them. Didn't want to frighten anyone."

"That's hardly the point," Sarah retorted. "If you had an ounce of good in you, you'd be calling for an ambulance right now. Kelly's in a terrible state."

"If we've got a deal, I'll call."

"And you want us just to forget Vicky McCormick? You're a monster!" Sarah walked back to her sister, muttering, "If it was just me, you wouldn't get a deal."

Matt felt like an intruder. He wasn't a Keating and he didn't feel that he had the right to make or break any bargains. He kept his thoughts to himself. Kelly would have had an opinion but she was hardly capable of expressing it. They all looked at Evan.

"First, I've got a few questions," Evan said. Henderson was the one with the weapon, but Evan was in control. "How did you know we were here?"

"Some responsible citizen saw the floodlights. Thought it odd at this time. She took the telephone number from our hoarding and called to let me know. I was working late in the office," he explained. "I didn't believe that the rats had set off the security lights."

"What about George McCormick? You've been avoiding mentioning him."

"He's got nothing to do with us, here and now."

"So, you *did* kill him. Presumably because, once Mum's body was discovered, he realized you'd used sub-standard materials and murdered Mum because she threatened you. Tried to bribe you to stop work on the factory."

"You *have* got this notion about me firmly fixed in your brain, haven't you? As if I'm the only bad guy. No, I didn't kill him."

Evan wasn't so sure. Even if he hadn't murdered McCormick, he was certainly in on it, otherwise he would have claimed that Vicky's husband had committed suicide. "It's down to this … certain person again, then?"

"That's right," Henderson smirked. He reminded Evan of a naughty schoolboy who always managed to get someone else into trouble while avoiding the flak himself. "OK, tell me why he killed Mum and McCormick," Evan continued.

Henderson's face crinkled. "Why? You want to know *why*, not *who*?"

Evan surprised everyone by announcing, "I know *who*, but I've no idea *why*. Has he just flipped his lid?"

"Just a minute," Sarah interjected. "Who are we talking about?"

Evan turned towards his sister. "Who – apart from Vicky McCormick – could have told him", he jabbed a thumb towards Mr Henderson, "that Kelly was on the warpath tonight, and where she'd be?"

From behind Sarah, Kelly's pained voice muttered "Daniel Perriman."

"Right," Evan responded.

Together, Sarah and Matt cried, "Perriman?"

Henderson watched them with some amusement on his face. He didn't spoil his fun by confirming or denying it. He simply listened.

"Who else could it be?" Evan argued. He turned to Eric

Henderson and said, "You knew Mum was having an affair, didn't you? Must have heard it on the grapevine at work."

Henderson gave the merest nod. It was meant to encourage Evan to continue.

"But you didn't know who with, did you?"

"Bingo!" Henderson replied. His twisted smile looked like a black hole in his bushy beard.

Matt was puzzled. "What's that got to do with it?"

"Don't you see?" Evan said. "It explains why Perriman's description of the man in the restaurant was wrong, and why he identified McCormick later. It's all falling into place."

"You what?"

"Mum met Henderson that night, not McCormick." Evan ignored Henderson's sarcastic laugh. "It was a bit late in the day but Mum tried to blackmail him to abandon Mr Warr's extension, using the letter she must have just found. Apparently, she decided to tackle him away from the office – over a meal at the seafood place. Or maybe that was Henderson's idea. Anyway, between them Perriman and Henderson killed her and hid her body. They knew she had a lover, so they cooked up this story about her meeting her mystery man in the restaurant. But they didn't know who he was, so Perriman just gave a vague description of an imaginary diner. Told the police they looked like scheming lovers and, hey presto, Tatton put two and two together and came up with five, just like he was supposed to. Mum had run off with another man."

"So, there is a brain of sorts inside that head of yours," Eric Henderson sneered.

Evan turned back to him. "Bit risky, wasn't it?" he remarked. "You must have worried about what her boyfriend would do when he heard that he was supposed to have run off with her."

"Yes, but we had to take that risk. We reckoned that, if he was a married man, he'd probably say nothing. For all we knew there might have been more than one lover. Each would think she'd taken off with the other. It was a calculated gamble."

"But McCormick did crack it eventually. Made a nuisance of himself," Evan deduced, "probably by threatening to tell his wife that you had the motive to murder Mum. Or maybe he said he'd expose your bad workmanship and have you closed down. Either way, he had to go. By then it must have been obvious to you that he was the mysterious boyfriend."

Sarah joined in. "You and Perriman poisoned him and wrote that suicide note. The rejected lover story wrapped it up neatly. Inspector Tatton made two and two add up to five again," she concluded.

"Very good," Henderson scoffed.

"Yes," Evan muttered. "But why? I understand your motive, but why did Perriman kill Mum?"

"Ask him yourself." Henderson nodded his head in the direction of the track where a pair of headlights searched out the pot-holes and bumps. "But before he arrives, what about our deal?"

"What evidence are you offering that Perriman did it?"

"Do we have a deal?"

Evan glanced at the others. They were silent. It was up to him. To Sarah's relief, he pronounced, "No deal. You tried to kill Kelly. You've killed Vicky McCormick in front of our own eyes. At best, you're implicated in the murder of George McCormick and Mum. All to protect your second-rate building business. No deal."

Henderson sighed theatrically. "I'm very sorry about that. You'll be sorry too. You leave me no choice."

Daniel Perriman picked his way distastefully across the site, avoiding the tools and works vehicles. He looked like a worried man. Before he joined the small crowd, he hesitated, surveying the scene. He was trying to gauge the extent of the problem. The expression on his face suggested that he'd concluded it was a big one. He shook his head sadly, then trudged up to them and stood alongside Eric Henderson. "What's going on?" he inquired.

Henderson was brief. "They've worked it all out."

Kelly staggered forward and fixed Mr Perriman with her eyes. She asked, "Why did you kill her?"

"Is that what *he* told you?" He meant Henderson.

"That's what we've worked out for ourselves, and what he confirmed."

"I didn't kill her."

"What?" Sarah exploded as she helped to prop up her trembling sister.

"There's no one else," Evan reasoned. "It must have been you."

Perriman shrugged. The pressure on him was beginning to tell.

"You might as well know the truth," he said. "I *didn't* kill her. Not really. No one did. She was the first customer to have a new batch of shrimps."

"Shrimps?"

"Yes. Shrimps. They ... er ... weren't good." Daniel Perriman seemed to be genuinely sorry, as well as afraid. "Have you ever heard of blue-green algae?" Without waiting for a reply from his stunned audience, he continued, "Apparently huge numbers of them suddenly grow, and shrimps graze on them. The trouble is—"

"Is this for real?" Sarah interrupted.

"Yes," Perriman replied with as much force as he could muster.

"Let him finish," Evan said. "I think I've seen a programme about this, or read about it. Blooms of algae. They're poisonous, aren't they?"

Mr Perriman bucked up on hearing Evan. He took his comment as support. "Yes. The chemicals from the algae – they're called toxins – concentrate in shrimps. I had a load of Philippine shrimps. They were good value, but I didn't know then that they'd been collected when there was an algal bloom in the area. I checked afterwards and destroyed the remainder. It's not easy to monitor absolutely everything that I buy for the restaurant, you know; something as rare as this is easily overlooked. An amount the size of a pin-head can kill a human being. That's what did it," he concluded.

"That's horrible!" Sarah exclaimed. "You two just watched her die! Why didn't you do something, like call an ambulance?"

"She went very quickly," Mr Perriman said in his defence.

Henderson agreed. "One minute, she said she had a funny tingling in her lips. She didn't take it too seriously. Then she said she was going numb in the mouth. A few seconds later, she collapsed."

The restaurant owner took up the story. "She was paralysed by it. Couldn't swallow or breathe. That's what this toxin does. An ambulance couldn't have done anything for her, I'm afraid. It was all over in a couple of minutes. I would still have reported it, but *he* stopped me."

Henderson looked at his accuser sternly. "That's nonsense, and you know it. All I did was point out that we were both in the same boat. Cheap products had got the better of us. I had to use them or

go bankrupt; you chose not to check your raw materials properly."
Addressing Evan, he added, "You see, your mum was threatening
my business, and a case of food poisoning would certainly have put
paid to a restaurant's business. We were both against the ropes. You
have to protect your livelihood. There's not a lot of hope if you go
bust these days. So I just pointed out that it was in both our interests
to cover up your mum's death, that's all. I didn't want the police
sniffing round the building yard. And you", he said to Perriman,
"didn't want them closing you down. We agreed it was for the best."

Mr Perriman gazed at the ground. "Yes, we agreed. But now it's
getting out of hand."

"You both sorted out George McCormick when he twigged
what was going on."

"Only because Henderson forced me," Perriman insisted. "He
took me to McCormick's house, intent on setting up a suicide. He
had it all planned. He said it was common knowledge that
McCormick kept himself going with pills. We found bottles of the
stuff in his bathroom. Henderson held him down and made me
feed him the pills," Perriman snivelled. "A whole bottleful."

"How could you be forced to do that?"

Perriman glanced nervously at the builder, then replied, "He
said he'd take some evidence to the police if I didn't cooperate."

"Evidence?" Evan murmured. "I think it's time we heard about
this evidence."

"My dinner guest died under my own nose," Henderson
explained. "I put some of her uneaten meal in my pocket when *he*
wasn't watching. Just in case it was the food and I needed a little …
persuasion power. I've still got it in my freezer. I'm sure a decent
forensic scientist would find traces of that toxin stuff in it. It gets
me off the hook, that's for sure. And", he continued, talking to the
restaurant owner, "it means you'll help me clear up the mess here
and now."

"Clear up? What do you mean?"

"These", he said, indicating his four captives and the motionless
policewoman, "are the loose ends that need tidying up."

"No!" Perriman objected. "It's gone too far. It went too far with
McCormick. This is too much."

"Be careful what you say," Henderson growled. "You're a loose
end as well."

"I ... er..."

"Look. They won't run away because they won't leave Kelly. We can finish it right now. Don't you want to see the back of this affair? Remember your nice little business. Remember I've got the evidence on you."

"I don't know," Perriman dithered.

"Well," Matt said, "there's something else you both should think about. When I went to Vicky's body, I felt a police radio in her inside pocket. I turned it on. There's another loose end for you. And judging by the cars coming..." He pointed towards the track.

Perriman spun round but Henderson spluttered, "Don't be daft! He's bluffing. No sirens..."

Matt and Evan glanced at each other. Suddenly Evan knew that Matt was bluffing, but he also knew what he was thinking.

Catching Perriman off guard, Evan dived on him, pushing him violently into Henderson. The flailing piece of tubing crashed into the restaurant manager and not Evan. By the time Henderson was ready to strike again, Matt was behind him, pinning his arms to his chest in a bear hug.

"Hit him! Knock him out!" Matt screamed to Evan.

"But..." Evan had never hit anyone before.

"It's the only way!"

"No," Sarah said. "Use this."

She picked up a length of rope and offered it to Evan.

"No," Evan muttered to his sister. "You tie him. I'll help holding him. Just in case."

Swiftly, before he could be kicked, Evan ducked down and swept Henderson off his feet. Matt held down his top half and Evan took care of his legs while Sarah tied his hands behind his back, then coiled the rope round his ankles.

The three of them stood up and watched their victim writhing in the mud.

"He's not going anywhere," Matt declared, satisfied with the bonds.

"I know where I'd like to put him," Sarah mumbled, glancing towards the wooden frame.

"No," Kelly replied. "That's enough."

"Yes, I know really," Sarah muttered as she clung to Matt.

"What about you?" Evan said, standing over Mr Perriman, who

was whimpering on the ground. "It's over, isn't it? You're not going to try anything, are you?"

If Perriman said anything, it was gibberish. He wasn't a threat. He was finished – a broken man.

"What do we do now?" asked Sarah.

From behind her, a voice spoke. "You help me to my car, so I can radio for assistance." Vicky McCormick, one side of her face covered in blood, was sitting up by the side of the ramp.

"But you're..." Sarah turned questioningly to Matt. "You said she was dead."

"I thought if I told him she was dead, he wouldn't hurt her any more. I also hoped she'd recover and come to our rescue, like the cavalry."

"Sorry," Vicky mumbled. "Better late than never, eh? But I do feel like I've risen from the dead." She tried to get to her feet but failed. "I'm dizzy," she said.

"You might have a fractured skull," Matt suggested.

"So, are you going to help me up?" she prompted.

With Evan on one side and Matt on the other, they dragged her up and across the site towards the car. Halfway there, Matt said, "I really don't know why I'm doing this, Evan. You could give her a piggy-back. After all your practising with Kelly, you'd be good at it."

Evan grinned weakly. "Very funny," he muttered.

Behind them, Sarah had linked arms with Kelly and together they watched over the helpless culprits. "Won't be long," Sarah said. "Soon get you fixed up in hospital."

"Yeah," her sister replied. "I think I need it." She rested her head on Sarah's shoulder and, through her sobs, said, "It's hurting, Sarah." She took a deep breath and added, "Actually, it's agony."

Sarah put a hand on Kelly's head. "I know. But at least it's all over."

Kelly tried to find a smile for her war-torn face. "Yeah. Knowing what happened, it's almost like getting Mum back. We can't really bring her back, but she's ours again. We've got a memory of her now."

"That's not all," Sarah replied. "I think we've regained a brother."

16

Thump! Thump! Thump! Thump! Suddenly a cry went up behind him. "Evan!"

He spun round.

"You're wanted," the coach cried.

The Scorpion's first-choice forward was hobbling off the pitch on a damaged ankle and Evan was the only substitute who was a striker.

"Oh!" Evan left the practice football at the school wall and ran to the touch-line.

"Up front," the coach instructed him. "Straight swap for Colin. You've got ten minutes to show us what you can do, to show us you're a team player. A goal at this stage will finish the game, so get in there and do the business."

Evan ran tentatively on to the pitch, touching hands with Colin.

The coach turned to a spectator, the father of the goal-keeper, and whispered, "New lad. A bit young, but big for his age. A friend of Matt's. Didn't want to use him really. He's skilful on the ball but a loner. Keeps the ball to himself."

It took five minutes for Evan to warm to the pace of the game and settle into his position. Then, taking the ball from the half-way line, he dribbled expertly round three of the opposition.

"Pass it!" the coach screamed.

Evan ignored him, tangled with a defender and fell over.

"I knew it!" the coach muttered. "He's lost it."

Immediately, Evan scrambled back to his feet and, before the centre-back could get rid of the ball, took it off him again. The last defender was made of sterner stuff, though. He still couldn't separate Evan from the football but he forced him out wide to the right.

The coach buried his head in his hands. "Watch. He'll shoot from there," he groaned. "It's an impossible angle. Wasted chance."

Evan stopped and put his foot on the ball. He lined up for the shot. The defender rushed in to block it. Then, out of the blue, Evan dummied the shot, turned inside his marker and crossed the ball, chipping it over the keeper's head. The delay had given Matt, the Scorpion's big left back, time to charge upfield. No one else bothered. They thought they'd sussed out Evan's virtuoso style of play. It would be glory for him or, more likely, a lost opportunity for the team.

Matt leapt into the air and headed the ball down into the goal that was as open as the Scorpions' mouths.

Evan walked calmly back up the field ready for the centre while Matt shrugged off the congratulations of his mates. "Come off it," he said. "You saw who made the goal. Still think he's selfish, eh?" He ran up to Evan and slapped him on the back. "Now that's what I call a cross. Reckon you can do it again?"

Evan hesitated then smiled broadly. "I don't see why not."

On the touch-line, the coach was still trying to find his voice. At last he managed to murmur to his neighbour, "You've ... er ... got to hand it to him. Perhaps he'll be a part of the team after all." Cupping his hands round his mouth, he yelled, "Great play, Evan! Now you've learned how to pass the ball, do it quicker next time."

Evan glanced back at Matt just before play resumed. The left back shrugged. "Never satisfied," he called to Evan.

In the small band of spectators, Sarah joined in the celebrations. It was her first football match and she hadn't got a clue about the rules of the game, but she knew a goal when she saw one, so she jumped up and down and shouted joyfully with everyone else. She wasn't just cheering the goal, made by her brother and scored by her boyfriend – she was rejoicing in Evan's return to the real world.

Back at home, the mood was more sombre. Kelly's dislocated shoulder had been put back in its proper place and the bone in the forearm had been set. She was still strapped like an Egyptian mummy and she was under doctor's orders to take it easy. No parties, no driving, no football matches, just rest. One hundred per cent boredom.

While the others were at the match, she went upstairs to investigate the bumps and bangs coming from her dad's room.

Her father was kneeling in his bedroom, surrounded by all manner of odds and ends. Kelly noticed the briefcase, jewellery box, and lots of her mother's clothes among the big heap of things on his bed.

"What are you doing, Dad?" she asked.

"Ah, Kelly. It's ... I thought it was time to have a clear out."

Kelly nodded slowly and smiled at him. "Yes," she agreed. "I think you're right."

He got up and hugged his daughter briefly. "Thanks for telling me what really happened. I didn't realize how much I needed to know till you told me."

Kelly had hated every moment of the telling but she knew all along that she'd have to describe her mother's death. She'd picked the right moment – just after he'd driven her back from the hospital – and told him everything. Every messy detail. He had to know it all if he was going to come to terms with her death and learn to live without her.

Now, tears came easily to his eyes. "I knew all along she was seeing another man, but I shut it out of my mind. I just couldn't admit it." He wiped his eyes and exhaled. "Anyway, she's certainly not coming back, so it's no use keeping all her things. I phoned a charity that collects this sort of stuff. They'll be round later today. They're welcome to it."

"Good idea," Kelly replied. She didn't offer to help. She believed that her dad needed to do it himself. It was his therapy.

The police found the remains of the shrimp salad in Eric Henderson's freezer. The food and its toxin had not deteriorated, and analysis confirmed that the shrimps had been polluted by blue-green algae. It was a lethal salad.

The forensic evidence was interesting but unnecessary.

When Kelly had gone out that night to meet Detective Sergeant McCormick, she'd taken a small cassette recorder in her pocket, intending to tape their conversation. During the confrontation with Henderson, she'd managed to slip the recorder into Evan's hand, and Evan had moved close enough to Henderson and Perriman to get the whole conversation on tape. In police interviews, Perriman's silence and Henderson's wriggling were to no avail. Evan had already supplied the police with everything they needed.

Patched up and back at work, Vicky McCormick oversaw both prosecutions. As Henderson had predicted, she grabbed the glory. And that wasn't her only success. Through the post she received a photograph of a young man. On the back someone had written, "Pete. Runs gambling racket for kids. Revolvers." The information allowed her to wind up an unsavoury trade that had got many youngsters into trouble. When the Superintendent queried her source and excellent rate of success, she replied, "Having the right connections is one of the hallmarks of a good detective, isn't it, sir?"

The luckless Chief Inspector Tatton was moved to a different section and Vicky was promoted into his job. She had a lot to thank the Keatings for.

The extension to the video factory was declared unsafe. With Mr Warr in no position to argue, in case someone should spill the beans on the unlawful part of his enterprise, the wall at the bottom of the Keatings' garden was demolished and the view from the back of the house was restored. It wasn't the prettiest of scenes but it was a lot better than a lump of concrete.

Barbara Keating would have approved.

THE
SMOKING
GUN

For my grandmother

1

On your marks! The starter's pistol was raised aloft. One hundred metres down the track, two excited first-years held a ribbon across the lanes. In what the children called the Royal Box, the Head sat between his deputy, the unsmiling Mr Monk, and Dr Dearing, a representative of local business and Chairman of the School Governors. On the opposite side of the field stood the tall brick wall, topped by spikes and security cameras, that surrounded Dr Dearing's laboratories. Around the field, several elderly residents sat out on their porches, anticipating a good afternoon's competition.

Sports Day. David Rabin's mother and grandfather had turned up for the occasion. They had really come to see his sister, Ros, perform. She was the sporty one. David was not so athletic. He did have real strength – he had been forced to be strong since the death of his father – but it was strength of character in his case. There was another reason for the Rabin family's attendance at the school's annual event. As new residents in the area, they thought it appropriate to be seen for the first time at a school function.

Ever since their arrival in Northampton, Ros had been conscious of the wilder rumours circulating about them – the wealthy, fatherless newcomers. David himself was not aware of the gossip because he did not mix well at school. Perhaps it was because he was aloof that people gossiped. When Ros had convinced the rest of the family that they had become curiosities, David had decided that they should make this public appearance. He had not known then what an impact they would have on Sports Day.

Get set! The last shout of encouragement before the hubbub died away was Kevin's roar, "Come on, Ros – show 'em what you can do!"

In the third lane Ros arched on fingertips and toes, muscles tense. The silence invited a gunshot.

Suddenly, a noise broke the spell. Three of the sprinters set off, but pulled up when they realized that the starter's pistol had not fired. Not a shot, the noise was a cry. It sounded like the dreadful howl of a dog, mortally wounded. But it was emitted by a human. Someone in the crowd of spectators. Quizzical faces turned towards the massed ranks of parents.

In what used to be the caretaker's cottage, Mr Smith shuffled in his seat, curious to see what had happened. Further along the boundary of the school grounds, Mr Edriss exclaimed, "Good grief!" A half-smoked cigarette tumbled from his lips to the ground. When the shock of the noise passed, he smiled broadly. Delighted to witness a disruption of the event, he mumbled to himself, "Serve them right if something's gone wrong. Sports Day, indeed!"

Some inner instinct told David who had uttered the inhuman yell. It was not possible to recognize the baying as his grandfather's voice, but he knew all the same. From the senior pupils' benches, David dashed across the track. He had nearly reached his grandfather by the time his mother overcame her stupefied silence and began to scream, "Help! Help!" Ignoring her, David dropped to the ground where his grandfather had toppled from his chair. He nursed his grandfather's head in his lap as the old man gasped for air and clutched at his chest in agony.

"Grandfather! Grandfather!"

It was no good. He could not hear. His body was racked with pain. If David had not been holding him, he would have writhed on the ground like a worm sliced in two by the ruthless blade of a spade.

In less than a minute, the fit was over. The old man's body went limp. His eyes opened and, after a few seconds, he recognized David peering down at him in horror. He tried desperately to say something, but was too exhausted and breathless to make himself heard. Even so, there was a look of sheer determination in his drawn face. There was something he had to say to his beloved grandson. He gasped and tried again. "David..." he whispered, hardly able to move his blue lips.

"Yes?"

"I saw…" The voice became inaudible. Set in a cold white face, his eyes portrayed bloody-mindedness. Stubbornly, he refused to die before he had delivered his message. Again he struggled to speak. "David."

"Yes, I can hear you." David put his ear close to his grandfather's lips and listened intently.

His grandfather murmured his final words and gave a long sigh. David looked up and glanced around. He was surprised by the size of the audience that had collected about them.

Stunned, his mother stammered, "Has he gone?"

David said nothing. He just nodded.

His mother's hand darted to her mouth. She was too shaken even to weep. Through her fingers, she mumbled, "Oh, no! What did he say?"

David hesitated. "I … er…" He scanned the onlookers before he answered her. "I don't know, Mother. I couldn't make it out."

"What?" His mother was in shock and almost hysterical. "Did you see his face? Whatever he had to say was … so important to him. Are you sure you missed it?"

"Leave it, Mother. Now's not the time."

David continued to cradle his grandfather. He didn't need to check his pulse. He knew that the person he respected most in this world was dead. His death would be attributed to a heart attack, of course. But it wasn't that simple. David knew that the attack had been brought on by something his grandfather had seen, or thought he'd seen, on Sports Day.

He stroked the old man's white hair and closed his staring eyes. His grandfather had had a fraught life. Years of pain and bitterness had left their mark on him. But now that life had gone, his face expressed peacefulness. It bore the contentment of a man who had lived long enough to fulfil his ambition.

David was ashamed to cry before an audience. It betrayed a certain weakness that did not become the head of the family, and its only surviving male. But he could not help himself. His grandfather had meant so much to him. Now their relationship was over and the spent body lay before him like an exhausted runner who has successfully passed on the baton. David had not admitted it to his mother, but he *had* heard his grandfather's dying words. At least, he had heard enough of them to make sense. Now it was as though he held the baton securely in his grip and had no choice but to run with it. His grandfather's parting message seemed almost unbelievable, but he had struggled so much to deliver it that David had to take it seriously. A precious and gruesome heirloom had been handed down to him – a legacy that was too dangerous to share with his mother or with Ros. Even as he sat there, still holding the empty body of his grandfather, he knew that he would never benefit from this bequest.

And three weeks later, the sinister inheritance claimed its next victim.

2

It took Ros a few minutes to realize that the rocking sensation was not part of a dream, but that someone was trying to wake her. She opened her eyes and, in the dark, made out David's silhouette. "What...?"

"Wake up."

Ros glanced at the bedside clock. "David! It's the middle of the night." She turned away from him.

"Yes. But we have to talk. Not for long."

Ros groaned. As usual, though, she gave up the notion of a good night's sleep and gave in to her brother. Keeping the sheet up to her shoulders, she heaved herself into a sitting position. "What is it?" she asked grumpily. "An apology for this morning at school?"

David perched on the edge of her bed. "What do you mean?"

"You really don't know, do you?" Ros replied in exasperation. "This morning. Your ... outburst with Kevin."

"I'm not here to talk about that. This is something really important. Listen to me."

The remnants of sleep were pushed aside by Ros's anger. "Important! *My* life's important. You may be a tower of strength to Mother, but to me you're a pain. An arrogant..."

David interrupted her. "I was only thinking of you – protecting you..."

"I don't need protecting from Kev."

"You mean, you don't know that you need protection. There's a big difference."

Ros hated David in his Big Brother mode. He had taken exception to Kevin's interest in her and was determined to keep them apart. Kevin came from the wrong part of town. His family's income was inappropriate. And friendship with anyone having a criminal record was, to David, unthinkable. But Ros found him exciting, macho – and very good-looking. Her brother's attempt to break up their lunchtime liaison had ended in blows. Well, one blow. Kevin had delivered his direct and blunt response, a punch to the head, before David got to the end of a speech on how he failed to come up to scratch as a companion for Ros. Looking on, Ros had found it difficult not to gloat as David picked himself off the floor.

"Kev's all right," Ros insisted. "You've never tried to get to know him. You deserved what you got, acting like a complete idiot."

David sighed. "As I said, I was only doing what's best for you," he replied paternally. "And what's best is…"

"Leave me to get on with my own life, David! I'm not your little sis, needing advice."

"I think you do. You'll see. Kevin is … not going anywhere. He needs sorting out."

"What do you mean?" Ros asked.

"I mean … Never mind. Look, I didn't come to talk about him. I came to tell you I'm going out."

"What?" Ros was so disarmed by her brother's sudden change of tack that she didn't insist on an answer to her question. "It's one o'clock!"

"I told you it was important."

"What are you going on about?"

"I'm sorry but I can't tell you. It's too … risky. Best if you keep out of it." Usually, David was very sure of himself. Now, he seemed insecure. "I came to give you this," he said to her.

For the first time, she noticed that his hands were not empty. He was carrying a torch and holding something out to her. She could not make it out in the dark.

"What is it?" she asked. "A postcard? I can't see."

David stood up. "Don't worry about it now. It's a photo."

"A photo?" She squinted at it.

"Yes. Of Grandmother. But don't bother about it now. If all goes well, I'll have it back in the morning." He hesitated then added, "It's a memento. You should keep it if anything goes wrong."

"Goes wrong?" Unnerved by his air of mystery, Ros asked, "What *is* all this, David?"

"I told you. It's too…" He edged his way towards the door.

"Yeah, yeah. Risky. Too risky for little sis. I suppose you're protecting me again," she said sarcastically.

"That's right," he replied from the doorway.

Suddenly, Ros remembered the incident with Kevin that morning. "You're not going to do anything silly, are you? To get your own back?"

David was too far away for Ros to see the expression on his face but his hesitation told her that she had stumbled upon something. His reply evaded her question. "I have to go now." The bedroom door clicked shut behind him.

"David!" she called. But it was no use. He had gone.

Ros turned on the bedside light and stared at the photograph in her hand. It was ancient, black and white, and tattered. It showed a woman in her twenties – her grandmother, if David was right – standing against a whitewashed wall. She was shown in profile, wearing pyjamas. She looked unkempt and, if she hadn't been pregnant, she would have been unnaturally thin. Where it was visible, her skin was tight on prominent bones. Her hair, cropped short, hadn't seen a comb for some considerable time and her face was gaunt. The photo reflected hopelessness, sadness and resentment.

Shaking her head in perplexity, Ros put down the photo and slid out of bed. Pulling her bedroom curtain aside, just enough to peer round, she watched her brother's outline as he strode purposefully down the drive, carrying a plastic bag. She let go of the curtain when she could not make him out any longer. "What *is* going on?" she mumbled to herself. She knew that, despite the time of night, she must phone Kevin to warn him – just in case David was on his way with vengeance in mind.

3

"What's that, d'you reckon?" The two security guards at Dearing Scientific peered at the video screen. "It's ... er ... a shoe. Isn't it?"

"Mmm. Could be."

By the first light of day, the perimeter cameras normally picked out discarded crisp packets, empty Coke cans and dogs with their legs cocked against the wall. Items of clothing were a relative rarity.

The first security officer was still not satisfied. "The camera's panned as far as it'll go, hasn't it?"

"Yep," the other guard confirmed.

"Pity."

"Why?"

"Because I think there's a foot in the shoe."

"Yeah?"

"Yes. Look." He pointed at the extreme left of the screen where the black shoe was lying on a green background. "Isn't that a bit of sock?"

"I don't know. You might be right. Could have a drunk on our hands."

The other guard sighed. "Could be. You know what this means, don't you? Someone's got to go and check."

"Yeah, I know. I'll do the honours. You stay here and keep shop."

The school field was still damp with dew as the Dearings security officer marched to the patch of land monitored by video camera E5. He expected to find a sad, bewildered old man with a straggling white beard, wearing a greasy raincoat and clutching a dubious bottle of alcohol. He wasn't prepared for the cold, lifeless body of a smartly dressed young man.

Behind the screens that the police had erected in the playing fields, one man was taking photographs. Another was inspecting the body carefully with gloved hands. Detective Superintendent Whyte slipped into the tent and glanced at the victim, splayed on the grass. He groaned aloud.

His colleague, working on hands and knees, looked up. "Not very pleasant, Charlie. A lot of vomiting, evacuation of bowel and bladder."

Frowning, Detective Superintendent Whyte squatted down by the body. "So I see," he murmured. "Do we know who he is?"

"No. Nothing to identify him. He's still got his wallet, though – with money in it."

"Not a robbery, then. How about time of death?"

The pathologist shrugged. "I'll let you know."

"Best guess?"

"I'd say ... between two and three. Yes. Four hours ago."

"OK. Anything else yet?"

The pathologist lifted one of the boy's arms and pointed to red marks on his wrist.

"Been tied?"

"Yes. Both hands. At some point they were tied together. Probably behind his back. Maybe behind a chair. I need to examine the upper arms properly back in the lab to be sure."

"Tied with what?"

The pathologist shrugged. "More than string but not rope. Cord maybe."

"What about clothes?"

"Nothing very illuminating. Judging by the grass stains, he was writhing about here for some time."

Charlie Whyte mumbled, "Poor sod. How old do you think he is?"

"Seventeen? Eighteen at the outside."

"Not a nice age for this."

"No age is a nice age for this, Charlie," the pathologist replied.

"True, but the young ones are the worst. Anyway," the detective said, rising and stretching his legs, "what about the big question. Cause of death. Any answers?"

"Unknown at this stage," his colleague answered, looking up at him. "No obvious wounds. The only signs of violence so far are the marks on the wrists and a black eye."

"No one dies from a black eye or tied-up wrists. Any chance the black eye came from falling over here?"

"No. Not without breaking his nose as well. I imagine he's been thumped recently."

Charlie smiled wryly. "I thumped a few at that age. None of them died, though."

"Well, I've got a funny feeling about this one."

"In what way?"

"Cause of death," the pathologist answered. "It's a funny one."

"Great! That's all I need." Detective Superintendent Whyte headed for the gap in the awning. "Let me know. I'll be waiting. And don't make it too funny."

"There is one thing," the pathologist called after him.

Turning, Charlie prompted eagerly, "Yes?"

"By the smell, I'd say he was drunk."

"Drunk enough to kill him?"

"It's one possibility. It would explain the vomiting."

"OK," the detective superintendent said. "Keep me informed." He left to talk to the press and await a telephone call from some anxious parent wanting to report a missing son.

In the field an army of uniformed policemen inched forward on hands and knees, radiating out from the canopy and peering closely at the ground for clues. They looked almost comical, like a pack of dogs trying to pick up an intriguing scent. Charlie wasn't laughing, though. He too had a funny feeling about this case.

4

And then there were two.

Ros clasped her frail mother in a vain attempt to console her. Mrs Rabin was rocking to and fro, repeating over and over again, "Not David as well. What are we going to do now?"

After she had called the police to report his absence, she'd been put through to Detective Superintendent Whyte. He had rushed directly to the house. Even before he'd handed her the polaroid photograph of a boy to examine, she had known it was her David. Over the years she'd experienced so much misfortune that she had come to expect it. First, the exhaustion of caring for David's sick father and the tragedy of his death. Now, in rapid succession, both David's grandfather and David himself had died. This new blow was too much for her. She was drained.

Through her sobbing, she asked the policeman, "How did he … you know?"

Detective Superintendent Whyte spoke softly, with an air of business-like sympathy. "We don't know – yet. But we'll find out. Of course," he added, "I'll have to ask you to identify him."

David's mother took her handkerchief away from her tormented face. "But I already have! The photograph."

"I'm afraid you'll have to look at David himself. To make absolutely sure."

The policewoman who accompanied Detective Superintendent Whyte added, "It's made as easy as possible for you. It won't be as painful as you think."

Detective Superintendent Whyte nodded. "I have some questions for you as well." He glanced at Ros and added, "Both of you. I won't bother you too much now – I'll come back tomorrow. But, just to be getting on with, have you any idea what he was doing out in the middle of the night?"

Mrs Rabin shook her head. "He should have been here – safe," she sobbed.

"How about you? Rosalind, isn't it?"

"Yes. Ros." She hesitated, gulped and then said, "No. I've no idea what he was up to."

"OK. What about fighting recently? Did he get into a fight?"

David's mother shrugged, speechless. Ros felt her cheeks reddening, but replied, "Er ... I guess so. He had a black eye but ... I don't know about it."

The detective rose. "OK. Now's not really the time. Tracey here", he indicated the policewoman, "will hang on in case there's anything we can do. Or in case you want to talk about it. But just one more thing. Did David drink at all?" he asked.

"What? Alcohol, do you mean?"

"Yes."

"Certainly not," his mother replied, aghast.

Ros shook her head to confirm her mother's answer.

"Thanks," he said, keeping any views to himself. "I'm sorry about the questions but I have to…"

Mrs Rabin nodded, signifying that she understood.

"I'll come back later. OK?" He looked at Ros and said pointedly, "Then maybe you'll be ready to tell me who gave him that black eye."

Ros's head dropped as she blushed again.

Ros phoned Kevin from her bedroom, well out of Tracey's hearing. When he came on the line, she said, "Kev? Is that you?"

Recognizing her voice, Kevin leapt in. "Hi, Ros. Have you heard? Someone's found a body – a dead body – on the school field. Wicked!"

Ros tried to respond but was lost for words.

"Ros?"

"Yes," she said. "I'm here. It's ... It's David."

"What's David? What's up with him now?" Kevin sounded disdainful.

Ros felt awkward and foolish because the right words wouldn't come. She could only repeat, "It's David."

Kevin didn't reply immediately. It took a while for Ros's meaning to dawn on him. "David? In the field? You're kidding!"

"I'm not."

"Oh." Kevin paused again. "I don't know what to say, Ros. I'm sorry. It must be ... rough."

"Rough? Mother's absolutely devastated."

"I guess so," Kevin replied. "Look, I'd better come over."

"No!" Ros suddenly became animated. "The police are here."

"So what?"

"They want to know where he was last night, and what he was doing. I thought he was going to your place to get his own back. Remember, I told you on the phone."

"Well, he didn't turn up here," Kevin assured her. Then, as he realized the full implication of what she had said, he added, "You mean, he was done in and they suspect me?"

"I don't know. They haven't found out yet. But they were asking about his black eye. If they discover it was you..."

"Damn!"

"Kev? Are you all right?"

"Yes," he answered. "I just ... look, you believe me, don't you? We didn't get on, I know. We had a disagreement. But this is something else. I haven't seen him since school yesterday."

"Are you sure?"

"Ros!" He sounded indignant and defensive.

Ros wondered just how well she knew Kevin. She hadn't been seeing him for long and they had no friends in common. She hoped that her opinion of him wasn't as misguided as David had suggested. "OK," she whispered. "I believe you." She tried to make her voice sound free of doubt.

She must have been successful because he replied, "I should think so."

"What should I do, though?" Ros asked him. "They'll quiz me about what I know. Tomorrow."

"Well, don't say he was coming here, whatever you do," Kevin said sharply. "You can't be sure he did anyway. But the punch-up's a different matter. You might as well tell them about that."

"Really?" she checked.

"If you don't, someone else will. They'll ask around at school, no doubt. If it comes to a question of loyalty between me and Rabin –

sorry, I mean, David – the kids'll back me. But there'll always be one who says too much. Someone'll let it out. They'll find out it was me all right, so you might as well come clean on that."

"OK." Ros felt relieved to have his permission. She wasn't good at lying and dreaded trying to keep the truth from Detective Superintendent Whyte. "Of course," she added, "they'll be round to question you."

"Of course they will. I can handle it."

The more confident Kevin sounded, the more Ros's doubts about him returned. In his position, whether guilty or innocent, she would have been scared stiff by the thought of "helping the police with their inquiries". She didn't share Kevin's bravado in times of trouble. She hoped that their difference in attitude reflected nothing more sinister than a difference in upbringing.

"Ros?"

"Yes. Still here. Just ... thinking."

"You sound pretty ... shaken up. Not surprising, I suppose. I ... er ... I'm sorry, Ros."

Kevin had never seen eye-to-eye with David, and would never have done so. It was unlikely that he could summon up much remorse for David's death. It was quite likely, though, that he would feel genuine regret for Ros.

"What you need", he continued, "is a break. Get away from it for a while. How about the club tonight? I could pick you up. I just ... came across a new motorbike. Bit clapped out but I've fixed it up OK..."

Ros interrupted his flow. "Kevin!" she exclaimed. "It's hardly suitable." She almost bit her tongue when she realized how like David she sounded. Still, it was true. "I can't ... for lots of reasons. A disco's hardly the place for mourning. And, for another thing, I can't leave Mother."

"All right," he replied, apparently hurt. "I was just trying to help."

"Yeah. I'm sorry," she said as a peace-offering. "Guess we're all on edge."

She felt that Kevin's suggestion had been well meant, even if inappropriate. She could not believe that he didn't care, but realized that he must be finding it hard to pay his respects to someone for whom he had no respect. Ros wouldn't have admitted it to anyone, but she was having trouble coming to terms with her own feelings. She wasn't sure if her distress was caused by fear for the future rather than the tragedy of the present. Then there was anxiety for her mother. When she saw how her mother was suffering, Ros felt ashamed that she herself was not going through her fair share of grief. But, she told herself, someone has to keep a level head if the two remaining Rabins are going to pull through. She had to assume the responsibility that had come so naturally to David. She was no longer the free-and-easy one in the family. She found herself wondering what she felt for David himself. She knew what she was supposed to feel, but she'd always had problems conforming to family expectations. In the school relay team, Ros had run the last leg. The ultimate responsibility for winning the race had been hers. Now, she felt like the last runner for the family as well. She understood that there would be new obligations, but she was unaware of the nature of another baton that David had surreptitiously passed on to her.

"For a while", she said to Kevin, "I've got to be here. Sorting things out. Mother's not capable of doing anything."

"Are you saying you're not seeing me again?" Kevin asked.

"No," she replied rapidly. "Just give me a bit of time."

"So when will we get together again?"

"I can't tell," Ros admitted.

"How about after the cops interview us? We should compare notes."

"Yes. OK," Ros replied. "That makes sense. Give me a call and we'll take it from there."

"All right," Kevin concluded. "Knowing the cops, it won't be long. See you," he said. "And ... all the best. You know."

"Thanks, Kev. Hope it goes all right with the police."

5

What have you got for me, then?" The pathologist laid down the woman's arm he was examining and turned to see Detective Superintendent Whyte. "Ah, Charlie," he said. "Just a moment." He gave some instructions to his deputy, peeled off his gloves and put them in the bin. "Over here," he called to the detective.

At a large sink, he talked while he scrubbed his hands. "Want to see the boy's body again, or just my report?"

"The report will do. But first, just tell me the main points."

"OK. Prepare yourself," he began ominously. "Down the front of the lad's shirt was a stain." He indicated the place on his own white coat. "The lab confirmed my suspicions. Residue of rum."

"Rum?"

Drying his hands on disposable towels, the pathologist said, "Yes. And enough alcohol in his urine to fail the test."

"So he drank himself to death?"

"No. There was something else on the shirt – and in the body."

"What?"

"I told you it was a funny one."

"You've got that wicked I-told-you-so look. Get on with it."

"It was a lethal dose of nicotine that killed him."

"Nicotine?" Charlie queried. "As in cigarettes?"

"That's right. Tobacco leaf extract."

"He smoked himself to death?"

"No. That takes years, not a few hours. Besides, it's not the nicotine that gets you when you smoke," the pathologist explained while they walked to his office. "Anyway, this lad didn't smoke. The presence of both rum and nicotine in the same stain on the shirt suggests they were taken together."

"You mean, someone prepared a lethal cocktail of nicotine in rum?" The pathologist nodded. "Then forced him to drink it."

"Forced?" Detective Superintendent Whyte checked.

"Two things. Marks on the upper arms were consistent with his being held in a high-backed chair with his wrists tied behind it. And bruising around the mouth suggests forced entry – the bottle, presumably. The lad must have struggled a bit."

"So he was poisoned. Deliberately."

"You got it. Urine, blood and kidney – all riddled with nicotine." He took some notes from his desk and gave them to Detective Superintendent Whyte. "With the alcohol and loss of fluids, shock contributed to his death as well, but nicotine's the real villain of the piece."

The policeman glanced down the report as he asked, "Where do you get it from? And how much would you need?"

"It's all in there." The pathologist pointed to the papers. "The LD_{50} – that's the lethal dose, more or less – for someone his size would be about three grammes. But where do you get it?" He shrugged. "Any chemical suppliers, I guess. Nicotine used to be used as an insecticide, if I remember rightly, so it's not hard to come by – for someone who knows his chemistry." He hesitated, then added, "There's one other obvious place to get it from."

"Yes? Where's that?"

"A packet of ciggies, of course."

"Really? How? Is there enough nicotine in a packet?"

"I shouldn't think so. You'd need a good few packets, I suspect. I'm not a hundred per cent sure. You'll have to consult a tame chemist or toxicologist. But anyone who does a bit of chemistry would be able to extract it from tobacco."

"Wouldn't some special equipment be needed?"

"As I said," the pathologist went on, "better consult someone who knows. I'll tell you one thing, though. It's pretty neat as a murder weapon. Easy to get hold of. Ownership not illegal. And the forensic scientists can take as many samples as they like from suspects, it'll never prove anything. You'll get traces of nicotine just about anywhere and on almost everybody. Especially on – or near – smokers. Forget forensic evidence. It's like finding a drowned man in the middle of the Atlantic and asking exactly which bit of the water killed him."

"OK," Charlie groaned, "I get the picture. Just tell me. Have you come across a poisoning like this before?"

"No," he answered. "It's definitely a funny one."

"Just my luck!" Charlie waved the report and said, "Anyway, thanks for this."

"You're welcome," the pathologist replied as he prepared himself to return to the examination of another victim. "If I were you, I'd drag out my old chemistry schoolbooks. A bit of revision is called for."

6

When Detective Superintendent Whyte returned to Ros's house, he was not alone. He was accompanied by Tracey, who had the impossible task of comforting Mrs Rabin, and another policeman, who was there to help sift through David's belongings. Such a search was needed, they explained tactfully, because their inquiries had become a murder investigation. David's effects might reveal a clue.

Mrs Rabin did not take the news well, and it was not long before Tracey called in the family doctor to put her under sedation. Then it was up to Ros to deal with Detective Superintendent Whyte and his questions on her own.

"If you believe in TV cops," he said to break the ice, "you'd expect me to be called Super. But no one calls me Super. I can't think why not. Anyway, Charlie will do for me." He went on to ask her at length about her brother: his friends, his life, his state of mind, everything.

Eventually, he came to the topic that Ros had dreaded. "Now," he probed, "this black eye. You said you didn't know anything about it, but have you changed your mind?"

Head bowed, Ros simply nodded.

"Tell me about it."

"It was David's fault really," she began, from the outset defending Kevin. She knew she shouldn't speak ill of the dead, but it was the truth. Besides, there was nothing she could do for David now. At least she could protect the living. She explained how David had insulted Kevin by telling him that he wasn't good enough to mix with the Rabins.

Charlie Whyte made a note of Kevin's details then asked, "What did you think of this ... spot of bother?"

"How do you mean?" Ros asked innocently.

"Did you approve of your brother's action?"

"No. David gets ... He used to get too bossy. He meant well, of course. But he took his role as head of the family too seriously. We argued about it afterwards."

The policeman's ears pricked up. "Oh yes? When?"

Ros blushed. "It was ... late. He came to ... Anyway, we had a row about it."

"What time was this?"

"One o'clock."

"You sound sure. It's not a guess, is it?"

"No. I checked my bedside clock."

"And after you argued, he left? Left the house?"

Ros nodded again. "Yes. That's why he came into my room in the first place. To tell me he was going out."

"Strange at that time of night. It must have been important. Surely he said where he was going, or why he was going somewhere?"

"No." She dared not mention her suspicion that David had set out for Kevin's house. "He just came to say he was going out. That's all. He wouldn't tell me where when I asked him."

Detective Superintendent Whyte pondered for a moment. It was simple to deduce that Kevin might be involved. "Time, I think, that I had a word with Kevin Kingsnorth," he said.

"But he's not ... It wasn't Kev that did it."

"No?"

"No. He's ... not like that."

"I'm sure you're right, Ros," Charlie reassured her. "But I'd better check it out for myself. I have to."

"Yes. I know," Ros admitted sullenly.

"What did *you* do after David left?" Detective Superintendent Whyte asked.

"Me?"

"Yes. You quarrelled about Kevin, then he left. What did you do?"

"You don't think I...?"

"I just want to know what you did. Like, did you run after him?"

"No," she answered. "For one thing, I wasn't dressed. I'd never have caught him up by the time I'd got some clothes on." Until then, it hadn't crossed Ros's mind that she might be a suspect herself. She gulped at the thought. Suddenly, she didn't feel like answering any more questions. She wished there was someone there to advise her. Someone like David.

From that moment she decided to be less cooperative. She thought better of telling the detective about her phone call to Kevin. That would implicate him even more. He was in enough trouble without that. She also decided not to tell Detective Superintendent Whyte about the old photograph of Grandmother. It was something, she felt, that was private to the family, and telling the policeman about it would be a betrayal of some family secret that she didn't understand.

"I went to sleep. Nothing more," she said. "I took a while to settle, but that's all I did. Went to sleep feeling annoyed with him. Maybe even a bit worried about why he'd gone out. But it was the last time I saw him." She swallowed, trying not to show her weakness.

"It's OK, Ros," Charlie said warmly. "Look, I think I've bothered you enough for one night. I'll leave you in peace now. I'm sorry I've had to put you through this."

"I understand."

They both rose. On the way to the door, Detective Superintendent Whyte asked her, "How do you get on at school?"

"How do you mean?"

"Don't panic," he replied amiably. "Nothing to do with the inquiry. Just interested. What are your best subjects?"

Nonplussed, Ros said, "Er ... I don't know. History, I guess."

"History! My worst," Charlie replied in a friendly tone. "Could never concentrate on the past. Always wanted to investigate the present myself. Science was my best subject. Chemistry. Are *you* interested in chemistry? Any good at it?"

Thinking that his banter was altogether out of place, Ros wanted to bring the conversation to an end as soon as possible. "No," she replied tersely. "Flopped Combined Science last year – at my old school."

"You're ... what? First year of A levels?"

"Yes. History, English and Social Science."

"Well," Charlie said, opening the front door, "I hope you can return to normal studies soon." He looked outside and up at the clouds. "Mmm. Looks like rain on the way." Glancing back at her, he added, "Thanks for your patience."

She nodded, then shut the door with a feeling of immense relief. After a few moments savouring privacy, she made for the phone. She had to warn Kevin that the police were probably on their way – and that they were hunting for a murderer.

7

Outside the long terrace of grey-brick houses, there were two cars without wheels, several abandoned shopping trolleys, a couple of Jehovah's Witnesses, and a stray dog. A man whose bare arms were covered in tattoos was wagging his finger at a young boy and shouting, "How many times have I told you…?" Further down Curtis Street three boys were kicking a tin can across the road. Overhead, dark clouds drifted.

Detective Superintendent Whyte's car, driven by Tracey, meandered down the road to avoid first the footballers then the dog. It cruised past the tattooed man and his son, and pulled up outside number 37. The detective got out of the car and banged on the wooden door as if he were trying to waken the dead.

After a couple of minutes, Kevin answered the door. Neither of his callers were in uniform but he frowned and groaned. "Cops!" he muttered.

"Kevin Kingsnorth?" Detective Superintendent Whyte asked.

Before Kevin could reply, the black sky above them was rent by lightning, like a flashing blade slicing through a dark curtain. Almost immediately, ear-splitting thunder boomed and huge raindrops pelted down.

"Amazing!" Kevin cried above the clatter. "How did you do that?"

"Always like to make a dramatic entrance," the policeman yelled back.

"It'd be fun to keep you here on the doorstep," Kevin replied, "but I guess I'd better let you in." He stood to one side.

Already soaked, they stepped inside and dripped on to the living room carpet. "Thanks."

"What's it all about? David Rabin?"

Not responding straight away, the policeman introduced himself. "I'm Detective Superintendent Whyte and this is WPC Ashmore. And ... er ... Can I sit here?" He plonked himself down and tried to ease his wet trousers away from his skin. "I'd like to know why you think this is about David Rabin."

Kevin sat down opposite the policeman and smiled. "You must have asked around by now. Found out who his friends were, and how many enemies he had. I imagine my name cropped up."

"Would you imagine it cropped up as a friend or enemy?"

"We ... er ... You wouldn't say we were the best of buddies."

"What would you say?"

"I'd say he was a pompous twit. More money than community spirit."

The policewoman remained on her feet, walking around the room and peering into every nook and cranny. Whenever she stopped circling, she kept her eyes on Kevin as he answered the questions.

"What was the problem between you, exactly?" WPC Ashmore asked.

Kevin smiled again. "Why keep beating about the bush when you want to know if I was the one who clobbered him?"

"Clobbered?" Detective Superintendent Whyte queried.

"Thumped," Kevin explained. "And yes, it was me. I thumped him. But the thump was the only thing I did to him."

"Only?"

"Yeah. Nothing else."

"Should there be anything else?"

"You wouldn't be here", Kevin retorted, "just to investigate a schoolyard tiff."

The rain clattered against the window like handfuls of pebbles and the water sluicing the pane obliterated the view of the street. The next flash of lightning appeared at the window like the momentary glare of the headlights of a passing car. This time it took a few seconds before they were hit by a barrage of thunder.

"Police procedure is something you know all about, isn't it, Kevin? First-hand experience."

"Yeah, yeah. No need to go on about it."

"Arson, wasn't it?" the policewoman asked.

"You know exactly what it was," Kevin snapped. "You'd have checked up before coming."

"You see our problem, though," the detective superintendent said, leaning forward in his seat. "This is your second argument with some kid from the other side of town. The first gets a petrol-soaked rag and a match through the front door. The second ... ends up dead in a field."

"I was younger, then. Besides, no one got hurt," Kevin protested. "And I didn't hurt anyone this time, either."

"Are your parents in?" the detective inquired.

"You've got to be joking! Out on the town as usual. They'll be back about two in the morning, if form is anything to go by."

The policeman leaned even further forwards and ordered, "Show me your hands."

"What?"

"Show me."

Detective Superintendent Whyte examined Kevin's fingers for yellow staining. "Mmm," he said, letting go the hands. "You smoke."

"I used to."

"Judging by the stains, you've given it up very recently. Why?"

"Can't afford it. And Ros objects as well. Why do you want to know?"

"Where did you buy them from, when you did smoke?"

"All over. The newsagent's round the corner usually. So what?"

"Never mind." The detective superintendent sat back in his chair again, then asked sternly, "Friday night. Between midnight and three a.m. Where were you?"

"Friday?" Kevin stalled.

"Yes. The early hours of Saturday, actually."

"I was here."

"Tucked up in bed?"

"No," Kevin replied. "Watching telly. Big match. Live."

"Match? What match?"

Kevin answered, "American Football. At San Francisco."

"Who won?" the policeman inquired.

"The home team. The 49ers."

"Did you watch it on your own?" asked WPC Ashmore.

"No. A couple of mates came round. Graham Johnson and Darren Cook."

"And they'll confirm this?"

"Yeah."

"And when they're next in trouble, you'll provide the alibi, eh?" Whyte grinned wryly but not unpleasantly.

Kevin shrugged. "I just told you the truth, that's all."

Detective Superintendent Whyte changed the subject again. "Tell me why you thumped him. Rabin, that is."

Kevin looked puzzled. "Won't you have heard this already, from Ros? She was there."

"You tell me."

"Prince Charming told me I was too low on the evolutionary scale to be mixing with his Ros."

"Anything else?"

"That was enough," Kevin replied wickedly. "He said some other stuff as well, but that was enough for me."

"How did Ros react?"

Kevin shrugged. "Ask her."

"But what do you think?"

"I think you ought to ask her if you want to know."

Whyte wouldn't let go. "Did she congratulate you?" he queried. "Or have a go at you for hitting her brother?"

"She didn't seem too upset to see Rabin get what was coming to him." It suddenly occurred to Kevin that the cops might even suspect Ros, so he said no more. He didn't want to get her into trouble by implying that she was purring quietly over her brother's death.

"Have you seen Ros since the fight?" Tracey put in.

"No. Well, only across a crowded playground at break on the same day." To take the heat off Ros, he added, "She's been too upset to see me since ... you know."

Kevin was relieved that the accusing finger was not pointed only at him, but he was appalled that Ros was also under suspicion. Not Ros! She didn't get on with her brother, and she was now a lot closer to a fortune, but ... surely not! Ros was too full of life to take it from anyone else. Then it struck him that they might even suspect a conspiracy between Ros and him. After all, they were a lot better off without Big Brother watching over them.

"What's your relationship with Ros Rabin?" the detective superintendent asked, as if to confirm Kevin's assessment of his predicament.

"It's ... er..." Kevin shrugged. "We get along. Nothing too serious."

"But serious enough to annoy her brother."

"It didn't take much to do that," Kevin remarked.

The rain had ceased to batter the window. It had become a gentle patter and the thunder a distant rumble.

"How are you getting on at school?"

"School? Er ... All right. Why?"

"You're the same age as Ros, right? But a year behind."

"That's the effect of my last run-in with you lot. It put me back a year at school."

"Do you know what LD fifty is?" queried Detective Superintendent Whyte.

"What's this? Some sort of test?" Kevin groused.

"Do you know?"

"Sounds like a grade of engine oil to me."

The policeman did not ask another question straight away. He examined Kevin's face and let the silence force the boy into saying more. "Well?" Kevin said in agitation. "Am I close? What is this LD fifty stuff?"

"I thought you'd know."

Kevin shuffled uncomfortably in his seat. "No. No idea. Some funny questions you're coming out with – even for a cop."

"Well, you know how he died, don't you?"

Kevin hesitated, then grimaced. "No," he answered. "You didn't say, and it's not been in the papers." He was relieved to be back on familiar territory. The famous elephant-trap of a police question. He could cope with that sort of trick question all day long. It was the questioning that he didn't understand that made him feel uneasy. "What did he die of?" asked Kevin.

"He was poisoned."

"Poisoned? Wow! What with?"

"Oh, I don't think we need to go into that," Detective Superintendent Whyte replied. "But we may take a look around your house – just in case there's traces of it here."

"Feel free," Kevin retorted. "Search as much as you like. We're clean."

"OK, Kevin," the policeman said, rising to his feet. "We may do that. But not us. Some forensic chappies. Real experts. They don't miss a thing, you know."

Again, Kevin felt at ease with threats. He was used to intimidation. He would have been more anxious if the police had left without trying to panic him. "Fine," he replied in defiance.

"We'll be back," Detective Superintendent Whyte said as he went out through the door that the WPC had opened for him.

"Sure," Kevin called after him.

The storm had passed. It had gone to terrorize some other town. In the street outside number 37, rainwater had collected all around the parked car. As Tracey looked down at the puddles, she cried, "Oh, no!"

"What's up?" Charlie asked.

"Flat tyres. All of them. I'll have to call for back-up."

Charlie grinned at her and said, "As I've always told you, Tracey, know your environment. Know what you're getting into and take account of it."

"What?"

He walked to the back of the car and opened the boot. "The lads round here can recognize an unmarked police car by sixth sense. You should expect them to let the tyres down," he explained. He picked out a foot-pump and held it aloft triumphantly. "See? Forethought pays. I got the mechanics to put it in as soon as I decided to come here." He slammed shut the boot and said, "Come on. I'll do two tyres. You can do the other two. That's equality for you."

8

Ros was feeling vulnerable. She had always been sheltered from responsibility by the umbrella of the family. Now that umbrella had collapsed. If she didn't have the strength to hold it up, everything would collapse. Her mother hardly had the strength, or the will, to rise from her bed so it was Ros who had to take charge of the family affairs. Overnight, her freedom had been replaced with responsibility.

And on top of all that, there was Kevin. Was it right to be associating with someone suspected of her brother's murder? Should she be seeing him even before the police had released David's body for the funeral? Could she really be so certain of his good intentions? How on earth could she expect to run the family if she couldn't even make up her mind about Kevin?

After a little pressure from him on the phone, she'd agreed to see him. She wasn't sure whether belief in his innocence or curiosity about his encounter with the police had contributed more to her decision.

They met in the evening at Kevin's local youth centre, where a band of young hopefuls were playing cover versions fast, furiously and ineffectively. The singer cried to his colleagues, "Give 'em a belter. Let's have some life!" Even in a relatively quiet corner of the bar, Kevin and Ros couldn't make themselves heard without yelling at each other. "Come on," Kevin shouted. "I've got an idea."

They stood by the barricade to the swimming pool till no one was looking then, Kevin leading Ros by the arm, they vaulted over and into the changing rooms. "Here?" Ros queried.

"No," Kevin answered. "Let's go into the pool itself."

"What?" Ros objected. "You've got to be joking."

"No," Kevin explained. "I mean, sit by the pool."

"Oh. OK."

They went through the shower area and sat at the edge of the pool on the seats reserved for the attendants.

"Mmm," Ros said. "This is quite nice. Calm."

Only a faint repetitive thump from the hall penetrated the walls. One side of the pool, entirely windows, let in the moonlight which reflected off the uncannily still water. If it hadn't been for the reflection and the characteristic smell of disinfectant, they would have thought the water had been drained away.

"I've never seen the water like this before," Kevin said quietly.

"It's like … asleep," Ros replied. "Eerie."

"Yeah."

For a while they sat in silence. Ros was enjoying the tranquillity and Kevin was wondering how to break the spell. He was keen to talk about the murder, but before he'd settled on an opening sentence that didn't seem heartless, Ros chipped in. "Well, we can't just sit here, I guess. We'd better get started."

Gratefully Kevin agreed. "Why don't I go first?"

Ros shrugged. "If you like. What did they ask you?"

"Oh, some standard stuff – and some funny things as well." He went through as much of the interview as he could remember, interrupting his flow now and again to make conclusions or to answer Ros's questions.

"Why did he ask about smoking?" asked Ros.

"Search me," he responded.

"Do you reckon they'll check up on what you said about watching telly?"

"Sure to. But Darren and Graham won't let me down. They'll swear they watched the game with me."

"So you didn't really? You don't actually have an alibi."

"No," Kevin admitted. "And you've got the same problem. Remember, you're on their hit list as well. Perhaps we should have said we were together. Thinking about it, though," he added, "they might suspect we're in it together, so that wouldn't have helped."

"No," Ros said. "Anyway, I can't lie without turning bright red."

"Oh," Kevin recalled suddenly, "they asked me what LD fifty is. I didn't know. Do you?"

"LD fifty?" Ros replied. "Yes. We did a project on animal

experiments. It's the dose that's lethal for fifty per cent of a bunch of animals when they're fed some stuff that's being tested. They check out the LD_{50} of pesticides and things like that."

"So", Kevin queried, "it tells you how poisonous something is?"

"That's right," Ros confirmed.

"Ah, well. That makes sense, then. I passed that little test. They were trying to see if I knew how much of a poison to give someone to kill them. I didn't."

"You mean, David was poisoned?"

"Yes. Didn't you know?"

"They didn't tell me," she said. "I was in such a spin, I didn't think to ask."

"They wouldn't have said at first, anyway. They like to find out if a suspect knows the cause of death before it's publicized. Did this Whyte chap ask you anything about poisons, or something like it?"

"No," Ros replied. She hesitated then added, "Now you mention it, he did ask me something about chemistry. Whether I was any good at it. Was that my test? I guess it was. I hope I passed as well."

"Lucky he didn't give you the LD_{50} test. You'd have failed."

"No, he didn't ask me that one. Just as well, really."

"You'd better tell me what else they asked you," Kevin said.

To the barely audible heartbeat of the bustling life beyond the swimming pool walls, and hardly shifting her gaze from the becalmed water, Ros related her story. She also told him more of her encounter with David in her bedroom. "And", she finished gloomily, "a couple of hours later, he was dead."

Kevin squeezed her arm. "Yeah. I'm sorry."

"Are you?" Ros found herself saying. "Aren't you pleased to see the back of him?"

"That's not fair, Ros," Kevin replied, letting go of her arm. "He rubbed me up the wrong way, but…"

Ros looked at him askance, then wiped her eyes. "OK," she said. "I trust you. I'm sorry. I'm still upset. I still expect him to come through a door – maybe walk in here and find us together. He'd throw a fit."

"Of course you're upset," Kevin said as sympathetically as he was able. "The way I see it, you and me have got to stick together, though. We've got the cops after us. So the sooner we work out who … did it, the sooner we'll be off the hook."

"Us?"

"Why not?" Kevin answered. "We know about as much as the cops. And you know a bit more. What was the photo he gave you?"

"Grandmother. When she was young – and pregnant. Do you think that's got anything to do with it? David didn't say it was important, not in so many words. He just called it a memento."

Kevin shrugged. "No idea if it's important. But we shouldn't rule it out. We'll have to look at it together. She's not ... alive now, is she?"

"No," Ros answered. "She died soon after the photo was taken, I guess."

"This was the wife of the chap that died on Sports Day?" Kevin checked.

"Yes. Heart attack. Like Father when I was young."

"Your family's had it rough, hasn't it?"

Somewhere, a door opened then slammed shut. Ros didn't answer Kevin's question for a few moments. When the stillness returned and they were out of danger of being discovered, she whispered, "Yes. It's not a pretty history. But I don't know much about it. No one at home said anything. Not to me, anyway. David and Grandfather were close. They probably talked about it." Ross turned to Kevin and added, "The Rabin household could never have been described as a hotbed of feminism, you know. The men took care of the important things. Like a secret society, they were. I was left out in the cold – expected to help around the house and look decorative, that's all. They'd be regretting it now – keeping me in the dark – because I'll have to pick up the pieces."

"Well, what *do* you know?"

"I guess that photo must have been taken just before Grandmother had Father. She died giving birth." The quiet throb of the music relented for a few moments then started up once more, like a heart that stopped briefly, dangerously, before it began to pump life again. "It was a difficult birth all round, but I don't know the details. I bet David knew. Grandfather would have filled him in. They hid it from me. Made me feel ... I don't know ... bitter, particularly towards David. Perhaps that's why we weren't closer, because I felt isolated. Anyway, the birth left Father unhealthy for most of his life. Mother came along and helped him through – gave him a good few more years, I reckon. Strong in those days, she was.

But looking after him sapped all her energy. By the time he died – his heart packed up, I think – she was a nervous wreck. I was five at the time."

"So how come he earned a fortune?" asked Kevin.

Ros shrugged. "That was Grandfather and Father between them. You don't need to be healthy to play the money markets – to buy the right currency and the right businesses at the right time. They were good at it. Green fingers for stocks and shares and all that."

"All this wheeler-dealing!" Kevin scorned. "But at the end of the day they haven't made anything useful – except money for themselves." He paused, then said, "Sorry, Ros, but I can't stand that sort of thing."

"I'm not keen myself," Ros answered. "But the point is, has any of it got anything to do with David?"

"I've no idea," Kevin replied.

"Nor me. I don't see how it could."

"What about David himself, then? Any clues there? Did you say he was carrying a plastic bag that night?"

"Yes. But I don't know what was in it – if anything."

"And he had a torch?"

"Yes. So?"

"So, did the police say they'd found a bag or torch?"

"No. Would they, even if they had?"

"They'd probably ask you to identify them. Was the torch special at all? Or did it have his name on it?"

"No. Not as far as I know," answered Ros. "It was … just ordinary. I dare say there are lots of them around."

"But would you recognize the type if you saw it again?" Kevin asked.

"Yes, I think so."

"Good. So that's three leads we've got that the law hasn't: the torch, the bag and the photo. The trouble is, they've got the murder weapon. They know which poison…" Kevin stopped talking because he could see that Ros was distressed by his enthusiasm.

"You talk about David as if he was just … I don't know," Ros muttered. "He hasn't even been buried yet and you're all excited about some detective caper."

"I'm sorry, Ros," he replied, lost for any other words.

"Besides," Ros added, "what if we did find out something?"

"What do you mean?"

"Wouldn't it be dangerous?"

Kevin looked puzzled. "How come?" he asked.

"David said it was risky. He wanted to leave me out of it. If we go chasing a murderer, wouldn't he protect himself? Maybe we'd be next in the firing line."

Kevin hesitated then replied, "No worries, Ros. We'll be careful."

Ros didn't know whether to be reassured or dismayed at his confidence. She sighed. "I've had enough," she said. "I'm going home."

"OK," Kevin agreed. "Let's sneak out of here and I'll take you back on the bike."

They crept away from the dormant pool, passing through the turmoil of the disco and out into the cold dark night. "Want to risk a dodgy curry from the van?" Kevin asked, suddenly hungry.

"No," Ros replied quietly but firmly. "Just straight home."

9

Mr Monk, known amongst his pupils as Chipmonk because he seemed to have a chip on his shoulder, frowned at Detective Superintendent Whyte. "Yes. Rabin." He considered for a moment, wiping his perfectly bald head with his hand. "Not been here long and not one of my favourite pupils, I must confess. Bright, of course. Very bright. He'd have made it big, no doubt. Lucky lad."

"How do you mean," the policeman questioned, "lucky?"

"Some of us have to fight our way through life, Detective Superintendent," Mr Monk complained. "Even the able ones. Rabin was clever all right, but it wouldn't have mattered if he wasn't. The family business was always his safety net."

"Would you deny him his good luck, then?"

"When I was his age, we didn't have two pennies to rub together," the Deputy Head and science teacher replied. "It was hard to get even this far. Long hours, part-time jobs while studying – that sort of thing. Certainly no safety net. If I'd been free of those sorts of constraints, I'd have ... Who knows? I wouldn't have got bogged down in a dead-end teaching job, that's for sure. I'd have been out there doing science, not teaching it. And earning a worthwhile salary."

Detective Superintendent Whyte nodded sympathetically, encouraging Chipmonk to show his true colours. "I know what you mean. There's lots like us. Hard work, little reward. Then there's the privileged classes..." He shook his head, signifying unspeakable injustice.

Recognizing that bait was being dangled in front of him, Chipmonk refused to bite. "Don't get me wrong, Mr Whyte. Rabin certainly was privileged, but I didn't resent it that much. Anyway," he added, "neither of us would want to be in his shoes now, eh? Even Rabin deserved better than what he got."

"True," Detective Superintendent Whyte agreed. "Anything else about him?"

"Not really," the teacher answered. "I just couldn't get on with him, that's all. Neither did his peers. Rather arrogant, I found."

"In what way?"

"Sure of himself. Let me give you an example. Earlier this year he chose to do a project on the environment for his science studies. Before we knew it, he was round at Dearings, asking to interview Dr Dearing himself. Wanted to know if Dearings had an environmental policy."

"When was this?" asked the detective.

"I don't know exactly – before his grandfather died at Sports Day. About five weeks ago, I'd say."

"Well, did he get to speak to anyone in authority?"

"I'm not sure. We only found out he was making a nuisance of himself because Dr Dearing phoned the school. No one minds inquisitiveness, of course. They gave him some literature on the labs and sent him away, apparently. After he'd read it, he was back with questions. They refused to give him any more information. He would hardly take no for an answer. Persistence bordering on provocation. Unacceptable in any circumstances, but when Dr Dearing is Chairman of the School Governors ... It's just not on. They virtually had to eject Rabin from the premises. And I had to throw the rule book at him. You know," Chipmonk concluded, "if he'd lived, he could have become one of the worst sort of journalists. The objectionable foot-in-the-door type."

"A good investigator, then. Even if unpopular," Charlie Whyte prompted.

"That's right. Always delving into things. Whether he was wanted or not."

"Anything else he was working on that might have got him into trouble?"

"Let me see." The Deputy Head rummaged through the papers on his desk. "Nothing obvious," he replied. "Here's a record of the books he'd got out of the school library." He scanned the list. "A bit of fiction, environmental science, Stephen Hawking's *Time*, a history of the Channel Islands. That's probably a mistake. Sounds more like Rosalind Rabin's sort of thing. Anyway," he concluded, "nothing contentious."

"OK," Detective Superintendent Whyte said. "When his records are assembled, I'd be grateful for a copy."

"No problem."

"Just one more thing," Charlie added. "You teach chemistry, don't you?"

"Combined science at GCSE, and A level chemistry, yes."

"Do you ever do experiments on cigarettes?"

"Cigarettes? No. Why?"

"Oh, I just wondered."

Chipmonk's curiosity was aroused. "What's this about?"

"Nothing to do with David Rabin, but as you're a chemist, I thought I'd take the opportunity to ask. In one of my other cases I need an expert opinion."

"Oh, yes?" Chipmonk responded well to flattery. He liked being called an expert.

"We had occasion to raid a house. Found the usual drugs, you know. A right little den. But we also found quite a bit of nicotine. Odd."

"Very odd. It's pretty toxic. Same class of compound as strychnine."

"Yes," the policeman responded. "We want to know how it got there."

"And why?"

"Of course. Could it have been extracted from cigarettes, do you think?"

"I don't see why not," Chipmonk answered. "But ... er ... I think it occurs in tobacco as a complex, mainly."

"What?"

"Sorry. It's ... in a different form. You'd have to convert it to free nicotine before isolating and purifying it."

"So, this would need special equipment?"

"Ideally, yes. But not necessarily. It could be done in a kitchen with a bit of fiddling about. Only you'd need some chemicals. Mind you, they're not specialized either. Acid, base and a solvent, that's probably all. You might get by with some cleaning fluid containing ammonia. Lemon juice or descaling fluid for the acid, and something like petrol as a solvent. Yes," he surmised, "it might be possible."

"Mmm. Interesting. Well, thanks for the advice."

"Of course," the schoolteacher continued, "if your crooks were chemists, they could just buy it. Cut out the fuss. The real question is", he mused, "why they had it."

"I've got our forensic people on to that one," Charlie said abruptly, clearly wishing to bring the session to an end. "Thanks again. I'll send someone for Rabin's records tomorrow. OK?"

"Sure. You're welcome."

Back in his office, Charlie reviewed the findings of two officers on his team. One had interviewed Mr Smith who lived in the old care-taker's cottage, and the other had tried to make sense of Mr Edriss.

Mr Smith was retired. He spent his days collecting stamps and watching the activities at the school. He was particularly fond of whiling away the time on his patio that overlooked the field in which the body had been discovered. Mr Smith was in his seventies, but still reasonably healthy in body and mind. The kids at the school liked him because he always returned the balls that landed in his garden and he never blabbed to the teachers when he saw them sneaking out early. Voluntarily, he even acted as look-out for the school premises. He was known to Charlie because he'd once phoned the police station when he'd witnessed an attempted break-in at the school, from his bedroom window. On the night of David's death, he hadn't been so vigilant. He'd gone to bed at about eleven-thirty. Even if he had still been up, he wasn't in the habit of standing his patio after dark, and his bedroom window over-looked the school, not the playing field.

Mr Edriss was younger, about fifty, and a different kettle of fish altogether. He hated children. Their noisy games on the field drove him to distraction. He would stand, hands on hips, at the end of his garden overlooking the field and try to intimidate the kids by his presence. He was grumpy and frequently shouted incoherent abuse until he broke down spluttering and coughing. Mr Edriss was an unpleasant eccentric. At one time he'd been employed by Dearing Scientific, but there had been an accidental spillage of some nasty chemical and he had been exposed to it. On the grounds of ill-health, he had taken early retirement with a considerable settlement from Dearings. Mr Edriss was also known to the police. Charlie still remembered the events that had ruined his Christmas eighteen months ago. It was Boxing Day. Charlie was hoping to spend a restful day with his family, when he got called out to take charge of the incident. It was Edriss's birthday on Boxing Day and he claimed that the local kids, out riding their new Christmas bikes and kicking new footballs on the school field, were disturbing him. His attempts to have a quiet birthday got out of hand. His verbal abuse directed at the boys became obscenities. Obscenities became physical abuse. The result was a boy with a torn jacket, bruised arm and cut lip. Mr Edriss was convicted on a charge of actual bodily harm. From that moment, he had ceased to be a laughing stock and became a menace.

The officer reported that Mr Edriss seemed delighted that there would be one less pupil at the school. No remorse whatever, and no alibi. Not even an attempt at a weak alibi. Wished he'd killed some of them himself ages ago. He had no qualms about being a suspect. In fact, he seemed proud to be considered a potential child murderer. A nasty piece of work. The notes ended with the observation that Mr Edriss was a chain-smoker. The entire output of a tobacco plantation was lying around his house.

Charlie Whyte slapped the progress reports back down on his desk. All his fears about the Rabin case seemed to be well founded. It *was* a funny one. And he still had a final interrogation to conduct. He'd kept the juiciest one for himself.

On his FAX machine, a message had come in from the forensic science laboratory. "Nicotine. Found in dried leaves of *Nicotiana tabacum* and *Nicotiana rustica* at about 5% level, combined with various acids. Commercial nicotine available as by-product of tobacco industry. Simple extraction procedure given in several chemistry texts. It is a neuropoison; LD_{50} in rat for oral dose: 50 mg/kg. Symptoms of oral ingestion are extreme nausea, vomiting, mental confusion, uncontrolled bowel and bladder evacuation, convulsions. It has been used as a pesticide.

"Assuming the same LD_{50} in humans as in rats and given the victim's mass of 60 kg, a lethal dose would be about 3000 mg (3 g) by mouth.

"Regarding query about cigarettes, the average mass of tobacco in a cigarette is 650 mg, and about 5% of the mass is nicotine.

Therefore, one cigarette would contain 32 mg nicotine. If extraction were complete the lethal oral dose for this victim would require nicotine from roughly 100 cigarettes. Given incomplete extraction and doubts about the precise lethal dose, a batch of 150–200 cigarettes would be more certain to give sufficient nicotine to cause death by oral ingestion."

Charlie didn't have a degree in maths or science but he understood the main thrust of the FAX message. Just ten packets of cigarettes, a bit of chemical knowledge, and someone could have concocted enough poison to kill a healthy young man. He sighed heavily. He felt depressed, intrigued and angry at the same time. Even after years of contact with crime, he had never quite gained immunity from the shock of the next grim finding.

The security guards in the reception at Dearings were expecting Mr Whyte. They had a visitor's badge ready and waiting for him. He was asked to wear it at all times when on the premises and to hand it in on his way out. On the site of Dearing Scientific, he was to be accompanied at all times and should not enter any buildings or rooms without the permission of a supervisor.

Within a few moments, a secretary arrived to escort him to Dr Dearing's office. On the way, Charlie asked her, "What exactly does Dearing Scientific do?"

The secretary smiled at him, but replied, "Oh, you'll have to ask Dr Dearing that. I'm just a secretary."

"I find", the policeman observed, "that secretaries know an awful lot. All those letters and memos that pass before you..."

"I don't understand most of it," she answered. "And besides, I don't talk about my job here. Not if I want to keep it." She pushed open a door to a lobby. "Take a seat," she invited him. "Dr Dearing will be with you any moment."

The Managing Director of the laboratories was a small man, about fifty years of age, and probably hyperactive. He shook the detective superintendent's hand firmly as if he was greeting a new customer rather than an investigator. "Come on in, come on in. Emma," he called to the secretary, "protect me from callers while I have Mr Whyte with me. And bring forward the Management Team meeting. I want them all here immediately after Mr Whyte's visit. Say, half an hour."

Charlie smiled to himself. Dr Dearing was attempting to take control of the timing of their interview.

When they were seated in his immaculately orderly office, Dr Dearing said, "Your people interviewed my security guards. Did it help? Could they tell you anything about this unfortunate incident?"

Maybe, by asking the first question, he was trying to dictate their whole session.

"No," Charlie replied. "Only that when it was light enough to pick out detail, David Rabin's foot was in view of one of your cameras. According to the time of death, he must have stumbled into that position between two-thirty and three a.m." In wresting back control of the interview, Charlie launched into his first question without hesitation. "Exactly what does Dearing Scientific do, Dr Dearing?"

"What has that got to do with your inquiries?"

"Look. A dead body is found yards from your premises. One of your staff discovered the body. Naturally, I get curious about your business. In any investigation, the person who discovers a body is an immediate suspect. Usually, of course, they're rapidly eliminated from the inquiries. I'm here to find out if that applies in this case. So," he added before Dr Dearing could respond, "what is your business?"

"We undertake contract synthesis," the Director said unhelpfully.

"I'm not a scientist, Dr Dearing. Can you explain that?"

"We make the chemicals that people and organizations pay us to make."

"Like what?"

Dr Dearing laughed. "Mr Whyte. You may not be a scientist but, being in your profession, you'll appreciate the need for discretion in business. You can't expect me to reveal either our customers or their requirements."

"OK, but what type of thing do you make for what type of customer?"

"Is this relevant?" Dr Dearing responded impatiently.

"Yes," Charlie affirmed. "David Rabin died from poisoning."

"Are you insinuating that the poison came from my laboratories?"

"No. But I would like to find out for sure. Have you come across strychnine?"

"Of course." Dr Dearing explained, "I am a chemist." As if to prove his knowledge, he continued, "It's a toxic alkaloid from the plant genus *Strychnos*, used as a poison for rodents. And in small amounts, it's used medicinally as a stimulant. But", he added, "if Rabin died from administration of strychnine, I hate to disappoint you, but we haven't handled it for years."

"So what type of thing do you handle for what type of customer?" Detective Superintendent Whyte repeated.

"A huge range. Some difficult-to-prepare starting materials that a customer – maybe a pharmaceutical company or a government research station – will use to make a desired end product. Sometimes we make the end product itself if the customer doesn't have appropriate labs or sufficient resources. If the product is a new drug, you'll understand the need for confidentiality. Someone's livelihood will depend on its patent and marketing."

"When you say the government," Charlie inquired, "do you mean the military?"

"The government has many different research stations, studying food, medicine, fisheries, and so on. It's not all military, you know," Dr Dearing growled. "I really can't say which ones we deal with."

Charlie tried a different approach. "What about nicotine?" he asked.

"Nicotine?"

"Yes."

"Another poisonous alkaloid. Yet it's all around us, thanks to smokers. We're fortunate that it's not more toxic than it actually is."

"Have you ever made it?"

"Why would anyone ask us to synthesize it?" Dr Dearing said. "One would simply buy it from a supplier. That's much cheaper than getting specialists like us to produce it."

"Do you keep any of it?"

"Possibly," Dr Dearing replied. "We have used it now and again as a starting material for making more complicated alkaloids. I suspect that we may still carry limited stocks. Why?"

Ignoring his question, Charlie asked, "Who has access to your stocks?"

The Managing Director shrugged. "Several of my chemists. But being a poison, they would have to requisition it. Notes are kept of all users." He paused then added, "I guess that you wish to have a copy of our usage of nicotine."

"I certainly do," Charlie said with some relish.

"I'll arrange that."

"Thanks. Does it go far back in time?"

"For as long as we've used nicotine."

"Do you think Mr Edriss might be on the list?"

"Edriss?" Dr Dearing looked surprised. "Now, there's a name from the past. Why do you ask?"

"Because I want to know. You remember your ex-employee?"

"Yes. But he was just a technician. Not scientific, you understand. He would fix things in labs, that's all. I'm not aware that he'd have any knowledge of chemicals. He might have picked up a bit as he went around, I suppose, but chemistry wasn't his job."

"So he won't be on your list of nicotine users."

"Certainly not."

"Do you keep in touch with him at all?" asked Charlie.

"No."

"OK."

"Is that all?" asked Dr Dearing, looking at his watch. "Time presses."

The detective did not show any sign of leaving. "No," he said. "That's not quite all. You haven't mentioned your contact with the victim."

"Contact?"

"I have it that David Rabin came to this establishment on at least two occasions, some five weeks ago."

"Ah, yes. Indeed he did. An ... unfortunate episode." Dr Dearing shuffled in his seat. "I applaud vigorous investigation of any project. It's the sound scientific method. He came here as part of an environmental project and, because I applaud initiative, I granted him a few minutes and sent him away with some literature on standard methods for containing dangerous chemicals." Dr Dearing sighed. "Apparently that wasn't enough for this particular boy. He came back, wanting specifics. You know – what we make, waste disposal procedures, effect on local rivers. I refused to see him, and the security guards escorted him from the site. There's a point where curiosity becomes ... irksome, as I have indicated to you, Detective Superintendent."

"Mmm." Charlie was wondering if curiosity had killed the cat.

"As far as you know, he didn't come back again?"

"Indeed not."

The policeman could easily envisage David Rabin attempting to gain entry to the laboratories on the night of his death. It seemed an extreme step for a school project, but maybe the lad thought he had learned something sinister about Dearing Scientific and was determined to follow it up.

"OK," Charlie said, this time rising from his seat. "I'll need to send some of my people to talk to everyone present on this site on the night of the murder."

"But", the Director objected, "you've already spoken to the guards."

"I understand", Charlie returned, "that scientists are in the habit of always checking preliminary results. So am I."

Dr Dearing smiled faintly. "Yes. So you're not so ignorant of the scientific method as you made out."

"And, of course," the policeman continued, "there's the matter of any staff who have used your stocks of nicotine. I'll have them interviewed."

"Given your interest in nicotine, I assume that your comments about strychnine were designed to test my reaction to an irrelevant poison in this sorry affair. A red herring. Do I gather that *I* am a suspect?" His tone suggested that his good name should be beyond question.

"As you commented correctly earlier," Detective Superintendent Whyte responded, "in my business too, discretion is a blessing."

The detective left Dearing Scientific, feeling unfulfilled. He had on his hands a gruesome crime, plenty of suspects and several possible motives. Yet he had no obvious front-runner. His investigation had not so much hit a brick wall as opened up too many avenues to explore. There was the school chemistry teacher and the dreadful Mr Edriss. The connection with Dearing Scientific, though, was a particularly strong one. He could well imagine how an intruder to the site might be tied to a chair while the security breach was assessed. But force-feeding him a poison was the act of a sick mind. Of course, if there was something sinister about Dearings and Rabin, with his investigative instinct, had stumbled across it, then an over-zealous and over-protective worker might dream up a warped punishment. It was even possible that an ex-worker or sympathetic teacher might be paid to carry out the punishment. Maybe the nicotine was meant only to make him ill and the penalty was supposed to be nausea, not death.

Driving back to headquarters, Charlie's thoughts turned to Ros Rabin and Kevin Kingsnorth. Kevin's alibi had checked out. His two friends swore that the three of them had watched TV together till the early hours. Tracey, who had questioned them and who had a good nose for cock-and-bull stories, was convinced that they were lying. So, Kevin had primed them well. To prepare such a story, Kevin must have been tipped off about Charlie's interview with him. "Ros," the policeman muttered to himself. "She must have warned him I was on my way. The two of them in league. Sinister theories involving laboratories are all right as far as they go, but I like the tried and tested motives. An argument over a girl." True, Kevin Kingsnorth's tobacconist couldn't remember his buying a large stock of cigarettes, but there were plenty of other shops. And, as Tracey had noted, there was no rum among the small collection of bottles in one corner of Kevin Kingsnorth's living room. If he were the culprit, he would have ditched the bottle of rum. "Yes," Charlie mumbled, "the simple theories are still the best."

10

Kevin stepped into the Rabins' house for the first time and stood agog in the hall.

Ros shut the door, then said, "Are you OK, Kev?"

"Yeah," he answered. "It's just ... so big. You could fit most of our house into this hall."

Ros laughed. "It's not that big. You're exaggerating."

"But what do you do with all this space? Just a small family and an enormous..." Kevin stopped talking when he saw the hurt expression on Ros's face. "Oops! Put my foot in it again. I didn't mean..."

"It's all right," Ros said. She sighed and muttered, "We *are* a small family. Just that I'm sensitive to being reminded of it." She tossed her hair over her shoulder, pretending she could cast aside her cares just as easily. "Come on. Let's get it over with."

Kevin did not follow her immediately. "What about your mum? Will she mind us messing around in David's room?"

"I dare say she would," Ros replied. "But she's out of it. Knocked out by the tablets. You could ride your motorbike round the house and she wouldn't notice. So she can't be hurt because she won't know about it. We'll just have to leave his bedroom tidy afterwards, in case she's well enough to get up and wander in later."

In his own place, the stairs up to the meagre bedrooms were narrow and steep, as if they had been squeezed in by the builders as an afterthought. In Ros's house, the stairs were wide and plush, built to be a lavish feature of the hall. Kevin didn't see the beauty, only extravagance, but he kept quiet for fear of upsetting Ros even more.

"Let's check out that photo first," he suggested.

"OK. It's in my room."

They sat together on her bed and pored over the photograph of Ros's grandmother.

Kevin pointed to the striped pyjamas and asked, "This stuff was all the rage in those days, was it?"

"I don't know. It looks like fashion wasn't uppermost in her mind."

"You mean, she looks…" Kevin didn't want to offend Ros again so he didn't finish his sentence.

"Haggard's the word you're looking for," Ros said.

"Yes. Something like that. Where was it taken?"

"I'm not sure. Alderney, I guess."

"Alderney?"

"Yes." Ros explained. "My family used to live in the Channel Islands. Went there from France."

"You're French?"

Ros smiled. "No. But Grandmother and Grandfather were. After the war, Grandfather settled in the south – with Father, of course. They moved around a bit. A restless bunch, us Rabins. It's like Grandfather and Father were looking for somewhere, or something. But if they were, I was never told what it was, and I suppose they never found it. Anyway," she added, "we're as British as they come now."

Kevin took the photograph and turned it over. On the back, some writing was scrawled. They read, "Subject: Rabin 168/EAS. Twins eight days later. Mother did not survive."

"What's that mean?" Kevin asked, turning towards Ros. "Some sort of hospital code?"

Her face drained of colour, Ros stared at the writing. After a while, when she could speak again, she uttered, "Twins!"

"That's what it says." Kevin looked in her face, then asked, "Didn't you know? You've got an uncle."

"No," she stammered. "No one told me."

"Didn't you see the writing the other night?"

"I didn't think to look on the back," she explained. Then she murmured, "An uncle! Why didn't they tell me? Is he alive?"

Kevin shrugged. "You'd better ask your mum. She'd know. At least, I guess she would."

"Yes," Ros replied. "When she's better, I will." Then, looking at her watch, she added, "That reminds me, I've got to give her her next lot of medicine. You stay here, I won't be long. I just wish I could..."

"Ask her about this uncle?" Kevin suggested.

"Yes."

"Why don't you try?"

"I've asked her a few questions. Like, what she wants to eat. No answer, or just nonsense. It's the shock, the doctor says, and the pills. It's no use asking her anything." Ros trudged out of the room, shouldering a new burden.

Kevin could not restrain his curiosity for the five minutes that Ros spent with her mother. Getting up from the bed he strolled around her bedroom. On her dressing table there were photographs of David and what he took to be her mother and father in happier days. The photographs were not prominently displayed. They probably signified respect more than sentimentality. Her make-up looked expensive and trendy – not tested on animals. Her various sprays were ozone friendly. She had her own compact disc player, and shelves laden with books – and not just cheap and tatty paperbacks. She had a desk, littered with school files and pens. Kevin flicked open one of the files and read the title: "The Controversy of Animal Experiments". He groaned and let go of the cover so that it flopped back into place.

There were no posters on her walls or door, but a decorative rug, made of loosely woven coloured twine, hung from the wall over her bed. When he turned round, he noticed an upright chair with a cord stretched across its back. From this main cord dangled knotted chains of multicoloured threads, like washing from a clothes line. Just as Kevin bent down to examine it closely, Ros came back in. "What's this?" he asked her.

"Macramé," she replied.

"What?"

"The craft of making decorative knots from cord. I use the back of a chair as a support. You can make screens or holders for plant pots. That one's destined to be another wall hanging – like the one over the bed."

"I didn't know you did that sort of thing. Very arty, I'm sure."

"Not your sort of thing," said Ros, "but I enjoy it."

"Each to his own," Kevin replied. "How's your mum?"

"The same."

"What about the family business?" Kevin queried. "While you're under eighteen and your mum's … as she is, who's handling it all?"

"We've got an accountant to look after it, so I don't have to worry. Anyway," she added, "let's get this other business over with. It's bugging me."

"Why's that?"

Ros shrugged. As she led the way along the landing towards David's room, she said, "I suppose it's because I feel like a vulture, picking over his remains." She shivered. "It doesn't seem right, somehow."

"We're not the only ones," Kevin reminded her as they went into the bedroom. "The police have been through his stuff already."

Standing in the middle of the room, Ros spread her arms. "Exactly! So what are we going to find that they couldn't?"

"No idea," Kevin replied. "We have to hope that we recognize it when we see it. Something … out of place. Something that's not right for David, maybe. You'd be better at that than the cops. You knew him. Perhaps there'll be something about this mystery uncle. Bet the law doesn't know about that, either."

"I doubt it," Ros muttered unhopefully.

"At least it's something else we know that the cops probably don't. Anyway," Kevin prompted, "let's get started." He pointed to David's illuminated tank where tropical fish glided sedately. "You don't think they'll tell us anything, do you?"

Ros managed a wry smile. "I wonder if they miss him."

"What? Fish?"

"I don't suppose they care as long as someone feeds them. I do it now. Do you think they notice the difference?" She didn't expect an answer. She paused, then continued, "He used to sit in the dark – just the light of the aquarium – listening to a CD, and watch the fish. Relaxed him, I think." She breathed deeply and shook her head. "You know, you shouldn't think too badly of him. He had a lot on his plate. The family to look after. And he was well-meaning. All this protecting me. Just that he went about it the wrong way. He only wanted the best for me, and for the family."

"And I wasn't the best," Kevin remarked.

"In David's eyes, no. I'm afraid not. But", she added, "I didn't share his view."

"I hope not."

"Let's get on with ... this rotten job."

"OK," Kevin agreed. "Just a thought. He didn't keep a diary, did he?"

"No, not as far as I know. And if he did," she answered, "the police would've taken it."

"Yeah. Guess so. What about the computer?" Kevin nodded towards the desk where the keyboard and monitor gathered dust. "Any info on it?"

"The police took all the disks to check. He used it for business and school projects, I think."

"OK," he replied. "Keep your eyes open for a disk hidden somewhere. You never know." To Kevin, a computer was either a game or a device used by the rich to conduct a dishonest day's work. No honest sweat involved – not like digging, driving or decorating. In comparison, working with computers was hardly work at all. It occurred to Kevin that someone like David Rabin might have turned naturally to his computer if he had wanted to conceal a clue.

There was not a lot of data stored on the computer's hard disk, but they did find a section of a school report on an environmental project. Entitled "Disposal of Chemical Waste", it outlined David's discontent with the bland information given to him by Dearing Scientific.

"Interesting," Kevin murmured after he had read the section. "Might be worth bearing in mind. He was found near Dearings, as well."

"You don't think...?"

Kevin interrupted her. "You never know. It's a dodgy set-up. Not to be trusted. Did David push his luck too far with them? Was he trying to break in?"

"David?" Ros exclaimed. More calmly, she added, "It doesn't sound like him."

"Perhaps not, but ... maybe I'll check it out. Anyway, let's crack on."

His wardrobe and drawers revealed nothing more than the sort of dress sense that only the well-off can afford to have.

Tiring, Ros sighed. "It still doesn't feel right," she said. "It's like sacrilege."

"Even Tutankhamun probably wouldn't have cursed someone taking a gander around his tomb then replacing everything. We're not doing anything wrong. We're trying to help him – by getting to the bottom of it. Come on, Ros." He squeezed her arm. "Not much left. Don't give up now. Help me with his books and stuff, then it's all over."

Fiction, non-fiction, school books, magazines. "It's like his personal library," Kevin remarked.

"Mmm." Ros had picked up one book and, frowning, was flicking through its pages. "Now this is a bit odd," she said.

"Yes?" Kevin's ears pricked up. "Why? What is it?"

"History of the Channel Islands," Ros answered. "From the school library."

"So?"

"Well," she explained, "history wasn't really his thing. Economics, science, management – yes. But not history. And I can't see that he'd have any school work on it."

"Well," Kevin pondered, "perhaps it's something to do with the family. Interest in the background. You said your lot lived there once."

"Yes. Perhaps you're right," she said hesitantly. "If so, it's a recent interest."

"Keep the book," Kevin suggested. "You can go through it in case he's made any notes in it or marked something."

"OK," Ros agreed, closing it. "I'll do that."

"I hope it tells us something," Kevin said, "because it's about all we've got. One lousy book. Still, it had to be done."

Before she left, Ros checked the room carefully. She wanted it left exactly as they'd found it – as if David himself might inspect it for signs of interference. When she was happy that it appeared undisturbed, she pulled the door closed, like sliding the lid over his coffin.

Back in Ros's room, she asked Kevin, "What now? Any ideas?"

"Yeah. Some," he replied. "I reckon I should ask around at school. I know the cops have been putting their snouts in already, but the kids'll talk to me. They'll tell me things they wouldn't dream of telling the law."

"You think someone might know something?"

"Well, I'll give it a whirl and report back," Kevin replied. "Someone might just have seen something or heard something. But, for now," he added, "why don't you take me out for a drink?"

Ros hesitated. "I ... I don't know. There's Mother."

"Ah, yes. Mother," Kevin responded, almost mockingly. "David's ghost and David's mother. Between them, they've trapped you."

"Up to a point, they have," Ros replied wilfully. "But there's no need to be like that about it. These things take time, that's all. I can't be seen out enjoying myself – not with things as they are."

"I suppose you're right." In a more conciliatory tone, he added, "I just get impatient – for it to be like it was."

She kissed him lightly, like a sister kisses a brother. "Won't be long," she said. "I promise."

On his way home, Kevin stopped his bike some distance from the school then walked quietly the rest of the way to the playing field. It was a warm, damp night. He vaulted over the railings and on to the playing field. The school buildings were dark, but lights still shone in some of the homes at the edge of the field. Mr Smith's lounge and one of the bedrooms in Mr Edriss's house were lit. The blank wall at the far side of the field hid any activity at Dearing Scientific.

Kevin made straight for the spot where David had been found, careful to keep out of range of the security cameras. "David was poisoned," Kevin said to himself. "And behind this wall there's plenty of poisonous chemicals."

Kevin scrutinized the wall. Perhaps four metres high. Not easy to get over. Even with a good jump, outstretched fingers wouldn't reach the top. Besides, it was protected by sharp projections. But the spikes, Kevin decided, were also a weakness. It shouldn't be difficult to lasso one of them with a rope or cord and then scale the wall hand over fist. Rope-climbing to the top of the wall wouldn't have been beyond David, either. Of course, the cameras would be a problem. Or maybe not, if the night were dark and the climber avoided the best-lit sections of the wall. The drop on the other side would be ferocious but, if someone were really determined to break in to Dearings, it would be worth the risk. "Yes," Kevin muttered. "With rope, it would be possible. Worth checking out."

He turned and walked back across the field. When he drew level with Mr Smith's garden, the old man called to him, "Good evening, young man!"

Kevin started but, when he realized who had spoken, he replied cheerfully, "Hello."

"It's Kevin, isn't it?"

"Yes." Kevin strode to Mr Smith's fence. "What are you doing out at this hour?" he asked.

"Oh, just locking up the shed before I turn in," Mr Smith answered. "I could, of course, ask the same of you."

Kevin smiled. "That's true. I've just been over the field where … you know. Call it curiosity, if you like."

"Morbid curiosity."

"I guess so. Funny business, though, isn't it?" Kevin said. "A poisoning on our field."

"Poisoned, was he?"

"So the police say."

"Now, how'd a rogue like you know that? You haven't been in trouble again, have you?"

"No. But you know me, Mr Smith. Seem to attract the law's attention for no reason at all."

Once, when Kevin was dashing out of the school gates, he'd bumped into Mr Smith. He'd apologized, picked up the spilled shopping and carried it into his bungalow for him. Ever since, they'd struck up a casual friendship. Mr Smith seemed to enjoy Kevin's occasional visits. He was particularly fond of recounting his own childhood pranks and comparing them with Kevin's modern misdeeds.

"What you mean, young man, is that they suspect you of this terrible crime."

Kevin shrugged. "Yes. They know I had a row with him just before he copped it. The evidence was a black eye, I'm afraid."

The old man looked sternly at Kevin and asked, "Did you do it?"

"No."

"Mmm. You'll be fine, then. Nothing to worry about."

"I hope not. But I've decided to do a bit of investigating myself. See if I can turn up something."

"You be careful, my boy," warned Mr Smith.

"I can look after myself."

"Yes, I know." Mr Smith stretched his back and groaned a little. "Anyway, time for me to call it a day. Past my bedtime. Come and see me soon, when you have time off from your investigations. I'll make you a decent mug of coffee."

"OK," Kevin replied. "I'll do that."

The old man shuffled away and Kevin headed back towards his bike. By the time he'd ridden home, got a bite to eat, found some rope, and walked back, he expected that everyone would have retired to bed. He could test his theory that it would have been possible for David Rabin to scale Dearings' wall unseen.

11

The dustbin lid in Mr Edriss's garden clattered on to the paving stones. Inside the house, Mr Edriss opened his bleary eyes and cursed. "Damn cats!" He clambered out of bed and staggered to the window. Drawing back the curtain, he squinted to see in the dark. At the end of his garden he could just make out a figure, grovelling on the ground. "That's no cat," he exclaimed. "Blooming kids!"

He struggled to free the latch on the window then push it open. "Oi!" he yelled at the top of his voice. "What do you think you're doing on my property?"

Clutching a torch in his hand the intruder straightened up, glanced towards the house, then made for the gate. Hurriedly, he slipped through and into the school field.

Mr Edriss called after him, "Don't trespass on my property again. I'll be watching!"

He closed the window and went back to bed, still muttering curses.

Once Mr Edriss had settled down again, the calm of night was restored. The daytime drone from the distant motorway had faded away. No cars cruised along School Lane. There was barely a breath of wind. Overhead, faint flashing lights marked the position of an aeroplane flying too high for its engines to be heard. Beyond, a thin screen of cloud muddied the moon.

Kevin stood, rope over his shoulder, looking alternately at his watch and at one of Dearings' security cameras that swivelled slowly like an owl's head, scanning back and forth. From its starting point, surveying the wall, the camera panned over a sector of the

field, stopped, and swivelled back again in just two minutes. Anyone by the wall, Kevin guessed, would be out of shot for about one
and a half minutes while the camera executed its scan of the field.
It wasn't long. But was it long enough to throw and secure the rope,
then mount the wall? He doubted it. Not unless the lasso found its
target on the first attempt, which was unlikely. Kevin had never
been blessed with good luck before, so he did not expect it now.

He planned to dash to the wall as soon as the camera began its
outward sweep. Out of its field of view, he would fling the rope over
one of the projections set into the top of the wall. Unless the rope
caught first time, he wouldn't attempt to climb up within the same
camera pan. He'd withdraw, trusting that on a dark night the lens
would not pick out the dangling rope. Once the security camera
had turned away again, he'd sprint back to the wall and mount it
rapidly by pulling himself up with the rope.

As he waited for the right moment, he checked the loop that he
had already made in the rope. He tested the strength of the knot by
yanking on it. It held firm. When the camera began tracking to the
right, Kevin raced to the wall and, keeping hold of one end of the
rope, threw the other to the top of the wall. He expected the rope
to slither down the wall and collapse in a heap at his feet, but it
didn't. Amazed and delighted, he pulled on the rope to check that
it had found its mark on the first attempt. For a while, it held. But
when he put his weight on it, there was a wrenching noise and the
rope went slack. One of the metal spikes clattered down the wall
and struck him on the shoulder.

"Ouch!" he yelped.

The sharp metal had torn his jacket and possibly also his skin.
He swore under his breath at the pain.

He glanced up at the camera. It had reached its outermost
position and was beginning to swing back towards him. The
urgency made him forget his injured shoulder for a while. He took
the rope again and hurled it upwards. This time the lasso did not
catch anything firm and the rope fell back around him.

Leaving the rope in a heap on the ground, Kevin dashed away
from the spot before he found himself in camera shot. His heart
beating strongly and rapidly, he rubbed his shoulder and waited.
He was still determined to prove that David Rabin could have got
into Dearing Scientific by this route. He had to succeed. It was the

first step in proving that Rabin met his death inside these creepy laboratories.

Kevin's early confidence began to slip away when, on the next sweep of the camera, his four attempts to secure the rope all failed. Frustrated, he stood in the field getting his breath back. Suddenly, his throbbing shoulder suggested a different strategy.

When the camera next allowed, he sprinted back to the wall and dropped on to his hands and knees. Desperately, he searched for the metal spike that he had dislodged accidentally from the brick wall. When his hand stumbled across it, he grabbed it and, with the rope in his other hand, he withdrew. Sitting on the cold grass, he tied the long strip of metal securely to the end of his rope. He hoped that he could make the spike act like an anchor by lodging it between other projections on the wall.

The camera swung away and Kevin dashed in with renewed spirit. He flung the end of the rope, now heavy with the weight of his anchor, to the top of the wall. It crashed against something, making him wince at the noise, then plummeted down. Kevin side-stepped to avoid being struck again. He glanced at the position of the camera and tried again. This time, the rope did not end up at his feet. The spike had become wedged. He tested its grip by pulling with all his might on the rope but it remained firmly fixed. Kevin smiled. He was sure that it would take his weight. As long as the noise had gone unnoticed and the rope did not show up on the video, he was as good as in the Dearing Scientific compound.

He took a good, last look round the field to make sure that he had not attracted any attention, then dashed back to the wall. He jumped up, grabbed the rope with both hands and let out a cry of pain. In his excitement, he'd forgotten his damaged shoulder. The strain of heaving on the rope triggered pangs down his left arm. Resisting the temptation to let go, instead he tried to take more of his weight on his legs as he planted his feet against the brickwork. Groaning, he clambered up the wall, one step at a time, by yanking on the rope.

When his hands drew level with the top of the wall, he grabbed hold, keeping clear of the spikes, and scrambled up. The wall was not thick, but there was enough width to stand on without losing his balance. He glanced round briefly, noting that the camera would soon be taking pictures of his feet. He gulped when he saw the drop on the other side. He could jump, but there was a good chance that he'd break a leg.

Quickly, he squatted down, drew up the rope and let it down on the Dearing side of the wall. He adjusted the position of the spike to provide an anchor for the descent. Just before the camera caught him, he clutched the rope, let his legs drop down and, trying to ignore the agony of his shoulder, abseiled into Dearing Scientific's premises.

When his feet contacted the ground, he let go of the rope and crouched down. Automatically, his right hand felt his tender shoulder. He leaned against the wall for a few minutes, waiting to see if his entrance had gone unnoticed. He found himself on a narrow perimeter road. On the other side there was a building, made sinister by being in darkness. Further along the road there was another block. This one was brightly lit and, through its windows, Kevin could see that it contained laboratories.

No one came to arrest him. All was uncannily quiet. Kevin had proved his point: David could have slipped into Dearing Scientific to investigate their dubious operations.

Kevin stood up, then crept towards the laboratory building. He wanted to have a close look through one of the windows. If David had unearthed something corrupt before he'd been poisoned and his body dumped outside, perhaps Kevin could spot it as well. Perhaps Kevin could take David Rabin's place in exposing it.

Furtively, he continued along the road, keeping to the darker side. Just in front of the laboratories, a hedgehog shambled across the road, oblivious to Kevin's intrusion. Ignoring the animal, Kevin darted across the road and crouched for a while under one of the laboratory windows. Summoning up his courage, he raised his head slowly to peer into the room. There was movement in the lab but, eerily, it was empty of workers. To the right, a machine was shaking some flasks with yellow liquid inside. To the left, a robotic arm grabbed a syringe, filled it from a nearby vial then injected the liquid into some machine. By its side, a printer was churning out sheets of paper. Kevin was too far away to see what was written on them. He shuffled along the wall of the laboratories to get a closer look through the next window. At the top of one of the sheets he read, "ALKALOID DS5324. Average synthetic yield: 47%. Average biotechnological yield with tobacco enzyme: 61%."

"Tobacco," he murmured to himself. "Interesting." Thinking back to Detective Superintendent Whyte's strange questions about smoking, he whispered, "No way that's coincidence."

He sidled along the building to get a good view of the hard copy issuing from another printer, but before he reached the next window, he was stunned by a sudden dazzle. He froze, like a rabbit caught in a headlight beam.

"What...?" he exclaimed.

He glanced down and, by the floodlighting, saw some sort of sensor attached to the base of the laboratory wall. His foot must have set it off. There was no audible alarm, but spotlights blazed threateningly. Kevin looked round but the guards had not yet appeared. It would not be long, he guessed. No time to run back and escape over the wall.

He sprinted down the road, located the hedgehog and, ignoring the prickles, picked it up. He raced back to the sensor and dumped the frightened animal right in front of it. Then he dashed around the corner of the laboratories out of the glare of the lights. Just a few metres away, he found the fire exit of the building and, with a sigh of relief, huddled in its gloomy recess.

He didn't have to wait for long. He soon heard the heavy footsteps of three, perhaps four, guards as they ran to the scene of the break-in.

They trampled about for a while, then Kevin heard one of them report to the others, "Here he is! Our culprit. It's a hedgehog. Walked through the infrared beam. Poor thing's petrified."

"Great! Let's get back. My coffee's getting cold."

"No," another guard called. "Spread out and double-check. Just in case."

Kevin cursed under his breath. His diversionary tactic had not succeeded. His heart thumped in his chest when he caught the sound of one of the officers walking round the corner of the labs. He must only be a few strides away. His torchlight flashed here and there, probing the darkness. Kevin drew himself as far into the recess as he could.

Just as the man drew level and threatened to turn and point his torch directly into the fire exit, another guard called from some distance away, "Here! I've found something!"

The man near Kevin disappeared back on to the perimeter road.

But any relief that Kevin felt was short-lived. The first guard yelled, "I doubt if that hedgehog came over the wall by a rope!"

Kevin groaned. By discovering his rope, the enemy had cut off his retreat. Without an escape route, it was only a matter of time before he was ferreted out. Then what would happen to him? He wondered if David Rabin had been trapped in the same way. Was he now re-living Rabin's last few hours? The thought made him shudder.

He had no wish to cower in the doorway until he was cornered by the guards, but his exit over the wall had been blocked. He knew of only one other way out – the official one, by the gatehouse. It struck him that all of the security officers could be out searching for him, leaving the gatehouse unmanned. It was, he decided, worth a try. He'd never been inside the Dearings precinct before but knew that the exit must be along the perimeter road to the right, perhaps no more than a hundred metres away. He wished that he had Ros's speed but, even without it, he needed a burst of strength for just a few seconds. And, of course, a bit of luck. A sprint, a jump over the barrier, and freedom.

He stood upright and took three deep breaths. He accelerated out of the doorway like a greyhound from a trap, turned the corner on to the perimeter road, and immediately crashed into one of the security guards.

"What's this?" the man uttered as he spun round and expertly put an arm lock on Kevin. "Got him!" he called to his colleagues.

Kevin grimaced at the pain in his arm and shoulder.

As they converged on him, one guard said, "We caught ourselves a young one."

"What are you doing here, sonny? Come to get your ball back?" The voice was heavy with irony.

"No," Kevin replied. "I was out walking my pet hedgehog."

"Very funny," the chief officer retorted. "Come on. Back to base. Bring him." As an afterthought he said, "Jim, you stay and double-check – in case he came with a mate or has done any mischief."

Kevin was frogmarched down the road and into the security office. He was shoved roughly into a seat. His head hit the back of the chair and he yelped, "Ow!"

The man who was carrying Kevin's length of rope said, "Sit there quietly and don't make a move. If you do, I'll tie you to the chair with this." He dangled the rope threateningly in front of Kevin.

"All right, Frank. Let me get to him." The chief officer leaned uncomfortably close to Kevin and barked, "What's your name?"

Kevin's answer came out automatically, without really thinking. "David Rabin," he said. He guessed that he did it to test the man's reaction.

The guard didn't seem to recognize the name – or at least he acted as if he did not know it. "OK," he replied. "David Rabin." He drew up a chair and sat opposite his prisoner. "Now, while one of my officers phones for the police, why don't we have a chat? You can start by telling me why you were on our land."

"I did it for a bet."

"A bet?"

"A dare. Some of the lads said I couldn't do it – get over the wall. I said I could."

"So why did you go walkabout? Why not climb over and straight back?"

"I don't know. I just got carried away. While over here, why not have a look around? It's a mysterious place, you know, to us on the other side of the wall."

"Curiosity."

"Yes."

"Did you find it interesting, whatever you saw in the laboratories?"

Kevin shrugged. "Not really. Couldn't see much. It wouldn't mean anything to me, anyhow."

"You still at school, or working?"

"School."

"And what about your family? Any in the chemical industry?"

Kevin laughed. "No chance. Honest labourers, us."

"Sure?" the security officer asked. "The police will check what you say, remember."

"They can check all they like. I don't know anyone who does chemistry. Except the school science teacher."

"And who's that?"

"Chipmonk. Mr Monk."

"Ah, yes. The local school. Dr Dearing knows him, I'm sure."

"You think I'm some sort of industrial spy!" Kevin exclaimed. The notion seemed absurd.

"It had occurred to me," the man replied. "But there could be any one of a number of reasons for this bit of trespassing." His tone was still threatening.

"I've told you the reason."

"Yes." The word signified agreement but this man made it sound like disbelief. "Have you got a camera on you?"

"No. Search me if you like."

"Stand up," he ordered.

He ran his hands up Kevin's legs, feeling his pockets particularly, over his trunk and then down each arm in turn.

"He's clean," he said over Kevin's shoulder to his colleagues.

The man who had hold of the rope was scowling. "Kids!" he murmured. "We should teach him a lesson."

"We'll leave that to the police, Frank," the chief answered.

"If I had my way..." Frank began.

"Here they come!" a third guard said.

Kevin groaned when he saw who had rushed into the office. "Oh, it's you," he couldn't help saying.

Detective Superintendent Whyte frowned. "Who do you think it'd be when a message comes in that David Rabin's broken into Dearing Scientific?"

The senior security officer and Detective Superintendent Whyte went into a huddle for a few minutes to exchange information, then Kevin was led away.

In the back of the police car, Kevin faced yet more questions. "Why David Rabin? Why use his name?"

Kevin decided that there was no harm in telling the truth. "I wanted to see their reactions."

"Why?"

"Oh, come on. Bet you've checked out Dearings. This was my way of doing it."

"What was the reaction?"

"There wasn't one."

"And if there had been? What would it prove? That they'd read and remembered his name from newspaper reports. Big deal."

"Well, if one of them had turned bright red it would've told me something. There was one called Frank. He'd turned away when I said I was Rabin. Perhaps he turned red. I couldn't see his face."

"Why do you say that?"

"He seemed ... I don't know ... nasty. Threatened me."

"In what way?"

"You burst in before he got round to details. But he did threaten to tie me to the chair if I made any trouble."

"Oh yes?" the policeman put in, suddenly interested. "What sort of chair?"

Kevin shrugged. "An ordinary chair. Not an electric one."

Ignoring the joke, the policeman probed further. "Did it have a low back?"

"No. I hit my head on it at one stage."

"Mmm." Detective Superintendent Whyte said no more on the topic. Instead he asked, "Why did you do it, Kevin? Why go over the wall?"

"To show that David Rabin might have gone over that night. Hey!" Kevin said. "This isn't the way to the police station. Where are you taking me?"

"Home."

"Home?"

"What do I want to clutter the station with you for? You're not going to leave the country, are you? I can pick you up any time if I want to talk to you. Remember that, Kevin." The policeman glanced meaningfully at him. Then he added, "I've got all I need for a report. But if Dr Dearing wants it taken further, I'll pull you in again."

"OK," Kevin replied defiantly. "But there's something else you should know. Dearings is working on tobacco."

"Tobacco? Now, why do you think I'd be interested in that?"

"Because you asked me about smoking. There's something about cigarettes in all this, isn't there?"

Detective Superintendent Whyte took no notice of his question. "What makes you believe they're working on tobacco?"

"I saw a print-out in one of the labs. Something about using a tobacco enzyme. Whatever that means." The car took a sharp left corner and Kevin swayed on the back seat, clutching his injured shoulder. He added, "You're interested, aren't you?"

"In a case like this, I'm interested in anything."

"Sure." Kevin smiled to himself. The night had been even more useful than he'd thought it would be. He was learning a lot. "There's another thing, as well," he said.

"Yes?"

"It shows I didn't do him in. If I had, I wouldn't be going to all this bother. I reckon they did it."

"They?"

"Someone at Dearings. Strange place. David Rabin was suspicious about it. He could have broken in. They've got plenty of poisons. And there's the smoking business that you won't tell me about. They could've stopped him making a nuisance of himself by poisoning him."

"And that's supposed to let you off the hook?"

"Sure it is."

"Your prank tonight", the policeman replied, "could be construed as the actions of the villain desperate to put the blame on someone else."

"That's daft," Kevin retorted. "Can't you see? It wasn't me. It was them."

"We'll see," the policeman replied. "The truth will out."

The car pulled into Curtis Street and cruised to a stop outside his house.

Kevin got out and, through the open door, tried his luck once more. "David Rabin was poisoned by something in ciggies, wasn't he?"

The policeman shrugged. "It's too early to be sure. I keep an open mind on such matters." He paused, then added, "Don't pull any more stunts like this one, Kingsnorth, or you *will* be in trouble. I won't need much excuse to drag you in and make things deeply unpleasant next time. Understand?"

Kevin smiled. "Thanks for the lift."

12

The kids in David Rabin's class had plenty of theories. "Rabin never did hit it off with old Chipmonk. And, him being the science teacher, he'd know all about poisoning. I reckon it was Chipmonk." It wasn't the first time that someone had accused the Deputy Head as Kevin strolled around the playground casually asking questions or listening to the rumours. "No doubt about it. Edriss did it. He hates us all. Love to get rid of us. Bet he did it." There were quiet mutterings too about Craig Blackstock. No one dared to say why, but one girl suggested that Kevin should see him if he wanted to know who else might bear David Rabin a grudge.

Not many in the school would volunteer to go and see Craig Blackstock. Several were "invited" by his sidekicks to meet him at a certain time, in a certain place. Or Craig Blackstock might "interview" one of the children when he was least expected or wanted. Yet he had never sought out Kevin. He even had a degree of respect for Kevin – probably because he'd been in trouble with the law. Kevin didn't approve of the school bully, but he wasn't scared of him like everyone else.

When Kevin approached Craig Blackstock, he was flanked, as always, by two pals. "What is it, Kingsnorth?" he asked, adopting his usual tone which was meant to intimidate.

"The word is", Kevin said, "that you and Rabin had a ... confrontation before he copped it."

"The word is, so did you."

"Yeah. I can't deny that. Everyone saw the punch-up."

"So," Craig Blackstock replied, "who says I had a go at him as well?"

"No one in particular. Just a rumour. All I want to know is, who else the cops might be investigating."

"Not me. No one'll tell them about me. Will they, Kingsnorth?" he added pointedly.

"You know I don't mix with the law. I won't say anything. But if they come back and ask around ... you never know. Someone might let it out."

"Then I give them my alibi."

"What's that?"

"American football on the box that night."

"You too, eh?" Kevin couldn't help smiling.

"You mean, you've used that alibi?"

" 'Fraid so. I got in first. They'll never believe the same thing from you."

"But I *was* watching it. Were you?"

Kevin shrugged. "Can't you dream up another alibi?"

"Perhaps I'd say I was watching it with you."

"I wouldn't do that. I've already told them who I watched it with. You can't get added to the list now. It's too late. Anyway," Kevin said to change the subject, "all this suggests you did have an ... interview with Rabin."

"Yes, we had a little chat."

"What about?"

Craig Blackstock was built like a tank. And he had a business sense to match. Kevin knew what a little chat meant but he was hoping to learn more.

"I told him I'd heard that some of the lads were threatening to do him over. You know how enthusiastic some kids get for that sort of thing, especially with someone like Rabin. I told him I could help him out – stop the lads having a go at him – for a small fee."

Kevin nodded. It was much as he'd expected. "What did Rabin say?"

"You've got to give him credit. He told me where to get off."

"Really?"

"Yeah. Not many do that. Must've had a death wish. Judging by what happened, he did. Someone else gunning for him."

"It wasn't you, then?"

"It's not clever, or polite, even to think that." Craig Blackstock's minders each took a step towards Kevin. "I'd have had him the next day, of course. My reputation to think of. But I'd only have roughed

him up and made sure everyone knew it was me. Anyway," he
added, "I've had enough of this. Before you go too far, let's end this
... meeting. I wouldn't want to have to teach you a lesson as well."
Kevin left. He felt that Blackstock was probably telling the truth.
But everyone knew how he spent the money that he prised out of
the weaker schoolchildren. His ill-gotten gains funded his craving
for cigarettes.

Ros's mother was propped up in bed, sipping some soup. She was
pale and withdrawn. She would not speak unless Ros spoke to her,
and then Ros had to repeat all her questions before she got a
response. Her mother's eyes stared blankly when Ros asked about
her missing uncle.

"Mother! This is important. Do I have an uncle? Where is he?
Who is he?"

Her mother spilled some of her soup and fussed over the mess to
avoid answering the question. When Ros repeated it, she replied,
"Uncle? You mean your father's brother?"

"Yes. Did he have a brother?"

"He ... er ... We don't talk about him."

"So I *do* have one! Why don't we talk about him?"

Mrs Rabin shook her head, utterly distraught. "We just don't."

"Why not?" Ros repeated.

"Because it's time we forgot about him."

"What do you mean?"

"Forget him."

"Why? Why have you never told me about him?"

"Don't you get involved, Ros. Leave it be. It's time we stopped
living in the past."

Ros knew when to give up. Her mother had withdrawn into her
shell of remorse. If Ros wanted to learn more, she'd have to find out
for herself.

In her imagination, Ros could see a shadowy uncle, embittered
by being cut out of the Rabin family for some unknown reason.
Rejection had unhinged him. He was completely mad but, in Ros's
eyes, he was also very sad. And he was now wreaking revenge on the
family for being left out in the cold.

If it were true, if the Rabins were being stalked by a disgruntled
and long-since-disowned relative, would he stop at David's

murder? Was that enough to appease him? Or would he continue his vendetta until he alone survived and inherited the family's wealth?

One other thought troubled Ros. She wondered where honour lay – if there could be honour in such a family feud. Who were the heroes and who the villains? She dreaded the possibility that the Rabins might have committed an unforgivable wrong against her uncle. If they had, she would be counted as one of the bad guys. She didn't want to live the rest of her life with that on her conscience.

Before he died, David Rabin had been tied with cord to a chair with a high back. Following his escapade at Dearings, Kevin Kingsnorth claimed that one of the security guards had threatened to tie him to the same type of chair. Detective Superintendent Whyte was forced to give fresh credence to the involvement of Dearings in Rabin's death.

On Charlie's instructions, the forensic scientists had examined a couple of chairs from Dearing Scientific's security office for evidence of contact with David Rabin. Fresh from the FAX machine, the forensic report was disappointingly negative. No fibres from the victim's clothing had been found adhering to the chairs. The report concluded that it was most unlikely that David Rabin had been forced to sit in either of those particular chairs.

There was another explanation of Kevin's story. When the police checked it out, the guard whose name was Frank had denied all knowledge of the threat to tie up the intruder. It was possible that Kingsnorth had made up the whole story. If Kevin was guilty of Rabin's murder, he would have known that David Rabin's body bore the marks of being tied to a chair. He would have also known about the poisoning with nicotine. And he would want to deflect suspicion elsewhere. He could have broken into Dearings to invent the episode with the rope and the reference to tobacco in the laboratories. Very neat. He would have also known that industrial secrecy would prevent the police verifying his claim that the chemists were working with tobacco. He could make lots of allegations, knowing that they could not be checked. As long as they sounded real, Kingsnorth probably thought he could get away with it. He could make someone at Dearing Laboratories seem guilty and, at the same time, appear innocent himself.

Detective Superintendent Whyte knew that the lad was reckless. But was Kevin also sincere and blameless, or a cunning murderer? Charlie wasn't sure which, but he intended to find out. He decided to apply for a warrant to search Kingsnorth's house.

13

The spooky atmosphere of the deserted swimming pool was lost. Rain pelted down on the windows and the smell of disinfectant was too powerful to be pleasant. Somewhere, doors banged regularly, so Ros and Kevin kept thinking that their sanctuary was about to be invaded. Even so, they stayed long enough to compare notes.

When Kevin told her how he had spent the night, Ros shuddered. "You're playing with fire," she warned him.

Kevin smiled at her. "Yes," he replied. "Good, eh?"

He was right. Kevin could excite her and scare her at the same time. That was why she found him intriguing. Even so, she tried to express her doubts. "But the risk…"

"It was worth the risk," Kevin put in. "Just think what we learnt. David could have got into Dearings. I'm sure he was poisoned by something in cigarettes. And the law got all interested in me being tied up. I reckon David was tied to a chair at some point. Someone in those labs, maybe this character Frank, is my main suspect."

"But it's not certain. There are others."

"Yeah, too many. There's Dr Dearing himself, Craig Blackstock and his crew, and Edriss. According to the kids in David's class, Chipmonk's a possibility. And", he went on, "if you believe the cops, there's you and me."

"Yes, I guess so. But this idea of Chipmonk. It rings a bell. David had a clash with him not long ago, I'm sure."

"What sort of clash? What do you mean?"

"An argument. Some report that Chipmonk wrote on David. It wasn't very … complimentary. You know, full of damning comments. David thought it had nothing to do with his ability. Just that Chipmonk was smarting over David's antics at Dearings. He seemed to be trying to get his own back. And David wasn't afraid to say so. You know David – not one to duck a confrontation. He took his case to the Head and managed to convince him that the comments weren't deserved. Chipmonk had to admit they were influenced by personal feelings and climb down. He was in a dreadful mood for at least a week after, David said."

Kevin nodded. "That sounds like Chipmonk. And that puts him right up there with the rest of our suspects. He bore David a grudge. But", Kevin asked, "how about you? Any joy with your mum?"

Ros reported her short conversation and added a mysterious uncle to their list of suspects. "But", she said, "the Channel Islands book didn't help. I checked every page but David respected books too much to scribble notes in them."

"Pity."

"I've started to read it, cover to cover. Just in case there's anything relevant in it. Can't think what it might be, though. So", she asked, "where do we go from here?"

"What have we got?" Kevin thought aloud. "Lots of suspects, lots of motives. Not much evidence. You reckon there's a Channel Islands connection, and David used that photo to point the finger at some missing uncle. I reckon cigarettes come into it. And there's the torch. We need to find that torch – preferably on someone who knows his tobacco chemistry."

"You're not thinking of going back into Dearing Scientific, are you?" Ros asked in alarm. "To look for the torch?" She put her hand on his shoulder as if she could hold him back.

He winced at her touch. "Ouch! My shoulder."

"Sorry." She took away her hand. "How is it?"

"OK – till you wrecked it," he replied. Then he smiled and added, "No. It's all right. Strapped up."

"I thought you'd added a few inches. Padded shoulders."

"Anyway," he answered her, "I don't think I'd better go back – not yet. It's too soon. Too dangerous right now."

"So where do we search?"

Kevin shrugged. "I could do Edriss's place, some time when he's out. Or Chipmonk's. That'd be easier. I'll check his lab first. If he brewed up something in the lab, there might be some sign of it."

"You don't sound hopeful, though."

"I still think the answer's in Dearings," he said firmly. "Oh, I'm going to have a chat with Mr Smith, as well. You never know what he might have seen."

"Don't you think the police will have interviewed him already? And everyone else living round the field?"

"I guess so. But he'll talk to me as well – maybe more than he'll talk to the cops. He's all right, the old man. We get on OK."

Before they left the poolside they agreed that, after Kevin had seen Mr Smith, they would check out the school chemistry laboratory for clues together.

The door chimes didn't seem to work so Kevin banged on the glass of Mr Smith's front door. After a few minutes, the old man opened the door and his face lit up. "Ah, it's you, Kevin," he said.

"Well, you offered me a coffee the other night. I've come to collect."

Mr Smith laughed. "You're welcome, young man. Come on in."

Kevin pulled back from stepping inside when he saw an envelope on the floor. He bent down and picked it up. It was a small parcel addressed to Mr Edward A. Smith. "Here," he said, handing it to his host. "The postman's been."

"Oh, thank you." Mr Smith examined the package and murmured, "Good. I've been waiting for this. It's a packet of stamps. I collect them, you know. Fascinating."

"Yes. Fascinating." Kevin tried to sound fascinated.

"Heh, heh!" Mr Smith chuckled. "You don't have to pretend. To you, it's boring. But to me ... Well, when you get to my age, you'll see the attraction. Nostalgia mainly. Anyway, come in. I'll go and put the coffee on."

As always, Kevin found Mr Smith's bungalow oppressively hot. As always, Mr Smith asked him if he was warm enough. "Yes. Sweltering, thanks." He took off his jacket.

"There's a cold wind today. Difficult to keep the place warm."

The dining room table was awash with stamps, albums, a magnifying glass, tweezers, catalogues and notes. Mr Smith carried a tray with two large steaming mugs towards the table but changed his mind when he saw the mess. "We'd better have these somewhere else."

They sat on either side of a coffee table by the patio door that overlooked the playing field. After a few minutes of conversation about the weather, Kevin nodded towards the field and said, "All happening out there these days."

"Has something else happened?" asked the old man.

"Not really." Kevin thought better of telling him about his assault on the Dearing precinct. "Just this murder. Did you know him? David Rabin."

"Yes and no. I've seen him around, I think. Coming and going. Usually on his own. A bit of a loner, if I'm any judge. I didn't know him by name but I recognized his picture in the papers. Poor lad." Mr Smith shook his head sadly. "So young."

"Yeah."

"But you said you'd been fighting with him, or something. Not a friend of yours?"

"We had an argument about a girl."

"A girl? At your age?" The old man frowned playfully. "Hope she was worth it."

"It was his sister." Kevin tasted the thick coffee, which acted on his throat like paint-stripper on aged gloss. "Phew! That's … good."

"Mmm. When the coffee's good, you've got to have it strong to really appreciate the flavour. None of that decaffeinated rubbish." He gulped his own as if it were a draught of cold water. "So", he went on, "what had you been doing to this poor lad's sister?"

"Nothing. I just didn't match up to expectations."

"You mean, she's posh."

Kevin smiled. "And I'm not."

"Where does she live?"

"A big place up Laburnum Avenue."

"Ah. And you?"

"Curtis Street."

Mr Smith nodded knowingly. "I see the problem."

"Well, the main problem's … dead and gone." Gingerly, Kevin swallowed a small amount of his coffee and then added, "Now there's the law on my back."

"If you didn't do it, Kevin, you'll be cleared, sooner or later."

"Maybe. But this Detective Superintendent Whyte's a swine. Got it in for me. Has he seen you?"

"Me?"

"Yes. In case you saw anything that night."

"No," Mr Smith replied. "Someone came, though. A policeman, but his name wasn't Whyte."

"What did he ask?"

Mr Smith shrugged. "Just when I'd gone to bed and if I'd seen anything suspicious. That sort of thing."

"And did you?"

"No. Not so's I'd notice."

"Anything unusual going on at Dearings about that time – or since?"

"I'd like to help you, young man, but…" He spread his hands in a gesture of futility. "You seem to think that Dearing place had something to do with it. You were looking at it the other night as well."

"It's possible, yes. They're into chemicals. Bet they've got all the poisons you could want."

"But what do the police think? Does this … Whyte suspect them as well?"

"I think so," Kevin answered, "but I reckon he's got me at the top of his list."

"As I said the other night," Mr Smith cautioned him, "you be careful."

Kevin heard the advice but didn't comment on it. Instead, he quizzed the old man again. "You said Rabin was usually on his own. Who was he with when he wasn't on his own?"

"I've seen him with that grumpy teacher. What's his name? The Deputy Head or something."

"Mr Monk, the science teacher?"

"Yes. That's him. They seemed to be bickering."

"Anyone else?"

"Yes. The day before he came to grief. I don't know names," said Mr Smith, "but he tangled with two or three boys. Right outside my garden. One of them was trying to talk to him but he wouldn't have it. The others went to grab him but he pushed them away and shot off. Good for him, getting out of trouble."

"Sounds like Craig Blackstock."

"Who?"

"The school bully."

"That may be so. The main boy had that sort of air about him."
Kevin drained his coffee mug and found himself biting on some
grains that lay at the bottom like mud in a pond. "I wonder if you
can do something for me," he said.

"I should think so," the old man replied. "As long as you don't
want me to sneak about in the dead of night doing your
investigations. I wouldn't be any good at that sort of thing," he
chuckled.

"No, nothing like that," Kevin reassured him. "I just want you
to keep an eye open. Especially if anything funny's going on over
the field – in Dearings. OK?"

Mr Smith smiled. "Yes, I can do that. I haven't got much to do
but watch comings and goings anyway. Along with the stamps." He
nodded towards the dining table.

"Thanks," Kevin replied. "You can wave to me as I go past, if
you've got any news for me."

"Or I could phone. You're in the phone book, aren't you?
Kingsnorth, isn't it?"

"Yes. We're in there."

Mr Smith looked very cheerful. Kevin thought that the old man
had suddenly found a new purpose and relished the prospect of
turning detective.

"And I'll do something for you in return," Kevin said. "I'll look
out for stamps for you."

"Would you? I'm always grateful for them. It's something you
should take up, you know. Stamp collecting. It's not so dangerous
as investigating murders."

Kevin smiled. "I guess not. But ... er ... It doesn't turn on the
girls. You don't hear them say, 'Cor, I really fancy Kev. He collects
stamps, you know'."

"So that's why I've been short of female callers all these years."

Mr Smith was still chortling quietly as Kevin saw himself out of
the cottage.

It was break-time at school when Ros and Kevin slipped in to the
main chemistry lab when no one was looking.

"We're not allowed in here without a teacher," Kevin reminded
her in a whisper, "so we'll have to be quiet. Keep a watch on the
window as well, in case anyone looks in."

Ros was well aware that she was breaking the school rules. Her heart thumped and she had broken into a sweat. She'd decided to help Kevin only after much wrestling with her conscience. Kevin didn't expect to remain undisturbed for long in the laboratory, so he needed some help to search it quickly. In silence, they set about their task of looking for anything odd. They peered into each unlocked cupboard and tried each drawer, bench by bench.

They found nothing.

"Let's go," Ros urged.

"Let me just take a look at Chipmonk's stuff," Kevin breathed, determined not to miss anything.

As soon as he lifted the lid of Chipmonk's desk, he let out a gasp. "Bingo!" he said. "Over here."

Ros tiptoed to his side and glanced into the desk.

Lying on top of all his things, there was a chemistry book. Its title was *Tobacco Products*.

"Well, well," Kevin said quietly. "Whichever way I turn, the topic of the day is ciggies."

"There's a bookmark in it," Ros pointed out.

Kevin opened the book at the marked page. It was the beginning of a chapter on nicotine.

"Nicotine," Kevin murmured. "I wonder…"

Together they read, "Nicotine [3-(1-methyl-2-pyrrolidinyl) pyridine] is a colourless and highly toxic product obtained from dried tobacco leaves."

"Poisoned by nicotine," Kevin whispered to Ros. "It could be." He put the book down and began to rummage in the teacher's desk. "I wonder if there's any more incriminating evidence."

"Quickly, Kev," Ros urged, aware that Mr Monk could return at any moment. "And don't disturb it too much. If he knows someone's been rooting through his things…"

"He won't know it was us."

"But if he's … guilty, he'll try and find out. We could be skating on thin ice."

"Ah! It's worth it, though. Look."

Tucked between some laboratory notebooks and the side of the desk was a packet of cigarettes.

"Interesting. Especially because I'm sure he doesn't smoke himself," Kevin said, "but there's nothing else here. Let's get out."

Kevin poked his head round the door of the lab to check if the walkway outside was clear of teachers. He found himself peering at Mr Monk who was about to enter the laboratory.

"What do you think you're doing in there?" Chipmonk bellowed at him.

"Er…"

The science teacher grabbed the door handle and opened it fully. When he saw Ros, he seemed to calm down somewhat. "Rosalind Rabin. You as well. What's going on?"

"We … er … just came in to see if you were here." Ros tried to fib without blushing.

"Yeah." Kevin took over the explanation from her. "You weren't, so we were on our way out."

"You're not allowed in the laboratories under any circumstances without a teacher."

"I know," Kevin replied. "That's why we were leaving."

"What did you want to see me about?" asked Chipmonk.

"It was about David," Ros replied.

"David?"

"There's a couple of science books missing. The local library's been bothering us for them. We thought he might have left them in a locker or desk here."

Chipmonk didn't answer immediately. He peered at Ros, assessing her honesty. "No," he said eventually. "The police took all his effects from here. And I don't recall there being any such books."

"Oh," Ros said. "OK. Thanks anyway."

Eyeing them both as they made for the door, the science teacher commented, "Remember, in future, the rules about entering laboratories."

"Yes. Sorry," Ros returned.

Outside, Ros sighed with relief.

"Quick thinking," Kevin congratulated her. "You'll make a rogue yet."

"Great! Just what I've always wanted."

Kevin smiled at her. "Never mind. At least we got what we wanted."

"What do you mean?"

"Evidence. Chipmonk's tobacco book and the fag packet."

"So", Ros asked in a whisper, "are you going to call the police?"

"No!" Kevin shook his head. "Not a hope. We need more evidence than that. He could have just confiscated the ciggies from some unlucky kid."

"What other evidence?"

"David's torch, or that plastic bag he was carrying. A half-used bottle labelled poison. That sort of thing."

"But even if Chipmonk did it, how are you going to find them? They weren't in the lab, as far as we could see."

Kevin shrugged. "Maybe I should find out where he lives."

"No," Ros replied sharply. "If he's ... the one, it's too dangerous. He might suspect that we're on to him after that little affair." She pointed towards the science block.

"Mmm. True," Kevin replied. "But we need that torch – desperately."

He did not know then that David's torch was about to turn up – in the most unexpected place.

14

Detective Superintendent Whyte, bearing a search warrant and a businesslike frown, arrived at Kevin's door with Tracey and four other officers.

Kevin was taken aback. He hadn't expected the policeman to carry out his threat to search the house, but he couldn't prevent it, so he stood aside and put on a brave face. "It's only a small house, you know," he said. "No need to bring a complete squad."

"Last time I was here," Charlie replied menacingly, "you invited me to be thorough. We're going to be very thorough."

"I also said I was clean. I'm not scared," Kevin retorted. "Get on with it."

He stretched out on the sofa in the living room while the police crawled all over the place. He could hear them upstairs, emptying drawers and cupboards, even lifting the carpets. They brought in a small ladder and torch to look into the loft. They checked all of the obvious places and then every unlikely spot that they could find. Kevin sat tight as they turned over the whole house.

But it wasn't in the house that they found the evidence.

One of the officers came into the living room where Charlie and Kevin were waiting together and announced to his superior, "I think you'd better come and see this. In the garden."

"Come on, Kevin," Charlie ordered. "I think I'll have some questions for you in a minute."

The officer pointed to the gap between the garden shed and the brick wall. "Down there, sir."

Detective Superintendent Whyte peered into the cobwebby space. "Give me the torch," he said to the policeman.

Muttering to himself, he flashed the beam into the dingy hole to examine it again. Then he handed the torch to Kevin and invited him to take a look.

"There are two ways you could have got to know about tobacco being involved in David's death," Charlie said. "Either you deduced it from my questions, or you murdered him. Now, behind your shed, I count at least fifteen packets of cigarettes – all empty, no doubt – and a torch. Which of my two theories does this support, would you say?"

Kevin was noticeably drained of colour. "I don't know how they got there," he retorted defensively. "They're not mine."

Charlie turned to one of his colleagues and ordered him to call off the search. He pointed to the gap by the wall and said, "Just get that lot photographed, logged, and back to the forensic labs. I need to have a talk with this … young man."

As they went back into the house, Charlie said, "Now, we could go down the station, but we'd have to get involved with lawyers and that sort of thing. Have you got a lawyer?"

Kevin shook his head dismally. Lawyer's fees were well beyond his family's means.

"No. I thought not. So why don't we have a chat here? You can tell me all you know, and we can make it all official later. You *have* got something to tell me, haven't you?"

"Not really." Kevin was still shaken by the find. Since he'd worked out that nicotine had probably been used to kill David Rabin, he knew that he was in serious trouble. He dreaded another clash with the law. If they thought he'd committed another offence, they'd really lay into him. But this time it was murder, not arson. They'd send him down for good.

"So," the detective superintendent asked as they sat down at the dinner table, "how do you account for the haul behind your shed? How did they get there?"

Kevin clutched at straws. "I guess someone must have planted them there."

"Why would anyone do that?"

"To make it seem as if I did it."

"Really?"

"Yes. How else could they have got there?" Kevin said defiantly.

"Don't get hot under the collar," the detective replied. "I happen to agree with you."

"What?" Kevin could hardly believe his ears.

"I agree with you."

"Really? You're not having me on?"

Charlie smiled for the first time. "No. Scouts' honour."

"Why?" asked Kevin.

"Because you're not that daft. If you'd concocted the poison, you'd have got rid of the evidence by now," said the policeman. "And, besides, those packets haven't been there that long. Plenty of cobwebs around but hardly any attached to the packets."

The relief was clear in Kevin's face. The threat of a harsh and unjust punishment had faded. "So," he queried, "where do we go from here?"

"We? Well, you help me – by telling me what you know. Start with the torch behind your shed. What do you know about it?"

"Nothing for sure, but I guess it's David Rabin's." Helping the police didn't suit Kevin, yet he felt so relieved that he launched into the conversation without thinking about it. "Ros thinks he may have set out that night with a torch."

"Yes, that makes sense. We'll check it for his fingerprints. And for yours, of course. We'll still have them on file from your last offence. Now," he continued, "who'd want to pin his murder on you? Who have you upset recently?"

"Well, it could be someone at … No, it couldn't."

"Who were you going to suggest? Someone at Dearings?"

"Yes, but I told them I was David Rabin, so they couldn't have traced me here." He looked into the policeman's thoughtful face and added, "Unless…"

"Unless I told them who you were," Charlie spoke for him. "You see," he explained, "when Dr Dearing heard about your escapade, he was intrigued by a visitation from beyond the grave. He knew David Rabin, remember."

"So he found out from you who I was?"

"I'm afraid so," the policeman confessed. "It's interesting, though, isn't it? They find out it's you and almost immediately, some evidence turns up here."

"Yes, very interesting. I told you so – in the car that night."

"Let's not jump to hasty conclusions," the detective super-intendent said. "Is there anyone else who might have committed the murder and who'd like you to carry the can?"

"Possibly."

"Who?"

"Well, there's Mr Monk at school." Kevin recounted how the Deputy Head had caught him and Ros in his laboratory. He also mentioned that Chipmonk had cigarettes and a book on tobacco in his desk. "And he'd easily be able to look up where I live. Pretty suspicious, eh?" he concluded.

"Not necessarily," Charlie replied. "I talked to him about nicotine at one stage. Perhaps I aroused his curiosity enough to consult a book or try out a few experiments. Still," he added, "I'll bear it in mind. Have you confronted anyone else who'd know your address? How about that crackpot, Edriss?"

"No. Haven't been near him."

"Who else, then? At school, perhaps?"

"Well, just about anybody there would know where I live."

"But are there any particular kids who are crazy enough to get involved in a case of poisoning?" the detective pressed him.

Kevin hesitated. He was getting perilously close to being a sneak.

"What about Craig Blackstock?" Charlie prompted.

"Why him?"

"Oh, we've made inquiries at school. Quite a bully, that lad. And I heard a whisper that he'd had a disagreement with Rabin. Is that true?"

"I don't know. It might be."

"So, did you confront Craig Blackstock?"

Kevin wasn't sure why he was unwilling to incriminate such a boy. He was a nasty piece of work, and if he was a killer, he could be a threat to Kevin. "I ... er ... had a brief word with him, I think," Kevin said.

"You think. That's good enough for me. Have you got on the wrong side of any others over the Rabin business?"

"I don't think so," Kevin answered.

"OK," Charlie said. "I believe you. You've been quite helpful. I can only think of two other possibilities."

"Oh? Like what?"

"You really want to know?"

"Yes."

"Ros Rabin might want to sling some mud your way."

"What?" Kevin cried, rising to his feet.

"Don't get flustered again. I have to consider every possibility. She'd been arguing with her brother. They didn't get on. And you must admit, you'd be an ideal scapegoat for her – if she's been using you."

"She's not!" Kevin exclaimed resentfully.

"Even though you must seem pretty small to her – like David claimed."

"Look…" Kevin searched in vain for words strong enough to express his annoyance and deny the detective's charge. "It wasn't her," he retorted. "For one thing, David walked away from her that night."

"He could have gone back."

Kevin shook his head. He would never believe that Ros could either commit a murder or cheat him. "It wasn't her. That's the end of it. She couldn't."

"All right, then. Perhaps I should put more weight on my other theory."

"What's that?" Kevin snapped.

"That you've staged this whole stunt – in an amazing piece of bravado. A real double bluff. You put the evidence out the back, knowing we'd find it and think it had been planted by someone else. Which is why you've been going round bothering lots of suspects. To make enemies of them."

Kevin was dumbstruck for a few seconds. He wasn't in the clear, after all. "You … you've got a twisted mind," he growled.

"I prefer to call it devious," Charlie replied calmly. "That's why I'm good at my job. Anyway, you and I, we'll have another chat once forensic's finished with the treasure trove in your garden."

When Kevin eventually got rid of the police, he slammed his fist on to the dining table. It hurt quite a lot, but it helped dispel some of his anger.

15

The car plunged suddenly and accelerated alarmingly. Ros's head was thrown back against the cushioned headrest and her stomach seemed to leap, churning her insides. Involuntarily, she let out a scream as the car banked sharply, spiralling down. Despite holding tightly on to the rail, her body was flung sideways, colliding with Kevin. "Aaargh!" she wailed. The wheels clattered and the car jolted first one way, then the other. She slid back across the seat and Kevin slammed into her. A girl in the car behind them screamed at the top of her voice.

The roller coaster braked abruptly. In a series of jolts, it came to a halt. Ros groaned and, still queasy, rose slowly and unsteadily to her feet.

"OK?" asked Kevin.

"Just about," she answered.

"Told you it was a good ride."

"I'm not sure good is the word I'd use."

"Oh, you loved it really."

"Well … I must admit it's a break. Got me out of the house for a bit. But", Ros added, "I still feel guilty about it."

"How about something more leisurely?" Kevin pointed to the lake. "A rowing boat."

"OK," Ros agreed. "I can show you my rowing skills. Round and round in circles."

They stepped over the narrow-gauge railway line and headed for the wooden jetty.

In an effort to resume a normal life, Ros had decided to ride with Kevin to the leisure park at Billing. Besides, she needed a break after hearing of the find at Kevin's house and Detective

Superintendent Whyte's third session with her.

As they glided through the water, scattering the ducks, they talked about the interview. "So," Kevin said to her, "he showed you the torch and asked if you'd seen it before."

"Yes."

"And what did you say?"

"Well, I said that David had one like it. He asked me if David left the house with it that night and I said something along the lines of, 'Now you mention it, I think he did have a torch.' I asked him if he was sure it was David's. He was. Said David's fingerprints were all over it."

"Then, no doubt, he enjoyed telling you where he found it."

"Not exactly. He assumed you'd already told me. He just asked me if there was anything else I'd forgotten to tell him about that night. In an unpleasant sort of way."

"That was my fault. Sorry. I told him you'd mentioned the torch to me. He was grumping because you'd told me but held back the information from him. Anyway," he asked, "you didn't tell him about the photo, did you?"

"No. But I'm no good at this game. I probably blushed."

"Mmm." Kevin looked beyond her and said, "Pull more with the left or we'll end up on dry land."

Ros gave a few strong strokes with her left arm, then said, "If someone planted that stuff on you, who could it have been? Who knows where you live and would want to drop you in it?"

"Well," Kevin replied, "Whyte suggested you."

Ros stopped rowing and exclaimed, "Me!"

"Sorry, but I thought you'd better know," Kevin said. "Of course, I don't ... Anyway, it's a silly idea. I reckon the list's Chipmonk, Craig Blackstock, or someone at Dearings – maybe Dr Dearing himself or that Frank character."

Ros didn't reply. She was still smarting from the policeman's slur on her character. Absent-mindedly, she resumed rowing.

Kevin changed the subject. "How have you got on? Anything more from the photo or that Channel Islands book?"

"Not really," she replied, trying to forget the accusation. "But there was something in the book about Alderney at the time the photo was taken. Doubt if it's got anything to do with it."

"What?"

"Well, it would have been taken in the early 1940s..."

Kevin interrupted, asking, "Wasn't there a war on then?"

"Yes. The Second World War. The Nazis took over the islands. But records of exactly what happened have never been released, according to the book."

"So there was something underhand going on."

"Possibly. No one knows. It may have been some of the islanders co-operating too closely with the enemy. That's what the book suggested. And there was a slave labour camp on Alderney. Many of the prisoners died. I don't know how."

Kevin thought about it for a moment, then said, "You don't think your grandma...?"

"Was a prisoner? I don't know. She could have been, I guess."

"That'd explain why she looked so miserable."

"Yes. It occurred to me, as well. But even if she was, what's it got to do with David?"

"Yeah," Kevin agreed. "And that was fifty years ago. Who's interested in what happened fifty years ago?"

Ros looked at him seriously. "Some are, Kev. Some were hurt so bad they can't forget."

"Look out!" Kevin cried.

It was too late. The prow of the rowing boat parted the reeds at the edge of the lake and ran aground in the mud.

Ros cursed under her breath and Kevin laughed.

He stood up in the boat and said, "Give me one of the oars. I'll get us off."

He positioned the paddle against the bank and pushed hard till the boat floated free of the bottom. Before he sat down again, he glanced at the people on the path who had stopped to watch him wrestling with dry land. For an instant, Kevin caught sight of one particular man just before he turned his face away.

Kevin dropped on to his seat heavily and the boat rocked alarmingly.

"Careful!" Ros chided him. "Come on. Give me the oar."

He handed it over without a comment.

"Are you OK, Kev?" Ros asked.

"Yes. Just get us out of here."

"Why?"

"Because the security guard from Dearings – Frank – is just over there."

"What?" she exclaimed. "Are you sure it's him?"

"Yes. He's behind you. Watching us. Don't turn round. Just get us back."

Ros spun the boat round and headed towards the jetty. "Why?" she said. "Why's he watching us?"

"How should I know?" Kevin replied. "But if he murdered David, and planted the evidence at my place, he could be disappointed that the cops haven't carted me away."

"How do you mean?"

"His ploy didn't work. I haven't been arrested. So he's trying something else to stop me proving he did it."

"You mean he's gunning for you now?" Ros looked petrified. "I told you it was too dangerous, Kev. Ages ago."

"It'll be all right," he assured her. "But we'd better lose him – just in case. And to do that, we need to be on land."

"OK," she mumbled.

As she rowed back, she thought to herself, "Even if we can lose him here, he knows where Kevin lives."

Back on land, they stood at the edge of the lake and pretended to watch the people playing crazy golf. Ros whispered, "Well? Have you seen him? Is he still watching us?"

"Yes. He's near the entrance to the amusement arcade. Pretending, like us, to be interested in what's going on."

"So how do we lose him?"

"I think we'd better take the train."

"The train?"

"Yes. The trip around the lake."

"But", Ros objected, "he'll just get on one of the carriages."

"Maybe," Kevin replied. "But I don't think so. There are only three small wagons to sit on. He'd have to get too close to us. Blow his cover. My bet is, he'll stay here and watch. The train's in view the whole time and it doesn't stop till we get back here."

"So how are we going to get away from him?" Ros hesitated when she saw the glint in Kevin's eye. "Oh, no!" she murmured. "You're not thinking of jumping off."

Kevin nodded. "I am. Bet it doesn't go that fast. Trust me, it'll be OK."

They got on the train just before it chugged away on its circuit of the lake. As Kevin predicted, the security guard who was tailing them did not attempt to sprint to the train and board it. He stayed at the terminal.

"OK," Kevin said as the train rattled and bumped round the track. "We'll jump when we get to the caravan site. We can run among the caravans. It'll be like a maze in there."

"Yes," Ros agreed. "It's in the opposite direction from the car park. If he sees us jump for it, he'll think we're headed away from the bike so he'll run after us. We could double back to the bike and ... off we go."

"Exactly," Kevin said, impishly.

The wagons lurched round a corner near the caravan park. The train was going no faster than jogging pace. "On your marks," said Kevin. He glanced across the lake and commented, "I can't be sure, but I think he's watching us. It doesn't matter. Get set!" Discreetly, he removed the rope that stretched across the opening. He looked across the lake once more then cried, "Go!"

The train driver turned round and shouted, "Oi! You can't do that!"

But it was too late. In turn, Ros and Kevin had jumped. They were both running as they hit the ground. The other trucks trundled past them and, out of the corner of his eye, Kevin saw the man from Dearing Scientific begin to dash around the perimeter of the lake.

Kevin yelled to Ros, "He's coming after us! But he'll never catch us."

They darted between the closely spaced caravans. Ros swerved to avoid crashing into a dog that was sprawled in their path and, behind her, Kevin jumped over it.

After a burst of sprinting, Kevin called breathlessly, "I'm not as fast as you, remember. And we need to double back."

"OK," she replied. "Let's turn left down here."

They ran on for a short distance, then turned left again and slowed to jogging pace. Among the forest of caravans, Frank would never find them. Besides, by now he'd be going in the wrong direction.

When they reached the car park, there was no sign of Frank. Quickly, they donned crash helmets and got on the bike. Kevin kick-started it into life, engaged first gear and they rode away at speed.

Before going to his own house, Kevin took Ros home. When she leaned on his good shoulder and swung herself from the bike, she warned him, "Take care, Kev. He knows where you live."

"I know," he replied. "I'll be OK."

"I've been thinking. It could be just that Dr Dearing told him to follow you after you broke in. Maybe that's all it is: checking, in case you try it again or get up to any more funny business."

"That's right. It makes good sense if they still believe their industrial spy theory. Maybe they're tailing me to see who I hand over their industrial secrets to. He might not be after my blood at all." He didn't sound convinced but he smiled at her reassuringly.

"By the way," he added, "have you got any stamps?"

"Stamps?"

"As in stamp collecting."

"Yes, I think so. Why?"

"I want them as a bribe to Mr Smith for keeping watch on Dearing Scientific for me," Kevin told her.

"Mother keeps used stamps in a bag. Gives them to charity. I'll see if I can find them for you."

With Ros's bag of stamps in his coat pocket, Kevin rode home via Mr Smith's bungalow.

"Hello, young Kevin," Mr Smith greeted him. "How are you?"

"OK, thanks," Kevin answered. "Got something for you."

"Oh yes? You'd better come in."

In the lounge, Kevin produced the packet of stamps and the old man's eyes lit up. "Why, thank you!" He took the bag and peered inside.

"Have you got anything for me?" asked Kevin.

"A cup of coffee, perhaps. And a biscuit?" Mr Smith replied.

"No. I mean, anything on Dearings."

"Oh. Are you still into your investigations?"

" 'Fraid so."

"Well," Mr Smith said, "I haven't seen anything out of the ordinary. A few more of their vans coming and going, possibly. That's all."

"What sort of vans?"

"Just the usual. All white with that little code on them. Skull and crossbones, with 'Toxic' written underneath."

"Nothing else?"

Mr Smith had been distracted by the contents of the bag of stamps. He was taking them out and examining each one closely as he spoke. "No. Not really."

"How about activities around the school?"

"Er... That bully's been up to his usual tricks. Yesterday he pinned one youngster against my wall when the teachers weren't looking."

"How about Chipmonk? Mr Monk, the Deputy Head."

"He's been around, looking sulky. Nothing unusual about that." Mr Smith picked out one of the stamps particularly carefully with tweezers and murmured, "Nice."

Kevin felt he wasn't getting anywhere. He got up to leave. "I'll leave you to get stuck into the stamps – or whatever you do to them."

"Yes. Thank you. Thanks very much," he replied, his head almost inside the bag.

"You'll keep a look-out for me still?"

"Yes. Of course I will."

16

Kevin picked up the spare rib, dripping in barbecue sauce. "Mmm," he said as he tucked in. "That's good." He looked around the American-style café and observed, "It's good in here. Never been able to afford it, though."

Ros, who had agreed to pay the bill, smiled at him. "Wait till you tuck into the chocolate dessert they serve up here."

Kevin glanced at the menu, written on blackboards hung from the ceiling.

"'Death by chocolate', they call it," he remarked.

"Yes. Until recently, I liked the name."

"Well, I'll leave some space for it anyway," Kevin replied, glee-fully licking the spicy sauce from his fingers.

"Anyway," Ros said seriously, "I only volunteered to bring you here so we could talk something through."

Kevin looked at her and asked, "What's that?"

"Since yesterday at Billing, I've been thinking about this Alderney connection."

"The long-lost-uncle theory?"

"Possibly," Ros answered. "I wonder if we've been barking up the wrong tree."

"Oh?"

"Well, we've been trying to figure out who'd want to kill David." Ros leaned forward and whispered, "But what if David went off to kill someone?"

"How do you mean?"

"If there was a family vendetta of some sort, maybe David set out to end it. He could have brewed up the poison. He was OK at science, you know. But perhaps his intended victim overpowered him and gave David some of his own poison."

Kevin had stopped eating as he listened to her. "So… ?" he prompted. Clearly, he wanted to hear more of her line of reasoning.

"So, it could almost have been self-defence. We've been after the murderer. Perhaps we should be looking for an intended victim. That night," she said, "when David walked out, he … reacted when I said something about getting his own back. I was thinking about you, but perhaps he had someone else in mind."

"The missing uncle?"

"Well, it all began on Sports Day, didn't it? Grandfather could have seen his other son," Ros speculated. "He might have whispered it to David. David would have investigated – hence the photo and Channel Islands book. If there really was some bad blood resulting from the Alderney days, David could have confronted him – to settle an old score on behalf of Father or Grandfather. He did love Grandfather, you know."

"Yes," Kevin replied. "But I don't know if you're right. Would your grandad recognize a son after all these years?" He hesitated, then added, "Hang on! Of course he would. Your dad and him were twins. Was there anyone at Sports Day who looked like your dad used to?"

"Not as far as I know. But they may not have been identical twins. Just a bit of family likeness would be enough."

Kevin nibbled at a chip thoughtfully. "He must have changed his name as well. If you're right, at least we know how old this uncle is. You'll even know his birthday. When was it?"

"Boxing Day. Twenty-sixth of December. And he'd be fifty."

"Did you have someone in mind? I think we can rule out Craig Blackstock!"

"I guess so," Ros replied. "There's Edriss, though. And Chipmonk's getting on a bit. I imagine he's about fifty."

"So's Dr Dearing," Kevin put in. "He'd be pretty near perfect – but do you reckon there's a family resemblance?"

"Not really," Ros murmured.

"But there's something I don't understand, if you're right," Kevin said. "How come the fag packets ended up in my garden? If David cooked up the poison, they'd be more likely to turn up in yours."

For a second, Kevin's thoughts turned to Detective Superintendent Whyte's comment, *Ros Rabin might want to sling some mud your way.* If, all along, the family feud had been between Ros and David, maybe she *had* dumped them on him. After all, she had admitted that she felt bitter towards David. Was she so bitter that she was driven to murder? *No*, he told himself. *Don't be ridiculous. It wasn't Ros.* But he couldn't prevent his mind suddenly thinking back to Ros's hobby of macramé. David had been tied to a chair, and Ros was an expert in tying knots in cords that were attached to a chair. She also knew about LD values.

Ros shrugged. "I don't know how they got there. But nothing's really changed on that score. I'm only suggesting a different motive for the murder. The victim-turned-murderer would still want to put the blame on someone else. It's still got to be someone who knows where you live and that the police are investigating you. Minus Craig Blackstock."

"That rules out Edriss. Unless he's been nosing about without me knowing about it. But we've got nothing on him, just that he smokes and doesn't like kids."

"There is someone else, though."

"Oh?"

"Mr Smith."

"Mr Smith?"

"Yes."

"But", Kevin objected, "he's my mate. And he's nearer his sell-by date than fifty."

Ros shrugged. "He's a nice man, I know, but how much did you tell him? Does he know you're the police's prime suspect?"

"Yes."

"And does he know where you live?"

"I doubt it," Kevin replied.

"In that case, perhaps he's not…"

"Just a second," Kevin interrupted. "He does know which road I live in. We chatted about it. So he could've got the house number from the phone book. But…" He shook his head. "I can't believe it. If I had a list of people in this world who didn't do it, you'd be number one. He'd be number two." He wiped his fingers on a serviette and then screwed it up.

They sat in silence while the waiter cleared the table. They resumed their conversation once he'd gone to get the chocolate dessert.

"No," Kevin continued. "He's too old and he doesn't even look like a Rabin."

"That's true," Ros agreed. "But I think he's got to be added to our list."

"You sound like our chum, Whyte. Got to consider every possibility, and all that."

Ros shrugged. "That's true as well."

"OK," Kevin said, somewhat frostily, "I'll go back tomorrow and ask him when his birthday is. But I bet it's not Boxing Day." Kevin paused before adding, "Hey, that reminds me. Why don't you check out Dr Dearing's birthday? Bet he's in ... what's that posh people's book called?"

"*Who's Who?*"

"Yeah, that's it. I bet he's in it. And it'll give birthdays, I should think."

"All right, I'll try it. I don't suppose Chipmonk's done enough to get in it as well."

"No," replied Kevin. "That's probably what bugs him."

"Anyway," Ros said, nodding towards the waiter, "here comes the pudding. Just look at that. Hope you've left enough room."

"Wicked!" Kevin said as the bowl of brown stuff was slapped down in front of him. "Do you have this often? How come you keep in shape after this?"

"I run it off."

They waded into the dessert.

When they left, neither of them noticed the security officer from Dearing Scientific sitting in a car outside the restaurant. As they strolled along the road towards the shopping centre, the car crawled along behind them at a discreet distance.

17

When he left school the next day, Kevin saw Mr Smith out on his patio, waving to get his attention. Kevin jogged over to the fence and asked excitedly, "Have you seen something?"

"No, not really," he replied. "I just wondered if you could do me a favour."

"Oh?"

"You know those stamps I got the other day? Not yours, the ones that came in the post. Well, I've sorted out what I want and I've got to post the rest back. Would you take the packet to the post office for me? You go past it on the way home, don't you?"

Getting over his disappointment, Kevin answered, "Sure. I'll do that."

"Come round, then. I'll get it for you."

Kevin walked round the garden to the front door. He knocked, then pushed it open and went in. He found Mr Smith in the living room.

"Just sealing it up," the old man said. "Only take a minute."

"You don't collect every single stamp, then?"

"No. That would get out of hand."

"What sort of stuff do you collect? I could keep my eye open for it." Kevin glanced at the table and saw an album open at a page full of old Guernsey stamps. "Guernsey? That's part of the Channel Islands, isn't it?"

"Yes. That's one of the countries I collect."

"I'll see what I can do," Kevin said. "You haven't got a birthday coming up, have you?"

"Birthday?" Mr Smith finished taping up the small parcel and handed it to Kevin.

"Yes," Kevin replied with a smile. "I could put together a packet for your birthday."

The old man returned the smile, genuinely touched by the offer. "No need, lad. Besides, you'd have to wait for next year before I have another birthday. I don't bother with them now. When you get to my age, you forget these things – if you don't have a family to remind you."

Kevin held up the packet and said, "Well, I'll post this for you, anyhow."

"Thanks," he replied. "You're a good lad."

It was only afterwards, as Kevin rode to the post office, that he looked at the address that Mr Smith had scrawled on the package. It was directed to the Channel Islands Stamp Company on Guernsey. Kevin shook his head. He didn't want to make the connection between Mr Smith, the Channel Islands and the Rabins. He hoped it was just coincidence. Even so, when he got home, he called Ros to tell her about his conversation with Mr Smith.

"Why was he interested in the Channel Islands?" she inquired.

"He might not be. It might be just their stamps. I don't know."

"Didn't you ask?"

"No. Sorry. But he's not your uncle," Kevin argued. "He's ancient. And his birthday's some time early in the year – not December. Unless he was lying, and I don't see why he should be."

"I do," Ros replied. "If he's our man and if he knows we're on to him, of course he'll lie."

"But…" Kevin struggled to put into words his objections to her accusation. "Anyone could collect Guernsey stamps. It doesn't mean … I just can't believe it's him."

"I know," Ros replied. "And I hope it's not, either. But we've got almost as much evidence against him as anyone else."

"Yes," Kevin admitted unenthusiastically. "You're right. I'd better look into it."

"What will you do? Nothing daft, Kev."

"No," he said into the mouthpiece. "I'll go back tonight and check it out."

"You don't mean break in?"

Kevin had to have the freedom to look around the house without Mr Smith's interference. As the old man hardly ever went out, Kevin would have to give the bungalow the once-over while he slept. He didn't want to worry Ros so he didn't admit it. "No, I'll go and have a chat with him. See what I can find out."

"Be careful, Kev."

"OK."

"I'll try my luck with Mother again. She's not as doped as she was. I'll see if I can get her to talk about Grandmother and all that."

"Good idea," Kevin answered. "Let me know straightaway if she comes up trumps."

"All right."

"Hopefully, we can clear Mr Smith and then get on to Dearings again. Which reminds me – did you find out Dearing's birthday?"

"Yes," she answered. "Second of May. But there is one thing, Kev."

"Oh yes?"

"His piece in *Who's Who* says he was educated for a while in the Channel Islands."

Kevin perked up. "Really? That's … useful to know. I told you – the evidence against him gets stronger all the time. Anything else?"

"No. That's all."

"He's definitely number one, you know. Him, or one of his people."

"You don't think that Dearings man is still following you?"

"I don't think so," Kevin replied. "I think I've shaken him off. Or he's getting better at it."

"Watch out – just in case."

"Every day, Ros, you sound more like a mother!"

Ros giggled nervously. "Sorry. But this is serious stuff. I don't want to lose you, too."

"You won't. I'll be OK. This one's a doddle."

"Yes, I know. But… Oh, never mind."

"I'll see you tomorrow," Kevin said. "We'll compare notes then."

"Yes. Sure. 'Bye."

Kevin put down the phone and went to get tea. Then came the eternal wait for nightfall.

Kevin glanced at his watch. Eleven-thirty. He drew the curtain slightly to one side and peered out. Curtis Street was dead. No kids played in the road. Even the men who had spent the evening in the pub had returned to their houses. A few windows glowed by the light within, but most of the terrace was dark. There was not a sound. He scanned the street in both directions, but could see no unfamiliar cars nor any other signs of his watcher. But if Frank was determined to tail him all round the clock, Kevin knew that the guard could be lurking in any one of a hundred shadowy nooks in the street. Kevin let the curtain fall back into place. He sneaked out of the house and closed the front door quietly behind him. He started his bike and accelerated towards School Lane.

He liked the deserted, eerie streets. He could ride fast and cut corners on the wrong side of the road. He even jumped one set of traffic lights.

He stopped and padlocked his bike in the lane beside Mr Edriss's house. Glancing at the living room window, Kevin noted Edriss silhouetted against the light curtain. "It's late for him to be still up," Kevin murmured. "Good job I'm not wanting to do his place tonight – but why should I? I've got nothing on him." Kevin stole past the house and walked towards the bungalow by the school.

18

Ros's mother was sitting up in bed when Ros knocked lightly at the door and stepped inside.

"How are you?" asked Ros.

Her mother shrugged in response.

"Mother," Ros began, "I have to talk to you. I really do. I have to know what happened."

"When?"

"When this photo was taken." Ros showed her David's heirloom. "I need to know if I have an uncle. I need to know what happened to Grandmother. I need to know it all."

"No," her mother replied, refusing to look at the photograph. "Let bygones be bygones. Why can't you let it be?"

"Because it – whatever it is – won't let *me* be."

"What do you mean?"

"I mean, whatever happened to David is getting close to me and Kev."

Her mother looked petrified. "You too? I couldn't bear it if…"

"Then you must tell me."

Mrs Rabin didn't reply immediately. She looked everywhere in the room, except at Ros. Then she sighed and said, "It was a long time ago."

"But it's still going on. You have to admit it."

Something inside her mother finally, unwillingly snapped. She nodded tearfully.

"Mother," Ros asked quietly, "do I have an uncle?"

Mrs Rabin covered her face with both hands, shaking her head. "No," her broken voice said.

"But on the back of this photo, it says Grandmother had twins."

"You don't have an uncle." Her mother uncovered her haunted face and whispered, "He died when he was still a baby."

"But..." Ros stopped herself. She had a million questions and she didn't know where to start. And her theory about the long-lost uncle was shattered. She sat on the edge of her mother's bed, took her hand and said, "You'd better tell me."

Her mother swallowed. "It's not a nice story," she said. "I don't want you to get hurt as well. But I suppose you have the right to know." Uncomfortably, she began, "Your grandfather told me something of what happened. It was a bad time for people like him and your grandmother in Alderney."

"When? In the war?"

"Yes. Your grandmother and grandfather were put into a prison – a labour camp on Alderney."

"Why?"

Mrs Rabin shrugged again. "Because they weren't to the soldiers' liking." She squeezed her daughter's hand and continued. "It was a dreadful place, they say. Many died, you know. No one knows quite how many or exactly how they died, but they did. Buried five at a time in unmarked graves, they were. That's where your grandmother and uncle are. Sharing some patch of earth with strangers. At least we know how they died."

"Yes?" Ros prompted sympathetically.

"Most of the islanders hated what was going on during the occupation, but not all. Some helped the soldiers. There was one young man in particular. A new doctor. Doctor Somerton, he was called. He wasn't a bad man, originally. But just before the occupation, he did something both kind and awful. He ended the life of a dying woman. She wanted to die, you understand. She was in great pain. Dr Somerton put an end to her suffering. And his reward? He was struck off. If it hadn't been for the war and the occupation, he'd have been prosecuted. All he had to look forward to after the war was a trial for murder. Under that sort of pressure, he cracked. Maybe he also felt guilty about what he'd done. Maybe it was bitterness about the way he'd been treated. Anyway, he cracked." Mrs Rabin cleared her throat, sniffed and carried on. "They wanted a doctor at the labour camp. He volunteered. The soldiers didn't care that he'd been struck off. All they wanted was someone to make sick people fit for more work and to be experimented on." Her mother wiped her eyes and nose, unable to continue.

Ros waited for a while and then queried, "Experiment?"

"In the war, there were all sorts of atrocities, Ros. The soldiers wanted to know the effects of drugs and chemicals on the human body. Dr Somerton found out. He used the people in the camp as guinea pigs."

"What?" Ros cried.

"They were particularly keen on knowing the effects on pregnant women, apparently. This Dr Somerton fed people with all sorts of pills and potions. Made them breathe all sorts of gases, just to see what happened to them."

"Including Grandmother?" Ros asked in a whisper.

"Yes. She was separated from your grandfather. He was made to work on the island. She was part of the experiment. Dr Somerton did more and more experiments on her and she grew weaker and weaker as her time came. She just had the strength to give birth, but no more. She died afterwards. But", Mrs Rabin sobbed, "that wasn't the end of it. The soldiers and the doctor continued the experiments on the babies."

"No!"

Her mother nodded slowly. "Your father's brother didn't make it. He died after a week, poor little thing! Your father survived, of course, but he was never a well man, as you know. Afterwards, after the war, the hospital tried to find out what he'd been given. They thought he'd been tested with nerve gases, and chemicals from plants like tobacco and deadly nightshade. But they never got to the bottom of it. He'd probably been given all sorts of different things. Ruined his health."

Ros had read about the war. It was part of the curriculum. Yet it had always seemed so distant. It was history. It had happened to someone else, somewhere else. Now, it seemed so close. It involved her family. It had caught up with her as if the whole dreadful business had taken place only yesterday. Its echoes reverberated all about her.

"What happened to Dr Somerton?" she asked.

"No one knows," her mother replied. "After the war, he disappeared. The whole thing was hushed up, but I understand that the authorities did try to find him for a while. They never did, of course. He probably changed his name and … just vanished. He got away with it."

"Grandfather tried to find him, too," Ros guessed.

"Yes. And, when he could, so did your father. They searched and searched." She began to sob again. "They wouldn't let it be. Their hate even infected David. They passed it on to him."

"So, after all these years, Grandfather spotted Dr Somerton at Sports Day," Ros surmised. "Could he really have recognized him, fifty years on?"

"You never forget the face of someone who killed your wife and baby. Your grandfather always swore that he'd recognize him any time, any place."

"And he told David who it was."

She nodded. "He must have done. But what's the point, Ros? Whoever he is, he's an old man now. How can you punish him now for what he did then? I don't say he should be forgiven for what he did, but there's nothing that can put matters right now. He'll have God's judgement soon enough."

"David didn't think like that. He went out to do something about it." Ros was talking to herself really, but she did so aloud.

"Taking the law into your own hands never did any good," her mother replied. "And it won't now."

"But that's what Kev's been doing all along. And", she said, glancing at her watch, "what he might be about to do again right now." She was surprised how long she'd been with her mother, listening to her dreadful story. It was midnight – much later than Ros expected.

"What do you mean?"

"I've got to go and make a call, Mother. But before I do, another question. Do you know who Dr Somerton really is? Did Grandfather or David tell you?"

She shook her head. "No." Her mother called after her, "Don't you get involved as well, Ros. No good can come of it."

Ros hesitated at the door. She looked back at her mother and said, "Just one last thing. Why on earth didn't you tell me all this before?"

Broken, her mother replied, "Because I wanted you to be free of this … curse. We tried to protect you."

19

Mr Smith's bungalow was in darkness. The nearby street lamp lit the front porch so Kevin decided to get into the house from the back. Glancing about him to make sure he wasn't being watched, he climbed over the fence and slipped past the garage to the patio at the rear.

Kevin yanked on the patio door in an attempt to slide it back, but it would not budge. It was firmly locked. He crept further along the wall to a window with a fanlight above it. The window itself was not made to open but the fanlight, hinged at the top, was designed to swing outwards. Kevin put his fingers as far as they would go under the lip of the fanlight, and gently pulled outwards. The window didn't move but the wood came away in his hands. It was rotten. He poked at the frame and the end of his finger sank into the crumbling woodwork. "That", he said under his breath, "makes life easier."

From the inner pocket of his jacket, he produced a thin screwdriver and pushed it up under the lip of the wooden frame. It needed only a little force and twisting to go straight through the rotten wood. The tip of the screwdriver emerged on the other side of the window pane, near the catch. Kevin manoeuvred the blade sideways until it was directly under the latch. He thrust it upwards and the bar leapt off its catch.

He put the screwdriver away and pulled open the fanlight. It was only a narrow hole into the house but it was enough. Before he grabbed hold of the decaying frame and heaved himself up and into the bungalow, Kevin hesitated. He didn't doubt his ability to squeeze, head first, through the small opening. He was thinking about what he was doing. Breaking into his friend's home to pry felt like a betrayal. But Ros was right, Mr Smith had become a suspect. He had to be checked out somehow, and Kevin didn't know any other way.

He wriggled through the gap, slowly working his way into the house like a dragonfly struggling to emerge from its larva. With his feet still hooked on the window ledge, Kevin found himself upside down, his outstretched arms reaching down to Mr Smith's old sofa. He was grateful for the soft landing. He freed his legs and collapsed on to the couch with barely a sound.

He took a small torch from his pocket and flashed the beam about. It was the same old lounge – familiar, unexciting, almost beyond suspicion. What was he looking for? He wasn't entirely sure. Evidence of time spent on Alderney. Evidence of a poison. Anything.

On the table, the torchlight picked out two stamp albums. Kevin flicked the pages. One of the books seemed to contain stamps from Herm, Alderney and Sark and the other from Guernsey and Jersey. Each stamp had a small tag with a number, the year of issue and a brief description. He stopped at a page that bore the title, "1941–44: Issued under British authority during the German Occupation." Kevin groaned and shook his head. "It doesn't mean anything," he reflected. "Doesn't prove he was there. Just that he's interested in the period." He couldn't resist the afterthought, "Like David Rabin."

He flashed the light round the walls and furniture. For the first time, he realized that they were bare of the usual keepsakes – no photographs of a young Mr Smith, of friends or family adorned the room. It was almost as if its occupant didn't have a history – at least not one that could be displayed. That struck Kevin as sad. He wondered what Mr Smith had done before he retired. The book-shelves revealed an educated man: poetry, plays, natural history and medicine, as well as a variety of stamp catalogues.

In one corner, a few bottles of drink stood on a cabinet with a glass panel. Inside, models of old aeroplanes were displayed. Next to the cabinet, there was an old writing desk and chair. Kevin moved the chair to one side and tried to pull down the front of the bureau but he found that it was locked. Immediately he was curious. There was no key in the lock and the oak front held firm to force. He took from his pocket a length of copper wire and poked it into the lock. After a minute of unsuccessful fishing about in the mechanism, the wire hooked on to the stud. Kevin twisted the wire to imitate the turning of a key. The stud clicked satisfyingly into the unlocked position and the small bolt was withdrawn.

He put the wire away and pulled down the front of the bureau. He sat on the chair as he sifted through the items inside: paper, pens, bills and receipts, a cheque book and a couple of insurance policies. There was a British passport that had never been used and a medical card. Right at the back of the bureau Kevin found a letter, the paper yellow with age. The creases had almost become tears. Obviously, it had been unfolded and read many times over the years. It was from the General Medical Council, dated June 1940, and was addressed to Dr Somerton of Alderney. The letter informed Dr Somerton that, for purposely ending the life of one of his patients, he had been struck off the medical register and would no longer be permitted to practise medicine.

"Doctor Somerton," Kevin pondered. "Who's he?"

Ros let the phone ring and ring but there was no answer. As usual, Kevin's parents were out till the early hours and obviously Kevin himself wasn't at home. She guessed that he was still at Mr Smith's house. If she wanted to speak to Kevin, she'd have to call Mr Smith.

She put down the phone. While she wondered what to do, she examined the photograph of her grandmother, reduced by Dr Somerton to a physical wreck, and a code number – Rabin 168/EAS. Ros sighed. She had to decide. Was it right to bother an old man by telephoning him at this hour? She guessed that he must be sitting up late with Kevin, so a call wouldn't be too much of an intrusion. She thought that her information was too important to wait till morning, so she really had to talk to Kevin. She was worried about calling, though, because there was a chance that Mr Smith could be Dr Somerton. But if he was, Kevin was in great danger. That would make it even more important to tell Kevin what she knew. She decided to take the risk of telephoning.

First, she had to find Mr Smith's number. In the telephone book, she looked in horror at the sixteen columns of Smiths. Suddenly, it struck her that if someone wanted to disappear by hiding behind a new name, Smith was an excellent choice. A Smith was as safe from discovery as a needle in a haystack.

Ros didn't know the old man's initials, so she ran her finger down the endless list, carefully looking for a Smith that lived in School Lane. It took time but, of all the Smiths, she found only one: Smith, E.A.

Her spine tingled with excitement and fear. It wasn't just the finding of his name and number that thrilled and scared her. There was something else.

"Mr E.A. Smith," she said to herself. She looked again at the back of her grandmother's photograph and read, "Rabin 168/EAS. I wonder if they're initials. EAS. Does it stand for Dr E.A. Somerton? And now Mr E.A. Smith!" It was too close a match to be coincidence. "It's him!" she said to herself. "He just changed Somerton to Smith."

Her hair seemed to stand on end. It was like the sensation before a big race – the excitement, the nerves. But now the stakes were much higher. Ros knew that a phone call wasn't enough any more. Kevin was in trouble. Real trouble. She grabbed a coat and dashed out of the house. She had no idea what she had to do. There was no plan in her head. She knew only that she had to get to Mr Smith's house. She was running the most important race of her life.

Kevin was so engrossed in reading the letter that he didn't hear Mr Smith coming up behind him. He nearly leapt out of the chair when the gun was placed against the back of his neck.

"Don't move!" the old man ordered. "Put your hands behind the chair."

Kevin didn't dare speak. He simply obeyed.

"I'm going to put the gun down and tie you up. Don't think I can't pick it up if you make a move."

Kevin let out a yelp as the cord from Mr Smith's dressing-gown was tightened roughly around his wrists, anchoring them to the framework of the chair.

"Right," said the old man, retreating towards the doorway and the light switch. "Let's see what I've caught."

When the room filled with light, both of them blinked but Mr Smith was the first to react. "Kevin!" he cried in surprise.

Kevin looked at his friend but said nothing. He didn't know what to say.

"So," Mr Smith said, as he recovered from the initial shock, "you've figured it out. You know." The old man put the revolver away in the pocket of his dressing-gown. "I did wonder – when you got inquisitive."

Behind his back, Kevin tried to loosen the knot by twisting his wrists, but there was no play in the cord. Mr Smith had secured him well. There was no chance of escaping from the chair.

His captor sighed heavily and approached the writing desk. He took the letter and waved it in front of Kevin before replacing it in the bureau. "You've read this, as well," he murmured. "I wish you hadn't. And I wish it wasn't you. But you leave me no choice."

Reaching into a cupboard, Mr Smith produced a bottle of rum. He unscrewed the top and smelled the liquid. He turned up his nose and said, "This is a little something Rabin made for me. It's your turn now."

20

With his arms bent round the chair, Kevin's shoulders were forced backwards. A dull ache had set in, especially in the left shoulder that had been injured by the spike. The back of the chair dug into the tops of his arms and his muscles blazed with pain. Tied tightly at the wrists, one hand had become numb. Pins and needles jabbed at the other.

"It's my own fault," Mr Smith mumbled, partly to himself, partly to Kevin. "I destroyed every trace of my former life. Everything except that letter. I should have got rid of that as well. But I couldn't bring myself to burn it. I needed it to remind me of what they did to me. They destroyed my career before it had hardly begun. *They* started this whole thing."

"You were Dr Somerton?" asked Kevin.

Clutching the bottle of rum to his chest as if it were a new-born baby, Mr Smith glanced at Kevin. "You don't know everything, then."

"I don't know anything."

The old man sniggered. "Don't try and wangle your way out of this by pretending to be ignorant. It's too late for that. You wouldn't be here if you weren't on to me." He ambled restlessly round the room as he spoke. "Why did you come here in the first place?"

Kevin nodded towards the table. "The stamps."

"Stamps?"

"It connected you with the Channel Islands and Alderney."

"Is that all?"

"No. You knew where I lived. You could've planted the torch and fag packets on me. But", Kevin reasoned, "it doesn't matter now. I'm here. Plenty of people know I'm here. They'll come for me. You can't get away with it. You might as well let me go."

"You're wrong," Mr Smith replied, approaching him. "I *can* get away with it. The police don't suspect me. They suspect you. You told me. They think you made this." He held up the bottle. "When they find you, it will all make sense. You were filled with remorse and the police were closing in on you. You took your own medicine." He brought the bottle to Kevin's lips and tilted it. Kevin kept his mouth shut, but the old man grabbed him by his hair and yanked his head back. Kevin let out a cry and at that moment his mouth filled with the vile liquid.

"Ugh!" He spat out most of the rum on to the carpet but couldn't help swallowing some of the poison. It left an acrid, burning sensation in his mouth and his stomach churned.

"I had the boy Rabin tied up in this same chair," Mr Smith said, standing back and examining his prisoner. "Found him here in the dead of night. He'd obviously found out who I am. After all these years. The Rabins hadn't forgotten. They'd stumbled on me here. The boy thought he could get his own back, putting something in my rum. But I surprised him. Tied him up, and turned the tables on him. I fed him his own cocktail. Just a little at a time," Mr Smith said menacingly. "A lot at once and it would just come up again. That'd do no good."

The old man jammed the bottle into Kevin's mouth again, ramming it painfully against his teeth. Kevin swallowed a little more. His mouth and throat felt foul.

This time, as his head went back, his eyes were open and he spotted something – a face at the window. He couldn't see who it was – the face appeared dimly for an instant, then it was gone. But Mr Smith had his back to it. If someone had come to rescue Kevin, the old man was fortunately unaware of it. Kevin prayed that the person at the window would come in quickly, before he was forced to drink any more. He tried to keep Mr Smith talking, knowing that if the old man was speaking there would be less time for poisoning.

"Why did you kill David Rabin?"

"I had no quarrel with him, it's true. But he was trying to kill me. He failed. If he'd lived, he would have turned me in. I'll not be exposed by the Rabin family or by anyone else." He stared at Kevin for a moment, then added, "I won't be tried as some inhuman war criminal. I won't be humiliated. I'll do anything to avoid that. Anything!"

"How come you got hold of those fag packets and put them in my garden?"

"Ah, yes. When he came here – Rabin – he had a plastic bag full of cigarette packets. It didn't take much imagination to work out what he'd put in the rum. Nicotine! And he'd brought the packets, so his plan was to force me to drink it and then leave the packets here to make it look as if I'd killed myself," Mr Smith ranted. "Suicide! He'd have revealed my past, no doubt, to make suicide seem credible. Well, I gave him a good dose of the rum he'd doctored and threw him out. I kept his torch and the packets. I knew that old Edriss up the road has a reputation for hating kids – everyone knows it – so I left the evidence in his garden. I thought the police would check him over as an obvious suspect and find them. Only a matter of time before the clues were found. But, then, one night you came along. Pity it was you," Mr Smith muttered. "Anyway, you volunteered the information that the police were on to you. Ideal! I went back to Edriss's garden that night – the silly fool nearly caught me, actually – and got them back."

"Then you planted them at my place," Kevin deduced.

"Yes." Mr Smith smiled. It was no longer the smile of a harmless pensioner, but that of a scheming madman. He approached Kevin again. "Time for more!"

"No!"

But the neck of the bottle was in his mouth and the evil drink hit his throat like acid. Spluttering and coughing, some of the liquid trickled from his mouth, down his chin and on to his shirt. Kevin felt his body twitching. He couldn't control it. He was on the point of vomiting but he couldn't quite bring up the fluid. His eyes flickered and his head ached. He felt dizzy with the alcohol that had been forced into him. Just as he was beginning to think he must have imagined the face at the window, there was a loud thump at the front door as someone barged into it, smashing a way into the house. Kevin sighed with relief. His rescuer! "Quickly!" he urged.

Mr Smith stumbled across the room and hid behind the living room door. The gun was in his hand again.

The door swung open slowly then, suddenly, someone stepped into the room.

Kevin cried, "Watch out!"

It was too late. Mr Smith slammed the butt of the gun down on the back of the intruder's head and the figure slumped on to the floor.

The old man turned the body over with his foot so it lay on its back, staring at the ceiling. "Who's this?" he asked Kevin.

Kevin stared across the room. For a moment, he didn't recognize the body lying on the rug. He thought it might have been Ros coming to his rescue. After all, she knew where he was. But it wasn't Ros. It was Dearings' security guard who lay, stunned, on the floor. Even though Kevin hadn't noticed him earlier, he must have followed him to Mr Smith's home. "Frank," Kevin replied. "He's from Dearing Scientific. I thought he was the murderer." At least, Kevin thought to himself, it wasn't Ros who had been slugged. He wanted to escape, he wanted her help – but he didn't want her to get hurt as well.

Mr Smith surveyed the body littering his living room. "Mmm. How very convenient."

"What?" Kevin whimpered.

Mr Smith left the room briefly. When he returned, he was carrying a syringe.

"What are you doing?" Kevin asked in a slurred voice.

"I'm glad I kept David Rabin's concoction," he replied, "but there's not much left." He tipped a little of the deadly rum into a glass and filled the barrel of the syringe from the tumbler. "It's far more potent by intravenous injection. My own experiments years ago confirmed that." He held up the syringe and examined it. "I need enough for you to drink so this fellow will have to have it by injection."

"No!" Kevin cried. "Why? He's done you no harm."

"He's seen you and me. And", Mr Smith added, "he's your second victim."

Kevin was confused. He couldn't figure it out. "How do you mean?" he asked.

"You're the murderer and you've been pestering Dearings. In response, one of them started to pester you. So, to get him off your back, you kill him. I'll make sure your fingerprints are on this", Mr Smith indicated the syringe filled with brown liquid, "before dumping his body on the field. It's the second murder that makes you finally snap. That's when you decide to kill yourself with the poison. You'll be found on the field as well."

Kevin couldn't concentrate on words. He could take in one sentence but missed the next altogether. Even so, he understood enough of what Mr Smith was plotting.

The old man was warped, consumed with malice over a fifty-year-old decision to end his career. He wasn't Ros's uncle but in some way he'd tangled with the Rabins on Alderney. David had planned to finish the whole rotten business by killing him. Yet David's attempt had backfired. Now, the feud between Dr Somerton and the Rabins was as keen and alive today as it was all that time ago. They all felt aggrieved by past events. They had all been tormented too much to forgive and forget.

Kevin couldn't focus properly but he saw Mr Smith kneeling where Frank was laid on the floor and then rising. He seemed to be wiping the syringe with a handkerchief. Next, Kevin felt Mr Smith behind him, pressing the syringe into his palm and closing his numb fingers around it.

The old man reappeared in front of him, clutching the bottle in one hand. He peered closely into Kevin's eyes and said, "You won't need much more."

The rum ran into his mouth again. Kevin was beyond struggling. He had no resistance. He gulped down the whole mouthful and immediately retched. He was not sick enough, though. Most of the nicotine stayed in his body. As he neared the lethal dose, the poison sapped his strength and robbed him of his control and capacity to reason. His head lolled helplessly to one side.

Breathless, Ros arrived at Mr Smith's front door. She was surprised to find it ajar. She peered into a darkened hall. She was tempted to call out to Kevin but, fearing that he was with Mr Smith, she did not want to forewarn the man who had once been Kevin's friend. She pushed the door open and stepped quietly into the hall. She didn't know where they were, so she had to try each room in turn. Noiselessly and nervously, she opened the door of the first room on the left. It was dark inside. Even so, she realized that it was a bathroom. She left straight away. On the other side of the hall, she tried another door but found herself in another unlit room. This time, it was a bedroom.

She turned into the main corridor. At the far end, it led into the kitchen where a striplight shone brightly. She could not hear voices, though, so guessed that Kevin and Mr Smith were in one of the two rooms between her and the kitchen.

Slowly and carefully, she turned the knob on the first door and opened it a crack. A band of light appeared. The room was lit and muttering issued from the other side of the door. Her heart raced. This was it. She took a deep breath and walked into the lounge.

Kevin was writhing horribly in a chair and Mr Smith was standing over him like a vulture. Realizing that someone had entered the room, the old man spun round, his hand darting to his dressing-gown pocket.

Ros saw the gun in Mr Smith's hand. She tried to dash for cover but she tripped over a body on the floor and landed in a heap.

The gun exploded. The bullet, missing Ros, thudded into Frank's body. Ros screamed.

"You're David Rabin's sister," the old man barked. An insane grin came to his face as he aimed the gun at her again.

Ros winced. She wanted to cover her head with her hands and cower on the floor but some inner strength prevented terror taking over. She fixed her eyes on him and said, "Why are you hesitating, Dr Somerton? Why not shoot? You killed most of the rest of my family. Why not me as well?" She crouched on the floor defiantly and answered her own question. "You were good once. You cared. Cared too much, maybe. You got punished for it. You got your own back by punishing those poor people on Alderney. You used up all your hatred on people like my grandmother. You haven't got enough left after all this time to kill me as well." Sweat gathered on her brow. The gun was still pointed at her but it hadn't been fired. At least Mr Smith was listening to her so she carried on talking. "I haven't come for revenge like David. I'm not here to judge you. I only came for Kevin. I'll walk out of here with him. That's all I want." She clung to the sofa and, shakily, pulled herself to her feet. "Let me take him."

"No." Mr Smith still held the bottle of rum in one hand. With the other, he thrust the gun directly towards Ros and began to squeeze the trigger. "You're lying. You're Rabin's sister. You're like him. But I won't let you drag me through the dirt."

"No," she said in a quaking voice. "It all happened years before

I was born. I've got no right to sit in judgement. And I know you didn't start it. I can't condemn you – or forgive you. But I'm not going to let you finish it by killing Kevin."

"I don't need your pity, young lady. And, as for him," Mr Smith gestured towards the sad figure tied to the chair, "he's already had a lethal dose. It's too late."

"What?" Ros shrieked.

"It doesn't finish with him," he said to Ros. "It finishes with you." His forefinger pulled the trigger. He was so close to her, he couldn't miss.

Behind him, Kevin jerked upright. He was too confused to work out what was happening but, with Mr Smith distracted, he saw an opportunity. He lifted his right leg and rammed it into Mr Smith's thigh.

The old man twisted and crumpled. The gun went off. The shot hit Ros's shoulder and then slammed into a wall-clock. The clock chimed ridiculously twice, then fell silent. The bottle slipped from Mr Smith's grasp and rolled towards Ros. As it moved, the remaining liquid spilled on to the carpet, leaving a brown trail across the floor like a bloodstain.

Mr Smith's head appeared over the sofa and he prepared to fire again at Ros. Ros bent down, hardly noticing the pain in her shoulder, picked up the bottle and hurled it at the old man.

With a sickening thud, the glass caught him directly on the forehead. The gun flew out of his hand. His eyes stared in surprise and some rum ran down his cheek. He collapsed, unconscious.

Ros rushed to Kevin. As soon as she untied the cord that held him to the chair, he keeled over. Ignoring the agony of her wound, she helped him to his feet and shouted, "Kev! Kev!"

He groaned, barely aware of her.

"Don't let me down now," she bellowed at him. "Come to!"

Kevin croaked, "Ugh! Got to be sick."

"What? How?"

"Got to get it out of my system," he spluttered.

Ros glanced around the room as if looking for something to make Kevin vomit. There was nothing. "Oh, well," she said, steeling herself, "here goes." She held him up with her left arm and swung her right as hard as she could, landing a heavy punch in his stomach.

Kevin uttered a deep inhuman moan, "Ugh!" He slipped from her grasp, dropped to his knees and was immediately sick.

Ros knelt down, fearing that she had finished him off herself. Clutching his heaving shoulders, she lamented, "What have I done?"

Kevin, his face completely drained of colour, twisted towards her and gurgled, "You might have saved my life." He looked away, wailed involuntarily and was sick again.

When he'd finished, Ros yanked him to his feet. "Can you walk?"

"No," he replied.

Ros glanced at Mr Smith, who was beginning to stir. "Tough," she said. "You'll have to." Then she added, "Just a second." She kicked Mr Smith's gun under a sideboard where it was out of sight. "Don't want him shooting at us down the street."

Supporting Kevin as best she could, she guided him out of the room. She steered him as rapidly as possible through the hall and out into the blissfully quiet night.

"There," she said, pointing to a telephone box about a hundred metres up the road. "We'll call for help from there. Can you make it?"

"I don't know."

Together they staggered along the pavement, away from Mr Smith's bungalow. Kevin stopped to vomit painfully yet again. "Good," Ros encouraged him. "The more that comes up, the better."

Eventually they made it. Propping him up in the telephone box, she called for an ambulance.

Ros didn't have to call the police. Neighbours, awakened by the gunshots, had already alerted them. But when they arrived at the bungalow, there was no one to arrest.

Mr Smith had emptied the dregs of the bottle of rum into his own veins. The syringe lay a few centimetres from his frozen, outstretched hand. He had injected the poison directly into his bloodstream. It had killed him rapidly and efficiently.

He had turned the smoking gun on himself.

21

Ros looked through the window into the corridor. There were some people milling about, but the way seemed clear. She slipped through the door and padded along to Room 216. She gripped the handle, looked about to make sure that no one was watching her, opened the door cautiously and edged inside.

"Hi!" Kevin said brightly from the bed.

"Sssh!" Ros closed the door before speaking. "They told me I couldn't see you. I shouldn't be here."

"Why not?"

"You need to sleep it off. You need rest, they said."

"Well, they let Detective Superintendent Whyte in, a while back."

"That's because *he's* important. He saw me too, by the way."

"To take a statement?" asked Kevin.

"Yes."

"How's the shoulder? The sling looks impressive. Do you really need it or is it a new fashion thing?"

Ros laughed. "No. The bullet made more of a mess than I thought at the time. When I injure a shoulder, I'm not like you – I make a real job of it. They've plastered it so it keeps still while it heals. How about you, though? How do you feel?" Ros sat on the hospital bed to hear his reply.

"I'm OK," Kevin answered. "My arms feel like they've been in a strait-jacket for a year. My head feels like a huge boulder that's about to roll off my shoulders. My stomach ... Well, it feels like I've had two curries from the salmonella van outside the club."

"Oh well," Ros replied cheekily, "no problem, then." She glanced round and asked, "How come you got a room to yourself? I didn't."

"It's not for my benefit. It seems that the other patients wouldn't have enjoyed seeing, hearing and smelling the effects of the treatment I had to have."

"Ugh! Don't tell me any more." Changing the subject, she asked, "Did Detective Superintendent Whyte tell you about Frank?"

"Yeah. He didn't make it," he answered gloomily. "Pity, because he must have seen through the window that I was in trouble and came in to help me. Whyte found out that we were right about him, by the way. He was following me because, after I broke in, Dearing ordered him to. Thought I was some sort of industrial spy or troublemaker. Must be paranoid about security. He wanted to know who I talked to, in case I was passing all his secrets to an environmental pressure group, a rival, or to the press. Anyway, Frank would have survived the shooting, Whyte said, but the poison got him."

"And Mr Smith? Or should I say Dr Somerton?"

Kevin nodded. "I should hate him, I suppose, after what he did to me but … I don't know … I just feel sad for him. He'd flipped his lid, obviously, but even so…"

"I know what you mean," Ros replied. "It was something that should have been left behind fifty years ago. But it all happened yesterday. Think of it as something left over from the war. That way, it belongs to history. Makes it more remote. It's easier that way."

"I guess so."

Standing up, Ros commented, "I'd better go. Before I get caught." She pointed to the anti-smoking poster on the wall opposite Kevin's bed and said, "Promise me you won't ever take up smoking again."

Kevin smiled. "I don't want to see another ciggie for as long as I live."

"Good."

"Before you go," Kevin called after her, "promise me you won't ever take up a career in boxing." He rubbed his tender midriff.

"Don't worry," Ros replied. "I haven't got the stomach for it, either."

If only he had felt fit enough, he'd have thrown one of his pillows at her. Instead, he groaned and pulled the sheet up over his head.